KING PENGUIN

THE LAST OF THE JUST

André Schwarz-Bart was born in France in 1928. He went to the Sorbonne, and at the age of fifteen he joined the French Resistance. While writing, he has worked in a factory and in Les Halles, the large vegetable market in Paris.

He has also written *Un Plat de porc aux bananes vert* (1967; with his wife, Simone Schwarz-Bart), which was awarded the Jerusalem Prize in 1967, and *A Woman Named Solitude* (1973). *The Last of the Just* won the Prix Goncourt in 1959.

D0921767

ANDRÉ SCHWARZ-BART

THE LAST OF
THE JUST

TRANSLATED BY STEPHEN BECKER

How am I to toll your death?
How may I mark your obsequies,
Vagabond handful of ashes
Between heaven and earth?

M. Jaztrun. THE OBSEQUIES

A KING PENGUIN
PUBLISHED BY PENGUIN BOOKS

Penguin Books Ltd, Harmondsworth, Middlesex, England
Viking Penguin Inc., 40 West 23rd Street, New York, New York 10010, U.S.A.
Penguin Books Australia Ltd, Ringwood, Victoria, Australia
Penguin Books Canada Ltd, 2801 John Street, Markham, Ontario, Canada L3R 1B4
Penguin Books (N.Z.) Ltd, 182–190 Wairau Road, Auckland 10, New Zealand

Le Dernier des justes first published in France 1959
This translation first published by Martin Secker & Warburg Ltd 1961
Published in Penguin Books 1977
Reissued as a King Penguin 1984

Printed and bound in Great Britain by
Cox & Wyman Ltd, Reading
Set in Monotype Times

CONTENTS

BOOK ONE

THE LEGEND OF THE JUST MEN

1

OUR eyes register the light of dead stars. A biography of my friend Ernie could easily be set in the second quarter of the twentieth century; but the true history of Ernie Levy begins much earlier, towards the year one thousand of our era, in the old Anglican city of York. More precisely, on 11 March 1185.

On that day Bishop William of Nordhouse uttered a great sermon, and to cries of 'God's will be done!' the mob moiled through the church square; within minutes, Jewish souls were accounting for their crimes to their God, who had called them to him through the voice of his Bishop.

Meanwhile, under cover of the pillage, several families had taken refuge in an old disused tower at the edge of the town. The siege lasted six days. Every morning at first light a monk approached the moat, crucifix in hand, and promised life to those Jews who would acknowledge the Passion of our very gentle Lord Jesus Christ. But the tower remained 'mute and closed', in the words of an eye-witness, the Benedictine Dom Bracton.

On the morning of the seventh day Rabbi Yom Tov Levy gathered the besieged on the watch-tower. Brothers, he said to them, God gave us life; let us return it to him ourselves, by our own hands, as did our brothers in Germany.

Men, women, children, dotards, each yielded a forehead to his blessing and then a throat to the blade he offered with the other hand. The old Rabbi remained alone before his own death.

Dom Bracton reports: 'And then rose a great sound of lamentation, which was heard from here to the Saint James quarter . . .'

There follows a pious commentary, and the monk finishes his chronicle thus: 'Twenty-six Jews were counted on the watchtower, not to mention the females or the herd of children. Two

9

years later thirteen of the latter who had been buried were discovered in the cellar; but almost all of these were still of suckling age. The Rabbi's hand was still on the hilt of the dagger in his throat. No weapon but his was found in the tower. His body was thrown upon a great fire, and unfortunately his ashes were cast to the winds. So that we breathe it; and so that, by the agency of mean spirits, some poisonous humours will fall upon us, which will confound us entirely!'

There is nothing remarkable about the anecdote itself. In the eyes of Jews, the holocaust of the watch-tower is only a minor episode in a history overstocked with martyrs. In those ages of faith, as we know, whole communities flung themselves into the flames to escape the seductions of the Vulgate. It was so at Speier, at Mayence, at Worms, at Cologne, at Prague, during the fateful summer of 1096. And later, during the Black Plague, in all Christendom.

But the deed of Rabbi Yom Tov Levy had a singular destiny; rising above common tragedy, it became legend.

To understand the process of this metamorphosis, one must be aware of the ancient Jewish tradition of the *Lamed-waf*, a tradition that certain Talmudists trace back to the source of the centuries, to the mysterious times of the prophet Isaiah. Rivers of blood have flowed, columns of smoke have obscured the sky; but surviving all these dooms, the tradition has remained inviolate down to our own times. According to this tradition the world reposes upon thirty-six Just Men, the *Lamed-waf*, indistinguishable from simple mortals; often, they do not recognize themselves. But if even one of them were lacking, the sufferings of mankind would poison even the souls of the new-born, and humanity would suffocate with a single cry. For the *Lamed-waf* are the hearts of the world multiplied, into which all our griefs are poured, as into one receptacle. They occur in thousands of popular stories. Their presence is attested everywhere. A very old text of the Hagadah tells us that the most pitiable are the *Lamed-waf* who remain unknown to themselves. For those, the spectacle of the world is an unspeakable hell. In the seventh century,

Andalusian Jews venerated a rock shaped like a teardrop, which they believed to be the soul, petrified by suffering, of an 'unknown' *Lamed-waf*. Other *Lamed-waf*, like Hecuba shrieking at the death of her sons, are said to have been transformed into dogs. 'When an Unknown Just rises to Heaven,' a Hassidic story goes, 'he is so frozen that God must warm him for a thousand years between His fingers, before his soul can open itself to Paradise. And it is known that some remain for ever inconsolable at human woe; so that even God Himself cannot warm them. So from time to time the Creator, Blessed be his Name, sets the clock of the Last Judgement forward by one minute.'

The legend of Rabbi Yom Tov Levy proceeds directly from this tradition of the *Lamed-waf*.

It owes its birth also to a singular occurrence, which is the extraordinary survival of the infant Solomon Levy, youngest son of Rabbi Yom Tov. Here we reach the point at which history plunges into legend, and is absorbed by it; for exact details are lacking, and the opinions of the chroniclers diverge. According to some, Solomon Levy was one of about thirty children who received Christian baptism during the massacre. According to others his father did not quite succeed in butchering the boy, who was saved by a peasant woman and handed over to some Jews in a neighbouring county.

Among the many versions current in thirteenth-century Jewish lore, we note the Italian fantasy of Simeon Reubeni of Mantua; he describes the 'miracle' in these terms:

'At the origin of the people of Israel there is the sacrifice of one man, our father Abraham, who offered his son to God. At the origin of the dynasty of the Levys we find again the sacrifice of one man, the very gentle and luminous Rabbi Yom Tov, who by his own hand slit the throats of two hundred and fifty of the faithful – some say a thousand.

'And there is this: the solitary agony of Rabbi Yom Tov was unbearable to God.

'And this too: in the charnel-house swarming with flies was reborn his youngest son, Solomon Levy, and the angels Uriel and Gabriel watched over him.

11

'And finally this: when Solomon had reached the age of manhood, the Eternal came to him in a dream and said: Hear me, Solomon; listen to my words. On the seventeenth day of the month of Sivan, in the year four thousand nine hundred forty-five, your father, Rabbi Yom Tov Levy, touched my heart with pity. To all his line therefore, and for all the centuries, there shall be given the grace of one *Lamed-waf* to each generation. You are the first, you are that one, you are holy.'

And the excellent author concludes in this manner: 'O companions of our ancient exile, as the rivers go to the sea, all our tears flow into the heart of God.'

Authentic or mistaken, the vision of Solomon Levy arouses general interest. His smallest deeds and acts are reported by Jewish chroniclers of the time. Several describe his face, narrow, thoughtful, somewhat childlike, and leaved about with long black curls.

But the truth had to be faced: his hands did not heal wounds, no balm flowed from his eyes; and though he remained in the synagogue at Troyes for five years, praying there, eating there, sleeping there, always on the same hard bench, his example was commonplace in the minute hell of the ghettoes. So they waited for the day of Solomon Levy's death, which might put an end to the debate.

It occurred in the year of grace 1240, during a disputation ordered by King Louis the Saint, of precious memory.

As was customary, the Talmudists of the Kingdom of France stood in one rank facing the ecclesiastical tribunal, which included Eudes de Châteauroux, chancellor of the Sorbonne, and the celebrated Nicolas Donin. In these singular disputations, death hovered over each reply of the Talmudists. They spoke in turn, in order equitably to distribute the threat of torture.

A question from Bishop Grotius, relative to the divinity of Jesus, produced an understandable hesitation.

But suddenly they saw Rabbi Solomon Levy, who had effaced himself until then, like an adolescent intimidated by a gathering of men. Slender and slight in his black gown, he steps hesitantly

12

up to the tribunal. If it is true, he whispers with constraint, if it is true that the Messiah of which our ancient prophets spoke has already come, how then do you explain the present state of the world? Then, with anxious little coughs and his voice on one thin note: Noble lords, the prophets surely stated that on the coming of the Messiah wails and moans would disappear from the world ... ah ... did they not? That the lion and the lamb would lie down together, that the blind would be healed and the lame would leap like ... stags! And also that all the peoples would break their swords, oh yea, and beat them into ploughshares ... ah ... would they not?

And finally, smiling sadly at King Louis: 'Ah, what would people say, Sire, if you were to forget how to wage war?'

And these were the consequences of that little oration, as they are revealed in the excruciating *Book of the Vale of Tears*:

'Then did King Louis decide that our brothers of Paris should be condemned to a Mass, to a sermon, to the wearing of a yellow cloth yoke and a sugar-loaf hat, and, as well, to a considerable fine. That our divine books of the Talmud should be burned at the stake in a wind-swept field of Paris, for being querulous and full of lies and dictated by the Devil. And that finally, for public edification, into the heart of the Talmudic flames should be cast the living body of that Just Man, that *Lamed-waf*, that man of sorrows, oh how expert in sorrows, Rabbi Solomon Levy, since then known as the Sad Rabbi. A tear for him.'

After the *auto-da-fé* of the Just Man, his only son, the handsome Manasseh, returned to that same England his ancestors had once fled. Peace had been reigning over the English shores for ten years, and to the Jews it seemed permanently enthroned.

Manasseh settled in London, where the renown of the Just Men set him at the head of the resurgent community. And because he was very graceful in form and speech, he was asked to plead in defence of the Jews who were daily accused of sorcery, ritual murder, the poisoning of wells, and other affabilities. In twenty years he obtained seven acquittals, which was indeed remarkable.

The circumstances of the seventh trial are little known: it concerned a certain Eliezer Jefryo whom rumour accused of having stabbed a communion wafer, thereby putting the Christ to another death and spilling the blood of the Sacred Heart, which is the dry bread of the Host. This last acquittal disturbed two powerful bishops. Soon after, Manasseh was arraigned before the tribunal of the Holy Inquisition, and accused of the crime from which he had so recently exculpated Eliezer Jefryo.

He was obliged to undergo the Question Extraordinary, which was not repeated – that being forbidden by the legislation in force – but simply 'continued'. The court records show him infected by the evil spirit of taciturnity. And therefore on 7 May 1279, before a gallery of some of the most beautiful women in London, he was made to undergo the passion of the wafer by means of a Venetian dagger, thrice blessed and thrice plunged into his throat.

'It is thus,' a chronicler writes naïvely, 'that after having defended us in vain before the tribunals of men, the Just Manasseh Levy rose to plead our cause in Heaven.'

His son Israel did not seem bound to follow that dangerous path. A suave, peaceful man, he had a small cobbler's shop, and forged elegiac poems at the top of his hammer. So great was his discretion that his rare visitors never arrived without a shoe in hand. Some assure us that he was well versed in the Zohar; others that he barely had the intelligence of a dove, just as he had its gentle eyes and liquid voice. A few of his poems have become part of the Ashkenazi ritual. He is the author of the famous Seliha, *Oh God, cover not our blood with thy silence.*

So Israel was thus fashioning his little world, silently, when the edict of expulsion burst upon the Jews of England. Always level-headed, he was among the last to leave the island; first they made for Hamburg, but later resigned themselves to the Portuguese coast. At Christmas, after four months of wandering, the caravel ended up in Bordeaux.

The little shoemaker made his way furtively to Toulouse, where several years passed in a blessed incognito. He loved the southern province where the Christian customs were gentle,

14

almost human. One had the right to cultivate a bit of ground, to practise trades other than usury, and even to swear an oath before a court just as if, though a Jew, one had a real man's tongue. It was a foretaste of Paradise.

The only shadow in the picture was a custom called the *Cophyz*, which required that every year on the eve of Easter the president of the Jewish community present himself in his shift at the cathedral, where the Count of Toulouse, to the strains of the Mass, gave him a slap in the face with great ceremony. But over the centuries the custom had been singularly refined: in consideration of fifty thousand écus, the Count was satisfied with a symbolic slap at six paces. This had already happened when Israel was recognized by an emigrant from England, and duly 'denounced' to the faithful of Toulouse. They plucked him from his shop, blessed him, his father, his mother, all his ancestors and all his descendants; and willy-nilly he accepted the presidency, which had become a position of no danger.

The years flowed by with their train of griefs and small joys, which he continued to translate into poetry; and on the sly he also turned out a few pairs of shoes now and then. In the year of grace 1348 the old Count of Toulouse died; his son had been raised by excellent tutors, and decided to administer the Easter slap.

Israel presented himself in a long shirt, barefoot, wearing the compulsory pointed hat, and with two vast yellow circles sewn to his white front and back; on that day he had seventy-two years behind him. A huge crowd had gathered to see the slap. The hat rolled violently to the ground. According to the ancient custom Israel stooped to pick it up and thanked the young count three times; and then, supported by his co-religionists, he made his way through the yelling mob. When he arrived home his right eye smiled with a reassuring sweetness; it is only a matter of getting used to it, he told his wife, which I am already. But over the cheek marked by four fingers his left eye wept, and during the night which followed, his aged blood turned slowly to water. Three weeks later he displayed signal weakness by dying of shame.

*

Rabbi Mattathias Levy, his son, was a man so well versed in the mathematical sciences, astronomy, and medicine that even certain Jews suspected him of trafficking with the Devil. His agility in all things was notorious; in one of his anecdotes, Johanaan ben Hasdai compared him to a ferret; other authors describe him even more vividly as perpetually running away.

He practised medicine in Toulouse, Auch, Gimont, Castelsarrasin, Albi, Gaillac, Rabastens, Verdun-sur-Garonne. His condition was that of the Jewish doctors at that time. In Auch and Gaillac they accused him of poisoning sick Christians; in Castelsarrasin they accused him of leprosy; in Gimont he was a poisoner of wells. In Rabastens they said he used an elixir based on human blood, and in Toulouse he was curing with the invisible hand of Satan. In Verdun-sur-Garonne, finally, he was hounded as a propagator of the fearsome black death.

He owed his life to his patients who warned him, hid him, and spirited him away.

He was frequently reprimanded, but he always found, ben Hasdai says, 'strange reasons for opening his door to a sick Christian'. His death was reported in several places. But, whether he was thrown into the Jew-pit at Moissac, burned alive at the cemetery in Auch, or massacred in Verdun-sur-Garonne, the ferret would always, one fine day, make his sad appearance in some synagogue. And when King Charles VI, well advised by his confessor, published the edict of expulsion for the Jews of France, Rabbi Mattathias Levy was hidden away in the neighbourhood of Bayonne; a step or two and he was in Spain.

There he died very old, in the middle of the following century, on the vast white slab of the *Quemadero* in Seville. Around him, scattered among the faggots, was the daily ovenful of three hundred Jews. It is not even known whether he sang in his agonies. After an ordinary life, this somewhat dreary death casts doubt on his quality as a Just man ...

'Nevertheless,' writes ben Hasdai, 'he should be counted in the illustrious lineage; for if evil is always brilliantly manifest, good often dons the clothing of the humble, and it is said that many Just Men die unknown.'

On the other hand his son Joachim bore eloquent witness to his vocation. He was still under forty when he composed a collection of spiritual decisions, as well as a dizzying description of the three Cabbalistic Sephiroth: Love, Intelligence, Compassion. 'He possessed,' legend says, 'one of those faces of sculpted lava and basalt, which the people believe have been modelled by God, truly in his own image.'

At those spiritual heights the persecutions did not reach him. Always grave and dignified he reigned over his disciples, who had come from all corners of Spain, and he spoke to each of them the language of his death. In a polemic which has remained famous, he definitely established that the reward of the persecuted is the Supreme Delight. In which case it is obvious that the good Jew does not feel the horrors of torture; 'Whether they stone him or burn him, whether they bury him alive or hang him, he remains oblivious; no complaint escapes his lips.'

But while the illustrious *Lamed-waf* discoursed, God for his part, and through the agency of the monk Torquemada, divinely concocted the edict of permanent expulsion from Spain. Through the black night of the Inquisition the decree fell like a streak of lightning that meant, for many Jews, immediate expulsion from earthly existence.

To his great shame, Rabbi Joachim managed to reach Portugal without bearing personal witness to his own teachings. There John III charitably offered the exiles asylum for eight months, in return for a mutually agreeable entrance fee. But seven months later, by a singular aberration that same sovereign decreed that he would now spare the lives of such Jews who left his realms without delay; and this in return for a mutually agreeable exit fee. For lack of savings, Rabbi Joachim was sold as a slave with thousands of other unfortunates; his wife was promised to the leisures of the Turk, his son Chaim promised to Christ and baptised with abundance in several convents.

A doubt hovers over the Rabbi's death. A sentimental ballad locates it in China, at the point of a paling stake; but the most cautious writers admit their ignorance. They suppose that his death was worthy of his teachings.

The infant Chaim had a prodigious fate; raised in a convent and ordained a priest, he remained a faithful Jew beneath the cassock; but his superiors, satisfied of his apparent good conduct, delegated him to the Holy See in 1522, with a sizeable group of 'Jewish priests' assigned to the edification of the Papal retinue. Leaving for Rome in cassock and biretta, he ended up in Mainz with the black caftan and sugar-loaf hat; there the survivors of the recent holocaust welcomed him with pomp.

Treated and regarded as animals, the Jews were naturally avid for the supernatural. Already the posterity of Rabbi Yom Tov had spread far beyond the frontiers of the Ghetto. From the Atlantic coast to the interior of Arabia, every year on the twentieth day of the month of Sivan a solemn fast took place; and the cantors chanted the selichoth of Rabbi Salomon ben Simon of Mainz:

> With tears of blood I mourn the holy community of York.
> A cry of pain springs from my heart for the victims at Mainz.
> Heroes of the spirit who died for the holy name.

The arrival of Chaim Levy, come surging from the depths of monasteries, seemed as miraculous as the deliverance of Jonah; the Christian chasms had rendered up the Just Man.

Blessed, cherished, circumcised, he lives like a canon monk. They present him generally as a tall, thin, cold man. A witness alludes to the unctuously monotonous flow of his voice, and to other ecclesiastical traits as well. After eight years as a recluse in the synagogue, he marries a certain Rachel Garson, who shortly offers him an heir. A few months later, betrayed by a co-religionist, he is escorted back to Portugal. There, his limbs are broken on the rack; lead is poured into his eyes, his ears, his mouth, and his anus, at the rate of one molten drop each day; finally they burn him.

His son Ephraim Levy was brought up piously in Mannheim, Karlsrühe, Tübingen, Reutlingen, Augsburg, Ratisbon, all cities from which the Jews were no less piously chased. In Leipzig his mother died, with fast last breaths. But there he knew the love of a woman and married her.

18

The margrave was not at all devout, neither was he greedy or wicked; he was simply short of money. So he fell back on the favourite game of German princes, which consisted of chasing the 'infamous' and retaining their worldly goods. Young Ephraim fled with his new family to Magdeburg, whence he set off for Brunswick, where he took the death-road of the Just Men, hit by a stone thrown at him in Cassel.

He is hardly mentioned in the writings; the scribes seem to avoid him. Judah ben Aredeth devotes barely eight lines to him. But Simeon Reubeni of Mantua, the gentle Italian chronicler, evokes 'the bobbing curls of Ephraim Levy, his laughing eyes, his graceful limbs moving as if in dance. They say that from the day he knew his wife, whatever befell him he never ceased to laugh; so the people named him the Nightingale of the Talmud, which indicates perhaps an excessive familiarity towards a Just Man.'

These are the only lines to describe the charming person of the young Ephraim Levy, whose happiness in love seems unworthy of a *Lamed-waf*. Even his last agony failed to soften the severity of Jewish historians, who do not mention its date.

His son Jonathan had a more commendable life. For many years he criss-crossed Bohemia and Moravia – a job-lot pedlar, and a prophet. Whenever he entered the gates of a ghetto he would start unwrapping his glass trinketry; then, the day's small business over and the bundle done up and knotted at his feet, he would challenge passers-by on the Torah, on the angels, on the imminent arrival of the Messiah.

A reddish beard covered his face even to the periphery of his eyes, and, by way of a more cruel disgrace, his voice had a falsetto resonance; but he possessed, the chronicle says, 'a story for each of our sufferings'.

In those days all the Jews in Europe wore the uniform of infamy ordered by Pope Innocent III. After five centuries of this catechism, its victims were curiously transmuted: under the pointed hat, the *pileum cornutum*, solid citizens thenceforth imagined two small horns; at the base of the spine, where the cloth yoke began, the legendary tail could be guessed at; no one was any longer unaware that Jewish feet were cloven. Those who stripped their corpses were amazed, seeing yet further witchcraft in these bodies now so human. But as a general rule no one touched a Jew, dead or alive, except with the end of a stick.

During the long voyage that was his life Rabbi Jonathan often met cold, hunger, and the ordinance of Pope Innocent III. All the parts of his body testified forcefully to that. Judah ben Aredeth writes: In the end, the Just Man no longer had a face. In Polotzk, where he turned up in the winter of 1552, his pedlar's bundle was taken away from him. A happy indiscretion having betrayed his quality of *Lamed-waf*, the sick man was looked after, he was married, he was admitted to the seminary of the great Yehel Mehiel, where eleven years passed for him like one day.

Then, Ivan IV, the Terrible, annexed Polotzk in a thunderclap!

As we know, all the Jews were drowned in the Dvina, except for those who would kiss the Holy Cross, prelude to the saving aspersion of holy water. The czar, having expressed a desire to exhibit in Moscow, duly sprinkled, 'a couple of wriggling little rabbis', the methodical conversion of Rabbi Yehel and Rabbi Jonathan was undertaken. When all else had failed they were tied to the tail of a small Mongol pony, and then their remains were hoisted to the thick branch of an oak, where the bodies of two dead dogs awaited them; finally, to this oscillating mass of flesh was affixed the famous Cossack inscription: TWO JEWS TWO DOGS ALL FOUR OF THE SAME RELIGION.

The chroniclers prefer to end this story on a lyric note. Thus Judah ben Aredeth, usually so dry: 'Ah, how the mighty have fallen!...'

On Tuesday, 5 November 1611, an aged servant rang the bell at the Grand Synagogue of Wilna. Her name was Maria Kozemenieczka, daughter of Jesus, but she had raised a Jewish child; and perhaps, she finished timidly, the Jews would make a collection to save him from conscription?

Assailed with questions, she first swore by all the saints that the child had been *engendered* in her by a pedlar, *casually*, on the roadside; then she admitted having picked him up, the day after the Russian annexation, at the gates of the former ghetto of Polotzk; and finally she offered what was accepted as the truth: once cook in the household of the late Rabbi Jonathan, she had received the boy from the young wife's hands as the Russians broke down the door. In the night, she had fled to her native village. She would be old some day; she was moved to pity; she kept the *innocent* for her own; that was all. And may you all forgive me, she concluded in a sudden shower of tears.

'Return to your village,' the rabbi said to her, 'and have the young man come here. If he is properly circumcised, we will pay for his release.'

Two years went by.

The prudent Rabbi of Wilna had breathed not a word to any man, and congratulated himself on it.

But one night as he left the temple, he bumped into a young peasant standing under the porch, haggard, his features drawn with fatigue, his eyes gleaming with an emotion in which arrogance battled with fear: 'Hey, you, old rabbi, I seem to be one of your people, so tell me what do I do to become a Jew-dog.'

The next day, bitterly: 'Pig in a sty, Jew in a ghetto, we are what we are, huh?'

A month later: 'I'd like to respect you but I can't do it, I have a feeling of disgust, there in the belly.'

Started on the way of frankness, he told them of his anger and his shame, of burying himself in the army. He had deserted in the middle of the night on an irrevocable impulse. 'I woke up, just like that, and I heard them all snoring, good Christian snores. Jezry, Jezry, I said to myself, you didn't come out of the belly you thought, but a man is what he is and if he denies it he's a pig . . .!' After that violent thought he had knocked out the sentry and then a passer-by, whom he stripped of his clothing, and like an animal flung out into the night he had headed for Wilna, a hundred and twenty-five miles from his garrison.

Men who had known his father, the Just Jonathan Levy, came rushing from all the provinces. Repelled at first by his coarseness, they tried to get to know him, they analysed his expression. They say it took him five years to resemble Rabbi Jonathan; he burst out laughing when he found that he had Jewish hair, Jewish eyes, a long nose with a Jewish curve. But they were always worried about the crazy peasant who slumbered in him; now and then rages shook him, he spoke of *getting out of this hole*, uttered blasphemies at which they stopped their ears. After which he enclosed himself in an attentive, studious, suffering silence for weeks on end. In his famous Story of a Miracle the prudent Rabbi of Wilna reports: 'When he did not understand the meaning of a Hebrew word, the son of the Just Men would crush his head in his heavy peasant hands, as if to wrench the thick Polish veinstone out of it.'

His wife revealed that he cried out in his sleep every night, calling now upon Biblical figures and now upon a certain Saint Johannus, the patron saint of his Christian childhood. One day, when the service was at its height, he fell full length on the floor, beating at his temples with his huge fists. His madness was immediately recognized as holy.

According to the Rabbi of Wilna: 'When the Eternal at last took pity upon him, Nehemiah Levy had replaced, one by one, all the pieces of his former brain.'

The life of his son, the quaint Jacob Levy, is nothing more than a desperate flight from God's implacable 'benediction'. He was a creature with frail, elongated limbs, a languid head, the long fearful ears of a rabbit. In his passion for anonymity he hunched his back as low as he could, as if to mask his height from men's eyes; and as a hunted man buries himself in a crowd, he became a mere leather-embroiderer, a man of nothing.

When the talk turned to his ancestors he claimed that there had been an error in his case, arguing from the fact that he felt nothing within himself, except perhaps terror. I am nothing more than an insect, he said to the prattling fawners around him, a miserable insect; what do you want of me? The next day he disappeared.

Happily, heaven had joined him to a talkative woman. A hundred times she had sworn to keep silence, but one fine morning she would lean towards a neighbour and whisper: 'He doesn't look much, does he, my husband?' she would begin slyly. And under the absolute seal of confidence the secret made its way like a fired train of powder; the Rabbi sent for the modest leather-worker and, although he did not offer him his own ministry, he made him one of the Blessed, dangerously radiating glory. And it happened thus in all the towns through which the couple passed. 'So that he could never savour the quietude of obscure men,' writes Meir of Nossack, 'God placed a female tongue at his side, as a sentinel.'

In the end Jacob's patience was exhausted, he repudiated his wife and hid in a small alleyway of the ghetto at Kiev, where he quietly carried on his trade. They found him soon enough, but out of fear that he would disappear again they only verified his presence now and then, with a discretion equal to his own. Observers record that he straightened up to his full height, that his eyes cleared, and that three times in less than seven years he gave in to unfeigned gaiety. Those were happy years, they say.

His death fulfilled everyone's expectations:

'... The Cossacks locked up a group in the synagogue and demanded that all Jews present strip naked, men and women. Some had begun to take off their clothes, when a man of the people came forward whom a subtle rumour had linked with the famous dynasty of the Levys of York. Turning towards the tearful group, he hunched his shoulders suddenly and, in a quavering voice, broke into the seliha of Rabbi Salomon ben Simon of Mainz: *With tears of blood, I mourn* ...

'They cut short the chant with one blow of a hatchet, but other voices had already taken up the plaint, and then still others; then there was no one to sing, for all was blood ... Thus did things come to pass among us in Kiev on 16 November 1723, during that terrible Hadaimakschina.' (Moses Dobiecki. *History of the Jews of Kiev.*)

His son Chaim, called the Messenger, was bequeathed his father's modesty. He gleaned instruction from everything, from rest as from study, from things as much as from men. 'The Messenger heard all voices, and would have accepted the reproach of a blade of grass.'

And yet in those days he was himself a fine blade of a man, built like a Pole, and so hale that the ghetto-dwellers feared for their daughters.

The evil-minded insinuate that the young rabbi's celibacy was not unconnected with his sudden departure from Kiev.

And it was indeed at the express injunction of the Elders that he was obliged to take his place near the Baal Shem Tov, Rabbi Israel ben Eliezer, the divine master of renown, in order, they said, to add to his knowledge and to refine his heart.

After ten years of retreat on the most savage slopes of the Carpathians, the Baal Shem Tov had established himself in his natal village of Miedzyborz, in Podolia, whence his light streamed forth on all Jewish Poland. They came to Miedzyborz to have ulcers treated, to resolve doubts, or to cure themselves of demons. Wise men and fools, the simple and the depraved, those of noble reputations and the lowest of the faithful, all mingled around the hermit. Not daring to reveal his identity, Chaim Levy did his chores as a handy-man, slept in the barn reserved for the sick, and awaited, trembling, the luminous glance of the 'Besht'. Five years passed in this way. He became so thoroughly like a servant that pilgrims from Kiev did not recognize him.

His only visible talent was dancing; when the reels formed to lighten the heart of God, he leapt so high in the air and cried out so enthusiastically that many Hasidim were offended. He was relegated permanently to the ranks of the sick; he danced among them, for their pleasure.

Later, when everything was known, he was also nicknamed the Dancer of God . . .

One day the Baal Shem received a message from the old Gaon of Kiev. Immediately he had it proclaimed that a Just Man was concealed at Miedzyborz. All the pilgrims were interrogated: the sick, the wise, the possessed, rabbis and preachers; the next day it was noticed that the handy-man had fled. Testimony streamed in immediately, each contributed his own anecdotes: the vagabond of the barn danced, at night, took care of the sick, etc. But the Baal Shem Tov, wiping away a tear, said simply: That one was healthy among the sick, and I did not see him.

News filtered in as if drop by drop.

They learned that poor Chaim was wandering through the countryside, preaching in public squares or practising odd and humble crafts, for example that of the bone-setter, who used only his two hands (and who treated both humans and animals). Many chronicles point out that he only preached reluctantly, as if under the domination of an officiating angel. After fifteen years of that mad solitude, his personality became so popular that a number of stories identify him with the Baal Shem Tov himself, of whom he was said to have become the wandering incarnation. In the abundance of ancient parchments we cannot separate entirely the commonplace from the miraculous. It is certain nevertheless that the Messenger often stayed in a village without delivering himself of any message but his medicine, so that he passed doubly unnoticed.

But his legend travelled faster than he did, and soon they recognized him by certain signs: first his woodchopper's big build and his face ridged with scars; and then the famous missing right ear, ripped off by Polish peasants. From then on it was noticed that he avoided the larger cities, where his description was too well-known.

One night, during the winter of 1792, he arrived in the neighbourhood of the small town of Zemyock, in the county of Moydin, province of Bialystok. He collapsed at the door of a Jewish home. His face and his boots were so worn, so hardened by the cold, that at first he was mistaken for one of the innumerable pedlars who criss-crossed Poland and the 'zone of Jewish residence' in Russia. They had to amputate his legs at the knee. When he was better they came to appreciate his manual talents and his skill as a copyist of the Torah. Every day his host transported him to the synagogue in a wheelbarrow. He was a human husk, a poor unfortunate, but he performed small services and was consequently not a great burden. 'He spoke,' writes Rabbi Moshe Leib of Sasov, 'only of material things like bread and wine'.

The Just Man was in his wheelbarrow, like a living candle planted in a dim corner of the synagogue, when it happened that the village rabbi erred in the interpretation of a holy text. Chaim

25

raised an eyebrow, rubbed his one ear, cleared his throat carefully, rubbed his ear again; to hold back the truth of God is grave, grave ... Finally, rubbing his ear one last time, he supported himself with one hand on the edge of the wheelbarrow, and requested the right to speak on the text. He was then assailed with questions. Suffering a thousand deaths, he answered them all brilliantly. To complete the disaster, the old Rabbi of Zemyock was transported into a sobbing ecstasy:

'Lord of the worlds,' he cried between two sobs, 'Lord of souls, Lord of Peace, admire with us the pearls that drop suddenly from that mouth! Ah, no, my children, I cannot now remain your rabbi, for this poor wanderer is a far wiser man than I. What have I said: far wiser? Only far wiser?'

And advancing, he embraced his horrified successor.

BOOK TWO

ZEMYOCK

1

How Chaim tried to throw them off the track and was finally unmasked; what happened when he was married, and the diplomacy he exercised in order not to be carried to Kiev in triumph – no, lest the reader see a romance in it, none of this can be the object of a historical narrative.

It is nevertheless true that in spite of his most subtle hairsplitting, he soon had to give up being pushed to the synagogue in a wheelbarrow.

A pious artisan had conceived a sort of rolling armchair, a veritable throne upholstered in velvet even to the inner faces of the wheels; they installed the Just Man in it with great pomp; a brocade quilt, placed across his thighs, covered his infirmity. The cantor walked on his right, and the outgoing rabbi somewhat intimately on his left, so that he could command the attention of the Just Man's good ear. And the High Priest pushed the rolling throne, leading a procession of the faithful who offered their homage to the Dancer of God.

At first the children displayed respect; but one day, doubtless emboldened by a young ringleader, they posted themselves along the line of march and burlesqued the old wheelbarrow.

Men rushed at them, but Chaim was exultant: 'Leave them alone,' he said. 'They're making fun of the throne, but they never laughed at the wheelbarrow.'

That reflection was small consolation to the Jews of Zemyock, who felt that their dignity had been impugned. They took counsel, they spoke of wooden legs, and the carpenter was ordered to construct a thoroughly dignified pair padded with leather and trimmed in fine silk. Solemnly offered to the Blessed of God – who had to train himself immediately to their use – the pair of legs proved to be a frightful instrument of torture; the stumps, instead of hardening with their use, became more tender, more

29

sensitive; until finally they became infected. There was nothing for it: an ark was erected in the Just Man's room, which became a place of worship. So ended the humiliating journey to the synagogue.

Still infatuated with their great man, although, they admitted privately, a bit *put out*, the villagers thought to glorify him still more with the reputation of a miracle-worker (a campaign supported by the local businessmen). Chaim claimed immediately that he possessed no such power, except perhaps, *perhaps*, he emphasized, the power of tears; nevertheless he received the sick, prescribed simples or other rural nostrums; and he also received animals in a near-by barn.

And still, even when he could do nothing for a sufferer, he always conversed with him; not on higher matters, as one might have hoped, but on very insignificant affairs, entirely devoid of interest, such as the married life of the sick man, his work, his children, his cow, his chicken. Strangely enough, people went away happy, saying that he knew how to listen, that by following your little tale he uncovered the grieving thread of your soul. When he could not hear you well he turned his left ear towards you, cupping his hand, behind it, blinking with kindliness: 'How do you expect me,' he asked, 'to be interested in your soul, if you don't trouble yourself about my ear?'

One day, to a poor old lady who was thanking him: 'My old friend, don't thank me: my soul goes out to you, for I have nothing else to give you.'

He might have established a school, for solemn doctors of the Law, rich zaddikim in marten-lined capes or penniless wanderers sparkling with holy fire, hurried from great distances to *dispute with a Lamed-waf*; but they encountered only his silence, or else a bad grace which unreeled itself in banalities on the mystery of knowing.

When the day was sunny, he would not let anyone in who wore the beard of a Talmudist, but would drag himself to the window and sniff the air, breathing deeply and looking sad. On those days a discreet watch was kept on the house, for the urchins of the neighbourhood liked to tiptoe even into the Just Man's room. They came because of his pillow, under which there was a heap of dried raisins, assorted nuts, almonds, and sugar-candies that the Just Man dispensed to his young admirers. But in exchange the old man engaged the children in interminable conversations on the rain, the good weather, the quality of the snow, the tenderness of cherries eaten straight from the tree. 'Ah! You give me back my legs!' he cried occasionally, in the middle of a rowdy discussion. And sighing with pleasure, 'My legs, yes, and *maybe even more . . .*'

Once they found two little boys under his bed; surprised by the arrival of a group of Cabbalists, they had spent the whole afternoon munching, and the sound of it made the wise men's hair stand on end. When the little jaws became too noisy, Rabbi Chaim said simply: 'Now children, do not forget that I am holding an important conversation.'

Bewildered, the visitors believed that he was admonishing familiar demons.

It caused a small scandal. They would have liked the Just Man to devote himself to occupations more worthy of him, and above all more worthy of the respect in which they held him. Shortly after this painful episode, they noted a certain improvement: he asked for ink, rolls of paper, and goosequills in great number. They rejoiced, and believed that the peasant had mended his ways. Informed persons announced that he was preparing a vast commentary on the treatise Ta'anith; according to others, it was a fundamental exegesis on the Tzedeka.

In the end it turned out to be simple tales for children; he went on writing them for the rest of his life.

At the birth of his first male child, Rabbi Chaim rejoiced, thinking that all was now consummated, and the cycle of his life at an end. And how would he present himself before the Eternal? In a wheelbarrow, ho ho! And then his heart a little gripped with fear: Oh Lord, what a wretched gift I am offering you; and how will you put me to the sword? What death awaits me? Outside, for the villagers, all things flowed cheerfully under the cloudless sky of Zemyock; but musing on the multiple dooms of his ancestors, Chaim told himself that God's resources are inexhaustible.

He was approaching forty; few Just Men had lived so long.

At first it was a matter of days, then weeks; after six months the horrifying reality was borne in on him: Zemyock was so peaceful a town, so sheltered from the world, that even a Just Man could only die in bed!

The holocausts of life, they say, often follow the roads laid out for commerce and industry; but Zemyock was huddled in a valley, hidden from the world's eye; regional traffic went by beyond the hills, and as there was neither a nobleman nor a priest for at least a league in any direction, the peasants lived on human terms with these Jews, artisans and cutters of crystal. From time immemorial, perhaps more than a hundred years, the faithful here had died gently, between two sheets, fearing only cholera, the plague, and the holy name of God.

Chaim became a dreamer. Each night he took to the highroad on wooden legs, or fled in a little wagon for the legless, that travelled like lightning. But always the villagers found him in the end, tucked him willy-nilly into his great feather-bed, and to the triumphal sound of the shofar, the bed hoisted on four shoulders like a coffin, carried him back into their city of perdition.

When his wife's belly swelled again, all Zemyock was perturbed. There were anguished confabulations, followed by a consistorial assembly. Finally a delegation comprising the principal personages of Zemyock arrived at the Just Man's bedside, to make the general apprehension known to him. They said, in substance: O Venerable Just Man, what have you done, what have you done? ... *Your ancestors gave the world one son and then died* ... And tell us now, if this next child is also a boy, which of the two will be your spiritual heir? Which of the two will be the *Lamed-waf*?

'My good friends,' Chaim answered, 'I refrained from knowing my wife for over two years, because I was afraid to hinder the design of the Most High. And then I thought that it is not right

32

for a man so to conduct himself towards his wife. If God wills it, this will be a daughter.'

A young student of the Law insisted: 'And if it is a boy?'

'If God wills it,' Chaim repeated calmly, 'it will be a girl.'

A few months later it was a boy, and the delegation demanded immediate audience of the Just Man, whom it found prostrate in his bed of misery, his eyes grim, looking as if he himself had painfully given birth. 'Why do you harass me?' he complained. 'It is not I who decide these things. I have done nothing to retard my death.'

'Or to retard this second child,' the student remarked in obvious irony. 'Your wife is pretty . . .'

'She is also a good woman,' the recumbent protested. 'Possibly,' he sighed, 'I am not a *Lamed-waf*; you built a throne for me, but I sat on it reluctantly. I have never received any confirmation from within, not the least sign, no voice telling me that I was a *Lamed-waf*. As far back as I can remember, I have believed that the dynasty ended with my father, the poor Jacob, may God warm his soul! Have I accomplished miracles for you? All I asked was a wheelbarrow.'

'But you sat on the throne too,' the student went on skilfully; 'you could have told us that you felt nothing!'

'What can I say, my friends? I am only a man, alas!'

'Alas, yes,' the student said with a certain smile, 'and you made that quite clear to your wife.'

A heavy silence fell over the room.

Two tears slipped from the hollow eyes of the *Lamed-waf*; slowly, one by one, they were lost in the wrinkled scars of his face.

'It is written,' he answered calmly, 'that God will satisfy those who revere him. And here he is satisfying your desire to find an opportunity of mocking me.'

Those words transfixed the hearts of his audience. To everybody's astonishment the student of the Law began uttering shrill screams, standing frozen in the attitude in which the Just Man's words had touched him. When calm was restored, each of them approached the bedside, kissed the Just Man's hand, and tiptoed out. Of all those who were present at that scene, none ever spoke of it again. But the rumour spread over all Poland that God could not make up his mind to kill Chaim Levy, whose heart seemed that of a child.

In addition to a few daughters, his wife added three more sons to his perplexity.

The future Just Man, he judged at the beginning, would be easily distinguishable from his brothers, like a cygnet among ducklings. But as they all grew up, Chaim was forced to admit that the divine presence was not apparent in any of them. A mutual loathing usual among heirs divided the first four, who intrigued for the title; sufficient proof, Chaim thought naïvely, that they had no right to it.

The fifth was beneath any consideration: a pagan, an imbecile, an authentic *Schliemazel*. They called him Brother Animal; he could not read, and the wings of thought barely touched him once or twice. He was devoted to the soil, and rather than pray or cut crystal he just planted those stupid vegetables that grow alone and require no skill save in the eating. He lived in a smelly hut, with many dogs, tortoises, field-mice and other abominations which he treated as brothers – nourishing them, teasing them with protective gestures, blowing into their faces. He was misshapen from birth, with a glazed eye and a hanging lower lip. The arrival of an idiot is a manifest omen; poor Chaim saw in it a confirmation – God had rescinded his promise.

The brief last agony of the Just Man was made sadder by the absence of Brother Animal, who was wandering peacefully in the fields, walking his beasts.

The patriarch had admitted only his sons to his bedside; these latter were wrangling over the succession, and Chaim only wondered if there would be one. And as they were also wrangling over the meagre estate, it is said that Chaim wept to hear them, beating his guilty breast with both fists, indicting himself for having lived so long only to die in bed like a woman, like a Christian.

Suddenly, dropping back on his pillow, he gave way to little chortles of happiness.

'That's the last straw,' the eldest son said coldly, stroking his beard in irritation; 'now what are we going to do?'

But already, with a sort of calculated slowness, the dying man was recovering his breath and giving gentle sighs of content, as beads of froth formed at the corners of his dark mouth. Finally, his eyes sparkling, his face lightly flushed: 'My children, do not be misled,' he said in an uncharacteristic tone of malice. 'Only the smallest drop of life is left in me, but my mind is sound.' Then lowering the wrinkled veil of his eyelids over his blind eyes, he seemed to withdraw into a region of being where his bones, his dead flesh, and the enveloping night ceased to cohere. 'My sons,' he said dreamily, 'sons of this clay, does a man not have the right to smile at his death, if God makes it gentle for him? No,' he went on into his grey beard, already matted in a terrible sweat, 'I have not yet felt the fluttering ... on my forehead ... of the wings of imbecility.

'Listen, open your ears, for I will tell you now why I was laughing. Amid my tears I heard: Well-beloved Chaim, your breath is thinning; hurry therefore and announce that the *Lamed-waf* is he whom your sons call Brother Animal; and so it will be for him at his last breath.'

And laughing again in delight, old Chaim choked, gasped, exhaled a thin sigh, 'Do you know? God enjoys himself,' and died.

2

WHEN he returned from the fields that night Brother Animal wept idiotically at his father's bedside, when he should have been rejoicing at that marvellous crown which was his legacy.

From the next day on, he threatened to leave Zemyock if they insisted on naming him Rabbi.

It was useless; neither veiled threats nor the promise of all earthly wealth could bring him to modify a single one of his cherished habits. Every morning, after swilling down his bowl of rude soup, the new Just Man would swing a spade to his shoulder, whistle for his dogs, and make for a strip of land granted him by a Polish peasant. The gifts rotted in his hut: exquisitely baked tarts, honey-cakes, pastries made with real cow's milk butter – whatever the dogs declined went to the children of the neighbourhood. For himself, he brewed enormous pots of vegetable soup in which he soaked black bread – or, lacking that, bun cake.

Although he was thoroughly ugly, thoroughly dirty, thoroughly stupid; although he urinated as the spirit moved him (except in the synagogue, where he sat rigid, as if paralysed by terror), the most beautiful girls of Zemyock now dreamed only of him; each of his faults glowed now in the idealizing light of his title. Anxious, ashamed, secretly glad, even the men yielded to the charm. It is impossible to say just what, they agreed, twisting their curl-papers in sheer vexation, but he undoubtedly has *something*.

The most desirable matches were offered him; motionless and enraptured, clasping his hands or foraging in a nostril with his index finger, Brother Animal would stand in contemplation before each beauty in all her finery; but he did not approach her. The mere word marriage sent him into strange excesses. Hoping to bring out unformulated desires, a bold father one day bends to the Just Man's ear, gesturing towards his daughter: 'Ah, Brother

Animal,' he whispers in an appropriate tone, 'have you no desire to put that pigeon in your bed?'

The Just Man casts a wet glance at the girl, reassures her with a beatific grin, and, raising his fist in the manner of a mallet, brings it hammering down on the skull of the foolhardy father. The question was not raised again.

He had only one friend, Joshua Levy, called the Absent-Minded. Little Joshua was still a child, and though he was normal in all respects (leaving aside a pronounced tendency towards day-dreaming), he sometimes accompanied his uncle into the fields and watched him work. Later on, it was stated that the idiot and the child indulged in long conversations; still, no one ever saw them other than silent, the one digging, the other dreaming. One day the idiot gave his nephew a little yellow dog and that was all. But later, much later, it was also remembered that the child never called his uncle Brother Animal, like everyone else, but by a singular aberration addressed him simply as Brother. And what was first attributed to childish inattention was later illuminated in a strange light . . .

When Brother Animal lay down to die, on a fragrant evening in May, he called for his dogs, his goat, and his pair of young doves. But the Levys insisted that he first name his successor, and as he claimed to know nothing about it, they kept the whole menagerie at a distance howling, bleating and cooing to death.

They say – but is it true? – that as Brother Animal obstinately refused to give them a name, the Levys persecuted him to his last breath. Pity, pity, he wailed, I swear to you that I hear no voice!

However, a long time after the tragedy some uncharitable tongues claimed that the idiot roused from his comatose state and fearing that they might retard his death indefinitely, only then gave in and named his little nephew Joshua Levy – 'you know, the one who has my yellow dog?' – before falling into the last sleep of the Just.

After that, they knew that the crown of glory could 'fall' upon any head; cliques sprang up; a pitiless pressure was brought to bear upon the reigning Just Man; the life of Joshua Levy was but one long calvary. He promised his second wife, 'so young, alas', to designate a son of her flesh; and in the end, in his agony, the name of an undistinguished nephew escaped his lips. Nothing more is known. Nothing. The unfortunate Levys sought vainly to identify the signs by which God made his choice. Was it necessary to engulf oneself in prayer? To work in the fields? To love animals? Men? Accomplish noble deeds? Or simply to live out the wretched but so sweet existence of Zemyock? Who will be the Chosen One?

So from then on the childhood of each Levy was lived under the new sign vouchsafed by God to his people: a question mark, hovering over their skulls like an uncertain halo.

While the sand of days ran on, gently, grain by grain, the Jews of Zemyock persisted in thinking that the measureable time of man had stopped in Sinai; they lived, not without grace, in the eternal time of God, that passes through no hour-glass. What was a day? Even a century? Since the creation of the world the heart of God had pulsed only half a beat.

From those sublime heights, no one had eyes to see what destiny was weaving in the time of the Christians: a newborn industrial Poland, nibbling away steadily at the mainly artisan life of the Jews; like an iron heel, each new factory crushed hundreds of independent workers. The elders often remembered better times, more propitious to the founding of families and synagogues. But they were unable to resign themselves to these sinks of iniquity, the factories – where the Sabbath was not respected, and where one could not observe, in their plenitude and magnificence, as at home, the 613 commandments of the Law. So they died of hunger, piously.

Then a few souls, bold and unstrangled by religious scruples, took flight towards Germany, France, England, often reaching even the two Americas. It was thus that about a third of the Polish Jews came to live essentially through the post office; which is to say, by the money orders from their 'envoys' abroad. It was the same for the inhabitants of Zemyock, where crystal-cutting could no longer feed a Jew.

But the Levys received no support from the mails, and expected none.

It was known that to leave one's homeland was to place oneself at the mercy of American idols: to exile oneself from God. And because God, for Polish Jews, was nowhere more at home than in Poland, the Levys judged that he felt particularly comfortable in Zemyock, in the territory assigned to the Just Men. So they would not leave him, and all of them remaining, all were with God, and all were miserable.

As they were the poorest and shabbiest of Zemyock, those who ranked a bare second to them in poverty spared them some kind of alms; for the rich pity only each other, do they not? In season the Levys hired themselves out to small farms; but the Polish peasants scorned the frail arms of the Jews and paid them a pittance in kind.

Towards the end of the nineteenth century, the Levy children were recognized by the pallor of their faces . . .

Mordecai Levy (grandfather of our friend Ernie) was born into a needy family of crystal-cutters. As a boy he had a narrow head, a clear bright eye, and a big hooked nose which seemed to draw his whole face forward. But his adventurer's vocation was not yet very evident.

On the day when even the traditional herring of the poor was lacking at the table, Mordecai announced that he would seek work the next day among the neighbouring farms. His brothers stared at him astounded and his mother cried out shrilly, swearing that the Polish peasants would insult him, would beat him to death and God alone knew what else.

To begin with, he was refused all work; Jews were hired only with reluctance and under seasonal pressure. After long days of vain requests, he was taken on for the harvesting of potatoes but at a very distant little farm. The foreman had said to him: Jew, you're as big as a tree, and I'll give you ten kilos of potatoes a day. But will you be brave enough to fight? Mordecai met the foreman's cold glare, and did not answer.

The next day he was awake two hours before dawn. His

mother tried to hold him back; something bad would happen to him as it has to this one, and that one, and the other one, who had all come home bloody. Mordecai listened to her and smiled, remembering that he was a tree.

But when he found himself alone on the road, in the grey dawn, in the vanishing warmth of his breakfast of tea and potatoes, the foreman's words came back to him. My God, he told himself, he was going there to work, and would behave himself so well towards everybody that the devil himself wouldn't have the heart to insult him.

The morning was uneventful. Legs apart, he was lifting the instrument they had put into his hands, bringing it down with a fearful force all around the faded potato plant; then groping into the fibred soil and heaping its fruits on the edge of the open trench. To his left, to his right, the rows of Polish workmen advanced at much the same pace. Determined not to be left behind, he did not see the surprised and grumpy looks that his neighbours cast at him, vast Jewish adolescent, stiff and formal in his long black cloak, as he brandished his hoe with the industrious eloquence of a priest, the blind intoxication of a blacksmith.

When he reached the middle of the field he took off his velveteen hat and balanced it carefully on two potatoes.

But sweat still obscured his view, and ten yards farther along he stripped off his cloak and left it lying across the trench.

Finally, when the moving line of harvesters had almost reached the end of the field, a kind of spider with numerous cutting claws came down on his back, arching it in sudden agony. Twisted and cramped, Mordecai lifted his hoe with a terrible slowness, saying in his mind, My God, then brought it down desperately to the soil as other words saw light in him for the first time: *come help thy servant*. It was to that invocation, renewed before each potato plant, that he attributed his heroic perseverance to the end of the row. He finished up dead level with the Poles.

At noon he went back into the field to recover his cloak and his hat, then, shivering with cold and with a formless fear, made for the fire round which the team was sitting.

The farmhands fell silent at his approach. He squatted down and slipped three potatoes into the embers. Those silent looks filled him with a deadly anguish. The foreman had gone back to his own chores; Mordecai felt caught in a wolf's jaws, posed delicately on its quivering tongue; at his slightest gesture the fangs would close, and tear him to pieces. Almost panting with fear, he plucked out a potato and juggled it in his palms.

'Some people use the fire without even asking,' a voice behind him growled.

Seized with terror, Mordecai dropped the potato and half rose to his feet, bringing his elbow fearfully up before his face, as if to ward off an imminent blow.

'I didn't know, sir!' he stammered from under it in his hesitant Polish. 'Forgive me, I believed I . . .'

'You hear that?' the 'Pole' asked jovially. 'Did you hear it? He *believed*!'

The peasant was about his age, but his arms were bare in spite of the cutting cold, and his half-open tunic unveiled the majestic beginnings of a bull-like neck. His knotty hands, fixed squarely on his hips, emphasized his look of a stocky animal. Mordecai shuddered; in the middle of a crude red face two delicately blue eyes were staring at him with a kind of grave loathing, placid, and very Polish.

'It's no good,' a voice came from somewhere, 'you've got to fight.'

Mordecai protested: 'Why? What for? Fight for what?'

And turning towards the motionless group of peasants, he undertook his defence according to the methods recommended, in such cases, by the most ancient authors: 'Gentlemen,' he began, spreading his arms significantly, 'by your leave, you are my witnesses . . . I had no wish to insult this gentleman in using the hearth for my potatoes. Can you believe otherwise?

'And since there was no offence,' he went on in quavering tones, kneeling but with his chest quite literally thrust outwards by the force of his oratorical breathing; 'and since there has been no offence, do you not think, farmers and gentlemen, that reasonable explanations would allow us to resolve the differences

41

between myself and ... this gentleman?' he finished on a sadly falsetto note.

'They do know how to talk, these kikes,' said the young Pole in a voice full of admiration. And sweeping the air with an eloquent gesture, he flung Mordecai to the ground.

With a swift process of his elbows, Mordecai moved a few yards away. The smell of the soil climbed into his nostrils. Far off in space and time, the peasants were in fits of laughter at his dazed and frightened posture. He removed a scab of mud from his jaw, which had hit the ground first.

The young Pole stepped forward. Mordecai placed one finger on his cheek, where the blow had landed. He would have to show these people that they were mistaken; they couldn't force a man to fight who was as religious as he was, a Jew whose principles set him against any manifestation so little in conformity with the teachings of the sages, a young Levy who had never witnessed physical violence and who knew a punch only by hearsay. But as his oppressor approached, rolling his shoulders absurdly, Mordecai had a dreaming presentiment that such a demonstration was doomed to failure.

'And how could he understand, *this monkey*?' he exclaimed suddenly, in Yiddish.

He was just getting up to run away when the kick caught him on his rump, depositing him face down on the dirt. The young Pole was calmly repeating: dirty Jew, dirty Jew, dirty Jew, driving his boot into Mordecai's buttocks every time he tried to rise. Such a strong note of triumph was running in his voice that soon Mordecai felt his contempt for the *monkey* turn into an aching flame that consumed all things within him and suddenly delivered him up to a human body flexed and sinewy as a bow.

He never knew how it happened; he was standing once again, and flung himself upon the young Pole crying. 'What do you think you're doing?'

He was indignant.

3

WHEN the peasants dragged him off his defeated foe, whom he was still hammering with his fists, his feet, his elbows – and, had it been possible, with the whole stiffened mass of his body – Mordecai, haggard and almost drunk on blood, discovered that he had conquered the whole Christian universe of violence in one blow.

'Well, he's a fine one,' said a peasant. 'He's not like the rest of them.'

Slowly a dry shame invaded Mordecai. 'Now,' he said with a naïve arrogance they liked, 'now can I use your fire?'

And that evening, home again, he knew that henceforth he had over his own people the oh, so despicable advantage of a body intimately bound to the earth, to plants and to trees, to all animals, inoffensive or dangerous – including those who bear the name of men.

At first, every new farm meant a brawl; but as he circulated around Zemyock his reputation as a 'tough Jew' won him sympathy. As for the gentle Jewish souls of Zemyock, they looked askance at him, with the compassionate respect due to a fallen Levy, and the secretly jealous scorn one feels for a great pirate. The Levys watched him suspiciously; his crude unshapely hands drew their dismayed glances and his posture, alas, no longer expressed the traditional hunch or the required detachment. They murmured – supreme scandal – that he had become stiff from the neck to the heels.

Seeing this, he gradually fell into the habit of returning to Zemyock only on Friday night, as the Sabbath drew exquisitely near. Saturday was given over altogether to contrition, then on Sunday at dawn, with his books and prayer-shawl carefully stowed away in his knapsack, he would lose himself again in nature.

One day on his way to a farm at some distance from Zemyock, he ran into an old Israelite seated at the edge of the road on his pedlar's pack, his eyes full of pain and weariness. He carried the load as far as a nearby town where the old man had, as he put it, 'a crumb' of family. The pack contained popular Yiddish novels, multicoloured ribbons, some glassware; Mordecai sold a little of everything, as a game, in the villages they passed through. The old pedlar watched him, smiling. But when they reached his home town, three days later, he said to Mordecai: My career is ended, I can walk no more. Take this pack and go. I give you my capital, my suppliers, my itinerary; you are a Levy of Zemyock and I risk nothing. When you have a few zlotys in hand, you can come back here and pay me back the capital. Go, I tell you. Go on.

Mordecai slung the pack slowly on his shoulders.

A pedlar could easily find lodgings in villages; for he brought a breath of fresh air into those settlements, withdrawn into themselves all the year round.

Mordecai affected nonchalance, laughed loudly, ate as much as he could, and argued with whoever looked dubiously at his merchandise; but when he was within sight of Zemyock the lively fire of his eyes went out and he felt himself invaded by a slow and peaceful tide of anguish. And it was with a sort of confused discretion that he put down his profits on the corner of the table, surrounded by the icy silence of the Levys.

'So you're back?' his father said rather ironically. '*They* have let you go again?' And as Mordecai bowed his head in shame: 'Come here you rascal, let me see how you're made, if you still have a Jewish face. Well, come on into my arms; what are you waiting for, the return of yesterday?' Mordecai was trembling like a leaf.

When he was back on the narrow country road, leaving behind the crumbling walls of Zemyock, strange questions came into his mind. One day, in a gesture of sympathy, a colleague offered him a date. Everyone had hurried to contemplate this rarest of fruit. Hastily they scanned the Pentateuch, to savour in it the word 'tawar', which means date; and Mordecai himself, though an experienced businessman by then, seemed to see the whole land of Israel in that single date. Now he was crossing the Jordan, reaching the tomb of Rachel and the Wailing Wall of Jerusalem; now bathing in the rich waters of the Lake of Tiberias, where the carp fatten in the sun ... And each time he came to himself by the side of the road, his little date all grey and wrinkled in his fingers, Mordecai wondered: My Lord, what does all this mean, a pedlar lost on the plain, a Levy far from Zemyock, a date, a tough Jew, the Lake of Tiberias, a young man facing life?

And a thousand other questions.

One day as he approached the town of Krichownice, more than twenty days from Zemyock, he even wondered why God had created Mordecai Levy. For several years there had been no reigning fool in Zemyock, and it is written: 'Every city has its wise man and its fool.' But what could be done, he wondered suddenly, sadly, with an animal like Mordecai, who was tiger-striped at random with both those virtues.

He was certainly tired at that moment. He had been walking since dawn, and now his fatigue made the hills of Krichownice dance, far off in the shifting light of dusk. Every few seconds he searched the sky in anguish, afraid of finding that first star which announces that the Sabbath has descended upon the world. Once, surprised by the first star of a Friday night, he had abandoned his 'capital' in a field, hidden in the tall grass.

At the city gate a young woman was filling a bucket from the communal well with a slow, almost animal grace that made light of the rope saturated with cold water. Her attire was Sabbatic: flat slippers with pearly buttons, a long dress of black and green velvet, and the traditional ruffs of lace at her throat and wrists.

Even from a distance Mordecai felt the allurement as of a wild animal within her; the supple beauty of her gestures suggested danger held in check.

Approaching quietly on the grass, he saw that she was a true Jewish beauty, almost as tall and slender as he. Three paces away, he was arrested by her cat-like profile: short nose, slanted eyes, small brow pulled back by the heavy tresses that gripped the back of her neck. God forgive me, he said to himself, she pleases me.

Flinging his pack to the grass almost at the woman's feet, he cried out in the tones of a hardened pedlar: 'Hey there, my dove! Can you show me the way to the synagogue?'

He had a cavernous, stentorian voice; the young woman started violently, dropped the rope, caught it up again, and finally, setting the wooden bucket on the lip of the well: 'What a beast of a peasant!' she cried, tossing her head. Almost immediately her frown softened at the sight of the lean, smiling young man, white with the dust of the road. 'Am I a horse?' she asked deliberately, in a pungent, sweet Yiddish. 'A donkey, a bull, a camel? It seems I must be.'

Steadying the wooden bucket on the stone lip, she threw her hair back with a quick motion of her head. Her jet-black eyes bore upon Mordecai with a burning and devouring curiosity, but below these she pursed her lips, determined to show the utmost disdain for him. 'Besides,' she said, 'I don't speak to strangers; but if you will follow me at ten paces, I can point out the synagogue as we pass.'

And measuring him with a haughty glance, her back arched proudly, she started off through the village paying no further attention to 'the stranger'.

Mordecai whistled, a long slow hiss between his teeth. 'God forgive me,' he sighed as he hoisted the sack painfully to his shoulder, 'I like her. I like her a lot, even, but . . . I'd beat her with pleasure.'

Moved by this contradictory sentiment, he concentrated (keeping his distance of ten paces) on verbal barbs, which had the effect of hastening her step and provoking angry tosses of her head. Her tresses then swept her lovely shoulders, side by side, like the ruffled mane of a mare, and the unconscious animal coyness of their heavy motion incited Mordecai to new sarcasms: 'So that's how you greet strangers in this town?' he bellowed. 'At ten paces? Do you know that God chose Abraham for having granted hospitality to beggars? Think a minute, maybe I'm a messenger from the Lord.'

46

But striding straight and firm down the centre of the road, the woman pretended to hear nothing, and Mordecai dared not diminish the absurd distance between them. As he broke into a forced laugh, over-loud, he was astonished to hear these words emanating from the cool dancing silhouette ten steps ahead of him, cold words, hardly softened by the breeze that bore them: 'To listen to you, my fine gentleman, one would think you were rather a messenger from the Devil!'

Mordecai could hardly believe his ears, and as he wondered whether to be angry, a smothered laugh reached him, and the black mane shook triumphantly.

'Not even the Devil,' she went on, 'he's too good for you . . .'

An odd sadness fell upon Mordecai; he decided to take offence, and was silent, suddenly aware of the pack rubbing against his spine. After which, probably for the first time in his life, he resented his lambskin tunic, the lining of which was unravelling, and his boots, worn and scuffed, and even the uncommon form of his velour hat, due to its use as a recipient for solids and certain liquids. What difference does that make, he suddenly decided. Am I a gold mark, to please everybody?

Just at that moment he saw that the girl had set down her bucket and had turned to him with a smile, shrugging ironically, as if to say, Come on now, don't be angry; you started it, after all. Then she shook her head and walked off again brusquely so that the wooden bucket, now at her side again, bobbed faster with her springy step. She seemed to carry it as lightly as a bouquet, but now the leaping spray was spattering the velvet of her dress, beading it with evanescent drops of light. The young man felt that the moment was sweet.

Behind the town church were the first Jewish homes, shabby and dilapidated, huddled together like fearful old women. Here and there a bearded figure in moiré caftan glided along a wall. Night came down suddenly, in a fine drizzle: that young lady, dancing along in front of Mordecai, was now no more than a shadow. Suddenly the shadow halted, and a thin white finger pointed to an alley opening; the synagogue was there, said that finger. Then it, too, disappeared.

'Who does she think I am?' Mordecai raged at himself. 'I'm not a dog that ... who ...' Dropping his pack he marched forward with the swift and burning impulse that flames up from a feeling of righteousness.

The girl, warned by the sound of his advance, had quickly taken refuge in a doorway. But when he saw her at ten feet, so beautiful in the shadow, he thought gently: Come now, why should she even thank me ...

Calm but wary she watched him, one hand on the latch, ready for anything.

'Would you,' he stammered suddenly, 'that is, would you allow ... may I carry your bucket?'

'You're a pedlar, aren't you?' she whispered breathlessly. 'Here today, gone tomorrow ... how dare you talk to me like that?'

And with a wide mocking smile (in which nevertheless he seemed to see a fine shadow of regret) she swung up her bucket, more than half empty, let it rest against her calf, saluted the young man with a brief bob of her mane, then suddenly broke into a trot and disappeared in a splashing of water; he could not tell which street she had taken.

Modecai lifted his pack wearily and turned to the synagogue. One star twinkled in the sky, between the suddenly black houses. But the star did not evoke the transparent glow of the Sabbath, for the patch of sky in which it winked – like a gold-headed pin – seemed to him cut from the nocturnal velvet of a Jewish girl's dress.

4

AFTER the evening office the faithful, coughing, chirping and gesticulating in the smoke of the small synagogue stove, argued as to who the signal grace of exercising hospitality would fall upon. The general feeling, on account of his appearance, was for offering Mordecai to a person of note whose immoderate taste for the external world was well-known; but on this night the rabbi, instead of shoving Mordecai in the category of 'happy pedlars', assigned him to that of 'pilgrims living by trade', and invited him to his own table.

'Rabbi, good rabbi,' Mordecai said, 'my place is not at your table. I'm not a good Jew; I'm just a little sad this evening. You understand?'

'And why are you sad?' asked the rabbi, surprised.

'Why am I sad?' Mordecai smiled. 'Because I'm not a good Jew...'

The rabbi was a little round man, goggle-eyed, with a tiny mouth that seemed to chirrup beneath his beard. 'Come along,' he shrilled suddenly, 'and don't say another word!'

The meal was regal; Mordecai could not have dreamt anything better: a fish-broth done in wine, a roast of beef, and an exquisite dessert of sugared carrots. Though delighted to be so well received, Mordecai uttered not a word, behaving with as much austerity as if he had been in Zemyock, at the meditative table of the Levys. But when the hostess passed a platter of carob-beans, he could not help tapping his belly with a comic air and saying: 'Ah, brethren, brethren, a bit of carob tastes of Paradise; it evokes the land of Israel. When we eat it, we become languorous, and we sigh, Return us, O Lord, to our own land, to the land where even the goats graze on teeming carob!'

With these words the gathering came to life, and the eternal interrogation began: When would the Messiah come? Would

49

he come on a cloud? Will the dead accompany him? And on what would we nourish ourselves, since it is written, On that day I will make an alliance for you with the beasts of the field? And how, my gentle lambs, can we hasten his arrival? This concluding question was offered by the rabbi, with a small, desolated sweep of his arm.

Everyone present, knew that here the two-thousand-year-old discussion reached its peak, an awesome summit from which all of Creation was visible.

'We must suffer,' began an ancient on the rabbi's right, hollow-eyed, with a hanging, pink lower lip; his head never stopped wagging; 'suffer, and suffer more, and suffer always, for . . .'

'Mr Grynspan,' his hostess interrupted angrily, 'and what do you think we're doing now? Isn't that enough for you?'

'Tut, tut,' the rabbi said timidly.

'For it is written,' the old man went on with no change of expression, 'for it is written: suffering becomes Israel like a red ribbon on the head of a white horse. For it is written: we shall bear the sufferings of the world, we shall take its grief upon ourselves, and we shall be considered as punished, stricken by the Lord and humiliated. And then only, when Israel is suffering from head to foot, in all its bones and all its flesh and all its nerves, prostrate at the crossing of the roads, then only will God send the Messiah! Alas,' Mr Grynspan finished, his eyes protruding as if in a vision of the terrible things to come, 'then only; not before.'

'Mr Grynspan,' the rabbi chirped sadly, 'I ask you: what pleasure do you take in terrifying us? Are we Just Men, to live with the knife before our eyes? You know what, dear Mr Grynspan, let us rather speak of something gay: what news of the war?'

Having said which, and though the *hoary* joke was known to all of them, the rabbi fell into such a coughing and sputtering and gasping that they were afraid for him. But after the customary exorcisms and aspersions the crisis of laughter passed as it had come, and he reseated himself at the common table. 'We were saying?' he murmured, embarrassed.

Then, noting the general disapproval, he composed a serious face: 'I am not unaware,' he modulated at last, 'dear Mr Grynspan, how shocking, even painful, my demonstration may have seemed to you, but I must point out that it was not directed at you, nor at what you said, and that this attack was due solely to the joy I feel on such a beautiful Sabbath. Do you believe that?'

'I believe you willingly,' the old man said with emotion, 'but allow me to bring this to your attention, that according to the school of the Rabbi Khennina . . .'

The conversation turned to the subject of laughter: its nature, its laws, its human and divine significance, and finally, by an insidious route, its relation to the coming of the Messiah.

Faithful to his role as a pedlar, Mordecai had kept silence until then. From time to time a black and green dress flitted before his melancholy eyes. How could he see her again? Staking everything on one throw, he leaned forward: 'For myself,' he offered gravely, in the tone his father adopted for such occasion; 'for myself, if I note that Yitz'hak means above all he who will laugh in the future; and if I observe that Sarah had seen the son of Hagar, Ishmael, when he was "Metza'hek", this is to say, laughing; I conclude humbly that the sons of Abraham, Ishmael and Isaac, are distinguished by the fact that the first knew how to laugh in the present, while it was reserved for Isaac, our father to weep until the coming of the Messiah, blessed be he, who will grant eternal laughter to all. And tell me, Brethren, how a truly Jewish heart could laugh in this world, if not at the thought of the world to come?'

On this noble envoi, Mordecai raised his liqueur glass to his mouth and, throwing his head back, swallowed its contents in one gulp, like a peasant, to the great stupefaction of all the guests. Then, clacking his tongue against the roof of his mouth, he added, not without finesse, 'Happily, our own hearts are not entirely Jewish; otherwise how could we taste such a serenity this evening?'

His final remark was much appreciated. The rabbi found a Hasidic flavour in it. Yet he was astonished at such marvels from a simple pedlar, and it was then that Mordecai put the finishing touch to his subtleties; bowing his head almost coyly he said that he was a Levy of Zemyock.

'I would have sworn to it!' cried the little rabbi.

'But I am far from being a Just Man,' Mordecai qualified modestly, even as he offered a wide and seductive smile to the company. God forgive me if he can, he said to himself at that moment; she is really too beautiful!

The next morning, waking in the big conjugal bed (where the rabbi and his wife had insisted that he sleep) Mordecai was prey to an uneasiness, a strange torpor, a difficulty in moving – all symptoms of the tertian ague. Equipped with a new jug, and supported by his distressed hosts, he went immediately to the nearby river and said to it: River, river, lend me a jugful of water for the trip that I must take!

Then amid the total silence of the many spectators, he brandished the jug seven times about his head, and poured the water behind him, crying: River, river, take back the water you gave me, and with it the fever that burns me. I beg this of you, river, in the name of our common Creator.

This was said with artistry, truly in the style of Zemyock.

Then the sick man and his attendants returned to the rabbi's house, where Mordecai took to his bed immediately. Many villagers appeared at his bedside, attracted by the renown of all the *Lamed-waf*. They found him doleful, his expression cadaverous; and the fact is that he had spent a sleepless night of anticipated remorse.

Gradually, and as the tertian became quartan ague, he agreed that to continue his journey would be madness; and as the fever persisted, he even condescended to take up his winter quarters in Krichownice, as a replacement for the beadle. This arrangement delighted everyone, beginning with the beautiful black-maned creature he saw a few days later, as he was loafing casually around the well. 'You know,' she laughed, 'your illness didn't worry me too much.'

'Is it possible?' he cried, lost.

'Then you were . . .' she stammered, 'you were *really* . . .'

As she spoke she stepped back, and stood against the edge of the well, with so much pity in her eyes that all her feline expression disappeared to be replaced at once by the wary tenderness of her young girl's flesh, Mordecai felt a sweet twinge in his breast; with a pedlar's gesture, he smoothed back his moustache. 'I was really ill,' he said, smiling slyly, 'and I still am, more than ever,' he finished in a hoarse tone laden with emotion.

She broke into endless laughter and Mordecai was allowed to follow her, that day, at five paces; which became three the following day, and then zero; happy as a child, he clutched half the icy handle of the bucket.

This last favour intoxicated him; he let himself speak unchecked, sweet words, and grave, and melancholy, such words as he thought would please a young woman of Zemyock, or Krichownice, or any place. But she soon made him understand that she preferred him as the 'happy pedlar', and, sick at heart, Mordecai complied; this puppet that Judith loved in him, whose strings he manipulated to please her – now he wanted to smash it!

'Why do you have to bay at the moon?' she said. 'When one loves, the great thing is surely to make oneself lovable. Am I a moon? I am Judith.'

One fine day she admitted, though playfully, that she had never seen a pedlar as big, strong, sweet, and amusing as he. And doubtless, she went on in the same tone, it was an honour for her to be noticed by a Levy of Zemyock; but there it was, she was an idiot, she didn't feel it, she would have preferred a plain ordinary Levy. What did all those fearful, bloody stories mean that they told about his family? Brrrr! they made her shiver!

And as he had begun to look prim, she exploded: 'I don't want any of *that*, do you hear? I want to live! Live! Live! What do I want with a Just Man?'

'But I'm not a Just Man!' Mordecai protested in accents of despair.

'We know you, we know all about your kind,' she answered;

'whoever says that he isn't one, that's the one who is. And why do you have to suffer for the world? Where do you get it from? And tell me this, does the world suffer for you? Does it?'

'But I'm not suffering, I swear it!'

But Judith was no longer listening; she was wringing her hands and rolling her wild eyes, the whole of her small nose quivered and a fine spray of saliva had formed on her lips, as with cats. She brought a strange look to bear upon the young man: 'And why,' she demanded, 'why must it happen to idiot me, Judith Ackerman, that of all the showers of men that God rains on the earth, I should choose the one bad drop? There aren't a thousand *Lamed-waf* on earth, not even a hundred, only thirty-six, thirty-six! And I, *mad from the land of Madness*, I no sooner catch a glimpse of one of them, than I fall in love with him, you hear?' she sighed, with a gentleness all the more poignant in the tall, savage girl.

And as Mordecai stood, dumbfounded: 'Do you hear me, murderer?' she shouted to his face.

At this Mordecai took on an expression so submissive, so unhappy, that flinging herself against her executioner and covering his eyes with her hands, the girl kissed him on the lips, unexpectedly, for the first time. Mordecai went half crazy, grinned, felt vaguely uneasy, and knew that there was such a breath of life in her that all the reason in the world was shattered against her lips, to fly off like chaff, far off, high off, in the grey unmoving sky of ideas. Straining her against him, he murmured, 'I'll do ... I'll even be your puppet, all right?'

The spirit of Zemyock that smouldered secretly within him burst into flame after the betrothal, which was a decisive turning-point for him; tamed already and radiant, the fierce animal quite visibly longed only to enter her cage, and beneath the tremulous lover the husband suddenly rose, the lord and master, protected by the laws as by so many iron bars. At the first skirmish the husband was victorious. 'If you don't understand me,' he cried acrimoniously, 'it's because you don't want to!' Then, opting for the truth, he put on a mask of pride that hardened his face and astonished Judith altogether: 'You see,' he explained, 'among *us*, before he marries, a man must recopy the book of our family, the whole history of the Levys, to give it to his children to read; and you want *all that* to end because of your pretty head of hair? I have to go back to Zemyock just once. You can see that.'

'Go on then,' she cried, 'but don't come back!'

Mordecai stared at her, hesitated, turned his back in absolute calm.

As he crossed the threshold two hands fell on his shoulders and he felt the uneven, excited breath of his betrothed against the back of his neck: 'Come back quickly,' the proud Judith murmured.

He promised, wept, promised again. If she had known how to turn her defeat to advantage, she could have kept him there. But Judith knew nothing of that weapon and Mordecai left for Zemyock, mounted on a cart-horse they had loaded down with slices of smoked beef, jars of preserves, a caged chicken with two weeks' feed, and a multitude of cakes, embroidered napkins, spools of thread, buttons, socks, and other gifts for the son-in-law's family.

So equipped, he looked magnificent, but on the outskirts of Zemyock three weeks later his enthusiasm disappeared. He found his family at table, around a single herring. Under the low, cracked ceiling, crossed by a beam for ever bare, those emaciated faces wrung his heart. His father did not deign to rise.

'I thought,' he jeered majestically, 'that you would marry without even writing your book.'

'I love her,' Mordecai said gently.

'Listen to that, he loves her!' exclaimed his elder brother, raising his skinny arms towards the beam, as if to call heaven to witness the enormity.

'And have I not loved also?' his father articulated slowly. 'But I thought,' he relapsed into sarcasm, 'that the wife must follow her husband; perhaps you are not of that opinion?'

'But she didn't want to come,' the lover said dolefully; in the same instant he bit his lower lip and blushed; a unanimous burst of laughter greeted his confession.

'*Peace!*'

Dissipating the uproar with that one word, the father rose to his feet, quite tall despite the curvature of age; and with his arms crossed upon his breast as immemorial symbol of duty, and his hollow eyes flaming like torches, he very distinctly pronounced these words – perhaps prepared in advance: 'Remember, my son: for the man whom women have destroyed, there will be neither judge nor justice.'

Then he sat down stiffly and ignored Mordecai's existence.

5

JUDITH did not recognize the 'happy pedlar' who had left her a few weeks before: his beard was longer, his aquiline face had taken on an ivory sheen; he took her absently into his arms.

'My flesh and my blood,' she whispered against his chest, 'how thin you are and how sad; are you ill?'

'He's ill with love,' Judith's mother said gaily; she was a strong woman with a reddish complexion who was generally busy in the kitchen, preparing ample libations. 'It's a good disease,' she stated, peremptorily; 'good for the spleen and the shine of the eyes!'

'Is that true?' Judith asked, palpitating with pleasure; and as Mordecai did not answer she tore herself away from him and cried out, with sudden insight: 'You don't love me now!'

Mordecai's gaze fell on her, but without force; the grey irises of his eyes were hesitant in the pale white membrane, like clouds lost very high in the sky. Then they filled with tears.

'My father did not give me his blessing,' he said at last, in a dying voice; and then he added violently, as his whole face reddened in passion: 'But God will look after us, won't he?' And he astonished them all by reverting to his casually gay pedlar's manner; he grabbed a long-stemmed glass and tinkled it gaily against the bottle of kvass, as one knocks at a door: 'Mother-in-law,' he thundered with authority, 'what's the meaning of this?'

And maliciously citing Scripture, he declaimed: '*Give strong drink to him who is dying, and wine to him who has bitterness in his soul!*'

He gulped down the kvass like water; he was laughing! Judith felt better.

But a few days later she realized that Mordecai was withdrawing into himself again. Just as he had loved movement and gaiety – before that cursed Zemyock – so now he fled all such occasions, going so far as to mortify himself for hours on end at the synagogue. Judith did not know what to think. It seemed to her that instead of drawing closer to her, with intimacy revealing more and more of the man, her fiancé was wrapping himself up in a cloak invisible to the eye, and against which her poor heart jostled painfully.

She advanced the wedding date. When Mordecai shattered the bachelor's symbolic glass, she wept. That same evening the ecstatic couple settled in the home of Judith's parents. These latter were bakers of bread, and were delighted with the heavy kneading hands of the son-in-law sent to them by the *providence of the aged*.

And Judith breathed easily; for with the passing days and weeks Mordecai never tired of his wife's body, a body that was always accessible and always distant, secret, woven of innocence. Each night they fell into the same astonishment; it was like a gulf of light, she thought, a heaven upside-down. Her mother teased her privately: 'Who ever knew love before you? Who else can even talk about it? No one.'

But for himself Mordecai wondered in shame whether such delights did not contain a certain excess, a pagan undertone; did they not cut him off from God?

An uneasiness grew within him, which he associated obscurely with his exile from Zemyock. The girls of his village had one admirable quality, in that their will wavered under a simple glance; any man, even as shy as a mouse, could keep tight reins on his wife. But to try that with Judith, who not only obeyed neither touch nor glance, but would reject a formal order from her husband as one brushes a fly from one's face!

All in all, incontestably the most troublesome problem was her tendency to flirt as before their marriage; for a yes, for a no, she would stubbornly refuse her favours; and in her passion for being desired was quite capable of going two or even three days without one tender word, without one sigh, was this a Jewish heart?

And so, although he could never accuse her of shamelessness, Judith used her charms to acquire such power over the poor

58

pedlar that he even went so far as to wonder if he hadn't married a demon in the guise of a marvellous woman. This gulf that they were digging night by night, where would it lead them?

More and more often, Mordecai was surprised to find himself expressing his homesickness for Zemyock.

This counter-offensive gathered momentum very slowly.

When Judith saw that her husband was taking on the look of a studious and meditative man, it was too late to revert to their old relationship of good grace shot with stormy civility; the words that Mordecai uttered now all seemed marked by the seal of God, his wishes all seemed to conform to the divine will; he claimed that his every act was performed in obedience to the commandments of the Eternal, even unto the act of love.

On this last point, Judith reserved her opinion. Yet the day came when Mordecai gave orders, and then the day came when his haughty wife obeyed; shortly afterward, he persuaded her to follow him to Zemyock, for good.

She immediately lost all control. Her looseness of speech, the arrogance of her bearing, were an affliction to both sexes: 'Look at that Bohemian!' they said. 'Oi, what a misfortune! That's what a husband gets when he wanders for a wife.' And the stranger was treated with the distance that separated the 'Judiths' from the proper wives of Zemyock.

At first she would often burst into tears, then into a tearing rage during which all the griefs she had recorded one by one on the scutcheon of her rancour were squarely blamed upon her husband, who was accused of delicately breaking her heart and life. 'From the first minute, from the first second, you deceived me, you made a fool of me! Ho, my dove, may I carry your little bucket, my princess? A pedlar, a grenadier, an Alexander devouring the miles! And stupid me, I thought we could enjoy each other and amuse each other every day, all our lives; and what was underneath all that! A snivelling little Levy with a prayer in the morning and a prayer at night and in between . . . nothing but one long prayer!

'But you kept it under cover, oh, you played the part perfectly, you tamed your little dove, didn't you? First I have to write my book, then my father didn't give me his blessing, and finally the last step: Zemyock! Zemyock! Ai, ai, Zemyock, I wouldn't wish it on my worst enemy! What kind of a town is it? Levys, everywhere Levys, nothing but Levys, half the town is Levys. Who could believe there were so many Levys?

'In my father's house you made good bread; and here? My lord cuts crystal, ha-ha, the pretty-pretty trade, and very soon you turn to crystal yourself, so people can see right through you! But who cares? As long as I babble, and gibber prayers at the synagogue, and gibber philosophy with all the wise old beards, zim zim zim, what do you think about heaven? Zom, zom, zom, what do you think about hell? And what good does that do anybody? Does it help God, maybe? As far as I know him, he feels the same way about it as I do: what flea can have bitten them? He wonders. And scratches his head.

'But all good things come to an end: I'm leaving. I'm going away, you understand? I'm going back to dear old Krichownice full of asses and illiterates! And I'll tell them you're dead, I'll go into mourning; and believe me, as your widow – do you hear, Alexander of Zemyock? – I'll be a thousand times happier than I was as your wife! And the plague strike me dead if . . .'

Mordecai watched her silently, raising a pained eyebrow, and murmured one word, always the same, with the expert, resigned patience one applies to animals: 'There . . . there . . . there . . .'

And as he spoke he would run one hand through that wild head of hair; and musing upon his wife with an infinite tenderness, raised his moustaches in a smile so young that poor frenzied Judith threw herself into his arms.

All their arguments ended that way. Mordecai never explained himself any further, for the simple reason that he did not understand the reproaches of his poor exiled wife. At night, while she lay beside him, he was taken by an obscure pity for her, for himself, Mordecai, for these two strangers whom the lightning madness of love had thrown into the same bed and who were still unable to address each other like creatures of reason.

'At least,' she would say sometimes in the communion of the marriage bed, 'if I knew what was behind all these stories about the Just Men ... Why do they have to suffer like that?'

Roused from torpor, Mordecai would stretch out an arm in the darkness and, encompassing what he could, draw nearer to the good odour of milk, spiced with cinnamon, that rose from Judith's languid body.

'Marvel of my nights,' he would exhale smiling, his lips against his wife's skin, 'and who does not suffer? Think,' he went on, continuing his wily way, 'of what you make me endure, and what you endure because of me. There it is: our suffering is heavy with sin, and drags itself on the ground like a worm, like a bad prayer.'

'What sin are you talking about?' Judith would ask, repulsing him, not without a perfidious gentleness.

'... But the *Lamed-waf* takes our suffering upon himself,' he would go on playfully. 'And he raises it to heaven, and sets it at the feet of the Lord – who forgives. Which is why the world goes on ... in spite of all our sins,' he concluded tenderly.

Judith loved to change his mood: 'Then tell me why the Just Men of Zemyock die in their beds?'

Irritated, Mordecai would detach himself from the undulating body – a river flowing with life – to find himself suddenly on the sharp, stony bank of reality.

'It's an old question,' he would say dreamily, to himself more than to his wife. 'But to answer it we'd have to know what goes on in the heart of a *Lamed-waf*; and he himself doesn't know, isn't aware that his heart is bleeding away; he thinks it's simple life passing through him. When a Just Man smiles at a baby there is as much suffering in him, they say, as in a Just Man undergoing martyrdom. And you see, when a *Lamed-waf* weeps, or whatever he does, even when he's in bed as I am, with the wife he loves, he takes upon himself a thirty-sixth part of all the suffering on earth; but he doesn't know it, and his wife doesn't know it, and half his heart cries out while the other half sings. So what can martyrdom add? Perhaps, who knows? God wanted the Levys to rest for a bit, who knows?'

'I must be really stupid,' Judith would observe gently under the blanket. Then she would burst out laughing and fling herself against him, prodding him with rare delight. 'Do you know I haven't understood a word of all that?' she would bubble into his ear, filling it with little kisses – so as to win forgiveness for that confession; 'do you know that I'll never understand? Tell me rather about a miraculous rabbi who pulls evil spirits out of you like a thorn from your foot. He says a prayer, it goes up to heaven, and oop! there you are! But the Just Men, where are their miracles?'

The man marvelled at her: 'A Just Man doesn't have to work miracles; he's like you, he *is* a miracle . . . a living miracle. Do you understand that, at least, little idiot?'

In the soft night Judith, for one instant, opened wide questioning eyes.

One day she went to find the incumbent *Lamed-waf*, Rabbi Raphael Levy, with whom she held a long confabulation. A few months later, that Just Man died in strange circumstances: his testimony being the sole basis of an accusation of theft, he could not bring himself to provide it, and spent the whole of the night before the trial battling with himself – torn they said later, between the contradictory angels of Mercy and of Justice. When dawn broke he lay down on the ground, closed his eyes, and died. That end pleased Mordecai prodigiously.

'But in what way is it worth two martyrdoms?' Judith wanted to know, intrigued. 'At home in Krichownice, the beadle before you also *took flight* like that; one day someone made him see what was up between his wife and Heschke of the Golden Tongue. He said, Poor little soul, if she knew that I knew – whatever happens, don't tell her, will you? He went home, he went to bed beside her, and in the morning he was cold. There's your martyrdom! And besides he looked exactly like your Rabbi Raphael: a sharp little man who trimmed his beard sloppily and stuck out his tongue when he talked. You understand? A *sharp* little man who doesn't sting!'

Mordecai's penetrating glance fell on her: 'And how do you know that the *Lamed-waf* (may God take him in his hands and

breathe gently upon him!), how do you know he was *sharp*?
He never appeared in public.'

Judith's nostrils twitched, she stormed, whinnied, confessed.
'You know how I am,' she began, tearfully, 'but just the same
I never wanted to shame you; so I went to him for advice.
I've been in Zemyock for two years, I told him and I haven't
changed an inch, I'm still as *mad from the land of Madness*.
What can I do? He who stands so well with God, he might
have had a little prayer for me, perhaps?'

Mordecai looked away, annoyed. 'And what did he answer?'

'Oh, silly stories!' she cried, furious at the memory of the
encounter. 'At first he couldn't answer at all, he was laughing
so much. Like a chicken, you know, kut-kut-kut. Then he stuck
out his tongue and he said, "You are Judith? Kut-kut, then
remain Judith, kut. The camel kut-kut who wanted horns kut-
kut-kut lost his ears, kut." There!' she finished, tossing her head
indignantly.

Abandoning all dignity, Mordecai burst out: 'Ah, you! My
crazy mare!' Then he strode towards her and gripped her firmly
by the nose, laughing in great gusts as he tugged at her curls with
his free hand.

Judith arched away and launched one of her marvellous furies;
but in her heart she was delighted.

She saw that she would remain 'stupid' all her life; she made
of it first a justification and then a glory. I, who have the wit
of a potato, she took pleasure in saying (thus announcing one
of her incursions into the kingdom of the mind); I who am not
intelligent, she went on, in tones so ambiguous that they wondered if perhaps she considered intelligence a flaw, from which
she was, thank God, exempt; I who am nothing at all, *I think
that* . . .

And yet, inexplicably, a sense of pride came to her at being
allied to the Levys; and with the aid of that subtle balm, she ended
by feeling as much a native of Zemyock as anyone else.

Judith's dowry had permitted them to move into a small
house of two rooms, not far from the workshops. But the slump

in crystal-cutting continued unchecked, and with unemployment came the misery of a new age. New-born babies succumbed to an unknown disease that attacked them in the second month, fresh and pink, to carry them a few weeks later into the corner of the cemetery reserved to children – but by then they were entirely blue, stunted, abominable larvae with extremities twisted like talons. Was it the cold, the hunger, or the blue sickness? The first three fruits of Judith's womb disintegrated within her, and she miscarried. Each time he felt the noble intoxication of progressing, even by a fraction of an inch, in his knowledge of the Talmud, Mordecai imagined that it was at the price of innocent blood. When Judith found herself pregnant again he decided – at the risk of cutting himself off from God – to take up peddling again.

It was on an ordinary winter morning. Confused, Judith added that she had known for two weeks, but had not dared to tell him.

The man's first impulse was to press, gratefully but prudently, that belly against his own. Why didn't you dare, he asked, smiling; it's not as though it were the first time.

Judith smiled weakly, in sweet desolation. 'I don't know ... My belly is full of joy, but the joy hasn't reached my heart.'

She had stepped away, and now she stood out of her husband's reach, behind the table, wrapped in the tattered shawl he had once loved. Invaded by his wife's fear, Mordecai turned dreadfully pale. And as his own happiness died, a chill of the soul glazed his eyes, and with a cruel clarity he saw the changes life had accomplished in the marvellous Judith since their arrival in Zemyock five years before.

Six feet from him, across the table, stood a woman whose face placed her in her thirties, and who was not yet twenty-five. If she seemed more, Mordecai understood suddenly, it was not that the years had weighed heavily upon her body, but rather that her character had been formed by the misfortunes of the times, and had stamped a sort of premature ageing on her features. She had a cat's face now, which would hardly change until her death. Wide and bony at the base, her forehead rose in an ivory curve, like a rock of which the peak alone receives the sun. Her brows took root above a firm short nose and the arc they traced, rising to mid-temple, was so perfectly designed they might have been the brilliant brush-strokes of a Torah copyist; two wrinkles ran from above her nostrils to the bitter corners of her mouth, supporting firmly-fleshed cheeks and imposing on the lower part of Judith's new face the watchful pout of an old cat.

She breathed gently, 'You're right. We must rejoice.'

And coming round the table in her long dancing stride, she embraced her husband warmly.

Awkward in her emotion, she had slipped her face under the man's beard, and left it buried there, like a furry, frightened animal; her hands were clasped together in the small of Mordecai's back; Mordecai barely felt her breathing against his neck, a humid breath, lulled to quietude already, perfectly gentle and regular.

He choked out, 'Yes, yes . . . let us rejoice.'

But his heart was petrified with sorrow; he could think only of the cold, the hunger, the blue sickness, of all the misfortunes waiting for that belly blessed by God and which already, like the previous times, he thought he could feel pulsing against his own. As he dared a timid caress, barely sensual, on Judith's white neck, a question crossed his mind: Does God, blessed be his name, wish the death of infants?

All that day, prostrate in the synagogue, he argued with the fathomless heart of God. Towards the end of the afternoon the faithful, surprised, saw him burst into sobs, and then rush out of the synagogue like a madman, his face dazzling in its joy: he had come to a decision.

6

THE house nestled at the far end of the village, beside the path
that climbed towards the Hill of the Three Wells; but the snow
was so thick, so thoroughly drifted over everything, that he had
to pick his way in the dark. Judith had been watching for him; she
opened the bolt as soon as he stood muttering on the threshold.
She had gleaned some dead wood, and the orange flickers from
the fireplace were reaching out to claim it from the yellow halo
of the old kerosene lamp that smoked benevolently in the middle
of the table. Mordecai was amazed to see Judith wearing her old
velveteen dress, the one she reserved for holidays; he had no time
to shake the snow from his cloak – already his wife was embracing him impetuously yet full of coyness, and smiling:
'Do you see what's on the table? Mother Fink lent me a lump
of butter, and I have an idea that the flour comes from Mrs
Blumenkrantz; well, now, are you pleased?'

Bringing his gaze back to her, Mordecai found her so desirable
he felt dazzled. He leaned towards the offered face. 'Woman,
this holiday is not on the calendar. My crazy mare, oh you ...'
Judith's mouth was burning, with a flame so bright that everything around her became night.

'Oh, my wife,' he sighed at last. 'Oh, my mare. And now it's
my turn to give you a surprise, isn't it?'

'Don't be silly,' Judith said, unbelieving. She laid her index
finger on his lips and he nibbled at it.

'Now,' he went on, holding her hand against his cheek, 'I've
just talked to Max Goldbaum. Er ... he had a money-order from
his brother – you remember him – the redhead with a nose like
that who left for America three years ago? Max is lending me
200 zlotys, and tomorrow I'm off to Zratow, where I can pick
up a little merchandise. I've worked it all out: with 200 zlotys I
can surely get back on my feet. What do you think of it, do you

like my own little surprise?' he finished, pulling Judith's hair in both hands to bring her beloved face beneath his own as in the nocturnal embrace. 'Well? Haven't you anything to say?'

Judith's features were hard, metallic, her expression frozen in pride: 'Yes,' she said flatly. 'I say that you haven't the right.'

'But you yourself . . . four years ago, you begged me to think about food for the . . . you remember . . . the first one?'

'Yesterday is not today,' Judith cut him off. 'You know very well that your place is in the synagogue of Zemyock, and not on the road like a tramp.'

Mordecai cried out, 'And the child? The child?' His distress was extreme.

Opening her shawl, the young woman placed her palms simply under the velveteen of her bodice, raising her breasts as an offering: 'Look at my breasts. Look at them. The trouble with our babies was never hunger; I've always had good mother's milk. And then . . .' she trailed off suddenly.

'And then?'

Now Judith's fingers curved like claws and her feline body, leaning slightly forward, seemed about to spring; then suddenly, with an indignant glare at her husband, she let her anger flow: 'And what would they say about me if I let you lead the life of a wandering dog? You, you, you, a man so pious now that Mother Fink was saying to me only this afternoon – only this afternoon – that I must feel closer to God since I married you.

'They'd be too happy, those gossips, those women with the tongues of serpents: Look, they'd say, madam eats caviar while he swallows his shame on the road. And they'd say, ah, too bad he married that doll of a peasant, he might have been a saint with the help of a real Jewish woman of Zemyock. Where will he say his prayers? On a haystack. With whom will he discourse? With the cows!'

Tossing her head furiously, Judith seemed to be resisting the arrival of a pleasant thought, which suddenly brushed her lips in the form of a moist thin smile: 'And *then* . . .'

Now Mordecai was really worried now: 'And then?'

Trying to escape his look, Judith threw her arms around his

neck; and in a tone of amorous confidence, her strong voice as transparent as a little girl's, she murmured into his lightly hairy ear: 'And then me, what would I think of myself?'

Mordecai threw up his arms in sudden humour: 'God in heaven: a miracle!'

While a woman neighbour sponged her thighs, heavy with flesh and blood, Judith waited anxiously for the cry of the newborn. It came only at the sixth minute. The midwife slipped a fat finger between the gums of the abortive creature, and to the great surprise of the prostrate mother, withdrew a clot of blood the size of a hazelnut. Filling her matronly lungs then, she forced her tongue into the creature's mouth and blew in a slow, voluminous mouthful of air. A trembling stirred the little mass of purplish flesh. In their efforts to hold on to the vital breath, the minute fingers and toes knotted, clenched, arched, like the talons of the blue disease; at last, the mouth opened for a thin little cry ... What's the use? grumbled the sceptical midwife, while Judith rolled over on her pillow, damp to her very soul, reconciled with life.

A frail plant, the new arrival offered no scope to disease; contrary to all expectations, he survived.

In a slender body that harboured barely a trickle of life, he displayed two round eyes full of hard malice, which hurt like pinpricks, as Judith put it, adding at once, But will he be a *sharp* one who pricks others, or *one* who pricks himself?

'I'm very much afraid he has the nature of a mosquito,' Mordecai murmured unhappily.

Shocked by the small size of his son, the father could not see him as an authentic and veritable descendant of the dynasty; there has been an error in heaven, he told himself in consolation. And then, Judith having presented him with three more Levys, one after another, all richly formed by nature, he forgot his first mortification, thanked a clement heaven, and forgave the mosquito.

The latter certainly seemed animated by an insect's frenzy: he never stopped moving, ferreting, fidgeting in all directions,

as if through his gymnastics he would fill all the space that his
skinny limbs left gaping about him. Judith was ecstatic: 'And
how can I stop him?' she asked a furious Mordecai. 'If I grab
him by an arm it may break off; what would we do with a baby's
wing? And you're being unfair to him; he didn't come into the
world all by himself; flesh of your flesh, he is.'

'Of the flesh only, worse luck.' Consequently Mordecai
neglected the mosquito's religious instruction, consecrating the
greater part of his time to the three later sons, who were already
beyond their elder brother in size as well as knowledge; and as
soon as Benjamin was eight years old, his father hurried him into
an apprenticeship with a tailor; which, though it brought in no
wage, at least saved them one mouth to feed at midday.

Benjamin was certainly a *sharp one*, as Judith said; but he
was one of those whose pointed souls were turned inwardly
against themselves. And because he was yielded so young to a
master's caprice, that point was sharpened: he suffered.

Although he worked assiduously, the immobility made him
nervous; he could hardly restrain himself, and all the animal
spirits dancing incessantly in his body kept him constantly
fluttering on the stool that was his prison. Thus reduced to
his own resources, and guessing that he was somehow segregated
from the deep community of the Levy's, he began to examine
the world with an eye not Jewish, but in some way passionately
personal. He knew now, for example, that although the Just
Man was king of Zemyock, there yet existed other powers in the
world; and perhaps, he told himself, not without malice, there
existed somewhere a Just Man greater than Zemyock's ... who
knew?

His doubts were crystallized on the day of his Bar-Mitzvah
when, according to custom, the young communicant was
presented to the incumbent Just Man. The latter had achieved a
septuagenarian dignity, stiffened by rheumatism. As his infirmities
kept him imprisoned in his room, the younger generation
knew of him only by hearsay, and consequently imagined him the
more solemn and wraithlike. His house was half-way up the

Glass-Blowers' Street at the foot of which the rusty chains of the former ghetto were still visible, wound about two stone markers.

Lost in the costume borrowed for the occasion, and exacerbated in all his senses, Benjamin made his entry into a very dim and very smelly corridor; he peered left and right, vainly trying to pick out some sign characteristic of the presence of a *Lamedwaf*. But when he entered a small, dark room, flanked by his pale father and poor Judith all excited at seeing the 'miracle' at close range, Benjamin had the marvellous sensation of discovering an attic: the stacks of dark air, the bizarre objects and furniture heaped in disorder; a trembling shaft of light as though from a dormer window; the subtle presence of dust ...

'Well, go on!' Judith cried, shoving him to the centre of the room.

'Tut, tut,' a disapproving voice said suddenly.

Straining his eyes, Benjamin made out an old man who had been seated in the dark recesses, behind a narrow iron bed: he wore a black skull-cap on a pink skull, and his robe was belted by a silvered sash; the old man was stepping forward now with the help of a stick; at each step he twitched it forward, like a frail and insufficient prop, while his body curved in the shadows panting like an exhausted animal. When he was quite close to the child, the latter discovered with piquant pleasure that the *Lamed-waf* was no different from the old crocks who muttered on the stone bench in front of the synagogue and who, if you passed within reach of their gnarled hands, could never resist caressing the back of your neck or tweaking your ears with a greedy little gesture. Reviving at once, Benjamin grasped the dangling hand of the old man and slyly placed it on his own head, which it completely covered down to the ears.

'My God, may the holy man forgive this rascal!' Mordecai cried in terrible alarm. And turning to the child who was smiling beneath the hand, he thundered, 'What did I tell you? You *kiss* the holy man's hand!'

'Oh, that's all right, it's all right,' bleated the old gentleman, who seemed greatly amused. 'Well, well ... the child has blessed himself.'

And caressing Benjamin's neck as foreseen, the hand descended to his chin, and raised it with a gentleness full of nostalgia: 'This is Benjamin, then, son of Mordecai?'

The child confirmed it with a friendly wink.

'This is then the new Jew that God brings us today?'

'Oh yes,' Benjamin answered condescendingly.

Under the shadowed vault of the brows the old gentleman's gaze sparkled in bluish irony; his eye was clear, unringed by wrinkles; but at the moment when the old man's eyes met the child's, Benjamin felt a slight burning sensation, and suddenly lowered his astonished eyelids.

'And tell me, Benjamin, tell me now: what do you know of the Pentateuch?'

The child was silent.

'May the holy man forgive us,' Mordecai said; 'this little fellow doesn't study much; he's a tailor's apprentice.'

A thick silence fell upon the room. Judith stared at her husband, who had stepped back a pace or two in shame, towards the door; Benjamin let out a plaintive sob.

'And I, what do I know of the Pentateuch?' the Just Man asked suddenly in a voice whose softness seemed aimed at the child.

Surprised, Benjamin raised his eyes; above him the bony white head nodded tremulously, as the old man's mouth opened in a sweet, dark smile.

'Tut, tut, tut. A little tailor, eh?' the Just Man bleated. Slipping his index finger under the boy's palm, he raised the small hand to his lips all smothered in beard, and kissed it.

Then, seeming to come to himself, he sent his visitors away with sweeping gestures that admitted of no reply; the interview was over.

They all wanted to inspect the hand that the Just Man had kissed; a yellow aureole was still visible upon it, a vestige of the old mouth stained with tobacco, and they made the child swear not to wash as long as it was still there. The aureole seemed in any case to have spread over the boy's whole personality;

he was spoiled by visitors, and his brothers made clumsy advances to him. The idea of placing a band round the hand was dismissed. Only Mordecai shrugged, saying that it was all incomprehensible, that it was doubtless one of these 'obvious oddities' which are commonplace in the lives of the Just Men. But Benjamin was rather inclined to agree with his mother Judith, who had let slip the thought that after all the Just Man seemed to her a 'good little old fellow like the rest of us'; secretly Benjamin agreed.

The faint illusions he still entertained of the Just Men were dissipated during his stay in Bialystok, where, several years after all this, he had gone to finish his apprenticeship, as a dim, well-bred young man, delicate of eye, with rough edges worn smooth and dull.

Bialystok was a true city, with apartment buildings, tricycles, cab-drivers identical in every respect to those he had seen in the one copy of a Polish newspaper possessed by his former master.

He remained for two years. They worked fifteen hours at a stretch in a small room drowned in the constant vapour of the gas-iron. Five commingled sweats composed a startling bouquet of perfumes. Benjamin was at once companion, apprentice, delivery boy, handy-man, nursemaid, and even now and then cook, when the master's fat wife felt excessively torpid. But he believed that he was living an adventure unique in the annals of the Levys, for everything, even the black air of the workshop, belonged to a world infinitely more real than Zemyock, that bazaar of dreams . . .

At noon he lunched with the presser, Mr Goldfaden, an ancient old boy whom the master was threatening to fire now that his emaciated arms had difficulty in lifting the huge gas-iron. Benjamin was bound to him in a wordless friendship made up of routine daily activities. One day when the awesome Mr Rosnek had gone out to deliver a precious frock-coat personally, Benjamin looked up from his needle and said without thinking: 'Pardon me, my dear Mr Goldfaden, but may I ask what you will do when you can no longer lift the gas-iron?'

The presser dropped the iron to its tripod, and his flaccid

face, puffed like pastry by forty years of sluggish, suffocating heat, took on an unpleasant expression. 'What will I do?' he articulated slowly. 'With God's permission, my child, I shall starve to death!'

'But you're a good Jew, Mr Goldfaden. And God will not . . .'

'I am not a good Jew,' the old man cut him short grimly.

On those words his face sagged in fear, and Benjamin recognized Mr Rosnek's masterly tread in the next room.

The next day Goldfaden became bolder and told the adolescent that he had ceased to believe in God almost six months ago. Benjamin stared at him uncomprehending; Mr Goldfaden, this cosmopolitan gentleman, had shown him more consideration than anyone except the *Lamed-waf*; assuredly, he was not an unbeliever. Then what could this mean? 'What do you mean, exactly, dear Mr Goldfaden, when you tell me that you don't believe in God? I am not entirely sure,' he added smiling, 'that I grasp the basis of your thought.'

The old man turned away; he seemed mysteriously irritated by Benjamin's tone. The boy went on with the same sceptical indulgence: 'Am I to deduce, dear Mr Goldfaden, that you don't believe that God created the heavens and the earth and all that followed?'

As he pronounced those words he was illuminated by a sudden insight, and Benjamin understood that the good Mr Goldfaden quite simply did not believe in God.

'But after all, dear Mr Goldfaden,' he went on, chilled with fear, 'if God did not exist, what would you and I be?'

The old man gave a compassionate smile, and his voice sought vainly for the lost tone of gaiety: 'Poor little Jewish workingmen, no?'

'*And that's all?*'

'Alas,' said the old presser.

That night, on his mattress set directly on the floor, Benjamin tried to picture all things as Mr Goldfaden must see them. Bit by bit he arrived at the terrifying conclusion that if God did not exist, Zemyock was only an absurd fragment of the universe. But then, he wondered, where does all the suffering go? And seeing again Mr Goldfaden's hopeless expression, he cried out, in a sob that ripped through the darkness of the workshop: *It gets lost, oh my God, it gets lost!*

He could go no further; he wept for a long time and then fell asleep.

Every day the presser became more awkward. When the boss was out, he took to raising the iron with both hands. Finally, he dropped it, in an acrid scorch of cloth and dry wood. The fire left only a black smudge on the floor, but the day after that accident the old workman was not at his place, and Benjamin met only Mr Rosnek's sombre silence.

In the afternoon, a young man appeared whose arms were as skinny as Mr Goldfaden's, but who seemed resolved not to drop the iron.

Benjamin did not become at all friendly with him. The young man told racy stories, wore a tie, and expressed scorn for 'pinheads' who did not see life as it really was. He was an authentic unbeliever, while Mr Goldfaden – Benjamin felt this strongly – had lost only the traditional outward aspects of the good Jew. It was nevertheless better not to set this man of the world against him, which is why, caught up in the toils of his own diplomacy, Benjamin found himself one night in an alley where women walked. The unbeliever made all the arrangements. As in a dream Benjamin ascended carpeted stairs and followed a corridor worthy of a palace. Then came an awesomely luxurious room, tapestried, it seemed with mirrors, then a fat lady who changed into a mauve, trembling, flesh-and-blood doll. Somewhere above the bowl of electric light the Song of Songs gently glittered:

Come with me from Lebanon, my spouse . . .

Squatting on the bidet, the flesh-and-blood doll bade him approach, crooking and uncrooking her index finger several times. Benjamin murmured in Polish, 'Excuse me, Madam,' opened the bolted door and fled.

7

WHEN he returned to Zemyock Benjamin had for ever given up
all search for the truth; all he wanted was to retrieve those
crumbs of daily purity he had abandoned two years before, and
which henceforward he would value above all things. Judith's
nose twitched, her fingernails flashed forward. When Benjamin
emerged from under her still-flapping wing, Mordecai in turn
welcomed him; he looked into his son's eyes, found them clear,
and pronouncing the prayer of welcome rubbed his moustaches
solemnly against Benjamin's forehead; Benjamin decided, in his
renewed plenitude, 'My God! If all this is error, I prefer it to the
small truths of the unbelievers!'

But the line of division was still hazy; if Zemyock was only a
dream then what was he, Benjamin, who no longer even belonged
to the dream . . .?

In the year he returned to his home town, a war broke out
somewhere in Europe.

The gentle souls of Zemyock were informed of this only in the
month of February, 1915, by letters arriving from Paris, Berlin,
and New York. Strange rumours spread. It was learned from
them that the Jews of France and Germany had been obliged to
don the uniforms of hate and to do battle, just like those cruel
beasts of Christians: they were *forced to!*

These horrifying facts were the subject of scathing discussions
among the elders, some of whom maintained that it was wrong to
cast a stone at the faithful who were constrained to bear arms for
the Nations. But all talk gave way to the blackest mourning, to
prayer and affliction, when they learned by the next mail that
boys from the same town, brothers who had settled in mutually
hostile countries, ran the risk, in these faceless massacres, of as-
sassinating each other most Christianly. Moaning, they repeated
the Just Man's gloomy pronouncement: 'All this is happening,'
he said in the Consistory of Elders, 'because Israel is tired of

carrying the sacrificial knife in its own throat; the sacrificial lamb has gone out among the Nations; he has knelt before their idols; he knew not contentment, he no longer wished to live with God. Our unfortunate brothers have become Frenchmen, Germans, Turks, and perhaps Chinese, imagining that in ceasing to be Jews they would cease to suffer. But behold: the Eternal sees today what has never been seen in the two thousand years of Exile: adorned with strange armours, speaking different tongues, adorning faceless idols, *Jews are killing one another!* Malediction!' And seated on the bare ground the Just Man heaped dust over his white hair and rocked back and forth, emitting shrill cries, like a wounded animal.

The women retailed a strange story (no one knew who had brought it to Zemyock): It is night at the front, a shadow, a shot; the Jew who has just fired hears a moan . . .

'And then, my dear lady, the hair stands up on his head, for only a few feet from him, in the darkness, the enemy voice is reciting in Hebrew, the prayer of the dying. Ai, God, the soldier has cut down a Jewish brother! Ai, misery! He drops his rifle and runs into no-man's-land, insane with shame and grief. Insane, you understand? The enemy fires at him, his comrades shout at him to come back. But he refuses; he stays in no-man's land and dies. Ai, misery, ai . . .!'

The war was not yet over when rumours of revolution reached them, and then rumours of pogroms, rumours which rose like a whisper in the fields. The Ukraine was fire and blood. 'As the buzzard and the kite share the heavens' the revolutionary bands of Makhno and the white-képi'd detachments of the Czarist Petlura came down, turn and turn about, on the Jewish communities of the Great Plain. Even the people of Zemyock, though sheltered behind their hills, no longer knew what to think. Several times, led astray by false reports, they fled into the wooded heights. Those who had stayed at home in bed made fun of the returning fugitives, so that at the hour of real danger a great many people, become sceptical, were taken in the subtle trap of false alerts preceding the real thing . . .

The night before the end, they saw a bright glow in the direc-

tion of the village of Pzkow. The month of August had been
torrid, and they reassured themselves with the thought that it was
a forest-fire. The first cries echoed at dawn. It all happened very
quickly. The Cossacks were already flooding through Zemyock
when many Jews, barely awake, showed themselves bewildered at
the windows, still in their nightclothes and with the skull-caps
askew on their heads, shouting at the panicky fugitives to find out
what was happening.

Accompanied only by their son Benjamin, Judith and Mordecai reached the peak of the hill of the Three Wells safe and
sound. Before following his parents into the forest, Benjamin
couldn't help turning back for a last look at the town given up to
the Cossacks. First he was moved by the beauty of the countryside. A ring of fog circled the little valley halfway up, and the
green slopes trailed off into the shrouding grey to re-emerge fifty
yards below. Black figures swarmed over the neighbouring hills
like so many ants. The pink roofs of the town stood out with a
blinding sharpness within the ring of fog. Benjamin was looking
for the open space of the church square when he heard the cries.
Then he saw many blackish flakes seemingly born of the pink
roofs as if by magic; the fires were now (thinned as they were by
distance) like the ludicrous cheeping of a nest of baby birds.
Above it all the sky remained motionless and blue. Benjamin
opened his mouth to scream, and then changed his mind. The air
was absolutely still.

'What are you waiting for?' someone had whispered; Benjamin turned and smiled mechanically. A few yards away, floating
up out of the underbrush, the pale, hollow face of his mother
Judith showed a mouth oddly open in mute appeal, while from
the thicket a dreamlike hand rose, its index finger, in beckoning
movement, reminding him of a child playing hide-and-seek. How
stupid of me to smile, Benjamin thought. Still smiling, he crossed
the ten yards of silent earth between him and the underbrush,
with what seemed to him a springy stride, and found himself
suddenly in the crackling shadows of the pines, whose indifferent
crests looked out over the smoking pink roofs below, in compli-
city with heaven.

77

'Did they follow us?' Judith gasped; she was trembling.

'Why should they follow us?' Benjamin said, absurdly. He sniffed the odour of resin. There were that world down below, and this one. Which was real? His mother Judith was bundled up in a coat of black cloth, and her feet were bare, and bare the upper part of her chest, which the tightly buttoned coat pressed lightly upward. The massive, square face of his mother Judith was white, yet patchy, as if sprinkled with a fine red powder that clung in ringlets on her cheekbones. Her eyes seemed lidless. Benjamin understood suddenly the reason for his smile; his mother Judith had not had time to snatch up her wig, the wig of a Jewish wife, and her bare skull, recently shaved, displayed only a stubble of white hair which gave her the look of an aged infant. Averting his eyes, Benjamin hoped that she was unaware of it. 'Come on, come on.' With a sharp tug Judith had pulled him into the thicket, while her heavy face turned scarlet and sweated with fear, retrospective breathlessness and a profound confusion evident even in her slightly demented gestures, her slightly mad expressions.

As he followed the tall, wide, nervous figure of his mother into the wood, Benjamin became aware of his father, well back in hiding, with his massive Torah woodcutter's body, and who was not only fully dressed but had found the time and the wit to bring along his great prayer-shawl, draping his chest with it as if with an armour against the evil raging in the air. All through their flight together Mordecai had made haste slowly, content to lengthen his stride, rather than rushing as Benjamin and his mother Judith had. Each time an impatient Benjamin turned towards his father, he believed he saw a delicate, dreaming expression on the majestic, emaciated old man's face, while the huge woodcutter's body accomplished, precisely, reflectively, and serenely, the actions necessary to flight. And half-way up the hill Benjamin had seen his mother Judith turn to Mordecai and say, in a curt, breathy voice, 'You're holding us up! Are you in such a hurry to die?'

The old man had stopped in the middle of the path and, as

peacefully as if he were amid the circle of faithful in the synagogue, had declared in sententious tones, 'Woman, woman, do you think that you can hold back the hour of God?'

Then he had set forward slowly through the fog, like a stone column moved by an unskilful labourer. Piqued by the pity so apparent in her husband's voice, Judith had answered angrily, 'And you, do you insist on setting it forward?' Panicky, Benjamin felt that she wanted to launch an immediate argument; but a shot from the bottom of the valley made her leap forward in confusion. And now his father Mordecai was moving calmly through the shadows of the underbrush, seemingly undistressed by the branches scratching across his face or by the shrill wails that reached them from the floor of the valley; or even by the hate-filled glances that poor Judith threw his way when she stopped every ten steps to wait for him and suddenly set off again like an arrow, straight ahead, indifferent to her feet, bloody now, and to her breasts, one of which had pressed up out of the coat. After a time she stopped short and whispered, 'Let's hide in a thicket.' The lines of her face had been distorted by terror, and Benjamin thought that she was frightful to look upon. Suddenly she seemed to notice the white pear of her breast, trembling outside the open cleft of her coat. Slowly she turned a wild look on the two men, and raising the collar of her coat held it tight from then on with two fists clenched in shame. Then she wept. Mordecai sat back against a pine. His heavy grey eyes stared aloft at the open branches of white and blue shifting against the upper branches, and his beard stirred lightly, as though he were muttering a prayer. Benjamin sat down and remained motionless. All three were so deeply plunged in thought that none heard the Cossack appoach. Each of them was alone. Now and then Judith let her haunting fear escape between her teeth: 'My God, what have you done with my other children? My God, only my sons and I... only us...'

It was learned later that individual Cossacks had searched particularly for the girls hidden away in the woods surrounding the valley of Zemyock. With no warning, Benjamin saw a fair-

haired man in cavalry boots come into his field of vision. A thin
ray of sunlight projected the Cossack's shadow almost to Benjamin's feet. He held his sabre straight before him like a jib; the
triangle of his chest was hairy; his moist yellow eyes glistened
slyly, and his square face was that of a Ukrainian peasant. He
moved forward raising each booted foot with infinite caution ...
His head still bowed against his knees, Benjamin wondered if his
parents were pretending not to hear the snapping of twigs just
behind them, or if they were truly aware only of their disquieting
thoughts. In the same instant Benjamin felt astonishment that his
own heart was beating no more quickly, that no sound escaped
his lips, that no tremor seized his limbs. Immediately the reassuring thought came to him that all of this was merely a spectacle in which he had no role, except a contemplative one. Mordecai was still sitting back against the pine and Judith was still
erect in the middle of the clearing, her eyes closed, trembling in
all her opulent flesh, her fist clenched on the collar of her coat.
Benjamin was suddenly aware of the Cossack's image making a
sort of sparkling leap across his retina, and landing with his feet
together between Judith and Mordecai, who started in terror. The
Cossack looked at his three victims scornfully, disappointed;
then, choosing Mordecai, he directed the point of the sabre slowly
towards the old man's throat. Until then Mordecai had not broke
out of his relative calm. But when the point of the sabre was a few
inches from his throat he threw his head back, flattened his hands
firmly against the pine behind him, and rolled furious eyes towards
heaven, as he shouted the first words of the prayer of the dying:
'Shema Israel!'

In his voice was a tone so dark, so desperate, that Benjamin
marvelled at such an attachment to life.

The Cossack suddenly pointed at Mordecai's terrified face,
seemed struck by an extremely comic idea, withdrew his sabre in a
convulsive gesture, and burst into a horrifying whinny of laughter. He was doubled over, shaken by spasms, clutching at his belly
with his left hand, the hilt of the sabre in his right hand, its point
stuck in the ground. No word had been spoken. Benjamin noticed that his mother Judith had come to life, and guessed that her

temper was rising. Suddenly he saw her angry, on the verge of breakdown, as she was so often at home. What followed was unclear. Taking a step forward, his mother Judith had swung her left fist (or perhaps simply the powerful flat of her hand) against the Cossack's face and, when he went over on his back immediately, she snatched up the sabre and struck blow after blow on the man's head and shoulders, as she might have with a meat-cleaver. The Cossack's hands went to his head. Distinctly, Benjamin saw the wide blade of the sabre cut through a wrist, which dropped away from the forearm with the passivity of a piece of kitchen meat . . . When his father Mordecai rushed to his mother Judith, it seemed to Benjamin that a layer of skin had been peeled from his eyes: was all that real? He could not yet believe it.

When darkness fell Benjamin ventured to the edge of the wood. Deep in the valley all was silent, but a bad smell was rising, and so were black spirals, writhing through the deep blue of the night.

As he descended the slope, tiny sparks of light appeared here and there. He crossed the washwomen's field and slipped into the shadows behind a house. A Jewish silhouette crossed the street – beard and caftan; in its hand was a candle. Trembling, Benjamin set out in the deserted streets of Zemyock. A sort of murmur rose from the centre of town. It came from the church square, where dozens of figures, candles in hand, were identifying their dead among the indistinct heaps of corpses. At dawn, Benjamin discovered his three brothers under a portico. The whole day was given over to grave-digging. They improvised a new cemetery beside the old one. Benjamin and his father made several trips there to tear Judith away from the mound under which her three sons were buried. For a week Mordecai shut himself into a room with her. She believed that God had punished her for the murder of the fair-haired young man; she felt she had murdered both her sons and their assassin; her hand plunged an imaginary sabre into her own breast. Then the fever fell.

They learned that the pogromists were White Guards, who had come through that lost town of Zemyock entirely by accident.

They were on their way to the Ukraine, under the command of German, French, English, and American officers, for the common purpose of destroying the new materialist regime. They were led by Kozyr Zyrko, a celebrated ataman. Many of the Jews of Zemyock had reached the hills. Kozyr Zyrko had assembled the others in the church square and, by way of encouragement to his men, had hoisted an infant on the point of his lance: 'This is nothing!' he shouted. 'Nothing! Nothing but seed for revolution!'

A singular thing: while families bunched together like grapes of blood, and died in each other's arms the old incumbent *Lamed-waf* was trotting among the corpses, begging vainly, 'Pierce, pierce, pierce me through, then' to the great happiness of the soldiers, who, finding him comical, confined themselves to slicing off his beard. Several times, too, they simulated his execution. Kneeling, his eyes closed, the old Jew submitted himself in a kind of ecstasy; but constantly disappointed in his human despair, and in his legitimate hopes as a Just Man, he remained the only survivor in the church square.

The pogrom at Zemyock passed unremarked among hundreds of others. Little by little, help came. The Jews of Europe and America banded together once more. But when peace was restored, before the decade of the twenties, the survivors of the pogrom discussed the miraculous survival of the Just Man. Some saw in it a measure of the celestial meekness; others scented out a mysterious and terrifying irony of God, hinted at in the sacred texts. A rancour stole into the hearts of certain inhabitants of Zemyock. The young ones were joining the Jewish General Union of Russian and Polish Workers and the desire to live and die in the forbidden land of Canaan suddenly flooded the Jewish soul like a powerful, voracious groundswell. Judith announced openly and sarcastically that the survival of the Just Man was an event so ridiculous that henceforth the Levys could abandon their pretensions. Benjamin agreed silently. Mordecai flashed them a glance compounded of astonishment and a nameless bitterness; he felt betrayed, but he could not have said whether by his own family or by God. His sons were dead, and the *Lamed-waf* was alive. Perhaps in that there was some particularly occult intention of the Most High?

In his doubt, he allowed Benjamin to exile himself abroad. And even had he not permitted it, his declining authority would never have stood up to Judith's henceforth inflexible will.

BOOK THREE

STILLENSTADT

1

BENJAMIN dallied for several days in Warsaw, undecided in his choice of exile. He felt as though it were a game, a childish fairy-tale. The name of the countries proposed seemed as frivolous, as altogether fantastic as the squares traced out by children in the Jewish version of hopscotch, which stood for a loaf of white bread, a sigh, a pound of chick-peas, an insult, a chicken-in-the-pot, a Polish slap, a million zlotys, typhus, a week among the angels, and, finally, a pogrom. The ball rolled about in his mind, crossing one by one the squares established by the Committee of Rescue and Emigration and returning sadly to its starting point, nothing settled.

Generally the ball rolled very quickly past the word 'England': an island, how would one escape in an emergency? But it lingered agreeably, with a tourist's curious yet scornful non-chalance, on the word 'America': that vocable first of all suggested the furious ocean which would separate Benjamin from his family; then it recalled the Biblical dance about the Golden Calf, to which his tailor-master in Zemyock had once compared the life of American Jews; and finally it evoked the fatted calf, salacious, rolling blind orbs on the Creation. As for the word 'France', it suffered the inconvenience of association with the word 'Dreyfus', which Benjamin had heard often; they said that the French had sent this Jew to Devil's Island: if the name alone stimulated a shudder, what must the thing itself be like?

Finally, after this painful tour of the world, Benjamin decided in favour of the word 'Germany'.

For the German Jews, he had heard, were so pleasantly established in that country that a number of them considered themselves 'almost' more German than Jewish. This was doubtless very strange, if not praiseworthy, but it demonstrated all the better the warmth and gentleness of the German character. Immediately, in a transport of enthusiasm Benjamin imagined a German personality so exquisite, so refined, in short so noble, that conscience-stricken and lost in admiration the Jews became German to the depths of their souls.

Berlin disappointed him immediately. The city had no beginning and no end. He had hardly been there twenty-four hours when he felt the desire to flee – but where this time, O Lord? The Committee had quartered him in a disused synagogue with hundreds of refugees from the East. Whole families lived in a great hall divided into apartments by lines of chalk. Cutting the hall in two, an aisle barely two feet wide gave the tenants access to the door. Each resident feigned unawareness of his neighbour's existence. To cross a chalk circle was to straddle the wall of a private life; to pay a visit one said, with a forced smile, knock knock, and waited politely until the host invited one to enter. It was as though they had all been driven crazy by homelessness. Some of them attached cords to the ceiling and hung up a mirror, a painting, a family photograph. Only the children obstinately refused to honour the 'walls' drawn by the adults, which occasioned constant squalling and squabbling.

'They're all waiting for an apartment,' said a young man standing in the chalk aisle on Benjamin's first day. 'They still have hope!'

'And what are you waiting for?' Benjamin asked smiling.

A face loomed out of the shadow above Benjamin, who raised his eyes uneasily. The young man had just left his bed. His unruly red hair seemed to slash at the surface of his forehead, where Benjamin saw a swollen wrinkle, like a scar, twisted vertically. The young man jeered: 'I'm waiting for the Messiah; but he's in no hurry. He has all eternity, no? Greetings.'

Such was Benjamin's first meeting with the young man from Galicia, whom he was to see often in the weeks to come, forever reclining or seated on the edge of his bed, plunged in a dream, his hands trembling like an old man's. Benjamin suspected that he was dying of hunger. When he received a package from the Committee, he invited the young man to share the soul-stirring omelette, the kosher frankfurters that inevitably made him think of home, or some other most rare viand that he stewed over the flame of the spirit-lamp. Depending on his mood, the young Galician followed him with a constrained smile or insulted him obliquely.

'Who will take you off my hands?' he said one day.

'Excuse me,' Benjamin stammered, 'I've just found work, so I allowed myself to prepare a little banquet . . . you understand?'

'Go on,' the other said more calmly, almost indulgently. 'I know how much you wanted to find a job, how hard you'll work, how happy you'll be to work: I congratulate you. What more do you want?'

Benjamin lamented sadly, in the ancient words, '*And who will not eat this night?*'

A gentle Jewish gleam rose to the flat eyes of the Galician; then the gleam wavered, and became a flash of incomprehensible nastiness: 'You eat for me.'

The words struck Benjamin like a slap. He retreated prudently, followed by the hostile comments of the 'tenants', all of whom were ashamed of the Galician, and seemed cankered by Benjamin's kindness to him, in which they saw an implied repudiation of their judgements of good men.

Back in his own room, Benjamin turned and noticed that the young redhead had fallen into his habitual attitude, head between his hands, prisoner of some unknowable dream which isolated him as thoroughly as if he had been truly alone and not at the continual mercy of two hundred hostile glances. What can he be thinking about? Benjamin wondered, not without the sharp uneasiness which the Galician's presence, or even the simple mental image of him, always brought on.

He probed into his pot and bit into a kosher sausage, without pleasure. Of course I embarrassed him, the poor sad young man, but he will never know what miserable pleasure I took in his company . . .

And ceasing to chew for a moment, he wondered for perhaps the thousandth time: Is he a sharp one who only pricks others, or does he prick himself too? There's the question.

Nevertheless, and though he reproached himself for it, he was much relieved the next morning, as he walked down the chalked aisle to go to work, to notice that the young Galician barely glanced his way. Already dressed, he lay on his bed, his bare, blackened feet splayed shamelessly at the eye-level of the tiny children who played near him, knocking at the invisible doors along the corridor. He never even blinked. He had cut the last thread of the frail mooring that united him with the synagogue, and it seemed to Benjamin from then on that every day the young man receded farther from the shoreline of his own people, lying on his bed, gliding towards a high sea known only to himself, and reflected in the gloomy roll of his eyes.

But the young Galician, of whom Benjamin now considered himself free, reappeared to him cunningly in the person of his fellow-workers, who were all victims, though to a lesser degree, of the same disease, the 'Berlin madness', as he called it when he had, painfully, come to know it better.

Mr Flambaum's employees were all fugitives from the pogroms, and bore some trace of the upheaval; but the workshop was suffused with an atmosphere of snarling mockery, ironic depreciation of the old life in Russia and in Poland. A demoniac spirit breathed in all of them, changing clear water to blood, killing off the delectable roots of goodness, showering rain and hail on every Jewish thought pointing from the soul. Benjamin would offer a hand to meet, it seemed, a claw. Although he contradicted no one, bent cautiously over his stitching, all the lances, the knives, the needles of their eyes seemed to turn against him. They started mocking at him. One day when the boss was out Lembke Davidowicz jumped up on the cutting table with the 'Berlin grin' twisting his lower lip: 'Listen,' he said in a voice that began gravely, then modulated into little acid hiccups, 'listen, if the little rabbi keeps his virginity too long he'll grow wings from his shoulder-blades. And then what? He'll be quite delicious. We'll all be able to feed on him. You, me, the last little German half-wit can reach out a hand and tear off a wing or a leg; they'll all want a bite,' he tittered. 'And better than that: when there's nothing left but the little heart of an angelic and delectable rabbi, (and who would want it, fellow-citizens, the soft, flabby part with no future on the market, not even listed on the Berlin exchange?), then we'll sit him down on a train and ... oh blow, ye trumpets of the Lord! a little Jewish heart is going home!'

This speech let loose a wild enthusiasm. The orator made suitable faces, jumped from the table, and shook the proffered hands with feigned avidity. They forgot about the victim.

'Look,' someone called, 'he's pricked himself. He's bleeding.'

Benjamin gazed flabbergasted at his thumb, bleeding on to the pale cloth.

The workshop was silent.

'We're the ones who pricked him,' Lembke Davidowicz said softly.

'We did it,' another said.

'Have we forgotten everything?' Lembke went on, looking at Benjamin as if he had never really seen him, his obese body sagging under the weight of the sudden discovery his own eyes had made, eyes almost feminine, with long lashes fluttering now over an entirely disarmed look, sad and naked. 'Have we become such perfect German gentleman?' he asked finally, with a disgust on his face that was immediately reproduced on the faces of all of Flambaum's employees.

'It didn't touch the bone, at least?' a worried voice asked.

Lembke approached Benjamin and gestured suddenly. 'Go ahead, talk!' he cried. 'Insult us, but say something: one word! Just one!'

But Benjamin, his eyes still glittering with suppressed tears, could only nod pensively, his thumb deep in his mouth, his appearance at once despicable and comic; but mingled with the acrid taste of his own blood, he was already savouring the startling thought that they would never 'prick' him again.

2

BENJAMIN stopped before the synagogue and, reflecting that
one brain was not enough in this world below, scraped his
Polish bootees vigorously on the mat crusted with snow and
mud.

Inside, beneath the high nave of shadow that failed to repel
the cones of light from the candles, the stripping bare of all these
lives upset him once again: here an old man groaning under his
blanket; farther along the young couple restricted to the motionless embrace of statues before the obviously interested eyes of a
pale urchin whose mother was squatting before a tiny spirit-
lamp, her shaky hands sheltering a finger of flame that seemed to
flee along the icy stone of the floor . . . And as for the uproar, as
for the horrible screaming of children, he could not be sure if it
was his ears that had become more sensitive or the young throats,
cloistered for so many months in this vast, airless, lightless dormitory, that had become more piercing.

'Home so soon, Mr Benjamin?'

Halting in the chalk aisle, Benjamin, who had recognized the
voice perfectly, pretended to be investigating the darkness of the
bed from which it had come.

'My dear sir, do you no longer wish to recognize me?'

Benjamin was upset: 'Forgive me; one can't see a thing in here.
So, Yankel, what's new since –'

The sickly face, the red hair, came out of the shadows. 'Nothing,' said the face, 'one lives.'

His adolescent slimness emphasized the gash of his nervous
mouth, his long, melancholy, hooked nose, his flat eyes so cold
that Benjamin had difficulty meeting them. 'But come in,' Yankel said quietly, as if it were the normal thing to do. 'No admission fee. My word of honour.'

Immediately Benjamin sensed a 'suffering in the soul' in the

92

boy's unusual behaviour; and, raising a foot modestly, he set it down on the other side of the chalk circle. 'Well, Yankel, how does life suit you?'

'It doesn't suit me at all,' the young Galician said. 'Several sizes too big for me. Or maybe too small; I don't even know any more. But you must be wondering: how come this young fellow who hasn't said a word to me for two months is suddenly talking to me again? Surely he must want a good omelette or –'

'No!' Benjamin cried. 'A thought like that would never have occurred to me.'

'Forgive me,' said the young Galician. 'I don't know how I get along. It's my tongue. I can feel it like a knife in my mouth. And when I use it, it has to cut someone. But it wasn't always like that, my tongue –'

'No?'

The young man laughed loudly. 'No, I swear it, once I had a velvet tongue. Once. But please sit down, and if you don't mind, not on just one buttock. Good. And now let me look at you, let me admire the new man! Ah, look, you've kept your fur cap, your bootees, your Hasidic caftan, and my God! you haven't even had those rabbinical curls cut! How can that be? Don't you know yet that you're in Berlin?'

'Do you think I don't know it?'

The young man smiled vaguely.

'That I don't *really* know it?' Benjamin went on emotionally.

At these words the fine hands of the young Jew rose before Benjamin's face, twisted in a brief, nervous, desperate dance. 'But then,' he whispered in extreme amazement, glancing at the neighbouring beds, '*if you know it*, then how do you get along, even just walking in the street, for example? Yes, frankly, when you walk down the street *like that*, don't you feel a kind of weight on your shoulders, like a cloak, that gets heavier every day?'

Benjamin started, alarmed to be so easily found out. 'Yes, yes, it's just like that: a cloak. And ... I can't even hurry along, because of the street-lamps.'

'I beg your pardon?'

'Oh, yes,' Benjamin said, with a touch of derision, 'in the beginning I walked right down the middle of the sidewalk you know, the way the Germans do, in a military stride. But they all looked at me, so I began to hug the walls, along the shopfronts. But even then, there was always somebody coming out of a doorway, or else it was a street-lamp.'

Yankel was quietly amused:

'So what do you do?'

'God forgive me,' Benjamin said, swept up in the humour of the situation, 'what do you suppose? I hug the walls quietly, and the shop windows, with a good little Jewish shuffle.'

'Ai, ai, a *good little Jewish shuffle!* But the people, do you think you can escape them that way?'

'Oh, the people,' Benjamin murmured, 'there's the real cloak, as you called it; and I can never take that off, that cloak, no, not even here, and not even when I think very hard for a long time about my home town, in Poland ... The people are really terrible here, worse than the cars,' he laughed. 'And even the Jews,' he added dreamily, '*they weigh on me*. So what can I do? Rip out my guts?'

Sitting on the edge of the next bed, a wrinkled man with a beard all ringlets was gazing down at a Bible open on his knees, lighting his way with a candle he held at the height of his temple, in the hieratic position of the nocturnal vigil. Benjamin felt that he was listening to their conversation. Intercepting his glance, young Yankel said scornfully, 'My dear Jewish colleague, pay no attention to that old fool; he thinks he's meditating, and he doesn't know that he's only an owl. At night he leans over to see if I'm asleep ...' The man with the book started slightly without removing his gaze from the text, as the candle, suddenly tilted by his emotion, released a drop of molten wax which fell on to the parchment, a fantastic, mute teardrop.

Yankel chortled wickedly. 'You see? We're all in the same soup.'

His voice had become shrill again, and his arm sliced through the dark air, snatching away in one quick gesture the thick shawl that had muffled his throat. Beneath his chin was a laceration. A thread of dried black blood ran down towards the thin growth on his bare chest. 'Aha! The latest gift from Berlin!'

Benjamin was upset but understood: the young man was forcing himself to hold back the heavy venomous secret coiled in his throat. He whispered gently, 'Brother, please, tell me what they did to you . . .'

A high-pitched laugh spilled into the shadows. 'Ah, what a pleasure to tell you secrets: nothing is lost, everything finds a home in your heart! Ai, my god, ai, ai, ai, the heart . . . Because you're a *little Jew from the old country*, do you know that? A little angel of blood,' he tittered. Then, noticing Benjamin's humble expression, the young Galician suppressed a shiver, and as his features softened, his back rounded to a hunch. 'Forgive me, forgive me,' he said tonelessly. 'And forgive my tongue, if you will; for two years it hasn't been able to keep still in my mouth. It moves. It does contortions. You'd think it wanted to get out!'

The hump rounded even more, and the young man's eyes were larger, glassier, in the shadow. His voice took on a childish inflection: 'Two years already,' he said. 'Is it possible? And in my mind, everything happened just yesterday. Yes. Every morning when I open my eyes it seems to me that the pogrom came last night. Is it the same with you, *dear brother*? Strange. Really strange the way time stops like that. Myself, you see, I'm still down in the well where I'd hidden; the same water reaches right up to my mouth, and I still see the same circle of blue sky; that hasn't changed either. And then I hear the silence. No shouts: silence. Because in my town, when I came up out of the well, there wasn't a soul alive in the whole village; there was no more synagogue; there was nothing. Only me, of course . . .'

The young man winked maliciously, as though that had been a prodigious joke played on him. 'Oh yes, oh yes,' he whispered smiling. 'And I buried them all, you know, the whole village without exception, didn't miss a fingernail. And for each one of them, even for that dirty little liar Moschele – he lived next door – for each one of them, I swear it, I said all the prayers from A to Z, because in those days I was a famous praying-man before the

95

Eternal, aiiii! It lasted eight days. And nobody came. The peasants were afraid. And when it was done, I felt queer all over, you know? It was in the cemetery. I woke up, and I grabbed a handful of rocks and began to throw them at the sky. And at a certain moment, the sky *shattered*. You understand?'

'Oh yes,' Benjamin murmured; he had been weeping silently. 'I see, I know, I understand.'

'Shattered like a simple mirror, and all the shards spread out on the ground! Then I said to myself, Yankel, if God is in little pieces, what can it mean to be a Jew? Let's take a closer look at that, my friend. But then as closely as I could look, I couldn't see anything but blood, and more blood, and blood again. But meaning, none. So what places does Jewish blood have in the universe? There it was. And what should a Jew do ... who is no longer a Jew? Eh?'

Now, in the half-light of the synagogue, the hallucinated gaze of the young man of Galicia seemed to spill out over his whole emaciated face, the face that fever had splotched with livid patches and reddish patches and patches dampened by a sweat that now and then reflected the yellowish light of the candles flaming near him.

Benjamin asked timidly, 'And why did you never look for a nice little wife from home? You're handsome and strong ...'

Astonished for a moment, the young Galician shook his head as if to throw off that incongruous change of subject; then grasping Benjamin's elbow, who cried out softly, he vociferated, 'Do you want to listen to me or not?' And without transition, as if hastening with his mad confidences: 'All right, listen, there was a rally this afternoon! No, no, not the Jews, what would the Jews rally about? Their nakedness, their weakness? Can you picture that, an army of little frayed bleeding hearts, marching, left, right, left, right, along Unter den Linden? Ha! you're delicious, and you know it, don't you?

'No,' he went on in a kind of contained fury, 'it was the Spartakists, the hammer and sickle. And when I saw them coming forward in the street, calmly, the way a river moves, and ... Ah, that red flag above the tallest of them! I ... I don't know why, even now! I ran out to join them! And believe it or not, at first they didn't *recognize* me. I was marching. I saw the flag in front. It was crazy . . . Do you understand? I was drowned in it for a minute,' he laughed, 'and then the man next to me turned to me and said, Jew, what the hell are you doing here, there's going to be a brawl, you know? He said it gaily, with a look of amazement. But the one who was marching behind me started to yell, He's a provocateur, it's the only explanation! And . . . they shoved me towards the sidewalk, and . . . and . . . *you'll see, I'll get them for it, I'll get them!*' he finished in a sudden shrill, bombastic shout, which woke the people in the dormitory and immediately surrounded their strange conversation with a high wall of silence.

'But what did they do to you?'

'Nothing. Exactly nothing. They stomp over you without seeing you. They're marching and you're on the ground; so they march right over you, what could be more natural? And all this time I was saying to myself, Yankel, dear heart, do me the great favour of never putting yourself into such a ridiculous position again! But there was the question: What can a Jew, who is no longer a Jew, do to avoid spending his life on all fours? I've thought about it all afternoon, and I think I have the answer; simple as hello and good-bye, and it's enough: *You want to make a calf of me, then I'll make myself a butcher!*'

'What? Whom do you want to kill?'

Yankel twisted his mouth into a knowing smile: 'Who said anything about killing? There's nobody to kill. Or maybe yes; you might fill the bill, but I'm not sure yet; I'll have to think about it!'

'But what's the good of talking?' he said suddenly in a distraught tone.

He was now sitting fully upright on his bed and was examining Benjamin curiously with his piercing gaze, like a bird of prey suddenly aware of the extreme distance separating him from this wan, sly, fluttering little nestling; his attentive stare seemed to say, Well, look at that, I've been confiding to this shadow! 'Never mind,' he said. 'Don't torture yourself trying to understand; you can't, you still have one foot in the old days. In . . . *the dream,*

97

eh? Like all these poor fools,' he added, sweeping the dark air with a lordly gesture. 'Go on, go on, grandpa, leave me alone now...'

Benjamin objected weakly, 'But you were the one who wanted to talk.'

'I know. Thank you. Because I still have in me a little ... *Benjamin* who flaps his wings. Aiii, he doesn't want to die; still, look how he struggles. But shh, shh, let us sleep now, him and me, will you?'

And not conscious of the hostile gathering grouped closely about his bed, the young man offered a wide salute to the world at large, tapped Benjamin's chest, smiling; then, raising his long arms above his head – as free and easy in his movements as if he had been within four walls – he peacefully peeled off his old sweater, under which he was nude, his torso barred with bones, and dirtied with blood.

Benjamin stared silently at him for a moment. What had happened? Scratching his temple in confusion he rose and went to his 'room' without a word. With a kind of gentle relief, he crossed the circle of chalk that marked the limits of his lair, and undertook the cooking of meatballs. He ate practically nothing. Stretching out on his mattress, he wondered if the bedbugs would bite as much as usual. Indignant murmurings persisted in the synagogue, and with night came the wailing insomnia of the small fry; Benjamin closed his eyes and imagined that the chalk circle was rising as a wall all the way to the ceiling. The wall seemed so solid, so marvellously thick, that soon he felt sheltered from the whole world.

Yankel's bed was empty the next morning. When he got back from the workshop, Benjamin found it occupied by a little old woman all harnessed up in black who looked like a turtle; as soon as he spoke to her she withdrew her head between her shoulders, as if to take protection as quickly as possible under the shell of her age. Benjamin laughed to see it.

Three months later the young Galician made a last appearance. He was seated on the edge of Benjamin's bed, with a distant expression, indifferent to everything and looking at no one. His hand fidgeted with a spool of thread lying on the blanket. He played with it gently. His long, ungainly body was crimped into a suit of English cloth; a stiff collar rose to the middle of his scrawny neck, adorned with a dazzling necktie. Slowing down his step, Benjamin noticed that what had once been an adolescent mop of red hair now covered the skull in a thin, iridescent film, carefully parted in the middle. The face seemed still unhealthily hollow and discoloured, but his mouth had hardened, thickened, and his lips thrust forward greedily.

The young man rose and proffered a well-kept hand: 'Forgive me. I took the liberty of coming into your room.' His eyes remained sad and cold, but the flesh around his lips trembled in irony.

'The plague take me,' Benjamin said, 'if you haven't become a real "gentleman"!'

Immediately he regretted his admiring tone.

'I have *become*, did you say?' Yankel asked bitterly.

'But how . . . by what miracle?'

'Rest easy, little Jew; I haven't killed anyone . . . It may be worse: I'm a merchant. I buy and I sell.'

'What? What do you sell?'

The young Galician smiled like an old fox; but the distressed upper part of his face contradicted the lower slyness. 'My dear little Jewish colleague,' he enunciated with a kind of childish affection, 'in Berlin, everything is bought and sold.'

At that instant Benjamin felt a deep surge of pity for the young Galician. His hand rose unwilled and like a frightened bird came to rest on Yankel's shoulder, as his mouth spoke words that came from he knew not where: 'Brother,' Benjamin's lips pronounced gravely, 'why all this shame and unhappiness? Awake, I beg you . . .'

The young man seemed not to hear, and Benjamin withdrew his hand hurriedly, surprised by the audacity of his gesture. But suddenly, moved by some terrible impulse, the redhead rose to his full height and, pasting that indefinable smile on his sickly face, murmured in a dragging, exhausted voice: 'Jew, little Jew from the old country, you're very sweet, do you know? So sweet that a man would like to bust your teeth in, one by one.'

And turning, the young man of Galicia found the chalk-lined aisle; crossed the synagogue in long, nervously jerky strides; disappeared for ever.

An hour later, slipping under the blankets, Benjamin found the envelope hidden between the mattress and the bolster. He judged that it contained a small fortune. A few lines were traced in Yiddish, in the elegant hand of a scholar: 'Dear little man, this money is the legitimate profit of a legal transaction. It was thieved honestly, according to the laws of commerce; with licence and I hope soon a thief's respectable business house. Leave this great Berlin for the countryside, and send for your family, if you still have one. For in Poland, my friend, a Jew can hold out all alone, with a herring and a synagogue. But here, believe me, if your two feet are your only roots, life soon ceases to reach your heart. Even yours, dear little man. Don't judge me. Thank you. Yankel.'

3

BENJAMIN set one foot on the platform of the little Rhenish station, pulled down the stringed up coffer that was his luggage, and found himself face to face with an individual dressed in the German manner who claimed to be the Rabbi of Stillenstadt. Suspicious, Benjamin refused to let him carry the 'valise', maintaining, against all evidence, that it was light as a feather. As they walked along the rabbi told him what a godsend the little shop on the Riggenstrasse would be. 'Mr Goldfuss, that's the owner, preferred to offer it to a victim of the Slavic persecutions, of which you are one, are you not, my dear co-religionary? A pressing-iron, a sewing machine, and several pieces of aged furniture are included in the, shall we say, "more than charitable" rent.'

All this proved true, with the slight reservation that Benjamin had not imagined the furnishings, or the place itself, in so advanced a state of age, as the rabbi had put it. 'But then,' the latter replied smiling, 'we don't look a gift horse in the mouth!'

As they chatted, the shop was invaded by eight or ten Germans who seemed to lunge forward, hands outstretched, towards Benjamin. He uttered a cry of fear; thought he would faint; and then recognized, with relief, two or three Jewish beards in the gallery of Germanic faces which surrounded him, bickering over him as over a piece of merchandise.

'Aren't you ashamed?' cried a woman's manly voice. 'You're crushing him, crushing him, squeezing the kernel out of him as if he were a piece of fruit!'

And cutting a path through to the 'victim of Slavic persecutions' a buxom Jewish woman, in a flowered-print dress and a plumed hat, displayed before Benjamin two smiling, outrageously rouged lips. 'If it comes to that,' she went on in the uncontradictable tones of the chatelaine, *'he belongs to me!'*

101

'What do you mean?' Benjamin breathed, as his hands flattened cautiously on the 'valise' over which he maintained an anguished guard.

'But leave your coffer here,' said the astonished goodwife; 'are you afraid that these gentlemen will run off with it?'

Benjamin felt his resistance rising again: 'It's nothing, it's nothing,' he stammered, 'you see? Light as a feather.'

But as he had practically disappeared under the weight of the coffer, gasping and panting beneath it, the excellent lady could not resist asking him, 'My fellow-Jew, what have you got in there that's so valuable?'

'*Everything*,' Benjamin said, dying of exhaustion.

Since his departure from Berlin the previous night, from the very moment when the train had plunged into the tunnel that foreshadowed his new plunge into the dark night of exile, Benjamin had not for one instant lost physical contact with that coffer, which indeed contained everything he owned in this world, the few rolls of remaindered cloth, the three or four flat-irons, the tailor's dummy with its unscrewed base, the presser's bench, and all the accessories he had managed to assemble thanks to the incomprehensible gift of the young Galician. Trusting the coffer, which was difficult to make off with, more than his own sensitivity to pickpockets, he had sewn the rest of his 'fortune' into the dummy's bottom. On the train his fear and anguish, the acute distrust which squeezed at his heart, were mysteriously transformed, on the level of thought, into resolves whose fiercely sentimental heroism forced him into attitudes of defiance; and at moments into brief interjections which startled his fellow passengers – provincials fascinated by this little man dressed in 'Russian style', rubbing his fists desperately against his scraggly goatee while his eyes, moist and glassy, seemed to throw off incessant sparks of suffering.

He even imagined, in the middle of the night, that henceforth he would look upon all things as the young Galician did: Yes, he blurted suddenly in Yiddish, to the great excitement of his neighbours, I say it and I proclaim it, in this world of iron the sword is the best answer to the sword!

An old lady smothered a cry and left the compartment; had she actually cried out, Benjamin, roused from his 'Berlinish' fantasies, might have fainted outright.

So armoured against the worst, terrorised, haggard, broken by exhaustion and inanition, all he saw of the Jews of Stillenstadt was their German manners and their strange preoccupation with his coffer. He never even wondered where she was taking him, this imposing woman who had taken possession of him. It's nothing, light as a feather, was all he managed to say, when she mentioned the burden under which he struggled.

He did not want to be without it even in the living-room, where Mr Feigelbaum, husband of the elegant plumed lady, tried vainly to dupe him with a hearty welcome, hearty certainly, but not good enough to fool our 'Berliner', wise in the ways of life; not even in the dining-room which he entered lugging his 'valise' behind him obstinately. Nevertheless, when he discovered right under his nose the steaming savour of a certain Jewish marrow-bone soup which he had believed the exclusive prerogative of his mother Judith, his nostrils suddenly began to prickle with 'the human happiness . . .'

And as he lowered the spoon into the plate, dreamily, a strange phenomenon occurred; first a light bubble, apparently elastic, was born in his breast, and rose to obstruct his throat exquisitely; and then, on the foaming yellowish ripples of soup, appeared the face of his mother Judith, the skull shaven and the eyes flashing in shame. Then there appeared in the soup the imperial profile of his father Mordecai, whose beard disappeared suddenly; the bloodless face of the poor young man from Galicia, whose red hair twisted and died like flames; and finally the three faces, embracing in the bloody doorway at dawn after the pogrom in Zemyock . . . And all that, coming to life and dying again as if miraculously on the shining film of soup, generated a beneficent warmth in Benjamin, hunched over the plate, fascinated . . .

'My God, he's crying!' Mrs Feigelbaum said.

Benjamin blushed, made a face, sketched a smile. 'Huh, huh, huh,' he managed in a shrill voice, 'this soup is hot!'

As he sensed rather than felt the intoxicating tear slipping along his nose, he brought the spoon close to his lips and blew on it at great length, with a kind of expert, though blind, application; then he introduced it into his mouth.

Straightway Mr Feigelbaum, who until then had expressed himself only through bearded and malicious smiles, set about insulting his wife, while his cheeks turned an incendiary purple: 'Don't you see that the soup is too hot? No? You don't see that? Animal, stupid animal that you are! A hundred times I told you, don't serve the soup too hot! Oh you stupid animal! A hundred times . . .'

Then changing his mood again Mr Feigelbaum began yelling loudly for his bottle, punctuating each of his demoniac cries with a shake of the fist, as drinkers do. But his wife was already repeating with him, 'The bottle, yes, the bottle,' and sat smiling, bursting with love. Finally, with one last oath, Mr Feigelbaum bolted to the buffet and came up with a green swan's neck bottle which contained, he said, some authentic and veritable Palestinian wine.

'It's been asleep too long,' he cried, lifting the bottle by its neck in a swaggering gesture. 'Ah, my children, I promise you that it will be drunk before the coming of the Messiah! Ah,' he declared emphatically, 'I'll swear to that!'

Surprised, Benjamin noticed that the bold Mr Feigelbaum was fidgeting terribly, and that his hand, so solid, trembled nevertheless in pouring the liquor of Carmel. But his host was already holding his glass at arm's length (a bit like a hussar, it seemed to Benjamin) and fiercely thundering an old Yiddish couplet:

> Sing, oh my Jewish brother,
> Sing, I beg you, sing . . .

As Benjamin marvelled at the ardour, the vehemence, brought to this rather sentimental plaint, he observed that at the end of each verse a brilliant gleam appeared in the corner of Mr Feigelbaum's eye, to disappear as soon as he had begun the next.

104

The singer interrupted himself suddenly: 'Good heavens, I'm stuffing you with discords and gorging you with flat notes!'

'Not at all,' said Benjamin.

'Not a word!' Mr Feigelbaum said.

After that, each new course was an exquisite dessert to Benjamin. But before the end of this love feast, some Jews invaded the dining-room in a long file. Insisting that no one must disturb themselves, they sat silently all round the table, and more especially opposite Benjamin, watching him masticate and shaking their heads in approval as if he were accomplishing a holy and mysterious function which indeed incarnated the invisible, the suffering and the death of the Polish Jews visible through him, in filigree. The discussion burst out before they could attack the fairyland *Strudel* that reigned in the middle of the table. It was at once passionate. After two hours of arguments, concessions, and counter-concessions, Mrs Feigelbaum, who intended to keep an iron hand on Benjamin's nutrition, arrived at the following compromise: all the noonday meals for her, and the evening meals to be shared among the other Jewish tables of Stillenstadt; if of course, she said, not without slyness, our dear brother really wishes to go elsewhere . . .

All aquiver with 'the human happiness', his nose low over his plate, Benjamin realized that every noon, every night, his place would be set at a Jewish table where he might, under cover of the traditional cuisine, gorge himself on tenderness. Unable to restrain himself, he rose suddenly and undertook to tell 'a good old Jewish joke from my hometown', as he put it, 'that would make a corpse shake with laughter'.

But he was a terrible raconteur; he giggled nervously at each word, lost the thread of the story wherever possible, picked it up and twined it with another of a different colour, and excusing himself over and over, took up his story from the beginning with, 'This time I have it . . . This time I have it . . .' which finally trailed off into, 'Well, there it is, I've lost it,' said plaintively, while with his right hand beating like a wing he sadly pictured for them the definitive flight of his good old Jewish story.

And yet – it mortified him a bit – they laughed throughout his strange narrative; and some of them, including Mr Feigelbaum, went at it so boisterously that they were even dribbling into their beards.

4

STILLENSTADT was one of those charming German villages
of a vanished age. A thousand dolls'-houses, pink-tiled, bedecked with potted flowers, made it seem like some secretion
of that old Germanic sentimentality which penetrates and binds
all things intimately, as the spittle of the swallow holds the twigs
of its nest by an invisible thread. But there was nothing aerial
about Stillenstadt. Simply set down on the plain, it lay in the fork
of a river which divided at the entrance to the town. The principal
arm of the river fed the shoe factories ranged on its banks as well
as the industrial dye factories where female workers faded slowly;
too thin and fragile, the secondary arm threaded its way delicately
through the fields. The Schlosse – that was its name – was only
good for fishing and summertime pleasures.

The tiny window of Benjamin's shop was boarded over by
ineptly nailed planks; an alleyway separated it from the two-
storey house next door. Hoping to win back the former clientele
quickly, he at once started to organize the 'shop' as he already
enjoyed calling it. And first of all, a moving moment, a sign
clumsily written in German announced the coming inauguration
of the establishment: THE GENTLEMAN OF BERLIN.

For the first three months he slept on a mattress spread out
on the floor of this retreat; then, as his anxieties diminished, he
began to think of touching up the 'apartment'. From the beginning, he saw himself established in the style of an American
millionaire: a sewing machine and a wing on the street. But
business being slack, he decided to alter his campaign. It was a
working-class district, the aftermath of a lost war lay heavily
upon the German people, and no one foresaw a quick end to the
depression; in view of all these things, Benjamin thought it out
so carefully and so well that enlightenment came to him. And
one fine morning, the astonished neighbours were greeted by

the little immigrant's new sign: an immense placard blocking half the shop window and rising like an arbour to the second storey windows, bore these words, drawn in handsome and noble Gothic lettering (a soft blue against a pink background): SPECIALIST IN PATCHING AND TURNING OLD CLOTHES – AMAZING PRICES – IT'S OLD, PRESTO, IT'S NEW!!!

In his desire to bring in business, he had set ridiculously low prices which bordered on unfair competition. On that first day he had more work than he could handle. The next day he plied his needle for sixteen hours and considered himself a happy man. He had seen himself on the edge of failure; this one stroke of genius established him in Stillenstadt. The days passed and the weeks, and he forgot the low origin of this infatuation with THE GENTLEMAN OF BERLIN, and even yielded to a dream – soft blue on a pink background – that his sewing machine had won the unanimous sympathy of the town.

As he worked at the local language, modulating each syllable with care, the day came when his customers understood a few snatches of his jargon. So he loved to engage them in conversation on any subject compatible with their German brains, with his dignity as a Jew, and with his extraordinary difficulty in pronouncing certain words. Fittings, particularly, favoured these idyllic relations between the church and the synagogue; inserting a pin, tacking a lapel, Benjamin eddied about his Christian like a fly, and to win that heart used all the politeness, all the grace, all the refinements that he might have employed in the seduction of a woman.

Receiving his customers called for a slow and painful elaboration: 'My dear sir,' he articulated shaking the hand of the newcomer tenderly, 'may I know to what happy circumstance I owe your visit?'

Whether they wore janitor's blue or a peasant's tunic or even the dignity of a necktie, his customers were all entitled to this same treatment, which nevertheless succeeded in disquieting several of them. But Benjamin, immersed in his urbanities, never saw the eyebrow raised, questioning, suspicious, or frankly acrimonious. He liked to think that these little people were renouncing their anti-Semitism for his sake, that they had been able to detect, under its Jewish envelope, that universal human nature which shone less vividly, perhaps, in the other Israelites of the town. One must set an example, he rejoiced secretly; the esteem they feel for me benefits all Jews; through me they can learn the simple truth!

Even better, after several weeks he tried to reproduce certain popular expressions that might establish his familiarity with the workers of the town; not, of course, that he would pronounce the impious phrase 'Shit' or oaths at that level; but he let himself go so roundly with expressions like 'Oh bother!' or 'You don't say!' or 'Don't make me laugh!' he put so much weighty conviction into these words using, like Germans, his whole frail body as he spoke, that he came to the conclusion he could honestly do without the word 'shit', however useful it clearly was. From time to time however, after making sure that no Jewish ear was lingering in the neighbourhood, he compromised far enough to swear by the holy name of God in German, like a man of the people: 'Eh, my God!' he would exclaim timidly, to the complete astonishment of his customer. Then he would mutter a mental prayer. Similiarly he felt the need to express, discreetly of course, a few modernistic ideas; he enjoyed referring to 'the big industrialists, sir, our common enemy,' without suspecting at all that certain workmen – particularly the unemployed – regarded him as one of the blackest capitalists of the street. And so it happened, after a fitting during which he had bathed in unadulterated 'human kindness', that he wondered how far his apprehensive sympathy for the working man would lead him; but on the next day a cold eye, a mocking smile, an outstretched forefinger in the middle of the street, fortunately reminded him that he was a kike, and nothing more.

In truth he found no true 'human kindness' but in the sweet company of the Jews of Stillenstadt, who had not only adopted him, but seemed moreover to revere in him some secret property, attached to his puny person and clothing it, like the cloak of

suffering in which the faithful of Zemyock clothed the *Lamed-waf*.
Was it possible ...? Benjamin wondered occasionally, uneasy.
But no overture was ever made to him, and if it happened that
the conversation bore on the thirty-six Just Men who haunted
the world, he was at least able to convince himself that the
German Jews had no knowledge of the mystery surrounding the
Levys of Zemyock. Only once, the rabbi alluded to a legend
according to which, yes, one of the thirty-six Just Men had been
chosen by God from the descendants of the famous Yom Tov
Levy, you know, of course, the one who died for the Sacred
Name in York? But few of them had heard about it, and Benjamin reassured himself with the idea that these 'Saturday Jews',
as they called themselves regretfully, revered in him only the
burning flame of Polish Judaism, and its great piteousness.

At the end of six months they disclosed to him, as they might
a shameful fault, that several Jewish converts to Catholicism
were thriving in the town. These inhabited the upper-class
residential sections, in those white six-storey structures that
gleamed behind the church. They were described to him as wicked,
perverse, apishly patriotic, and detesting especially the immi-
grants from Poland and the Ukraine whom they referred to as
'an Asiatic horde, the scum of the earth, foreigners, etc.' and
when one of them was pointed out to him, crossing the street
stolidly, as stocky and impenetrable as a German, Benjamin was
unable to repress a shudder.

The second apostate who was shown to him lived in the
Riggenstrasse, a few houses away from the shop; now and then
Benjamin saw him passing the shop window, with a sly look
flashing from his bent head. But on some days the apostate's chin
jutted forward, like a prow; on others it drooped humbly towards
his chest. His whole attitude was that of an incorruptible German
burgher, morose and well established, in his undistinguished
and dull clothing, of military cut and thoroughly buttoned
up over the stomach. He worked in a municipal office and had
been converted by patriotism, he said, and by grace. Benjamin
soon heard that the apostate was spreading rumours about
him, accusing him of eating the bread of German workers. 'He

said,' a woman neighbour slyly reported, 'that you didn't even know the colours of the German flag!'

'Me?' Benjamin cried indignantly; and then, unable to prove the contrary, he backed into his shop, overwhelmed by shame.

He waited for the apostate to come again, so as to give him a piece of his mind; but as he came up to him, trembling, the man went 'pffft' with an icy breath of contempt, and went on his way, chin high, swinging his walking-stick scornfully as though some vulgar public spectacle had been imposed upon him.

Now it happened that one day that apostate, named Meyer, appeared at the synagogue and threw himself at the rabbi's feet, kissing his knees avidly: I can't do it any longer, take me back, my heart has remained Jewish, etc. Great agitation on the part of the rabbi, who chased the man away angrily and urgently con-voked an extraordinary assembly of the faithful of Stillenstadt. Stationed at the doorway of the synagogue, the apostate saluted each arrival with a humble bow; he had set a skull-cap upon his head, his hair was full of earth and ashes and his clothes were rent: no one responded to his greeting. Not knowing which side to take, Benjamin entered the synagogue with his head held high, but gave the man an absurdly conspiratorial wink on the side.

The trial began.

Ensconced in the last row of the faithful, Benjamin was fascin-ated by the bizarre silhouette of the apostate, standing out against the central chair, before the ark of the holy of holies, where two lions, squatting on their golden haunches, seemed, at either side of the unfortunate man, to watch over him like policemen in a trial court. In the middle of his almost flour-white face, two red caverns gave him a terrible expression; and his sweat, diluting the ashes on his hair, drew black bars down his forehead, which gave his tortured face the mad look of a carnival mask. At each insult he bent his knees and jutted his head forward, to show that he confessed to all the evil; with his right fist he thumped his heart, like a metronome. His lips were pursed.

With eyes transfixed on the apostate, Benjamin was remem-bering that once in Berlin, unable to see any way out of his sadness, he had thought of yielding himself once and for all to the Christians (he did not know to whom, exactly, the Pope, a priest, or some mysterious dignitary of the Church) *so that it would be all over for him*. He could thus see himself now in the apostate's place, and each invective made him withdraw his head further into his shoulders, in a convulsive movement, as if he had been stunned by a blow. Suddenly, Mr Feigelbaum, livid with rage, climbed on to the chair and announced that as a childhood friend of the guilty man he had been present at the psychological martyrdom of the latter's parents: 'Not content with conversion, this mouthpiece of Satan lacerated his mother and father in their shop, calling them dirty Jews and other names which I do not wish to pronounce in this Holy House. Is he an apostate? That's the least of it! He is first of all, he is above all, a murderer!'

At this point in the debate, one of the faithful expressed the idea that, having been sincerely converted to Christianity, the apostate had become sincerely anti-Semitic: 'Since it is, alas, in the nature of that religion not to tolerate us, is that not so?'

'Do you think so?' Mr Feigelbaum cried; and turning towards the apostate whom he blasted with a look: 'Mr Heinrich Meyer, formerly Isaac, can he be so bold as to claim that excuse?'

Then something occurred which escaped Benjamin's understanding; for, instead of seizing upon this providential justification through faith, the apostate rose slowly, with unconcealed pride, and sarcasm on his suddenly heavy lips: 'How can you think,' he declared, hammering out the words acidly, 'tell me, how can you think that I believed for one instant in a God who, to relieve poor mankind, could think of nothing better than to pass through the body of a virgin, become man, suffer a thousand tortures and then death ... and all that, without a single noticeable result?'

And once again with a look of submission: 'My former friend Feigelbaum is right; I *pierced* my father and my mother because I wanted to live as the Christians do. I was ashamed of being a Jew; very simply ashamed.'

'And what have you gained?' Mr Feigelbaim asked scornfully.

'A greater shame.'

After that admission, they deliberated the penalty, out-bidding each other to find the most humiliation. In the end they decided that the apostate would lie at the entrance to the synagogue so that the entire community could step over him. The apostate beat his breast and begged a greater penance; he declared himself 'resolved to suffer'. Suddenly someone pronounced Benjamin's name: 'Our brother who has come from Poland, perhaps he can give us a useful opinion, point out a precedent; why has he not spoken?"

Benjamin sank back upon his bench and tilted the skull-cap down over his eyes, as if to protect himself from the unanimous gaze converging on his small figure, piercing it as with a single ray of flame.

'Well,' he stammered finally, 'I don't know, really. Back home in Ze— at any rate back home, nothing of this kind has ever happened. But I remember, yes, in the fifteenth century, Rabbi Israel Isserlein ... he said that he who returns to Judaism, you follow me, don't you? – he imposes upon himself a continual penance. Yes, that was it: a continual penance.'

'So what?' cried one of Benjamin's neighbours, a solid, red-faced man, whose eye-glasses jigged suddenly in the middle of his enervated flesh.

'So what?' Benjamin repeated in a thin voice. And carried away suddenly: 'But don't you understand?' he squeaked, pointing in despair to the apostate. 'Look at him, he has turned his back on the advantages and felicities of Christianity, and he has taken upon his shoulders the ... all the suffering of ... is that not so? And therefore he is expiating his sin, by the simple fact that he has come back ... no? Then why add a stone to his burden?' He finished in a painful tremolo that surprised the faithful more than all the rest.

Then, glancing about the assembly, now reduced to silence, the little man seemed to remember his true size. Trembled. Twisted his frail shoulders. Put his arms back under the prayer-shawl and sat down again so abruptly that his skull-cap fell forward again over his forehead.

Nevertheless, his voice came out in a trembling rivulet from under the skull-cap: 'Ah yes . . . it was the Rabbi Israel Isserlein . . . Rabbi Israel Isserlein said it . . . I swear it to you . . . and is there one among us who never thought about it? One?'

An incredulous silence greeted these words, followed immediately by a fair-ground tumult from the centre of which, sunk back on his bench, Benjamin could vaguely hear the astonishing bits of phrases: 'Now that's talking like a Jew! Have we already forgotten everything?' etc. And rising from the elders grouped about the oratory stove, a piercing voice came like an arrow: 'Is there one of us who has never thought of it, one? . . .' With calm finally restored, the Rabbi of Stillenstadt begged the apostate gently to take his place among the faithful: 'As before,' he said.

It was then that the event occurred.

The apostate, who until then had remained sombre and silent, suddenly burst into loud mocking laughter, demoniac even, according to some; and from the eminence of the chair deserted by the Rabbi, set about insulting the whole assembly, already terrified by this theatrical reversal. His face was convulsed with rage. He uttered words of death towards where Benjamin was sitting. In a blasphemous flight, he took his skull-cap and flung it to the ground with scorn, trampling and stamping on it as if it were a thing to be killed. Now laughing himself breathless, now flinging out a stream of obscene insults: 'Don't you think it stinks of Jewish flesh here?' he pushed through the dumbfounded gathering and left them.

5

THEY learned the next morning that he had left the city. Tongues wagged freely. The Rabbi went so far as to say that Benjamin should not have stopped the apostate from expiating, and our good apostle was looked at with suspicion; they accused him of flights of fancy, of manias. Only the Feigelbaums admired, admitting that strange circumstances were involved which escaped human understanding.

Banned from the best tables, looked upon as a bird of evil omen, Benjamin bought a sumptuous sheet of paper, and composed the letter he had been thinking about since his departure from Zemyock.

That letter which is still in the records, began like this: 'My very dear and venerable father, and you, oh, my so dear and so venerable mother. It is now nearly two years since your obedient son left you in search for a nest somewhere in the world. Today it is with a heart overflowing with joy that he tells you: Come, oh my loved ones, for the moment is finally here when the bird, with the blessings of the Most High . . .'

When she was able to discern, under the flow of images and biblical comparisons, the immediate and precise meaning of that invitation, Judith cried out joyfully: 'And now, Zemyock is over!'

'Which makes you very happy, doesn't it?' Mordecai answered bitterly. 'All right, what are you waiting for, why aren't we already on the train?'

He remained silent and impassive throughout the trip. Judith was less preoccupied by the absurdities which the windows of the iron monster offered her than by those wrinkles of grey resignation, that helpless prostration, which weighed so heavily upon Mordecai's hook-nosed mask, dissolving the majesty of his features. Now and then the old man shook his head as if he were unable to believe what was happening, and Judith heard him mutter feebly into his beard: 'But how was it possible ... a Levy from Zemyock?'

Benjamin was waiting for them in the little station at Stillenstadt. Two years before he had been a young man whose features were entirely dominated by an amusing little goatee, a rather nimble person, although tiny; in any case, indubitably Jewish. Judith had expected to find a similar Benjamin, drowned in the traditional garb: Polish boots, a black cloak, a velour hat with a flat brim. To tell the truth, she could hardly remember his features; and when she evoked his image, it was primarily through his small size, which was easy enough to hold in the imagination. Stepping down from the train she found herself facing a small German gentleman who had long ears, a curved nose like a rabbit's, fine and bony jaws, and the facial expression of Benjamin. That apparition made a painful impression upon her. Was it perhaps this beardless face? ... But she had the distressing feeling that Benjamin was a kind of skinned rabbit still grazing and jumping about, as if nothing had happened, all his muscles and nerves exposed; but with a constant grimace on his face. What could have happened? 'Ah, I've been lucky,' Benjamin repeated miserably. She could get nothing more out of him and was suddenly aware that she did not know him, that she had never known him.

Coldly, Mordecai pressed this piece of Levy to his breast, and allowed himself to be guided to 'the house', as Judith was already calling it.

The old couple made a sensation in the streets of Stillenstadt. Both seemed to have sprung from another age. Black from head to foot, girded with the naïve majesty of figures in old prints, they moved forward with slow, assured steps, entirely self sufficient, and looking at nothing but the small figure of Benjamin who pranced about three paces from them, his frail arms embracing the numerous bits of luggage which Judith had insisted on keeping with her. Mordecai was carrying a small fur-covered trunk on his right shoulder, and his left hand lay

gently on the back of Judith's neck. Both were still handsome,
with that hieratic splendour that accompanies strong creatures to
the end of their lives.

Benjamin had planned the reunion dinner in detail. In his fear
that Judith would be exhausted by the trip, he had begged Mrs
Feigelbaum to prepare a banquet. 'What's all this?' Judith cried
as she entered the kitchen gleaming like a new penny; 'You no
longer trust your own mother, and you have to have your meals
prepared by I don't know what local imitation Jewess?' Suspiciously, she sniffed the dishes at length, finding one a bit
overcooked, another composed of badly kneaded dough, etc.
Benjamin noted excitedly that his mother examined everything
up to and including the fruit.

It was just after the soup that the mysterious bout of fever
began.

Sitting at the foot of the table, Benjamin had Judith to his
right and Mordecai to his left, as it had been during those last
days in Zemyock, after the emptiness of the pogrom. Framed by
these two black pillars, he felt more at home in his own kitchen;
the walls white-washed by his own hands, the tile floor he had
almost licked clean, the utensils bought one by one, all products
of his own sweat, became slowly a part of him now; he delighted
in them suddenly, finding in them a thousand unsuspected virtues.
Something was simmering softly on the three-legged stove, but
Benjamin, ashamed, dared not lean forward to identify the pot's
delicious-smelling contents. His father was sucking a wisp of his
moustache; he set his spoon across the plate and grumbled, with
lassitude: 'So that's how it is. No one in Stillenstadt knows who
we *really* are?'

To Judith's great surprise, Benjamin was not in the least upset:
'No,' he said with authority, 'no one knows. And no one will
know,' he finished on a somewhat acid tone of command.

Mordecai said simply, 'All right, all right.' His arms crossed
on the tablecloth, he became a figure of profound and dignified
sadness. Opposite him, Judith swallowed a little soup, clacked
her tongue with an expression half approving, half disgusted, and

then, turning to the ecstatic Benjamin: 'Not too bad for a German woman; but myself, I always put a little parsley in it. So this Mrs Feigelbaum, you were saying ... ?'

As poor Benjamin considered the peaceful rectangle of the table, itself inscribed in that of the kitchen which, without any doubt, was held in the strictly enclosed volume of the house, he seemed suddenly and finally to shake off the nightmare which he had shouldered in Berlin, in the narrow and fragile rectangle of chalk. To recover countenance, he began to fiddle with an infinitesimal crumb of bread. At the same instant he felt the beat of a heavy blood awakening in his veins, after a long, cold sleep ...

'But it's impossible! He's covered with sweat!'

'Me?' Benjamin asked disbelieving; but bringing his hand to his forehead he felt his whole arm shiver.

A few minutes later, a grumbling Judith was tucking him into bed.

On the third day of that curious fever, he awoke enthusiastically and began work immediately. His eye was lively, his complexion fresh, and he brought to all things a sort of loving gaiety which rejuvenated his features and made him more perky than ever. Judith concluded that there had been 'a change of blood'.

Since the pogrom in Zemyock, Mordecai had taken on the appearance which would remain his until his death. His hair would whiten, his body would bow, he would become more wrinkled; but the main characteristic would remain intact – the tall and thoughtful mass of his body, whose slow movements suggested a preference for immobility which he broke only with an effort, with that kind of heavy regret expressed in the tread of an old elephant, each step seemingly torn from a vast stretch of stillness. On that enormous structure was grafted, in Stillenstadt, a thickening of the waist which reinforced the impression Mordecai gave of a huge animal or a massive hoary tree. But his face remained innocent of fat, as if the exercise of the spirit continually redeemed his threatened features, maintaining the long curved crest of the nose and the hard shelf of the cheek bones

118

beneath the slightly staring gaze of his heavy grey eyes which, without the slightest vagueness or distraction, always seemed to look and to see beyond visible things.

Although Judith adapted herself rapidly to her third existence, it was not the same for Mordecai, who was no longer more than half alive now, rolled up within the shell of his piety that hardened a bit more each day.

Even back in Zemyock, she had noticed that the death of his three 'real' sons had been more than a mortal wound to him, destroying in him all hope of seeing the line of Just Men perpetuated by his blood; taking no further part in the world, Mordecai trusted himself to her advice like a child who takes refuge in obedience.

Shortly after Benjamin's exile, she believed nevertheless that she was witnessing a rebirth: Mordecai watched her with a dreaming eye, declared smiling that she was still as beautiful as ever; and also began to demonstrate such a mad ardour that Judith, torn between her so recent mourning and the joy of seeing a man return to his body, could but reserve her judgement by using ambiguous phrases, like 'the noontime demon', 'the swansong', etc. But soon Mordecai put ever more searching questions to her, going so far as to ask outright if she felt nothing 'on the way'; poor Judith understood that her old tree of a husband was hoping for a last fruit. She reminded him that she was fifty years old. Nevertheless, she added, all is possible with the aid of the Most High. Who would have said to Abraham: Sarah will suckle a child? And yet she bore him a son in his old age, etc.

It was in Stillenstadt that they ceased altogether to be husband and wife.

One night as he was holding her forcefully, she felt herself flung back by the shoulders and sensed that her rough lover, changing his mind, had turned heavily towards the wall of the alcove.

'Good night to you, my wife,' said Mordecai's voice in the blackness.

Judith's surprise was extreme; she could hardly understand the abruptness of that decision; and yet upon reflection she had to admit that Mordecai's withdrawal had not taken her entirely by surprise. For in her husband's always strong passion she had often felt something like a secret rancour, a secret reproach to her for being so beautiful and so desirable. The more he aged, the more his effusions seemed to be forced by desire and not freely consented to, joyfully called forth, as during the first years of their union. But from that night when he ceased to express his desires she noted that he showed her instead a deeper friendship in daily life, a better and softer indulgence, a kind of new respect.

Certainly he became more distant each day, a cold star orbiting relentlessly in the peaceful heaven of his prayers and acts of contrition; but Judith sensed that at that distance, from which henceforth he looked upon his wife with his eyes grey and slow and heavy as clouds in winter, there was now nothing but love for her. And although she was still a woman, that voluntary detachment pleased her; she saw in it secret homage to her beauty, a last bouquet laid upon her body.

The last thread which tied Mordecai to daily life was broken insidiously by Benjamin's nimble and delicate little fingers.

From the day of his arrival in Stillenstadt, Mordecai had undertaken to find work; for he did not wish, he said, in an odd tone, to be a charge upon his son. He was in the habit, was he not, of earning his own living.

But the unemployment which had devastated Germany offered no hope to an old man, an alien and, worse, a Jew; after humiliating attempts, seeing himself thrown out upon the sands of life, he came round one day to his son's shop, filling it altogether with his cumbersome body. He wished to learn to sew buttons, to iron, to remove basting stitches, etc. – all tasks within the capacities of a ten-year-old apprentice.

But the work of his fingers – 'stiff as wood' he said in excuse – had to be redone by Benjamin's nimble hands. The son complained to himself at the old man's mania for usefulness; and then protested out aloud. At that, Mordecai gave up earning his living.

'Not to abandon,' he said to himself, 'a world which has

abandoned you, is to add madness to your misfortune. Should I be a laughing-stock?'

He left the shop and retreated to the small room on the second storey, behind his sacred parchments.

Benjamin reassured him, cajoled him, sprinkled him with unctuous little phrases, saying that in a Jewish home it was necessary to have a man of purity who would intercede with God for all. And willingly, at table, Benjamin emphasized the pre-eminence of prayer over basely material activity (meaning by that his daily work of 'a cutter on paper', as they said in Zem-yock, in contrast to the noble work of cutting crystal).

So cradled in words, and burying himself deeper each day in his interior world, old Mordecai finished by slowly forgetting the open wound to his manhood: his son plied the needle, his wife held the purse-strings, and he laboured for the souls of men.

And yet one day, while he was dreaming, between two verses, on the obscure path of his life, and on its inglorious conclusion, he resolved as a last resort to have grandchildren. That thought rejuvenated him. Rapidly he investigated the marriageable girls of Stillenstadt. A tiny Miss Blumenthal was among them, who seemed made to order for the little twenty-five-year-old tailor. Mordecai hardly investigated more than the size of his future daughter-in-law or hoped for more than the promise hidden in her rounded haunches. Benjamin was frantic, but then understood that his father wanted to console himself for the loss of his three 'real' sons; he accepted the interview which had been arranged for him with little Miss Blumenthal.

She did not displease him. She seemed so confused by him that he considered sympathetically her rather long face, her well filled dress, and above all her eyes, unmalicious eyes where, on a background of bluish fear, almost of terror, danced the multiple mischievous sparks of childish curiosity. When she began to blush, he found her desirable.

'Well?' Mordecai asked when he returned.

Benjamin stared at him in silence.

'No?' the old man asked, uneasy.

Benjamin smiled slyly: 'Yes.'

121

And without waiting for compliments, he plunged once more into the daily course of his life, running upstairs to change and dashing into the shop afterwards, where he started jumping about, nervous and indecisive as to the most urgent task, 'All this doesn't put any butter in the soup, does it?' he asked himself aloud, with an affectation of importance which surprised him; but when he least expected it something in him fell apart, and he burst out laughing.

6

An hour later, Benjamin was sitting crosslegged on the cutting table, with a jacket across his knees; vigorously he pushed his bent thumb and index finger against an invisible needle. The bulb, lowered close to his head, wrapped him in an aureole of harsh light.

'Why don't you wear glasses?' his father asked him affectionately.

Benjamin raised his reddened eyelids, their lashes made all sparse by the work of the needle: 'So you're happy?'

'I'm happy,' Mordecai said. 'I'm only sorry they don't know; we'll have to tell them soon!'

'Oh, they saw right away that I liked the lady ...'

'It isn't that, my son,' Mordecai said in an oppressed tone.

He was breathing noisily, and his moustache lifted with the passage of his breath, as he emerged timidly from a long and suffocating descent into himself begun the day of his arrival in Stillenstadt. 'We shall have to tell them who we are. Who we *really* are, do you understand?'

At this dizzying word 'really' Benjamin had interrupted his needle work, and his hand remained hanging in the air, as if floating in the electric light. Finally he declared: 'I'm sorry, but we will tell them nothing at all.' His eyes were blinking from fatigue, as well as from the old fear that his father inspired in him.

'Nothing at all?'

'Nothing at all,' Benjamin confirmed dryly.

'And her, you won't tell her either?'

Benjamin pursed his lips.

'I was afraid of it,' Mordecai growled low. 'You are an abominable pagan; but ... and the children?'

'What children?' the little tailor asked coldly, while Mordecai's mouth distended and gaped open over the shattered yellow

123

stones of his teeth, as if to make way for the rumbling torrent that suddenly rolled out over the terrified Benjamin: 'When there is a marriage, children are a possibility, aren't they?'

Two curious figures froze into immobility in front of the shop window.

Benjamin hunched his shoulders and with a discreet pressure of his heels retreated a little from the wave of fury that was breaking over him; then, in a voice as thin as a thread, he answered humbly: 'The children will know later, if they become men. I will not bother them with stories in which, I must tell you, my venerable father, I no longer believe . . .' He added immediately, on a note of bitterness: 'In which I no longer want to believe! Oh, father!'

As he ended this odd profession of faith, prudently withdrawn to the end of the cutting table, his head so low that it almost touched his knees, his father, Mordecai, began to cry out so piercingly that Judith ran in from the kitchen, a saucepan in her hand.

She got the gist immediately, and swinging her saucepan with fiery gestures plunged into the discussion, immediately speaking of the future Levy as if he were already present on her breast instead of the saucepan she was hugging so lovingly: 'Who's going to tell who?' she cried indignantly. 'If the good Lord, blessed be he, has made a decision one way or another about his little bird (and what shall we name him?), the little one will know about it when the time comes, soon enough, alas. But may God spare us,' she finished shrilly, 'from having a Just Man!'

'Oh father, father!' Benjamin went on emotionally. 'You know very well that to be a *Lamed-waf* is worth hardly anything in this world . . . and maybe even in the next.'

Outnumbered, Mordecai retreated slowly towards the door; he opened it, pointed a thick accusing finger out of the shadow, and said in a tone of supreme derision: 'Will you lose, for life, all your reasons for living!' Then he withdrew, cut off from his son for good.

On the wedding day he barely acknowledged the presence of the bride's parents; as for little Miss Blumenthal, he pretended not to see her, she was no longer any use to him, she no longer played a part in the Dream of his life. This time he had completely withdrawn into the pit of his age.

Judith always said of her husband from then on, That old elephant, that old solitary, that rock.

Although tiny and quite thin, Miss Leah Blumenthal was well made; but no one noticed that until her wedding day, a woman neighbour having helped her to emphasise all her beauty. She seemed totally lacking in natural coquetry. Her face was always clean, but not engaging; her hair always in order but not really styled; and her appearance always soignée, but neutral.

Mr Benjamin Levy, her husband, wondered how it came about that she had such slender white hands, with the fingers of a rich woman. He never suspected that this virgin whiteness required an amazing quantity of daily attentions and small cares so subtle that no one noticed, when she peeled a vegetable, what precautions she took not to chip a fingernail, or scratch the precious ermine of a patch of skin.

Judith would proclaim that her daughter-in-law handled all things with tweezers. But Benjamin was delighted with her hands; while his wife was asleep he loved to play with one of those bony mechanisms which took on in his palm, in the blackness, all the forms which his imagination might give it; animal, vegetable; and even, intoxicatingly, the form of five thick hairs which he combed against the supple skin of the pillow-case.

Still, in those first days of marriage he was astonished at the amount of time she spent indefatigably 'licking herself like a cat'. After each embrace, she went down to the kitchen to wash herself all over. This might have annoyed him in the end if she had not, each time, touched her armpits with a drop of perfume, which lent balm to all her freshly soaped body. And then when she reappeared, draped in her nightgown and holding the candle as far as possible from her hair, the childish, confused freshness of her person suddenly illuminated the room with a quivering clarity, bounded by shadows, and causing Mr Benjamin Levy's heart to beat rapidly.

'Ah, Miss Blumenthal,' he said to her, smiling agitatedly; 'have you had a nice walk?'

'I wanted to give you a surprise,' she said submissively; and sitting at the edge of the bed she would place an apple on the lips of her humble lord, or a slice of bread and butter, or a lump of sugar, by which she earned forgiveness for her desertion of the conjugal bed.

One day he surprised her undulating and simpering all alone in the middle of the room like a hairdresser's assistant. She was holding her nightdress tight about her waist, her hair was spread wildly over her shoulders, giving her an air of animal luxury which both aged her girlish face and recalled its childhood coyness. Benjamin burst out laughing ... From the sole example of his own wife, he knew now that all women are little girls getting on in years, each endowed with a body greater and more important than her mind, and all of whom adore surrounding themselves with meaningless mysteries. It was only much later that he learned that Miss Blumenthal lived in a narrow universe haunted by fear and by two or three sentiments equally terrible in their simplicity: the love of a few beings, the repressed pleasure of having a body.

The fear came to her in a direct line from her mother, a woman of imperial aspect and character who had made herself a perfect slave to Mr Blumenthal. She suffered accesses of cruelty, she found a voluptuousness in those things. But when Mrs Blumenthal died of the disease which had made her so shrewish and cruel, Mr Blumenthal could think of nothing better than to marry immediately a person of equal wickedness. Miss Blumenthal then suffered the yoke of the stranger, until her own marriage, towards which her stepmother had laboured frantically.

Soon afterward, this lady discovered that Berlin was a city with a future, and Miss Blumenthal was abandoned to the Levys. She watched her father leave as one watches someone die: this time she was altogether lost.

Naturally the one person in the world whom, from now on, she feared more than any other, was Judith; an order from her

made her tremble; and even though 'Mother Judith's' violence
was distributed solely in words, little Mrs Levy always hunched
over and raised an elbow gently, as if, one day or another, she
expected a real slap. And yet she stared directly into Judith's
eyes, to the point where Judith was occasionally upset by this
gentle gaze focused on her violence like a beacon on an absurdly
agitated sea. But until her first child arrived, Miss Blumenthal
bowed to the slightest frown of those terrible brows. Mother
Judith alone was mistress of the house and, in the fear that someone might encroach upon her territory, she preferred two precautions to one, assigning a task to her daughter-in-law only with
reluctance; and she never hid her opinion that she would have
performed it better herself. It was that way until Miss Blumenthal's first confinement.

Already during her pregnancy (which was immediate), the new
Mama Levy was offended that Mother Judith should treat her as
the mere repository of a precious object belonging primarily to
the Levys; or more exactly, like a perfume jar unaware of the
value of its contents. Mother Judith watched over the infant
being nurtured in the young woman, ordered the jar to recline, to
drink as much beer as possible, and to realise at all times the
undeserved honour of being the vessel for a Levy.

Be careful of the child, she would say, in a tone which meant
almost: remember that you are carrying our posterity.

In a movement of instinctive revolt, little Mrs Levy turned the
trembling but stubborn beam of her eyes (the eyes of a domestic-
ated bird) upon Mother Judith; and leaning forward she surrounded her enormous belly with her two arms in the solemn
gesture of a gravid woman, a gesture which had become familiar
since the child had started moving within her.

Open warfare broke out in the hospital. The mother, thin and
milky, lay back on her pillow, her bust raised slightly; at the foot
of the bed, the swaddled thing in her arms, Mother Judith
received the congratulations of visitors. They admired the infant,
they listened to the sage comments of Mother Judith; now and
then one turned towards the exhausted mother as if to say: 'Ah,
it's true, a bit of the credit goes to her.'

127

Suddenly little Miss Blumenthal half rose up, and gave out a piercing cry: 'Give him back to me, he belongs to me!' There was a moment of embarrassment. A murmur rose from the nearby beds in the ward. Mother Judith had reddened, and she frowned on her pale daughter-in-law, who was gasping, her body arched up on her forearms, entirely hardened by her new hate and her new love. And still, when they yielded the baby to her, setting it in the hollow of her breast, she lay beside it and fell asleep almost instantly, so much had that exceptional explosion of energy exhausted her.

Mr Benjamin Levy exulted secretly, while Mordecai declared in a tone of tender respect: May God protect us, we have a she-wolf in the house. Mother Judith was silent: until they were weaned, Miss Blumenthal would remain the mother of her children.

The drama was revived later on. Children respect only the supreme authority. Mordecai was always wise enough, in their presence, to efface himself before Mr Benjamin Levy; but it was not so with Mother Judith, who became mother-in-chief as soon as the children were old enough to obey her. Miss Blumenthal found herself relegated to the suckling babes. In the end she got used to these successive surrenders; she saw in them an ineluctable destiny, Mother Judith representing in her eyes only the first step towards the final detachment of the adult, which was for her mother's heart an ascent into nothingness. She even borrowed her authority from that of Mother Judith; and when she was not obeyed quickly enough, she went to fetch the Mother Superior in person. She never suspected that she nevertheless remained the true spring, the sole well of maternity, hollowed out in a mysterious fashion in the heart of each of her children. It was in the kitchen, close to her skirts, that the ungrateful creatures came to sit when they were seized by a sadness without reason, or by one of these indefinable anxieties that come from the depths to be appeased only by the sound of a certain voice.

Her husband was no different from the rest of humanity; quite obviously, he thought of her as something insignificant, and spoke to her only to tease her, as if she were a child.

Once, as a foolish young girl, she had dreamed of a man for whom she would be important, beside whom she would play a role, however slight.

But Mr Benjamin Levy cared for her as he did for a length of thread, and several times she bit back the desire to ask him suddenly, point blank, what was the colour of her eyes. She thought that he would be unable to answer, she imagined desperately his nonchalant manner: Ah yes, your eyes, they're . . . and will you please go away and not bother me with these children's games? She was quite sure that he had never really looked at them.

In which she was mistaken, as in the rest; for the tender Benjamin was not only aware of the colour of her eyes, but of more and, if quizzed on that chapter, he could have expatiated infinitely on the slightest particularity of the lashes, the white of the right eye, slightly whiter than that of the left, on the infinitesimal grains of pink that flecked the greyish background of the irises, and which he was doubtless alone in the world in having noticed. But could a man say these things? Miss Blumenthal had brought herself to his bed out of duty, and in all decency it was a bit late to subject her to a courtship which she seemed not to solicit at all. So for a long time after the marriage Benjamin continued to call his wife Miss Blumenthal, half in affectionate mockery and half because of that insane inhibition that kept him from acknowledging the deep and final bond which united him with this wife of chance circumstance. Their lovemaking was deaf and mute but at times, from those great nocturnal depths of silence, a crest of foam and cries arose out of an embrace and both tasted an extraordinary heightening – to which they never referred, for in it there was obviously something which did not belong to this world. It required, later, old age and above all the approach of violent death in the concentration camp to make Benjamin decide to express his love to his wife: she did not grasp his meaning.

Hurried by all the members of the Levy family, she had given birth to her first prematurely. Nevertheless he weighed nine sumptuous pounds at birth. Whom did he resemble? The question was never asked. It went without saying that here was the traditional form of the Levys, which little Mr Levy, the father, had transmitted so reluctantly. Mother Judith wasted no time in examining the eyes, the nose, the mouth, as she might have if the least doubt existed as to the 'resemblance' of the newborn. Addressing the old man, she summarized the situation in these words: 'He resembles *us*.' Miss Blumenthal might recall the strong personality of her dead mother, trace out a lip formed in tiny symptomatic points, emphasize a short nose which obviously came from the Blumenthal side: nothing made any difference, the child was not of her blood. And although the history of the Just Men seemed to her to include an unhealthy element, Mother Judith found herself almost tempted to throw it in her daughter-in-law's face, to stop her mouth for good of these claims on the child. In her fierce desire to appropriate it, she even came to identify herself with that illustrious lineage, clinging to certain domestic details of the cult; she made herself more than ever a Levy.

As he grew up, the living enigma set them at it again: it became obvious that he was neither Levy nor Blumenthal, but some indeterminate human creature, dotted by a touch of Germanic brute. The new arrival, Moritz, seemed above all not to let himself down among the little hoodlums who were his comrades, and incidentally succeeded quite well, helped by an appropriate physique. From the day of his birth he sported a round little belly which, like an expression of his animal joy in living and the quickly formed structure of his body, announced the true strength beneath the cheerful bon vivant's exterior. For years his face was like a doll's: regular teeth, a short nose with thick nostrils, and luminous, avid brown eyes always beaming forward, outward, towards the world, like a hand extended happily.

At first Mordecai thought that he could see in the child the scandalous young man he himself had been in Zemyock, and his indulgence was exaggerated by the conviction that the young devil would also, sooner or later, lay aside his horns. He nourished the boy discreetly on anecdotes of the Just Men, and secretly reckoned the young one's chances of measuring up to that honour. But as soon as Moritz was old enough to get about by himself, they never saw him at the house. The street attracted him. There he joined a gang of urchins among whom, alas, not one single Jewish nose could be seen.

Moritz was ringleader; he invented games and loved nothing so much as mock warfare on the banks of the Schlosse. When he prowled among the reeds, a half-drawn bow against his thigh, he knew that his destiny was not what they thought it at home. As when they undressed to dive into the river, the clothes of the presumed Moritz Levy would vanish in the air, revealing a naked savage in a menacing forest of reeds. He would fling himself wildly on the enemy. And when the two of them slid into the mud he could have wished their shouts genuine, the knives of real metal ... He came home with his face on fire, his knees and clothes in tatters; then he removed his braces, waiting patiently while Mother Judith finished her tantrum of temper. There was an immanent justice: they played at 'killing each other', as Mother Judith said weakly; then they got a good spanking. After which they could consider themselves even with God.

School finished the job of dividing Moritz's life into two irreconcilable halves. They never saw him except at mealtimes. Invariably he arrived late, sat down looking contrite, performed the necessary motions for giving thanks, and then leaned forward over his plate and forgot heaven and earth until it was emptied, the last stains mopped up with bread. Only then, raising his dishevelled head, did he become a presence in the world of the Levys.

'Has our pagan finished his soup?' Mother Judith asked sadly.

'And when will you find a moment for the study of the Talmud?' the old man asked him in a resigned voice. 'At your age I was already into the Midrash up to my ears. Aren't you Jewish?' Moritz, annoyed, murmured incomprehensibly: ... my fault ... homework ... school.

Benjamin, altogether astonished at having fathered such a scoundrel, came to his defence immediately: 'It's true, you know, in Zemyock there was no Christian school; but here, how can they become good Jews?'

'But you were the one who wanted to leave!' cried the old man angered by so much bad faith.

Benjamin smiled imperceptibly: 'Ah! don't I know it! But it's too late now and, as the Talmud says: Do not say, in the home of a hanged man, "go hang up this fish for me".'

'No,' Mother Judith said then, 'I can't see this child "sweating", either for us or for the Christians.' And she concluded with the strange comment: 'God has punished us, our little ones will be Sunday Jews.'

A thoughtful silence fell over the room. Then little Mrs Levy served the next course, and conversation rose again on another subject, grave or mockingly sentimental, as if the problem were solved. A slow wave invaded Moritz as he sank pleasurably into the warmly reassuring atmosphere of the family meal. What they were saying passed far over his head: birds tracing indecipherable signs in the sky, but whom he loved to watch.

An abyss separated this gracious little world from the vast universe that Moritz sniffed as soon as he set foot in the street. Occasionally it made him dizzy: like holding to the very top of the big chestnut tree at school, standing between two branches with an insupportable emptiness between them. Why weren't all the Christians Jews? And why weren't all Jews ...? Couldn't everybody enjoy this kind of happiness together? And what did the old man want of him, what was he scheming behind his bloody anecdotes, his tragic expression, his constant allusions to the *Lamed-waf*? Whenever he ventured out on these disconcerting paths, Moritz's brain was soon enough in a whirl; and his heart, it seemed, split horribly, with a dry ripping sound.

So he would venture out only very rarely.

7

ERNIE was Miss Blumenthal's second fruit. He arrived after the
full nine months. But when she saw that he was twice as paltry as
Moritz, Miss Blumenthal stifled a cry of happiness in her child-
bed: this one would not be claimed by Mother Judith, this little
nestling belonged indubitably to her.

It was easy to see that Mother Judith was in a difficulty. Several
months after the delivery, Miss Blumenthal surprised her again
examining the baby minutely: 'It's funny,' Miss Blumenthal
offered, 'I can't tell whom he resembles . . .'

And Mother Judith looked her up and down before adding,
perfidiously: 'He's built like his father, but his head . . . the head
comes from nobody. All this will be decided later,' she said almost threateningly.

Indeed, Ernie Levy's head offered no clue: at birth, his skull
bore a fine sheath of curly black down, that reached to the nape
of his neck; and his eyes, which were blue for three weeks, shifted soon to a midnight blue, sprinkled with brilliant, stellar
sparks.

Mother Judith did not understand whence came that thin
straight nose, with wings swept back to expose the open nostrils;
that long white dome of the forehead, and particularly the length
of the neck, 'no thicker than a finger', which supported the whole
edifice with the inimitable grace of a bird. But when she was
cradling the marvellous creature, Mother Judith would smile
into the void, wholly admiring; and her richly sensual gaze en-
folded that mysterious living thing tightly, the baby in whom ran
at least a drop of her blood, and who yet seemed to her so different from all known flesh that she called only him 'little angel'.

Forewarned by Moritz's example, the grandfather took Ernie
in hand at less than four years. From Poland he had sent for a
Hebrew alphabet in relief; he initiated the little angel through the

133

mouth, that ancestral method which is so sweet and pleasant; covered with honey, the rosewood characters were simply given to the young student of the Law to suck. Later on, when Ernie was capable of reading brief phrases, Mordecai offered them moulded on cakes, in the making of which Judith deployed all her cleverness.

Ernie began to trot along behind the old man. Their relationship became so intimate that Miss Blumenthal was moved. They held long conversations in the room upstairs; when she put her ear to the door Miss Blumenthal only heard whispering, now solemn, now so fine and lyrical that her breast tightened fearfully. One day she heard: 'So then, will you lend me your beard?'

More whispering followed, long and serious.

But more than anything else, it was their manner of being together that affected her strangely. From her kitchen she watched them now and then in the dining-room, during those awful Hebrew lessons; the old man's attitude seemed as reverent as that of the child; when Ernie asked a question, the patriarch nodded thoughtfully before answering, as if this were a learned Talmudic discussion. And once in a while his hand came to rest on the curly hair, straightening a lock.

Miss Blumenthal did not understand. She sensed a kind of umbilical cord between the old man and the child, but was unable to visualize the nourishing substance which ran through it. One day, peeking through the kitchen window, she saw the child hunched over a spelling book and stroking an imaginary beard with great dignity. An unexpected truth struck her: Ernie was *imitating* the old man. Alerted, she noticed other details; when he believed himself alone, the little one clasped his hands behind his back, his eyes became heavier, his head drooped forward, and with the heavy step of an old man he paced about the table, as if plunged in rabbinical meditation; at other times, seated before his spelling book, he would start intoning psalms with an inspired air, as do the angels and the pious Jews. She also surprised him in the act of trapping a pinch of wind, which he introduced delicately into his right nostril, sniffing it then in slow concentration, and lifting his head in the old man's manner.

One Friday night after the Sabbath Chants the old man climbed to his room and came down with an enormous volume bound in calfskin. Miss Blumenthal knew about this book through her husband, whose lips opened during certain moments of calm intimacy. She knew by hearsay a bit about the Just Men, about Zemyock, and about the variable money order sent to Poland every month. She might have been able to learn more, but she was not very curious about the subterranean world of the Levys' daily life; she never mentioned it to her husband, pretending to have forgotten. So she was as surprised as Judith and Benjamin when the old man slowly opened the book and began to read the first chapter. A heavy silence fell. The children watched Mother Judith, pale, majestically angry; suddenly she let out a raucous, guttural exclamation. The old man raised his eyes and blasted her with a look.

His voice was icy: 'These children don't know what a real Jew is.' And pounding the tabletop with a tormented hand, he added: 'And you, you don't even know that I'm still a man.'

Then he went on with his reading in the same slow, harsh, occasionally tremulous voice. It was the same on the following Friday.

Miss Blumenthal knew enough Hebrew to understand the linear lives of these martyrs. She made an effort to exclude the horror of them from her thought. And she was grieved to see that the little angel, leaning towards the reader, his eyes terribly wide, was 'imitating' the bloody characters of the book with all his heart. And then on the fourth Friday, when the old man had finished his reading, Ernie raised an obedient finger and asked him: '*if that all these stories are true . . .*'

A shrill, unpleasant laugh escaped Mr Benjamin Levy.

And then Mother Judith seemed to swell with fury, while her eyes turned imploringly on the old man, who hesitated, and chewed on his moustaches; finally he murmured in a dry, truly broken voice: 'Well, what do you think, my little birdlet, can such things really happen?' A fine line appeared between the child's brows. 'No, of course not,' he answered bitterly.

On those words the old man closed the book and left the

dining-room; late at night, Miss Blumenthal heard the echoes of the argument between him and Mother Judith; he never again brought down the book of the fabulous house of Levy.

Mother Judith had always cast a gloomy eye on Ernie's assiduity in learning from the patriarch. 'That one doesn't even need honey to chew up his abc's; but where's the good of it all?' She was afraid that by plunging that vulnerable consciousness into the 'old stories', Mordecai might insidiously communicate the virus of *Zemyockism*, as Benjamin called it. But the cure was close behind the disease, for soon attendance at school would lead little Ernie to the games of his own age: that, at least, is what the old lady hoped.

Events proved that the study of the Law had created a mechanism no less sensitive to pagan programmes than to the divine Torah and to the prophets. And Mother Judith found consolation in the fact that Ernie was wearying visibly of Mordecai's teaching, and devoting himself to profane studies.

He preferred to work in the kitchen, on a corner of the table set aside for him by Miss Blumenthal. Mother Judith would find some pretext for an intrusion; and as the boy stuck out his tongue in concentration the two rivals, watching one another, would each in turn subject him to the gamut of their uneasily curious glances.

On one fatal day he came home with an armful of prizes.

Neither Mordecai nor Mother Judith congratulated him disproportionately; although it was for diametrically opposed reasons, both evinced serious (and in some respects dramatic) reservations on what was for Benjamin an excuse for a thousand embraces. Miss Blumenthal, torn between panic and admiration, could only clasp her hands and beg: 'I hope only good comes out of it, my God, I hope only good comes out of it!'

As Ernie moved solemnly to the stairway, Mother Judith followed him on tiptoe; when she saw him mysteriously enter the young couple's room, she came up stealthily and heard the sound of voices. Glueing one ear to the keyhole, she heard these astounding words (pronounced by the little angel in a doctoral tone,

his German so curiously modulated by Yiddish inflections):
'You again? Congratulations, my boy, congratulations, my
young man. You again?'

Then she heard a mouselike laugh, and understood that the
little angel was strutting ironically before the mirror; the joke
was infectious, and she could not help launching into a huge
laugh of happiness herself – which produced immediate silence
behind the door.

Until that day the only books around the house had been
prayer books, Talmudic texts, or some classroom book forgotten
by the children. At first, when she saw Ernie plunged into one of
the prize volumes, Mother Judith suspected nothing; accepted
this as inherent to the modes of the country. But one night, in an
excess of scruple, she asked Benjamin to tell her something about
the little angel's latest reading. Her son's answer surprised her:
two collections of fairy tales, an adventure novel set in China, and
three tales of old German chivalry! After half an hour of confused explanations, she lost her temper:

'I don't understand a thing you've told me. What I want to
know is yes or no, did everything written in those books happen?'

'No,' Benjamin said resolutely.

'Then it's all lies,' Mother Judith declared with marked repug-
nance.

'It's not lies, it's stories.'

Judith's eyelids fluttered; the breath hissed between her pursed
lips: 'Why don't you tell me right out that I'm crazy?'

The conversation was over.

But Mother Judith's conviction was formed; and on that same
day she noticed for the first time that if Ernie was suddenly interrupted in his reading, he raised a blank expression, swollen by
dream and delirium, recognizing one only reluctantly.

'Where are you?' she asked him gently.

And as the child gazed at her without pleasure, she was sorry
not to be able to follow him into that sphere where things invisible to the naked eye are so beautiful, that anyone who can
read has no further desire to return to this world.

Shortly afterwards, without her knowing how, new books appeared in the child's hands, each more disquieting than the others. Certain of them were illustrated, and horsemen could be seen, and women in long gowns bedecked with diamonds, and curious beings and plants which doubtless came from China. But the volumes that Judith feared most were those which gave no hint of their content. When he emerged from them, the child seemed completely lost. After a few weeks, the rims of his eyes took on an unhealthy pink flush, while his tiny blue veins stood out clearly against the exquisite white of his skin. One night at table Ernie's eyes began to water with fatigue. In great agitation Judith called upon the whole family to witness this; no, no, things could not go on this way: 'Those awful books are eating out his eyes, and I wouldn't be surprised one of these mornings if they ate out his whole insides!'

Severe measures were voted that evening. As soon as she had rallied unanimous support, Mother Judith stalked into his room and expropriated all the volumes of 'lies', without exception.

In the next few days the battle became more bitter.

It transpired that the child was smuggling books home in the seat of his trousers.

With that ruse exposed, he redoubled his ingenuity and did so well that Mother Judith, as she put it, 'surrendered'. Still, though defeated as censor, she became a spy, keeping track of the little angel's activities and gestures, seeing to it that he did not succumb to his vice in the attic, or in the cellar, or even in the little corner of the room that now served him as a study. Driven from his last stronghold, Ernie tried to profit by the adult conversations which took place every night in the living-room. Slipping barefoot into the hallway, he managed to take advantage of the ray of light that gleamed from the doorway of the room – with the door left artfully ajar. They discovered him behind the door after midnight, haggard, his eyes wild, too tired to know what was happening to him.

But from then on, at the slightest sign of his approach, if the latch gave so much as a gentle, understanding sigh, Mother Judith's voice came to him from the other side: 'Ernie, my lamb of suffering, go on to bed.'

8

HAVING won the battle of the books, Mother Judith went so far as to hope that the little angel would follow the example of his pagan elder brother.

But soon enough, alas, she had to admit that in driving out one devil she had admitted another in its place, even more dangerous because totally elusive. Whether he was at table or doing his homework (and even during his rare frolics with the younger children), the little angel would suddenly freeze altogether, his features immobilized, a fine pink blur would fill his eyes, and he became as distant from all of them as though he were off in the land of books. She suspected that he was telling himself tales of chivalry. For – an astonishing thing – when he came out of those reveries he adopted an air of martial dignity, the detached, abstracted bearing of a hero.

She decided to use strong methods; if there was the slightest hint of sunshine, she shoved the child out into the street without ceremony; and one day, finally, it was learned that the little angel was forgathering with the other kids of the neighbourhood: she had won.

The gang headquarters were some way up the Riggenstrasse, in the backyard of an unused, dilapidated house. The grass and the rubble, the heaps of garbage and the unused well, composed a landscape rich in magic possibilities. Two of Ernie's classmates were also in the 'gang by the well'; one of them was a delicate little blonde girl named Ilse Bruckner, to whom Ernie never dared speak because her eyes were two lakes, and her golden hair cascaded in discipline and majesty over her shoulders, giving her the look of a medieval fairy princess. She wore a knitted sweater in red and white checks, and an iron necklace from which hung a cross; and when they asked her to, she sang, in a voice that made them lightheaded and giddy, some senseless little counting rhymes.

There was something miraculous about Ernie's admission to the gang. Since Mother Judith had started chasing him out of the house, he had fallen into the habit of wandering about, following the thread of his reverie, hands in his pockets, his body erect, and his head held high on that long neck that sprang like a stem from the open collar of his white shirt. Paying no attention at all to what went on in the street, he stumbled against pedestrians, crates, anything set out on the sidewalk; so that finally, made prudent, he preferred to walk outside the town, along the edges of the lush fields that bounded the Schlosse. But one day, roused by a voice recognizable among thousands, he slipped into the ruins of the old house. Huddled in the shadow, he watched Ilse sing in the middle of the group, her face drawing every gaze, and the sun sparkling in a cone of light on her corn-silky blonde hair. The next day he came forward openly, his hands deliberately crossed behind his back, showing by his whole attitude, that he was only a delighted little spectator of the gang's activities and laughter. They grew accustomed to his mute presence. They assigned small parts to him. He became a guardian of stone flocks, a referee of tournaments, a professional prisoner, a page to King Tristan; none of which duties demanded the wearing of a sword. When the game proved too violent, he cautiously left the field: the mere sight of bruises wounded him. And when they were swept up in the game, and whacked away at each other with wooden swords, Ernie wondered why they had to dream with their bodies, when it was so sweet to dream with the soul alone. One day Wilhelm Knopfer, a chubby little boy with laughing eyes and two chins, suggested that they play the trial of Jesus.

'But who'll be the Jews?' asked Hans Schliemann, who was the undisputed leader.

Each one protested. Finally they discovered Ernie Levy squatting behind a near-by wall, white with terror. Amid loud bursts of laughter he was dragged to the well against which Ilse Bruckner was already leaning, her arms wide above the mossy rim of rock, her head hanging in agony; she was on tiptoe, in imitation of the nailed Christ. Wilhelm Knopfer immediately improvised a pot-bellied, hilarious Pontius Pilate, who now and then rubbed his palms together significantly; and shooting a sly look at all of them: 'You understand? I'm washing my hands of it.' Now and then he slipped a hand into his shirt, in an inexplicable Napoleonic gesture.

'Ha, ha!' he puffed at Ernie. 'You're our only Jew, you're our only Jew, so you have to do it, otherwise who else can be *them*?'

Imposing silence on the excited gang, he frowned, raised a majestic lower lip, and announced gravely: 'Ho, Jews! What do you want me to do with Our Lord? Do I let him go?'

'It isn't like that,' interrupted a neatly braided little girl dogmatically, and in a tone that was incontrovertible. 'In the catechism, it's Barabbas first.'

Wilhelm Knopfer trumpeted: 'Shut up! You and your catechism! Here I'm the priest . . . All right then,' he began again, upset by the interruption, trying to win back his shaken prestige; 'Do I let him go, yes or no?'

A veiled sharpness shone cruelly in Wilhem's good-little-boy gaze, his pupils dilated by an interior vision, vindictive and heavy with reminiscence: Ernie fluttered his long lashes heavily. Firmly gripped by the two boys, and under the corrosive glare of all those eyes, it seemed to him that his fleshly self was dissolving into the air, to be reborn in some mysterious way in the spirits of his playmates, but concealed now behind a mask, wearing cheap and bloody finery, as in those nightmares where one sees oneself reduced to some sort of abject vermin. He threw a defeated glance at Ilse, whose golden head hung loosely against one shoulder, with an abandon as coy as it was moving. And as the cross swung against the girl's sweater, awakening the fabled memory of Christian atrocities, his knees seemed suddenly to weaken. 'Oh, let him go!' he breathed.

This evoked an immediate concert of protests: 'Ah no, it wasn't like that, not like that, not like that! You said to crucify him! Crucify him, you said! So say it, go ahead and say it, say it, say it!' They all took it up in chorus, while Ernie hung his head pensively, his lower lip already bleeding between the teeth which refused to part for the word of death.

'For God's sake!' Hans Schliemann cried furiously. 'Did you say it or didn't you?'

In the solemn silence which followed the leader's intervention, the melodious voice of the crucified girl was heard: 'Ah! the nails, the nails, they're hurting me . . .'

'Oh my God, have pity!' said a little girl in a tone of wretchedness that pierced the hearts of her unusual audience, freezing their blood, cutting their breath, agitating the girl's eyes, the long luminous lashes which blinked now, or trembled, or closed over shameful tears.

'But no, I didn't say it,' said Ernie, upset.

'Yes, you did say it!' Hans Schliemann growled in the voice he used for distributing justice, while his arm of iron came down mercilessly on Ernie's shoulder; Ernie sighed.

'And,' the little braided girl took up, 'you even said: Let Barabbas go, and crucify Jesus. Didn't he say that?'

'He said it! He said it!'

'I didn't . . . I didn't!' the accused stammered, a tear streaking one cheek.

'You said it, you said it,' the children repeated more violently, while Ernie Levy, hiding his face between his hands, murmured in a more and more hesitant voice, as if the others were convincing him: 'I didn't say it, I didn't, no, I didn't.'

A little girl's voice exploded against his ear: 'You dirty Jew!'

At the same time the viscous weight of a gob of spittle trickled down his ear.

And then Wilhelm Knopfer screamed indignantly: 'Murderer!'

And pressing down one of Ernie's hands, he gave him such a smack on the face from below, so hard that the child spun about, lost, in the air that was thick with shouts, fantastic fists, and sharp fingernails that the little girls were digging into the flesh of his shoulders and thighs as they fired plaintive insults at him: 'Wicked, wicked, you killed God!'

A hand stopped him in his dizzying fall and he saw close to his own the face of Hans Schliemann, grey with concentrated fury, unrecognizable: 'Look, what you've done!' Hans Schliemann cried pointing to little Ilse, who was weeping by herself, still leaning back against the rim of the well, her arms spread wide, her dying head twisted painfully, while in her pious imitation of Jesus Christ she let a thin thread of spittle drip from the corner of her pink mouth, twisted in pain. When she realized that they were watching her, she breathed in a touching voice: 'Oh, my God, what did I ever do to you, you Jews? Oh, my God, the nails, the nails...'

At which, no longer able to restrain himself, Wilhelm Knopfer picked up a rock, and slipping behind Ernie, hit him hard on the back of the neck, crying out: For Jesus! The Jewish boy fell in a heap on the grass, his eyes rolled back, his arms crossed. A red flower bloomed on his black curly hair. After a few moments of contemplation, the gang scattered silently. Only Wilhelm Knopfer stayed behind with a little boy of about ten who kept murmuring oh! oh! and stared in fascination at the red flower spreading on Ernie Levy's neck.

'He's dead,' Wilhelm Knopfer said, dropping his bloody rock to the ground.

'We ought to make sure,' the other one said, terrified.

'I don't dare.'

'I don't either.'

'He never did anything to us,' Wilhelm said in a strange voice.

'No, he didn't,' the second boy agreed.

'He was nice,' Wilhelm admitted suddenly, shaking his head as if unable to retrace the obscure road that had led to his act.

'Yes, he was,' the other one said with surprise.

'Shall we carry him back?' Wilhelm asked.

'We'll have to,' said the other one, who was already kneeling.

He took Ernie by the shoulders; and Wilhelm, between his legs, raised the body by the thighs. 'He doesn't weigh much more than a bird,' Wilhelm remarked in a tearful sigh. Then he began to weep silently, and went on weeping all the way down the Riggenstrasse, staring at Ernie's bloody neck, which juggled at each step, while a small group of curious bystanders formed a strange cortège to this even stranger hearse. Mother Judith was the first to know. With a shattering cry, she gathered up the child and carried him to a room on the second floor, followed by a silent Wilhelm. No one paid any attention to Wilhelm. When the doctor, called immediately, passed a flagon under the little victim's nostrils, Wilhelm made the sign of the cross mechanically and, stricken by the memory of their play-acting, he believed that he had made a sign of death. But the Jewish child, his head back on an already red pillow, suddenly gave a long sigh and murmured: 'I didn't say that, I didn't say that ...' Wilhelm slipped outside unnoticed. Once out on the sidewalk, he ran as fast as he could.

Although its origin was to remain a mystery, in time this attack on Ernie took its place in the series of anti-Semitic acts which announced Adolf Hitler's rise to power. Communists being scarce in Stillenstadt, and Democrats being altogether lacking, it followed naturally that the local section of the Nazi party directed the full fire of its propaganda against the few Jewish families which 'were rife' in the town. After Adolf Hitler's accession to the supreme office of Reichskanzler, German Jews felt trapped, like rats condemned to run in circles while waiting for the worst. 'We should never have left Poland,' Mother Judith admitted one day. 'I ask forgiveness, it was my fault, mine ...'

'Come, come,' the patriarch answered her gently, 'if evil is everywhere, how can you hope to escape it?'

It was the year 1933 after the coming of Jesus, beautiful herald of an impossible love.

BOOK FOUR

THE JUST MAN OF THE FLIES

1

IT was Ernie's father who gave the alarm. They had hardly left
the Riggenstrasse when Ernie sensed his father tense and alert.
It was that way every Saturday, on the way to the synagogue;
as soon as they set foot outside the Riggenstrasse, Mr Levy no
longer felt secure; twisting his head in all directions, he raised his
rabbit's-head, and Ernie thought he could see the ears quiver,
tall and projecting. But today the street was so calm and empty,
the red tiles of the roofs gleamed so gaily in the sun, that the
child could not help feeling an irreverent delight at his father's
agitation. Glancing up sideways, he noticed that Mr Levy's thin
lips were also trembling, closing and opening silently, like the
mouth of a suffocating fish. Suddenly Mr Levy's lips closed
altogether, and opened only to hiss.

'Shh . . .' said Mr Levy's mouth.

He froze in the middle of the street.

'What's the matter?' said Mordecai.

Once more Ernie was astonished at the calm of the patriarch,
who seemed never to be upset about anything that did not bear
on the observance of the Law. The old man took two steps
backwards, raised his hand slowly to his beard, and staidly
pulled at one of the strands. 'Well, what's the matter?' he
repeated, with a slight hint of impatience; but his heavy grey
eyes remained fixed, and did not seem to share the nervousness
of the younger Mr Levy. The latter brought a hand behind his
right ear and said: 'Do you hear?'

'I don't hear a thing,' said Mother Judith who had just
arrived, out of breath, gleaming and plump in her eternal black
taffeta dress.

'I hear . . .' Miss Blumenthal said feebly.

'I do, too,' said Moritz.

147

'They're coming by the Rondgasse,' Mr Levy continued; his right ear carefully straining to the waves of music that came closer every moment.

The Levy family stood paralysed beneath the sun, caught in the suddenly cruel yellow light that delivered them up to public attention.

'Come along, hop!' Mother Judith clucked. 'Everybody to Mrs Braunberger's house, quick!'

As she spoke she snatched up a child under each arm, then crossed the street and sidewalk like an arrow, and was already plunging into a near-by house, followed by the rest of the family. The patriarch was at the end of the line; his body moved forward heavily, and his spirit was remembering a former flight.

Ernie had reached the rear of the entrance hall when Mother Judith rushed down from the second floor, flustered, calling out that Mrs Braunberger's door was locked: 'She's already left for the synagogue,' said the patriarch, who was leaning calmly against the wall.

'What's to become of us?' Mother Judith cried; she stretched an arm towards the yellow rectangle of the street, and then dropped it gently about Jacob, who was pressed against her thigh.

'Come now,' said the patriarch, smiling in the semi-darkness, 'don't make a second hell for yourself . . . Of course if they catch you in the street, they knock you about. But they don't come into the house to look for you; they won't come here especially for you, will they?'

'Listen to him!' Mother Judith cried grimly; Ernie saw her teeth flash suddenly, in a brief mirthless smile. Then she made her decision: 'Come on! Up the stairs!'

She was already away, followed by the whole silent troop; even the old man, Ernie noticed, took each step on cautious tiptoe.

On the third-floor landing a closed window looked out over the street. Ernie managed to slip between the old man's bowed legs just in time to see the S.A. patrol appear at the crossroads.

148

Their song struck suddenly at the glass panels, and the thunder of their steps echoed on the wooden floor of the landing. Seen from so high, with their leather boots, their wide military belts whose buckles flashed every now and then in the sunlight, and above all their small cropped heads, they seemed a kind of inoffensive, clicketing insect crawling under the sun. When they reached the level of the building, their song died on a sudden beat and then a new song rose in the hot air, a song very familiar to the Levys, but which made them all shiver, nevertheless.

When Jewish blood splashes under the knife . . .

'One – two – three!' cried the platoon leader.

That does our hearts good, that does us good!

'One – two – three!'

Then the platoon slanted off into Aldermen Street leaving behind only a distant rumble, which seemed unreal.

'How wicked they look,' Miss Blumenthal said plaintively. 'Oh dear, oh dear . . .'

'All right, all right,' Mother Judith interrupted her, 'Let's not talk about it any more. We have to hurry now; we're a bit late.'

Jacob wailed, 'I don't want to go!'

'Go where?' Judith asked distractedly.

'To the synagogue.'

In reply the old woman grabbed his shoulder with one hand and made his head spin with an authoritative slap. Calmer then, and with her body well balanced on the two columns that were her legs, she decreed: 'Today they're out for Jewish blood, so we go to the synagogue in small groups. Each group will take a different road; there's no sense in being noticeable on a Saturday. You, Ernie, take Jacob and go around behind the Gymnasium . . . Yes, right now, go on!' And turning her back on the two little boys who had already clasped hands, she detailed orders to the others.

Ernie squeezed 'little' Jacob's hand and, as he found it wider across the palm than his own, he tightened his fingers for a better grip. With each step downward Jacob's snufflings diminished. When they reached the ground floor, Jacob was silent. 'All right?' cried Mother Judith from the stairwell.

149

'All right,' Ernie cried as quietly as he could.

But already, separated from his own by the three flights of dark stone, he was discovering his solitude; and when he emerged with hesitant steps into the dazzling sunlight of the street, his right hand tugging at Jacob's stubby, trembling paw (and he could guess at the kind, chubby face behind him, a bit swollen with fear and oddly crowned by the blue cap which Jacob always liked to tilt down over his forehead, like a jockey; a face on which he could sense already the returning fear oozing through the small bewildered sniffles, Ernie felt such a piercing anguish that he wanted only to go back upstairs, back to the first-floor landing, to return to that haven, so precarious and yet sheltered by the shadow of Mother Judith.

'Come on,' he said gently, 'I can't pull you all the way.'

Jacob stared at him without understanding, thrust his chest forward slightly and, hooking on to Ernie's hand at arm's length, as if harnessed in team with him, he followed heavily in his elder brother's footsteps. In almost the same moment he complained: 'You're walking fast . . .'

Ernie became impatient: 'You're bigger than I am,' he said dryly.

'Yes, but I'm smaller,' Jacob retorted, meaning: 'I'm younger.'

The one pulling the other in the sunlight, the two children set forth through narrow, darkened alleyways. All went well as far as Sparrows Street. Ernie had taken off that enormous, ornate purple handkerchief, duty gift of Mother Judith, which was obviously attracting glances from passers-by. Little by little the streets widened, the sun shone more brightly on the façades; they were approaching the better neighbourhood. The boys reassured each other; no one seemed to have evil intentions. Though he knew the way well, and could usually orientate himself easily, Ernie had more and more trouble finding his way among those beautiful homes, all so alike, and yet so different; around the Riggenstrasse, the houses were short, squat and truly identical, but they each had some distinctive sign by which he could recognize it at a glance. Ernie thought that the houses in the better neighbourhoods had no smell; they were like water.

Jacob gasped: 'Is it still far?'

'We have to get to the Gymnasium first,' Ernie said deliberately; 'I'll know the way better from there.'

'I don't know these streets, I never saw them before. Maybe we ought to ask somebody?'

'We can't ask anybody,' Ernie said after a brief reflection.

'Why not?'

'Because of our voices,' Ernie said, worried; 'we have Yiddish voices.'

Jacob waxed sarcastic: 'And you think that the people don't see that we're Jewish? We wouldn't have to open our mouths; they know it already, don't they?'

In one round look, Ernie compared the blond children playing in everyday clothes on the sidewalks near by with the short polished figure of Jacob, his shoes carefully shined, his clothes carefully pressed, his skin carefully washed, his thick black hair strangely covered by his checkered blue cap; his Jewish eye, the Jewish curve of his nose hooked fearfully over his upper lip: It's true, he said, it's Saturday and we've got our Sunday clothes on . . .

'And then we're wearing hats,' Jacob added in a meaningful tone.

'That's true too,' Ernie said. 'In summer "they" don't wear hats.'

'All right, all right then, will you ask somebody?'

Ernie did not answer; he was looking around, gauging the Christian world. Finally, after endless hesitations, he spied a tiny housewife sweeping her doorstep. Pulling Jacob behind him, he raised his beret and asked, in his prettiest German accent, 'if the Gymnasium might be along here . . .'

'Oh, it's straight ahead,' said the surprised little woman.

Then, taking a better look at Ernie, she laid her chin against the broom-handle and smiled a bit with her mouth, but even more with her small, light eyes: 'You're right, little ones,' she said understandingly, 'it's better to go this way because the main streets are bad for "you people" now that "they" never stop

151

marching around. But listen, it might be even better not to go at all, to your synagogue . . .'

Suddenly a second housewife emerged from the corridor: 'Oh! Them!' she exclaimed. 'Talking to them won't do you any good!' And then, turning to the two children, she added for their benefit: 'Cock-adoodle-doo, you Jews, watch out for trouble today!' And arching her back complacently, she set her hands against her comfortably swollen apron, and burst into easy laughter. Immediately the faces of several curious children appeared, surrounding the small group. Ernie and Jacob walked away hastily. They heard shrill cries and the sound of a race at their heels. Tightening his grip on Jacob's hand, Ernie began to run at full speed. At the corner, amazed that they had not been overtaken, he turned and saw in the distance a group of children making wild gestures of uncontrollable laughter. A small figure crossed the road, a broom in one hand and a child in the other. When it reached the sidewalk, the figure slapped the child and dragged it into the house. Ernie and his brother Jacob went on walking. Jacob was breathing heavily. He said in his high-pitched, breaking, slightly fluted voice: 'When I'm bigger, I won't go to the synagogue any more.'

'When you're bigger,' Ernie said, 'we'll all be dead.'

After a few moments Jacob went on innocently: 'If I take off my cap, they won't see that I'm a Jew, right?' And in a frightened tone: 'Oh, Ernie, my cap . . . I could put it back on just before we got to the synagogue, couldn't I?'

Ernie halted. Jacob's face approached his own; the good big black eyes gleamed with an imploring fervour, and Jacob's fleshy lower lip began to tremble so uncontrollably that Ernie felt seized with a stupendous sorrow. He raised his left hand and set it against his brother's cheek: 'But what about me? They'll still know I'm Jewish,' he said as gently as possible.

'Yes,' Jacob said in his fluted voice, 'you look a lot more Jewish than I do. But . . .'

Meanwhile, frowning, Ernie was thinking: 'Anyway,' he remarked suddenly, 'if you take off your cap, you die. So?'

'That's not true,' Jacob said, 'I've already done it many times.'

Ernie thought a bit more: 'God didn't want it, but he could do it to you any time.'

'You think so?' Jacob cried in fear.

'I'm sure of it,' Ernie said in a dream. 'But you know ... if you're so afraid ... maybe you could ... Oh, my God, why are you so afraid? Am I afraid?'

Jacob stared at him attentively: 'Of course not,' he said, '*you never feel anything.*'

At that same moment Ernie felt his back hunch, his head tilt slightly over his right shoulder; his eyes filmed over with dull weariness as he murmured in his usual soft and indifferent voice, 'All right then, give me your cap. I'll walk on ahead, and you follow along behind me. That way they won't know you're with me.'

Jacob removed his cap eagerly and Ernie took it from his hands, looking up to a heaven which he felt quite close, pricking his ears and all alert; he murmured solemnly: 'Oh God, let his sin fall upon me.' And then, to the astonished Jacob: 'This way,' he said indifferently, 'you won't die.'

'But you?'

Ernie smiled, embarrassed: 'Me? Me?' And then casually: 'Oh me, God can't do anything to me, since I'm not taking off my beret. You understand?'

And holding Jacob's cap under his arm as if it were a schoolboy's notebook, Ernie thrust forward his left leg, then his right, then the left again, with a spindly and fragile mechanical motion that gave him a feeling he was not truly walking. So that when he turned after counting exactly twenty steps, he was surprised to see Jacob trotting along behind at some distance, his bare head firm on his round shoulders, his eye calm, his face beaming. He winked at him discreetly, about-turned and went on walking, his head tilted and his thin back still bowed like an arch of distress.

As he looked about him, scrutinizing the sidewalk, the anonymous façades, and the sky which, like an immense blue arrow, tapered to an acute angle at the end of the street, Ernie felt fear coming to life in his belly and then slipping upward, into his chest, icy, boring into his heart like an earthworm. He was so alone in the street, so slight, so unimportant that no one would care if an S.A. gang beat him black and blue, which had happened the week before to poor Mr Katzman; or even if they chopped off his head.

As he walked, he began to listen closely. At first he concentrated on his right ear which told him nothing in particular; but when he turned his attention to his left ear, a disquieting patter vibrated for an instant on the ear-drum, then became faint music punctuated by an infinitesimal hammering of feet. Finally his right ear also vibrated. From then on he tried to pinpoint the songs, but failed, because they came sometimes from in front, sometimes from behind, from the left, from the right, and sometimes it even seemed that the music originated above him, in the sky. At a crossing he slipped along a wall, moved forward as far as the corner of the house and, peering around it with one eye, examined the side street. It was calm and almost deserted. 'Then where did all that noise come from?' the child wondered before starting for the other side. As he stepped out, a hand gripped his own. He cried out sharply, and turning, saw Jacob, white with fear.

'I'd rather stay with you,' Jacob said, sobbing.

Jacob's hand was crushing his own, but the contact between them was wet.

Ernie did not know why, but that wet thing between their palms terrified him. And as Jacob panted beside him, he made an effort to leave the present moment, as he had in the days when he played games with his soul. So he opened his eyes as widely as he could, in the thin hope that once again the houses, the sky, the bystanders, and Jacob, and even he himself, everything, the whole moment would begin to shimmer on his plane of vision, then sway quietly and slide into the fog of his eyes, into the gulf that was his throat. But it was no use; today neither the houses, nor the sky, nor the people blurred before his dilated eyes; all things remained clear, gleaming with a cruel visibility, and still he felt the slightly gluey stickiness in Jacob's palm.

'You're sweating,' a voice said.

' *You're* sweating,' Jacob insisted sadly.

Ernie glared impatiently: 'I don't sweat!' he declared forcefully; and at the same moment he realized that the oppressive unease spreading over his face was sweat. Then he became aware of the yellow light flowing slowly in the street, bathing in its soft water a cyclist, two hurrying housewives, baskets in hand, a young ruddy-faced man whose shirt collar was open; above the house, the dancing eddies of light threw off a fine blue mist. He turned towards Jacob and said, 'It's hot.'

Jacob was silent, and then spoke up in a thin voice. 'You're sweating because you're afraid.'

As Ernie turned to him, furious, he saw Jacob's face gently give way.

The two children were motionless on the sidewalk.

Suddenly Jacob's tearful eyes, his collapsed open mouth, the fist he was rubbing vigorously against one eye, his honest face, faintly ridiculous under that strange checkered cap; and the sobbing of his plump little chest beneath the white shirt, his helpless attitude, feet apart and arms dangling, all this flashed suddenly into Ernie Levy's widened eyes, and at that moment he became unaware of his fear and his sweat: a group of Hitler youths marched out of his mind . . . They were booted, helmeted, armed with long black-bone-hilted knives and they came screaming after little Jacob, who had no idea where to hide, where to squat the weak round flesh of his body . . . And now he saw the knight Ernie Levy rushing out among those wicked men and smashing their skulls while little Jacob fled into the distance safe and smiling. And from his gentle mind, a phrase sprang out like a sword, a white, vital, trenchant phrase: If they come, I'll spring at them. And as he set his trembling hand against Jacob's moist cheek, strong, hard words burst from his tightened lips: ' *Oh Jacob! If they come I shall spring at them!* '

155

Stunned, Jacob stared at his elder brother; and measuring him from head to foot with one look, he burst out laughing. Suddenly cheered up, he said between two gusts of mirth: 'Even when I push you, you go down like a feather!' And with a gentle thump, he shoved Ernie away.

Ernie's neck swelled, and he cried between his teeth, 'I tell you I'll spring at them!'

But Jacob was nodding and smiling, and it was with a kind of mocking condescension that he put his hand into Ernie's. Reassured now, his face shining with pleasure, he walked beside his brother with a springy step; his free arm swung cheerfully, and now and then he gave a little ironic chuckle.

Ernie had trouble in breathing. His hand lay in Jacob's as if dead. For the first minute he tried to repeat in his mind, I'll spring at them, I'll spring at them ... But the phrase no longer roused any conviction in him. Then with a more objective evaluation, he imagined that in flinging himself at the legs of the Hitler youth like a poodle, he would give Jacob time to flee. At last, hopelessly, he admitted that he could do nothing, and looked up calmly at the sky beneath which he was so small. Once upon a time he could easily imagine himself in heroic attitudes, either with a sword in his hand or naked to the waist and with beautiful, pious Jewish words adorning his lips. But all that was over a long time ago, and now he felt bitterly that if some noble opportunity occurred, not only would his tiny body forbid the slightest movement, but his courage as well would be strictly in proportion to his size. What could he do against all that? He was nothing, nothing at all, a little butt-end of nothing at all. And doubtless he did not even exist fully.

Jacob's fluted voice jolted him out of those reflections: '*So you'll spring at them will you?*' And without transition, Jacob yelled out: 'Idiot, here we are!' And dropping his protector's hand he shot forward along the wall, a little ball of joy flung through space.

Surprised, Ernie made out the grey, worm-eaten spire of the synagogue, fifty yards from the crossroads, above the gay German roofs surrounding the paved courtyard. A second later he recognized the plump black figure of Mother Judith dominating a group at the entrance to the cul-de-sac. He felt flooded with joy. The little ball reached the group and was lost in it. Ernie had a sudden desire to run; but he restrained himself, and he hunched his back again, nodding weightily in the manner of the patriarch; and lowering his eyelids over the uneasy fire of his eyes, he moved forward again with the flaccid thoughtful step of the true Jew impassive before death.

Mother Judith greeted him with no more emotion than if he were returning from a short walk: 'You took enough time,' she grumbled. 'All right, come here. What were you doing, dawdling along like a minister?'

Ernie reddened and tilted his head on one shoulder.

'And he lost *my* handkerchief!' the huge woman exclaimed.

Confused, the little boy pulled the purple square from his pants' pocket and transferred it, not without melancholy, to the pocket of his jacket over his heart.

'Hurry, hurry,' the patriarch enunciated clearly, as if nothing had happened deserving the slightest comment by a Jew; 'I tell you the Office is about to begin!'

'I can't,' Moritz announced with an air of importance. And with a gesture of his chin towards the menacing street, 'I'm on guard today.'

The crowd was already drifting into the courtyard of the synagogue, where the traditional separation of the two sexes took place. Ernie slipped behind the patriarch, whose hand suddenly lay across his shoulders like a gigantic necklace of tenderness; for one instant, one short instant, he closed his eyes in pure pleasure; and then the fabulous paw passed on, abandoned him distractedly, and the tall figure of the 'elephant' crossed the threshold. Retracing his steps suddenly Ernie went to the opening of the cul-de-sac where the three weekly watchmen were standing, hands against their brows as visors against the sunlight, scrutinizing the street with eyes that gleamed in the shadow. He poked Moritz's elbow, and Moritz, who was on guard, started in fright.

'I'm staying with you,' Ernie said to him, penitently.

2

'THEY won't come any more now,' said Paulus Wishniac.

'They might just take the trouble,' Moritz said. 'Still, I forgot we never sent them an invitation . . .'

He spoke absently, tracing out a six-pointed star with his shoe at the foot of the post he was sitting on. The three other boys were squatting in the shadow, behind the two posts at the entrance to the cul-de-sac. Drifting over the high wall, snatches of Hebrew melody dropped into the alleyway. The sentries' ears were dangerously lulled by those chants, which seemed to Ernie to be in some mysterious and final accord with the blue of the sky, the dazzling yellow of the house fronts, and the shadowed green of the avenue: as if nothing could ever disturb the dreams of things beneath the sun, as if God was there, outside, watching over the prayers of the synagogue, and not four glum and nervous boys, breathing uneasily.

Paulus Wishniac wiped his forehead and started again: 'If the bastards were going to come, they'd be here by now. It isn't right. I don't see why they should wait any longer; if they were planning to come today . . .' And then, turning to Moritz, who was still tracing meticulous stars in the dust from the top of his stone post: 'At least don't stay up there,' he begged. 'You know they can see you from the avenue!'

Moritz's square, fleshy face tightened. He murmured coldly: 'So what? They see us, we see them, we run back into the yard like rats. I say it's all pretty stupid. Especially that part about the gates . . .' He spat out his disgust in a long-shot gob of fury, and discovered Ernie who had been huddled behind the post from the beginning of their vigil, petrified. 'You still there, little bean?' Moritz's thick lips, barred by the bandage that crossed his face, sketched the shadow of a smile: 'My word, another hero!'

Ernie gazed at his brother's bruised face.

'You know very well,' Paulus said superciliously, 'that we're all heroes these days. God will remember it, it's guaranteed, the Rabbi swore it.'

'And I say that the whole thing is stupid, stupid, stupid,' Moritz answered with obvious weariness. 'What's the point of being stubborn, when we don't even have the right to close the gates any more? Why don't we let it go, abandon the synagogue, say our prayers in our homes . . . But no, that would be too easy, that wouldn't be worthy of Jews, would it?' And swelling his cheeks in a burlesque of the Rabbi's luxuriant, bland expression, he murmured: '*My dear brothers, the persecutions are increasing, but our hearts do not weaken; they may chase us from the House of God, but they cannot expect us to abandon it!*'

The third watcher, almost a young man, was continually sucking a wisp of his sweaty moustache. But he interrupted the mannerism to say: 'It's nothing to laugh about. With all the kids and the women, it could end up like Berlin . . .'

'Like Berlin?' Ernie cried in a voice shrill with fear, as his eyes leapt from one of the three suddenly embarrassed young men to the other; 'what happened in Berlin?'

'Nothing, nothing,' Moritz said placidly.

But the next moment, to Ernie's great surprise, his brother jumped off the post, looking bigger with the fury that animated his belligerent features; standing firm in his magnificent trousers of navy blue serge, he drove his right fist into his left palm like a sledge-hammer. 'Ah!' he shouted furiously, 'if I only had a pistol!'

'Not me,' Paulus Wishniac said slyly, his eyes narrowing with contained malice, 'give me only a million, a little million, you understand?' He raised his glasses and savoured the silent expectation of his three listeners; and suddenly he doubled with laughter: 'I'd *buy* them!' He got the words out with difficulty, 'I'd buy them all!'

'Very clever,' said the third watcher slowly; then he swung back towards the avenue, turning his back deliberately on that 'youth so unaware, so unaware . . .'

Moritz vaulted up on to the post again, and sat with his stubby hands on his carefully turned-up trousers. Two cyclists crossed the avenue, without a glance at the chanting synagogue; the steel of their vehicles made glittering straws beyond the shadow of the plane trees. Very high in the sky crows glided; they too seemed to be waiting, enjoying the spectacle in advance, the event that Ernie suddenly feared, wildly, like a madman, closing his eyes on the world and thinking in despair: God is not here, he's forgotten us . . .

Moritz's guttural voice snapped him out of it: 'And you,' it was saying with heavy good humour, 'what would you like to be given? A pair of scissors to cut them all in two, to bring them down to your size? You lucky bastard,' Moritz added, 'being so small. I have to fight, and I have to fight, and then I have to fight again. There are times when I'd be glad to make peace with them, believe me!'

'And they don't want to, do they?' said Paulus Wishniac. He went up to Moritz and slapped him jovially on the shoulder, like a fellow conspirator.

'Aii no, "they" don't want to! And yet,' Moritz added seriously in a sort of cracked voice, 'I'm beginning to have enough of fighting, no kidding.'

'You mean you're still going to the school?' the third sentry cried in amazement.

Moritz strutted naïvely: 'It's my last year. I'm not even fourteen yet; you'd think I was older, wouldn't you? Oh, you know, at first, I liked it, I enjoyed fighting . . .'

The third watcher commiserated: 'And then you were dropped by your gang, weren't you?'

And as Moritz averted a face stitched with scars, the third watcher went on rapidly: 'Oh, I remember, I remember too, *in the beginning* – a long time ago . . . yes, it was in the *old days.* Two years ago, it must have been! We had real brawls then, even right here, when the Office was over. I belonged to Arnold's group, you remember, the one who left for Israel? But whether we bled or made them bleed, we could no longer hold out, I swear! They brought along heftier lads of at least eighteen. Then it was the Steel Helmets, and one fine day we saw some S.A. men. So you see.'

Paulus Wishniac said, 'They won't be coming now.'

'You're right,' Moritz said acidly. 'But take a look at the crossroads, my friend . . .'

At that moment the nightmare burst upon them.

Ernie saw Paulus Wishniac peer over Moritz's shoulder and suddenly fling himself backwards as if the sunlit air had burned his face. And then the first strains of a Nazi tune came through to him, interlaced as it were with the terminal pleadings of the Sabbath Office – nostalgic Hebrew and rococo German mingling above the alleyway, which seemed to sway under the shock. 'And now, rats to the rathole,' said Moritz's guttural voice; he was suddenly erect, his teeth open over a flash of pointed tongue as he grasped his younger brother by the shoulder and pulled him, with a jolt, into the shadow of the cul-de-sac.

Paulus Wishniac and the third watcher were giant crows, with wings flapping against the narrow walls of the alley; Moritz in his magnificent trousers and his pearl-grey jacket had the heavy flight of a partridge, grazing the paving stones with each step as the alley suddenly began to clatter under Ernie's well-shined shoes, and the walls swayed first one way and then the other, as if they too were drunk with the fear which intoxicated Ernie, as if their heart too was spinning. 'Come on, you slug . . .' With a sharp flap of one wing, Moritz had thrown him between the gates and now Ernie was quaking in the court-yard of the synagogue, in the midst of the faithful, who fluttered about him for a few moments and then fell back steadily against the back wall where the largest families were already huddled, paralysed with fear. 'No, no, do not go back into the synagogue, everything must happen in broad daylight!' rose the Rabbi's strident voice; his thick arms were forbidding the doorway to several fat women jabbering in their finery who cried out in piercing shrieks of sudden enthusiasm: 'Broad daylight! Broad daylight! Broad daylight!' Then there was a great silence, things took on their normal summer colours, the floor of the courtyard oscillated a bit more, as if in a last burst of malice, and was finally still. Everything became strangely clear. A few steps from him, in the first rank of the faithful, his mother, dead white and sweating, her cheek against little Rachel swathed in pink, was whining timidly: 'Ernie...Ernie...Ernie...'

He took the three painful steps that separated him from her and buried his head in the silky warmth of a palpitating belly. Then he grasped his mother's hand and set it against his wet cheek. And as he calmed down despite himself, a vast sigh surging from the breasts of the faithful enveloped him; it was followed by a general gasp of anguish. No sound came now from the crowd, no breath, not even a baby's whimper. Turning immediately, he saw that the Nazis had arrived. They were blocking the gate, cutting off the cul-de-sac.

Stunned, Ernie thought he recognized the old grocer from the Friedrichstrasse in S.A. uniform, in front of the others, planted solidly on his black boots. Behind him, closing the trap, his men made a wall across the gateway; but dominating the scene was the sky, empty now of crows, unreasonably blue, and Ernie had a staggering intuition that God was hovering above the synagogue courtyard, vigilant and ready to intervene. One, two, three urchins slipped among the Nazi boots, armed with stones which they were already flinging at the congested mass of Jews. Miss Blumenthal gave a great shudder that brought her bony hip against Ernie's cheek. Raising himself on tiptoe, the little boy brought his mouth as close as he could to the tiny woman's ear and in his crystalline voice, wild-eyed, the shadow of a smile flitting over his lips: 'Don't be afraid, ma,' he said, suddenly imploring, 'God will come down in a minute...'

The windows opened and a few jeers toppled from the high crannied façade overlooking the synagogue courtyard.

Ernie had the feeling that the thirty yards of torrid space between the Jewish ranks and the Nazi wall, that was now stabilized before the gate as if hesitating at the silence of its victims, were now reduced to a thread.

Then he realized that the jeers were directed at the S.A. men who were looking up in annoyance, their hands swinging sharply to their clubs, so that the thread expanded dizzyingly in Ernie's mind, like a rope that would hold the Nazi flood back against the doorway. '*The windows bother them,*' he understood with an exaltation and a hope that made him raise his own head towards the adjacent building; it seemed ivied by the heads of men and women and even children, whose lively eyes shimmered under the parapets, in the white, saving light of the sun that fell full-weight on the stones of the façade and on their faces. 'How can it be?' he wondered in a joyful flash; until now, those windows never opened except for arms which tossed out garbage as the Jews came and went in the courtyard; so what could have changed up there? And then he saw, way up at the crest of the façade, like a bird on the platform of a pigeonhouse, the familiar, moustached face of Mr Julius Kremer, his teacher at the state school.

From that face came a shrill exclamation: 'Have you no shame!' Mr Kremer shouted at the petrified Nazis, with his index finger (Ernie noticed this with a kind of mocking happiness) clear-cut against the blue of the sky, as if to rebuke faltering schoolboys.

Around Ernie, not a murmur from the Jewish ranks; a thin whine rose in his mother's throat, but her lips remained tight. Ernie felt that God was there, so close that with a little boldness he might have touched him. 'Stop! Do not lay hands on my people!' he murmured as if the divine voice had found expression in his own frail throat. And closing his eyes, he imagined that the mass of the faithful was rising rapidly into the blue, together with the courtyard paving-stones that gave them the impetuous elegance of a stone flung into space and, paradoxically, the ceremonious dignity of a carriage, rising now to such fantastic heights, as a mere point in the slack, naked blue, that Ernie could distinguish only his mother's nose, as fine and precise, though infinitesimal, as the alert proboscis of a mosquito. And perhaps even now, he told himself smiling, his eyes still closed, the carriage of the Jews was whirling above the miraculous land of Palestine, bathed in honey and in the delectable asses' milk.

'*Hey, you up there!*'

Shocked awake, chilled, the scales fallen from his eyes, Ernie saw that the Nazi officer had taken a step sideways, towards the façade, and that his strong-man's torso was shaking with rage.

'Close those windows!' he added, raising his knotty fists above his fat, shaved head. And with his arms still stiffened towards the windows, he turned in a circle with the grave gyrating motion of a drunkard. But Ernie, terrified, saw clearly that the Nazi was drunk with his own anger, his own blood, which gleamed in reddish skin as his mouth opened and closed, spraying spume, searching for words of release.

'Tell me up there,' the man went on suddenly, whirling a furious arm in circles, 'tell me, don't you know these Jewish swine? Don't you know all the harm they've done? Oh my friends, they wanted to destroy our country, didn't they? Our country, the land of our ancestors,' he finished in a tearful voice which surprised the child more than all the rest.

The Nazi leader's mouth twisted in the middle of his face as he became suddenly speechless. Then he lowered his hairy arm, pointing at the frightened flock of faithful with a red index finger like an arrow springing from the first.

'*Tell me up there!*' he screamed in a voice which Ernie did not recognize, a muddy voice that seemed to squelch from his belly, 'ladies and gentlemen, if you want to make them welcome, these belly-aching pigs with their hell-dung; if you want to let this filth piss all over you. All right! what are you waiting for? Come on down here, and if that isn't enough you can crawl up their arseholes and worship at that shrine!'

In the fury of his diatribe he shook his fist at the windows, which closed, almost all of them, prudently, abandoning the Jews to the bare housefront. But some ten German witnesses remained leaning upon their sills, saying nothing, looking out over the courtyard, as if they felt the pleading gaze of the faithful, who now, one by one, the women and the children first, and then a few adult males, raised their trembling arms toward the compassionate windows. Caught up in the contagion of movement, Ernie set his heart's anguish in the cup-like hollow of his open hand: Oh God, he prayed fervently, Oh Lord, look this way just for a moment, please . . .

At that moment old Mrs Tuszynski stepped out of the Jewish ranks.

She was in a rage. Her long emaciated arms writhed about her head like a nest of snakes, and she flung imprecations at the suddenly paralysed Nazi wall: '*Was vhilh thyrh von uns*,' she screamed in her bastard German-Yiddish, 'what do you want with us, what have we ever done to you? Can you talk, at least, or have you become complete animals? The day of the Lord is coming, hear me, he'll take you in his hands, he'll crush you like that!' she finished with a pulverising gesture, while Ernie, suddenly sobered out of his fear, out of his mysteriously dissipated anguish, out of any religious feeling even, had become nothing but a pair of popping eyes fastened on the old woman who step by step, swearing and gesticulating, approached the menacing wall of brown shirts and gleaming, nervous, sharp boots.

When she was an arm's length from the Nazi leader, she flung at his face, weighing each word, in perfect German: 'You'll all roast for eternity! Yes, yes, yes, you'll roast!'

There was an endless pause. Then the Nazi took a step forward, restrained his men with a gesture, and smiled visibly at Mrs Tuszynski: 'But you,' he said, 'you're going to roast right now . . .' And as he slapped her brutally; and as the old lady's wig spun in the sunlight; and as Mrs Tuszynski fell backwards, hands covering the public shame of her carefully polished skull, Ernie took two short steps forward, giddy. 'No, no, no,' he repeated to himself, while his eyes registered the suffering of Mrs Tuszynski prone at the feet of the Nazi, her face against the earth, sheltering that strange eggshell with both hands. At the same moment he realized that he was shrieking. Miss Blumenthal, who had moved forward with him, clapped a hand over his mouth, but the boy freed himself almost at once and continued forward, keening shrilly. The thing happened so quickly that no one had time to react. The child was already six feet from the Nazi officer, his bare arms dangling beside his shorts; he was in the grip of so violent an agitation that despite the distance Miss Blumenthal, petrified, distinctly saw Ernie's reddish legs trembling at the knees; and heard his cry as though he had been standing beside her.

Two Jews stepped out in front of the group; their eyes were hard and yet dreamy . . .

At the end of the Office, Mordecai had been carried along by the violent jostling of the crowd, separated from his own family, pushed irresistibly back into the corner against the wall of the slaughter-room for sacrificial birds, so that his head touched the eaves in the triangle of shadows. The crowd's every motion surfed over him like an undertow of sad humanity, crushing him against the stones as he tried vainly to hold it back, while his gaze skimmed the tide of hats, skull-caps, headdresses, dishevelled hair-dos, trying to make out, in the hollow of a wave, some sign of his own family's presence. But only Judith's medusa-face with unkempt tresses was visible in the flood that swept her along like a groundswell. Resigned, Mordecai expected the worst. An ancient voice in his heart of hearts recalled the holocaust, since the beginning of time, since Zemyock, most of all since a year ago when Christian barbarism had started laying its claw upon German Jewry. But this, the madness of these women and all these children, come fearfully to stand against the Nazis – he had not wished for this; he had even opposed it; and it had required the unanimous delirium of Stillenstadt's faithful to make him accept, following their example, the need to make this offering of his own family to the synagogue. What mysterious instinct impelled them? he wondered, as their faces under his astonished eyes took on a more dignified look at the appearance of the S.A., even those of the most gossipy chatterboxes, even those of the skinniest children, who also seemed to be discovering a grandeur in the present moment. What harsh ancestral fire had ignited in the breasts of these tepid Jewish souls of Stillenstadt, lulled for a hundred years in that calm Rhenish province, who were discovering so abruptly, with persecution, the vertiginous significance of being Jewish? They who had forgotten even the simplest memories of yesterday's martyrs, they who seemed entirely disarmed, naked before suffering, faced the sudden event with readiness, stiffened already . . .

Soliloquising thus, Mordecai had witnessed the unexpected opening of windows and had wondered, as relief softened the pressure of the wave: 'What will happen, my God, when German windows no longer open upon Jewish suffering?' Then he had coldly analysed the growing fury of the Nazi; and had seen, not without melancholy, the casements close one by one, and the Jewish hands rise one by one towards heaven, as if suddenly discovering their utter weakness.

And as the crazy old woman flung herself forward into no-man's land, Mordecai had suddenly begun to clear a passage for himself through the heads bobbing up to his shoulders, through the women's sweating cheeks, through the men's bowed foreheads and the uplifted eyes of the children who were crying now, drowning in the adults' agonies, while above them the same reflex leapt from mouth to mouth: Oh Lord, oh Lord, let not Mrs Tuszynski's madness fall upon the heads of the children!

Ernie's cry reached him just when he was a few heads away from the burning gap that separated the two worlds.

The child was already standing before the terrible 'brown shirt', so small that he seemed servile at the man's feet; so puny that in the cruel splendour of sunlight on the stones of the courtyard, the man's shadow covered him entirely.

And suddenly, as Mordecai saw the trembling figure more clearly; as his heavy Jewish soul vibrated with Ernie's frail bleat of horror, a bleat that seemed to come from those thin, quaking legs, from those small black curls barely covered by that ridiculous German beret, the old man had a sort of vision: 'He is the lamb of suffering; he is our sacrificial dove,' he said to himself in despair, as tears clouded his eyes.

What followed took place far away, in one of those dream worlds of ancient legend, which the sparkling sunlight, beaming its mysteries on every detail of the scene, brightened with the lively colour of an old illuminated manuscript. First of all the Nazi burst out laughing, pointing at the child, and behind him the other uniforms joined in, whinnying and slapping each other with delight. 'Look at the defender of the Jews!' they cried. The sky, almost white hot above the hilarity, expanded the laughter to infinity; Mordecai understood that this happy wave surrounded the child with a protective veneer. Ernie seemed to know it too; he stooped suddenly, picked up the wig at his feet, and set it on Mrs Tuszynski's head; she grasped it avidly, then collapsed sideways again, her knees brought forward and touching her elbows; a long bony body drowned in her mourning clothes like a dead crow. But as the child stood up, the Nazi stopped laughing, and with a sharp blow sent him rolling against Mrs Tuszynski, whose skirt rode up on a whitish, wrinkled thigh. The Nazi blinked several times and stepped back embarrassed – his men flowing away behind him out of the alleyway. It was over for today. The crowd sighed with relief.

3

Mrs Tuszynski had broken her collarbone when she fell, but the child was unhurt; nevertheless Mordecai slipped an arm under the barely grazed knees, lifted Ernie to his breast and set off without a word into the alleyway, indifferent to the warnings offered by the faithful lingering in the courtyard. Though he coldly forbade her, Miss Blumenthal came stubbornly along behind him, bleak, tiny, mumbling, full of a vague religious fear.

A bead of sweat trickled down Ernie's temple; he protested he could walk by himself . . .

Meanwhile the patriarch moved silently forward in the sun-whitened streets, and the Germans stopped to watch the passage of that enormous old man bearing a little boy perhaps wounded at the synagogue.

They had no trouble; only a few kids following them down a street, with a refrain to which their limpid throats gave the unexpected grace of a nursery rhyme:

> Jews, Jews, matzoh-eaters
> The knives will come tomorrow
> After that the stake and faggots
> And afterward, heigh-ho
> You'll all be sent to Mephisto!

But his eyes were looking inward at his own dream, Mordecai was already planning the phrases of his 'revelation', and did not hear the thin shouts of the urchins who finally grew weary of his indifference. Only now and then, reminded of the lamb who lay in his flesh-and-blood arms, he lowered a distraught moustache to the curly, dusty, sweaty head of hair. Back at number 8, Riggen-strasse, he carried the child to his room and undressed him with unaccustomed awkward gestures. The boy's eyes looked terrified and Mordecai repeated hollowly, 'Don't be afraid, my little love, don't be afraid . . .' Then the child found himself tucked in bed, up to the neck like an infant. Bolting the door, Mordecai sat at the narrow bedside and in a hoarse voice, as if strangled by all the years of silence he had imposed upon it, he told the prodigious history of the Levys from beginning to end.

He interrupted himself often, trying to read on the child's face some sign of intelligent comprehension; then, adapting his words to the passionate blush of a cheek, to an attentive tongue peeking between first teeth, to the midnight-blue flash of a half-open eye, he would come down just a little further in order to reach and raise, to lift towards himself, Ernie's level of understanding. But at each of his attempts, and all through that strange monologue, the child who lay between two sheets in the half-shadow of daylight from the tulle curtains, seemed to take in nothing more than the memory of a thousand classic legends of the *Lamed-waf*. Only when he observed that the last Just Man of Zemyock had died three years ago without designating a successor (so that the Levy *Lamed-waf* were submerged now in the indistinct night of the unknown *Lamed-waf*), he thought he saw, in the depths of those bluish eyes, a small disquieting gleam which flickered and vanished immediately.

'And why,' he asked unexpectedly, 'did you do what you did – a little while ago – in the courtyard at the synagogue?'

The child blushed: 'I don't know, reverend grandfather. It . . . it hurt me, and so . . .' And lying back on the pillow he gave a little mouselike laugh, laid two fingers politely against his mouth: 'So I *sprang at him*! You understand, grandfather?'

'Don't laugh, oh don't laugh!' Mordecai murmured desperately, already regretting his foolish confidence, already sensing a shadow of remorse, the feeling of a crime as invisible as it was subtle, although, like any crime of the soul, irreparable.

The 'old elephant' leaned over the bed, kissed the astonished Ernie silently on the forehead, and moved towards the door which he opened slowly like a guilty man; a gentle call made him turn, all of a piece: 'Tell me, grandfather!'

Mordecai came back to the narrow shadowy bed with dragging steps, visibly weary: 'What is it, my soul?'

Ernie smiled first to reassure him; then an unusual colour enlivened his cheeks: 'Tell me, my grandfather,' he whispered, barely audible. 'What is a Just Man supposed to do in his life?'

The patriarch was at once seized with a terrible trembling, and had no idea what to answer. The child's face slowly became bloodless, pallid in the shadow; but his wide dark eyes, spangled with points of light, glowed passionately against the dim background of the pillow like Jewish eyes long ago, like the ecstatic eyes of Zemyock. Mordecai placed his hand on the oblong skull, clothing it in a shell of flesh. And as his fingers played among the young curls: 'The sun, my little love,' he murmured hesitantly, 'do you ask it to do anything? It rises, it sets: it rejoices your soul.'

'But the Just Men?' Ernie insisted.

His insistence softened the patriarch, who sighed, 'It's the same thing. The Just Men rise, the Just Men go to bed, and *all is well.*' And seeing that Ernie's eyes remained upon his own, he continued uneasily: 'Ernie, my little rabbi, what are you asking me? I don't know much and what I do know is nothing, for wisdom has kept far from me. Listen, if you are a Just Man, a day will come when all by yourself you will begin to ... *glow*: do you understand?' The child was amazed: 'And in the meantime?'

Mordecai suppressed a smile. 'In the meantime, be good.'

No sooner had the patriarch left him, no sooner had his slow, cautious tread faded on the stairway, than Ernie seriously undertook the dream of his own martyrdom.

The later afternoon shadows softened the rays of sunlight which traced uncertain forms, sashes and silken scrolls around the bed and the chair, and on the gossamer curtain fringe; a skilful narrowing of the eyes blurred it all, leaving only a pretty yellow filament which danced against the chair, and then dissolved in turn in the surrounding light. Sounds from the living-room died discreetly against Ernie's ears, while phantom

171

personalities, here and now, undulated at the foot of his bed. He switched away once more – this time deep within his brain – and the desired figure rose before him in the lunar clarity his eyes had distilled.

Sitting back against the pillow, Ernie was pleased to recognize dear Mrs Tuszynski, whose spider's fingers were steadying a whole scaffolding of wigs balanced on her gleaming skull.

Then the column fell apart, there was a confused flight of wigs, and Ernie suddenly recognized the bruised oval of Mrs Tuszynski's skull, set like a weird eggshell above her wrinkled face, above her angry open mouth. 'Come, don't be upset,' he said to the apparition, 'and first of all blow your nose calmly, Mrs Tuszynski. Because I am a Just Man, a *Lamed-waf*, you understand?'

'It's unbelievable,' she said smiling.

'It is as I tell you,' Ernie announced gravely.

Then, without waiting any longer, sitting squarely back against his pillow now and frowning severely, he gave birth to a troop of knights who until then had been hiding in the cupboard.

Waving their spiked maces, the plumed knights line up against the door and jostle about with a kind of metallic pleasure and a very serious air. 'And now,' says the grocer from the Friedrichstrasse, well protected by his iron mask, 'shall we avenge the Christ?'

At each end of the cross on his shield is the cruel mark of the swastika.

Obliged to reveal his secret voice, which he knows to be rolling and magisterial like the idea of a river, and not jumpy and timid like a small brook, Ernie fills his lungs with air: 'My dear sir,' he answers the grocer, 'I shall be at your service immediately.' And with a sigh that would rend a soul, he lifts the blankets, emerges in a dignified manner on to the floor where, in a slow parade step, he marches towards the door, towards his martyrdom.

The faithful remain motionless as a sign of respect.

But Mother Judith's inflexible arm stretches over the heads, and her greedy hand clutches at Ernie. To crown all, Miss Blumenthal has deliberately flung herself to the floor, blocking the

172

Just Man's way. Gently pushing away Mother Judith's hand, Ernie sets the extreme point of his bare foot on the summit of Miss Blumenthal's belly, and with a delicate spring leaps across the grieving obstacle.

'So you're the Just Man?' the astonished grocer mocks him. 'So you're the defender of the Jews?'

'I am,' Ernie Levy replies coldly. 'Come on, you savage,' he adds in a strangled voice, 'kill me.'

'Crack!' goes the grocer.

His gauntlet flashes out against Ernie Levy's neck, Ernie staggers under the blue sky of the synagogue; and with him, in the disquieting shadows seized by his filtering eyes even as he dreamed, staggered the sparse furnishings of the bedroom in the middle of which he was spinning, a small white phantom in a nightshirt. Then at last making up his mind to die, he stretched out romantically near the cupboard, his eyes still half closed, his face turned towards the ceiling where the figure of his executioner disintegrated suddenly and then disappeared, conjured away by a violent eruption of light.

'Little angel of heaven,' cried Miss Blumenthal in a trembling voice, 'what are you doing like that in the dark? You must be ill?'

Aware of Mother Judith's vigilance, Ernie feigned drowsiness. Then with sudden boldness, he let a languid sigh escape his lips. 'Are you asleep?' whispered Mother Judith after fifteen minutes. 'Bzzzz ...' Ernie's mouth replied subtly. Immediately the old woman rose, sighing and stretching her back. Through the screen of his lashes, amused, he saw her go towards the door on tiptoe in her slippers, with the halting gestures of a conspirator. The horrible light-bulb finally darkened, the stairway squeaked, then a door closed on the third floor and the silence was complete. The whole house was asleep but him.

Having learned to be cautious, he waited about an hour in the black and suffocating air of his first night as a *Lamed-waf*. The lightest breath, the least rustling, plucked at the taut strings of his body. But with discipline and penetration his thoughts followed the fantastic road laid out for them by his Just Man's consciousness and with his eyes wide in the night, twisting and turning on the rack of certain memories, he even managed to establish the marked differences between the varied deaths of his predecessors. For example, he arrived at the conclusion that to have been dragged by the tail of a mongol racehorse, like Rabbi Jonathan, had less value than to have been plunged naked into the stake's burning flames, as had happened to other, more deserving *Lamed-waf*. The flesh and the fat broiling horribly around the bone, and falling away in drops, in flaming shreds, oh my God! although he tried with all his might, he could not reach the point of tolerating even the idea of this particular torture. Resolved suddenly to put himself to the test, he slipped quietly out of bed.

He began modestly, by holding his breath.

At first this torture seemed to him paltry. But when his ears began to ring, and he felt a tearing burn deep in his thorax, he wondered, in a triumphant flash, if the thing was not comparable to the full martyrdom of a Just Man. Then he found himself on the floor, from failing to catch his breath in time.

'That's about enough,' said a small voice inside him.

'Oh God,' he answered immediately, 'pay no attention to what I just said; it was just a joke.'

Groping in the darkness, he went to the corner where he knew he would find Moritz's box of treasures.

With one hand, like a woman, he held up the long nightshirt in which his bare feet were tripping up, while the other came and went in the dark, waving its fly's antennae. He knelt near the table, opened the cardboard lid, fingered the strings, the lead soldiers, the six-bladed knife, and at last found the box of sulphur matches.

The point of the flame was blue.

'Now show us what you really are,' he murmured to give himself courage; and with a long sigh, he guided the match to the palm of his left hand.

As the delicate sizzle of flesh and the strong smell uplifted his soul, he was amazed at the slight reality of pain.

The match burned out at the end of his fingers and, with the return of darkness, tears flowed from his eyes; but they were tears of joy, lively clear, sweet as honey to the tongue.

'It's not possible,' he thought suddenly, in a flash of desolation; 'I couldn't have brought the match close enough!'

And when he wanted to strike a second match, he realized that the fingers of his left hand no longer obeyed him, rigid, splayed in spite of him like a fan about his burnt palm.

He raised his eyelids and he saw that all was dark; he replaced Moritz's paraphernalia and went back to bed. When he was stretched out he set his left arm, with great precaution, above the blankets, for the wounded palm gave off a furnace-like heat against his thin nightshirt. An immense joy wrung his heart. If he practised methodically, perhaps God would grant him later, at the hour of sacrifice, the strength to suffer an authentic martyrdom. Yes, if he hardened his body, perhaps he would be ready, when the day came, to offer it heroically to the holocaust, so that God would take pity on Mother Judith, the patriarch, Miss Blumenthal and Mr Levy, and Moritz and the smaller children and the other Jews of Stillenstadt; and also – who knows? – all the threatened Jews everywhere in the world! ... And as he wondered again at the ease of the operation, Ernie suddenly felt an extravagant shock at the end of his left arm, while his palm contracted convulsively and split wide open like water running over. 'All the same,' he said to himself delighted, 'I'm not crying out.'

Then he unclenched his teeth, and only then did he begin to feel raw, naked pain.

4

In the morning his palm displayed a splendid stigma, gaping
open as far as the wrist. No one could get any explanation out of
the little Just Man, feverish and half delirious with insomnia. A
burn from a red-hot iron according to the doctor, and the night-
descended wound gave much cause for exorcism; Mother Judith
hastened to slip under the patient's pillow a certain red sachet,
containing seven grains of ash from seven ovens, seven grains of
dust from seven door hinges, seven pea-seeds, seven pips from
seven cumins, and, oddly enough, a single hair. Then she lost
herself in conjecture.

'I don't understand,' she said later in the kitchen before the
assembled family. 'Yesterday the little angel jumped at the Nazis
like a heroic flea, and here he is this morning maimed. But not
content to make us suffer with his wound, the little gentleman lies
in state in his bed and stuffs himself and behaves altogether like a
general who has just won a battle. And if I, his poor grandmother,
ask him, "Little angel, what happened to you last night?" he
laughs in my face and drapes himself in some kind of mysterious
silence. Listen, I almost have the feeling that he's watching us ...
from up there!'

'Impossible,' said Benjamin.

'From *up there*,' Mother Judith repeated. And rubbing her
hands in despair, she cried to heaven: 'Good Lord, who could
have brought bad luck of such a size upon him?'

'It could be,' Miss Blumenthal interrupted, 'that he fell a little
on his head, yesterday, couldn't it?'

Equally frightened herself, she did not dare go on to finish her
thought, which was that the child was indulging in some new and
highly extraordinary 'imitation'.

As for the patriarch, who said not a word, he was suffering tortures. On the pretext of feeling queasy, he slipped discreetly into

the bedroom of the possessed, who greeted him with a triumphant smile and admitted, not without vainglory, that he had begun his training. His hollow eyes, his cheek bones radiating fever, and the enormous bandage that he held up like a pennant marked his confession with the obvious seal of madness.

'But training for what?' Mordecai asked trembling.

Despite the early hour, the curtains with their 'honeycomb' pattern kept the room in a false darkness through which the sunlight played. The patriarch's nose got a streak straight on its bone, and two or three spangles of gold skipped about on his beard. Ernie smiled reassuringly.

'To die,' he announced gaily. And he emphasized his smile, to show the patriarch that everything was going beautifully.

The old man bristled: 'Little Jew, what are you telling me?' he cried out as Ernie, suddenly conscious of a monstrous error, doubled up and disappeared in a flash under the blankets, which he wrapped quickly around himself as if to get lost in the very fibre of things, a frightened little animal. But suddenly a gentle caress, padded by the dark blankets, fell upon his shoulders. The patriarch's hand climbed along his neck, searched for his head, found it. 'All right, peace be with you, peace be with you. I could hardly believe my ears, that's all. But all the same, won't you explain to me why you did that? Did I say anything to you about dying?'

From the depths of his little night, Ernie hesitated: 'No,' he said, surprised.

'By the beard of Moses,' the old man grumbled, while his fantastic fingers became even softer, their touch almost sweet; 'by the miraculous rod of Aaron, what's the meaning of this story of training? Oh, men,' he finished in a sigh, 'who among you has ever heard of a thing so strange?' The thin voice beneath the blankets was broken: 'I thought, venerable grandfather, that if I die, you live.'

'If you die, we live?'

'That's it,' Ernie breathed.

Mordecai fell into a long meditation. His paw remained upon Ernie's hidden head, in a somewhat savage pose which the liquid revery of his eyes belied. 'But then,' he said at last in a very gentle voice, 'when I explained to you last night that the death of a Just Man changes nothing in the order of the world, didn't you understand what I meant?'

'That, no, I didn't understand.'

'And when I told you that nobody in the world, not even a Just Man, has any need to run after suffering, that it comes without being called . . . ?'

'Or that either,' Ernie said uneasily.

'And that a Just Man is the heart of the world?'

'Oh no, oh no,' the child repeated.

'And now do you understand?'

'That . . . that if I die . . .'.

'That's all?'

Ernie wailed in earnest: 'Oi, I think I do!'

'All right then, listen to me,' Mordecai said after a little more reflection. 'Open both your ears: if a man suffers all alone, it is clear, his suffering remains within him. Right?'

'Right,' Ernie said.

'But if another looks at him and says to him: "How you suffer, brother Jew . . .", what happens then?'

The blanket stirred, and revealed the sharp point of Ernie Levy's nose. 'I understand that too,' he said politely. 'He takes the suffering of his friend into his own eyes.'

Mordecai sighed, smiled, sighed again: 'And if he is blind, do you think that he can do that?'

'Of course, through his ears!'

'And if he is deaf?'

'Then through his hands,' Ernie said gravely.

'And if the other is far away, if he can neither hear him nor see him, and not even touch him: do you believe then that he can take in his pain?'

'Maybe he could sense it,' Ernie said cautiously.

Mordecai went into ecstasies: 'You've said it, my love, that is exactly what the Just Man does! He senses all the evil on the earth, and he takes it into his heart!'

With a finger against the corner of his mouth, Ernie followed the course of a thought. He sighed: 'But what good does it do to sense it, if nothing is changed?'

'It changes for God, don't you see?'

And as the child frowned sceptically, Mordecai suddenly became terribly thoughtful. 'That which is far off,' he murmured as if to himself, 'that which is deep, deep, who can reach it?'

Meanwhile Ernie was following his own idea, fascinated by his own discovery: 'If it's only for God, then I don't understand anything. Is it he, then, who asks the Germans to *persecute* us? Oh, grandfather! then we aren't like other men, we must have done something to him, to God; otherwise he wouldn't be angry at us that way, at just us, the Jews, would he?'

In his exaltation, he had sat up and raised his heavily-bandaged hand high above his head. Suddenly he cried in a bitter voice: 'Oh, grandfather! tell me the truth, we aren't like other men, are we?'

'Are we men?' Mordecai said.

Leaning over the bed, he was now gazing at the child with profound melancholy. His shoulder slumped. His skull-cap slipped to one side, so that he looked like a grotesque schoolboy. And then a strange smile lifted his moustache, and buried his eyes even deeper into their sockets. A smile of terrifying sadness.

'That's how it is,' the old man said at last.

Bending over, he hugged the child tight, pushed him away with violence, kissed him again and, with a sudden, incomprehensible start, fled. Ernie noticed that the old man's shoes halted for an instant on the stairway. Finally the door to the living-room slammed. Poor grandfather, Ernie said to himself, aiii ... Poor grandfather.

Seated on the edge of the bed, he brought his good hand to his neck; his spirits rose slowly. On his knee lay that enormous bandage which he suddenly found ludicrous. The old man's smile hung trembling before his haggard sleepless eyes. There were millions of words in that smile, but Ernie could not decipher them; they were written in a foreign language.

Bewildered, he considered his bandage again, examined it carefully, in the hope of finding some legitimate satisfaction in it. But his grandfather's smile blotted it out, and soon it seemed to him that, grandiose though he might imagine them, all his exercises in suffering would never be more than child's play. How had he dared to cause so much excitement about his own little person? To bring on so many worries? Two fine needles pierced his eyes, opening the way for two sandy tears.

'I am nothing more than an ant,' Ernie said gently.

The old man's nose appeared first. It seemed woven into the moisture of Ernie's eye, and its bony curve expressed a nameless rending. Then there was the majestic hill of the patriarch's forehead, topped by his black silk skull-cap. And finally the indescribable smile of his old eyes and his old beard: *That which is far away, that which is deep, deep, who can reach it?*

'You know,' Ernie said at once, 'I'll never touch matches again. And tomorrow I'll go back to school. And holding my breath too, that's over.' But the patriarch seemed in no mood to be consoled; and the sadness of his smile was so much bigger than Ernie's universe that the latter found himself once again become small, even more insignificant than before the 'revelation', diminished to the point of being nothing; not even an ant.

At that moment, when he had yielded to the idea that Ernie Levy did not exist, suddenly the patriarch rose full length before his awestruck eyes, metamorphosed into some ordinary old man, with all the marks of age inscribed upon his face, engraved in every wrinkle of his great elephant's body.

'So you're an old elephant?' Ernie said pityingly.

The patriarch agreed gravely: 'That is what I am.'

'I'll take your suffering upon myself, is that all right?' Ernie begged – his good hand clasping his bandaged hand in an imploring gesture.

Then he closed his eyes, reopened them; and delicately extracted Mother Judith from his brain . . .

When he had finished with her, he was sobbing at the surprising idea that she was a simple old woman; and bathed in his own tears he brought forward the person of his father; then that of his mother who smiled at him with her timid mouth, for a second, before slipping back into his brain. But when he tried to evoke Moritz, his interior vision fogged over so completely that he found himself sitting stupidly at the edge of the bed, before the window open on a torrent of sunlight.

'I'm not *small* enough before Moritz.'

'Still, you're nothing more than an ant.' At that moment, in slow exhalation, he succeeded in evicting all that remained of Ernie Levy from his own breast.

Then appeared a chubby boy, whose hair was cut short over a plump doll-like face, and whose brown eyes, set widely on either side of the nose, radiated a kind of joyful electricity. Dumb-founded, Ernie recognized his brother Moritz. But as he rejoiced to see him so alive, in those blue serge trousers, that pearl-grey jacket, that gentle paunch and his wide mouth open on magnifi-cently regular teeth, he suddenly discovered the scars of Moritz's cheek, his lacerated knees, and his trousers in tatters. Moritz took a step forward.

'You see,' he growled, 'I'm not the leader of my gang any more. They didn't like being led by a Jew. Er ... to tell you the truth, I'm not even in the gang any more. And tell me this, Ernie, why do the Germans hate us like that? Aren't we men like every-body else, aren't we?'

Ernie was flustered: 'I ... I don't know.' He added abruptly: 'Oh, Moritz, Moritz, Moritz, that which is far away, that which is deep, deep, who can reach it?'

'A little fish,' Moritz said.

At that, the vision of Moritz winked conspiratorially, saluted with an expert flip of the hand, and vanished on the spot, leaving behind it only the cloud of emotion caused by the wink.

Ernie realized then that his soul truly contained the faces of the patriarch and Mother Judith, of his father and mother, of Moritz and perhaps also the faces of all the Jews in Stillenstadt. Glowing with enthusiasm, he ran to the window, which he opened wide over the chestnut tree in the yard, the neighbouring roofs, the swallows with their tactile bat-like flight; the blue of the sky, so near. And stretching his neck towards the laughing face of the sun, 'Let me stay *tiny*!' he cried, imploring, inarticulate. 'Oh, my God! be good to me, let me stay *tiny*!'

181

Like the legendary idiot who one day discovered the keys to paradise on the road-side, so Ernie Levy, admitted to the banal yet extraordinary world of souls, and sniffing out their secret miseries, entrusted himself blindly to that ridiculous little key which the patriarch had passed on to him: compassion.

One may well begin to shake with laughter at the thought of him, brimming with joy at his discovery, his cheeks still sparkling with tears, dressing and going downstairs with a smile, to meet the souls he thought he was now in charge of.

The first he met was that of Mother Judith, sitting plumply in an armchair in the living-room, bending all her flesh to a minute sewing task. She had not heard him come down. He stood still, watchfully, on the last stair. And as he forced himself to become 'tiny', his dilated eyes became slowly intoxicated at the spectacle of the old Jewish woman crouching on her years, whose multiple wrinkles and crevices suddenly appeared to him as scars of suffering. An idea struck him: against all likelihood, Mother Judith had once had the body and soul of a girl. What evil then had come crashing in upon her? What immense suffering? he wondered, as he moved in small steps towards the armchair.

When he was close enough he reached a completely unprepared Mother Judith in one light bound; and grasping the heavy hand that was freckled like a dead leaf, he kissed it with fear and trembling like one touching at a forbidden mystery.

'What, what's going on!' cried the old woman. 'What are you doing here?'

But already an electrifying sweetness was tingling in her dulled and deluded blood, and it was with more surprise than anger that she went on: 'What new fantasy is this? What's got into you, to come downstairs and lick my hand? It's enough to drive a body crazy, in this house, since yesterday! Back to bed, now, hop to it!'

Her sea-gull shrieks brought Mordecai on the scene. Somehow he managed to separate her from her benumbed little victim. And as he held the old woman back with his arms spread wide, barring her passage, 'Please, please,' he repeated, 'don't be a stone on the heart of a child. You know very well he's been half "crazed" since yesterday, don't you?' And then turning to Ernie, who had been panting and clutching at his coat-tails. 'The anger of Mother Judith,' he announced emphatically, 'is like the roaring of the lion. But her favour is like the dew upon the grass. Stop trembling, look: the lion is smiling.'

'I am not smiling!'

'And I cannot believe you,' Mordecai said twirling his moustache affectionately. 'But you, you little monster, can you explain why you have to go around licking hands?'

'I don't know,' Ernie stammered, red-faced; 'I ... *it just happened.*'

'Just like that?' Mother Judith asked him. She laughed into her fist.

'Just like that, yes,' Ernie said solemnly.

Whereupon Mordecai tugged at his beard forcefully, to keep a straight face; but suddenly unable to hold out, he burst out into the proud laughter of his younger days. Judith followed with a loud whinnying. Altogether sheepish, Ernie slipped between the old man's legs and beat a retreat towards the kitchen.

Miss Blumenthal welcomed him with yelps of emotion. So he first had to calm her down: 'I was bored in bed,' he said smiling, half jesting, half in earnest; but his avid eyes were already off in search of his mother's secret face – the face he knew to be lurking under the paltry features that seemed grizzled with timidity, under her maidservant's appearance, even under the finicking and precautionary way she had of grasping objects, feeling for them with her long hands whose mysterious, sharp whiteness he noticed for the first time.

'Why are you looking at me like that?' she asked in surprise. 'What harm have I done to you?' She stirred the soup as she spoke, with a hand raised high above the steaming pot, while with her free elbow she went on expertly rocking the cradle that sheltered Rachel, the last-born. Ernie was hurt, and his eyes drank in his mother's features, unable to find in them a reflection of her interior face. But suddenly he had a dazzling insight into Miss Blumenthal's soul: it was a delicate fish, silvery and fearful, in perpetual flight under the exhausted wavelets of shallow, grey water that made up her face.

Still worried, she repeated, 'What harm have I done you?'

'Nothing,' Ernie said, upset. 'You haven't done anything.'

'Then it's your hand that hurts?'

'Oh no, it's not my hand,' Ernie said. Fascinated by Miss Blumenthal's anxious mimicry, he couldn't take his eyes off her, discovering abysses of virtue in her, an insignificance worthy of a Just Man. He was thus admiring her when she let the wooden ladle drop into the pot, cried out plaintively and, as if to mask the unease she felt under the steady gaze of her son's wide moist eyes, said to him abruptly, with a smile. 'You know, we need more bread, I'd love you a lot if you'd run and fetch me a loaf. But maybe you don't feel like it?'

Ernie jumped at the chance: 'Oh, yes! I do feel like it, I do!'

And as she handed him the money, bewildered, Miss Blumenthal noticed that the little man was holding on to her fingers and squeezing them, behaving generally like a lover overcome; then he seemed to resign himself to the worst, rose on tiptoe and, drawing the money towards him, touched her white palm with his lips and the point of his nose.

He scurried off quickly, hunching his shoulders in confusion.

The street was so fresh and alive that Ernie wondered if it, too, was not concealing a soul somewhere beneath the cobbles that were rounded like cheeks. The idea made him wild with joy: 'And all because now I know the secret: tiny, tiny, tiny, tiny!' Then he forced himself to be more serious, and moved along, his steps now solemn and majestic, now brisk and gay, towards Mrs Hartman's bakery, beyond Hindenburg Platz, where the Jews of the Riggenstrasse bought their bread ever since Mr Kraus had also set that strange announcement in his window: No Jews or Dogs Allowed In.

When he arrived cheerfully at the corner of Hindenburg Platz, Mr Half surged up like a figure from a nightmare.

Mr Half was nothing but a torso set upon its base, like a sculpture on its pedestal, and he propelled himself by the motion of his fists, the knuckles of which were horned over like shoe soles; his misshapen skull was no higher than Ernie's; a pointed helmet, lying pitted in the bottom of his wagon, served him as beggar's bowl. And his ragged clothes were speckled with multi-coloured ribbons and medals.

'Pity for a poor hero,' Mr Half intoned with a bitter grin that made clear the meaning of his chant. Moved by a sudden inspiration, Ernie took a step sideways, and stood firmly across the cripple's path, contemplating him with a sad expression, the proper expression he judged, to indicate what part of Mr Half's 'trouble' he was taking upon himself.

As he felt himself become 'tiny', an infinitesimal bubble, Mr Half's flaccid face swelled to fantastic proportions. The black cavities of his mouth came closer to Ernie. Then the blue marbles set in red flesh sprang in a painful double leap from Mr Half's face to take their place in Ernie's sockets, from which now trickled two thin threads of blood, clear and hot and horribly soulless.

'*You finished stethoscoping me?*'

Ernie jumped backward. The little blue marbles radiated hate in short flashes, followed by bleak, cold eclipses. The little boy discovered, amazed, that the cripple's flattened fist was being brandished in his direction. He retreated a few more steps and, terribly upset, explained, 'I didn't mean it, Mr Half. I only wanted to show you . . . I only wanted to tell you . . . I mean I really like you, Mr Half, I do.'

The veteran shrank further into his crate. His floppy head tilted to one side, tilted to the other; dropped to his chest. His features wavered between threat and appeasement. Ernie knew then that Half's soul was a kind of moon, gleaming with despair in the middle of the night.

Suddenly, in a single flight, the man reached the peak of rage; 'I still have my fists, you know!'

And as Ernie hurried off fearfully, his bandage tucked under his elbow in a thief's gesture, the cripple suddenly pivoted on the seat of his trunk, distorted his hairy lips, and savouring in advance the words he had chosen, 'Spawn of a Jew!' he spat out voluptuously, with the tone of supreme Christian scorn.

Ernie raced round the corner of Hindenburg Platz: then he

paused with his back to the wall, for his heart was beating very strongly. His legs too seemed to be throbbing, almost trenchantly, with pulsations sawing at his knees. Despite Mr Half's unpleasant character, it was terribly difficult not to visualize the place where his thighs had been ripped away by the French shell: that immense scar which supported the whole weight of his body. How were such awful wounds possible? And yet, the sky was its ordinary blue; automobiles grazed the kerbs; here and there human beings moved on their wholesome limbs, and the fountain in Hindenburg Platz was covered by a cloud of doves. Some of them, perched on the rim, were pecking at the water. And what had happened?

Ernie murmured remorsefully, 'Maybe it was because I looked at him too long. Then I'm supposed to take up people's troubles without their noticing it? Yes, that's the way I have to do it.'

But as the child praised himself for that new discovery, he noticed with some bewilderment that, instead of remaining 'tiny', he was growing suddenly, at such a rate that the whole world now came no higher than his ankle; and that all things, from the height of the compliment he had just paid himself, were disappearing at a prodigious rate from his own view. 'And now look; I am not a Just Man any more,' he said to himself, terrified.

5

ALL the other things that happened on that day when Ernie
found himself plunged, as into a bath streaming with marvels,
into the once unsuspected world of souls; the many twists and
turns which he imposed upon his heart, that magic key revealed
to him by the patriarch, for opening each of the doors and arriving at each of the hidden faces that surrounded him; his efforts
to encompass in one and the same affliction all the chickens, all
the ducks, calves, cows, rabbits, sheep, fresh-water fish and salt-
water fish, poultry or feathered beauties, including nightingales
and birds of paradise which he knew, by hearsay, to be daily
murdered for the pleasures of the stomach; his being's elastic
balance between the crystal smallness, the glorification of his tiny-
ness, and his irrepressible urge towards the shrouded peaks of
pride; the mass of domestic incidents occasioned by his desire to
take in evil through his eyes and ears, and by his inexplicable need
to touch it with lips and fingers – all these things, if reported in
detail, would make too many jaws drop. Let us point out, however, that towards the end of the afternoon Ernie's oddity became
intolerable; and that, scolded by everyone, discreetly threatened
by the patriarch, he beat a strategic retreat to his father's shop,
where the latter welcomed him with an undisguised wariness:
'What are you doing here,' he asked acidly: 'come to see if I
prick myself?'

Gripped by a strange panic, the child picked up the tailor's
heavy magnet and busied himself about the shop, his frail shoulders suddenly hunched; a thin black frown appeared between his
brows, his eye was wild, investigating, poking and ferreting even
under the cutting table in search of some hypothetical pin. When,
with his magnet he had prospected the planks of the floor one by
one, he laid a small heap of pins at his father's feet, who was sitting crosslegged on the pressing stand. Then with his jaw hanging,

his eyes rolling, he settled near the window and pretended to observe the traffic in the street. An unknown fatigue weighed upon his head. His hand imprisoned in the bandage, throbbed more and more sharply. And as he tried hard not to burst into tears, his thoughts galloped against his temples in a harrowing hammering of hoofs. But every time he hoped they were on the point of consolidating in one simple truth, they rushed headlong like desperate wild horses towards a huge black pit, which gaped in the middle of his mind; seized with anguish, terrified that he would understand nothing of the day's events, the little man shot a furtive look at his father, at that rabbit's face with the lips that seemed to be sucking at the needle; his desire was no longer to discover Benjamin's soul or to share his 'evil', but in an obscure way to hitch it with his own lost and floating soul, in the unreasonable hope of slaking his own misery, that inexplicable 'evil' which was aching in his brand-new consciousness as a Just Man.

Feeling observed, Benjamin responded to those timid advances by a look bristling with a multitude of pins that came to rest, as if upon a magnet, against Ernie's tearful eyes. Then he would give a disapproving sigh, hinting at tribulation; and Ernie blushed to his ears.

An hour passed in this way. In the middle of this manoeuvre the door squeaked and a customer came in; a worker, who humbly asked to have a patch put on his trousers. After many preliminary courtesies Benjamin let it be understood that he could not perform the operation on the customer's person. The honourable customer agreed, accepted the artist's suggestion, and settled down behind the cutting table, with a blanket across his hairy knees: jocularly grumpy.

When the patch was completed, it became clear that the man's feet were quite incapable of re-entering his shoes. Benjamin offered him a soup spoon, which did not have the desired effect. The unfortunate fellow panted and struggled and hammered the floor with his heels.

Benjamin said, 'Hang it all, I've been demanding a shoe-horn for so long, I ought to have a whole collection by now. But you can't depend on a woman's promise! Here, Ernie, instead of sitting there looking at me like a china dog, take this and go buy me a shoe-horn. But don't you start one of your crazy notions, now, or we'll all choke in our own bile and you'll be left alone in the world. Now shut up and go.'

The workman interrupted triumphantly: 'Don't go to all that trouble, Mr Levy. I've already got one foot into one of these damned beetle-crushers. The other one can't hold out much longer!'

'Go along just the same,' Benjamin went on. His arms flapped out suddenly to chase the air in front of him with brutal gestures. 'At least I'll be rid of you for a while.'

Ernie felt strangely empty. He went out without saying a word and found the Riggenstrasse plunged in twilight: blue, with purple streaks on the roofs, and yellow light floating like confetti in the channel between the houses. The confetti thickened in haloes around the streetlights and in the window-frames. Above this carnival, a sheet of dark, glossy paper undulated in the wind; he sensed its silky fragility; it was the sky.

Outside the grocer's lighted window he stared lovingly at a can covered with palm trees against a background of dancing monkeys. The label bore the mysterious word: pineapple.

Lost in reveries, Ernie opened the door mechanically and saw the grocer's daughter, a skinny little thing nine years old who often took care of the shop in her mother's absence, for her mother liked being absent. And recalling suddenly that shoe-horns were purchased at the ironmonger's, he cried out, 'Oh, excuse me!' and saw the alarmed little girl slip quickly back behind the counter. Full of remorse, crestfallen, he closed the door with the utmost gentleness, the kind of excessive precaution one takes for a dying man.

The grocery was next door to Mr Levy's shop, and on certain evenings they could distinctly hear the little girl's cries, shrill and continuous, under the grocer's fist; the latter was a fat man who was stirred by such music when drunk on beer and the cries were more delicately pitched, but sprang from interminable silences, when the blows were administered by the girl's mother, who had sensitive ears. So that Ernie, before walking away, looked longingly back into the grocery.

Only the little girl's head was visible above the marble counter, as if sliced off at the neck. A thick tongue emerged from her small thin-lipped mouth; and when she saw she was observed, she rolled white eyes, a bit cross-eyed, like those of the tadpoles in the Schlosse, and with exactly the same eternally uneasy expression.

'I must explain to her,' Ernie said to himself immediately, 'I must tell her everything: the shoe-horn, the can, the latch. She'll understand.' And reopening the door softly, he advanced into the shop with a friendly step, his bandaged hand discreetly hidden behind his back. 'It was nothing, I only wanted to buy a shoe-horn.'

'A what?'

He stared sadly at her, enraptured to find her so close and in such perfect communion with his soul. And yet, she had not attracted him at all until this day. She had not even the grace of a fly, only its laboured and timorous movements – always leaping at a piece of merchandise, crawling beneath a crate, or losing herself at the top of the ladder, glued to the ceiling. In a flash, he imagined her skin striped with blows, and realized with emotion that anything was capable of making her suffer; a sharp voice, an over-insistent look, and mere contact with the air perhaps.

'It's nothing at all,' he went on, smiling tenderly, 'I only wanted to buy a shoe-horn.' He had lowered his voice to an almost inaudible whisper.

'We don't have any,' she said resolutely.

'I know that very well,' Ernie said smiling even more. 'It was for exactly that reason...'

'Ah well, that's all right.'

'Because shoe-horns,' he went on cautiously, 'are found in the ironmonger's.'

'Perhaps. But we don't have any here.'

And she gave him a vague smile so greatly reduced by fear

that Ernie, already ill at ease, upset and half drunk with compassion, entirely lost his head: 'It's for a customer,' he stammered. 'He wanted a pair of pants, er ... So I opened the door ... er ... er ... er ...' Then, on a softer cadence 'I swear,' he said, smiling tearfully.

Resolved to reassure the little girl, he frightened her: *She knew nothing about shoe-horns; had never heard of them*; meanwhile, she was retreating behind the counter, making herself smaller and smaller in the shadow of the shelves. Did she take him for a madman, a criminal? These painful suppositions passed through the delicate brain of the Just Man, who resigned himself to beating a retreat.

He withdrew backward, trying to tell her clearly what a shoe-horn was and what it was *normally* used for; but swept up in his explanation, and obliged, he thought, to amplify it by example, the little angel went so far as suddenly to take off one of his sandals; inserting, under the wide eyes of his public, two fingers into the proper place; and, in a most convincing manner, scrupulously imitating the 'normal' use of a shoe-horn. 'And there you are,' he said in conclusion, straightening up with good humour. 'A shoe-horn is nothing more than that!'

The little girl's reaction chilled him: terrified by his unusual behaviour, she had half-buried herself in the sugar-bin; she plucked at her cheeks nervously with thin fingers.

'I'm going,' Ernie said.

Then with his sandal in one hand and his bandage round the other, he suddenly went back to the counter to explain that he wanted nothing more than to leave immediately. But as he approached the small bundle of terrified flesh, he felt he was growing prodigiously: his arms and legs were stretching to all four corners of the shop, while his head was splitting the ceiling. 'Oh, no,' he said in supplication, 'it's just what I didn't want ...'

At that moment the little girl set her hands flat against her cheeks, opened the circle of her mouth, took in a breath of air and launched her scream.

A spine-chilling creature surged from the trapdoor in the back of the shop. Two streaks of red widened her mouth, her eyebrows

arched right over her temples, apparently pushing back her eyes
like polished stones right into her cheek; an infinity of curlers
and dozens of pink ribbons divided up her hair into separate
strands that fell heavily on her cheeks, which were sweating
some thick cream. Interrupted at her dressing-table, she took
in the scene with one furious glance, then staggered out towards
Ernie; he closed his eyes philosophically.

When he was able to open them, stunned by the shock, his
good hand was still holding the sandal, but all he could see of the
grocer's wife was the impressive outline of her behind.

'What did he do to you?' she shouted shrilly.

Still huddled behind the counter, the little girl stared for
some time at the little Jew's piteous face: but it was useless,
she no longer saw in it whatever it was that had frightened her.
Then, raising her eyes at last to the maternal wrath, she was
suddenly seized with genuine fear and ... started screaming
again louder than ever.

'I see,' announced the grocer's wife solemnly, and pivoted
on her high heels, grasped Ernie by the back of the neck, and
yelped triumphantly: 'You vicious bit of filth!' Then she dragged
him outside like a cat by the skin of its neck.

Drowned in a painful dream, Ernie had only one care – not
to drop his sandal; for the rest, he would rely on grown-ups, from
now on: he felt utterly, unnoticeably, tiny.

Miss Blumenthal was leaning out of the first-floor window.
Down on the sidewalk, in the halo of the streetlight, a group
of housewives was causing a great commotion; one of them, in
curlers and a flowered peignoir, was screaming at the top of her
lungs: 'The Jew! The Jew! The Jew!' It was the grocer's wife,
who was shaking violently some inert object against the sidewalk.
The whole scene was imprisoned in the pale cone of light.
Between two convulsive shakes Miss Blumenthal recognized the
familiar ringlet of a curl that vanished at once, like a delicate fish
in a cluster of seaweed. Immediately she lost all awareness of
herself, her timidity, her appalling weakness. She had always
seen herself as a little woman; and yet she was out in the street

in less than a moment, her sharp elbows brought together like a cutwater that pressed irresistibly through the bawling, surging tide.

When she was within reach of Ernie, she tore him from the hands of the grocer's wife with one silent jerk, then fled without a word. She had clutched her child to her thin breast, and all her gestures betrayed an emotion so desperate and yet so resolute that no woman had the heart to impede her retreat.

A minute later Mother Judith made her appearance. They moved to give her passage, for her volume inspired respect. The women of the Riggenstrasse did not always restrict themselves to verbal bouts; so that all arguments, even the most trite, took place under the threat of the opponent's physical makeup, her well upholstered strength or her dried-up female's ferocity. The grocer's wife was regarded as one of the best 'grippers' in the street. Taking her stand, Mother Judith was an enigma. But her tough corpulence, her chiselled cat's mask, and the deadly fixity of the look she flashed upon the grocer's wife, augured well for her.

The circle closed about these two noted adversaries.

'What? What? What?' Mother Judith barked in a German limited to the simplest expression.

She crossed her arms majestically, and waited.

A pin could have been heard.

'Look at them, they're admiring each other!'

'Jesus Mary, and my soup on the stove! Come on, ladies, is it now or tomorrow?'

A third, disillusioned, said: 'What do you expect? *It's an even match.*'

Then the grocer's wife shuddered from head to foot, her shoulders shifting an invisible burden; only a thread, it seemed, separated the combatants.

'Be careful,' Mother Judith said coldly.

The grocer's wife seemed fascinated by the nostrils of the big Jewish woman, which were flaring in a sort of calculated rhythm.

'My ... my little girl,' she stammered wildly.

Then she retreated in disorder, fumbling for the shop door

behind her. But ten seconds later she surged out, transformed, dragging her child by the arm.

'What? What? What?' Mother Judith repeated, with a barely perceptible hesitation.

'Come on, tell her what he did to you . . .'

The crowd drew together again. Terrified by this solemn waiting upon her words, the little girl sighed, sniffled, and . . . was silent.

'Good God, will you tell them or do I trounce you?'

And rigid with impatience, the grocer's wife slapped the child, who crossed her arms and quickly bowed her head over her chest, in a penitent attitude.

'He . . . he was bothering me.'

'Tell them, tell them what he did!'

'I can't.'

'It was dirty, it was dirty, wasn't it?'

'. . . Y . . . es . . .'

'Not possible,' Mother Judith affirmed. 'He's not nasty.'

But in the pitying look she gave the skinny, weeping victim, all the housewives clearly read her true thoughts; and she retired amid a hostile murmur, silently, heavily, all arrogance dead, thinking sadly: still, he isn't very wicked, ordinarily . . .

She found Ernie in the kitchen, in Miss Blumenthal's arms. The interrogation ended with two majestic slaps into which she put all her former adoration as well as the obscure repulsion she would henceforth feel for this creature who had come indirectly from her own womb, but in whom she no longer recognized herself.

Ernie's head pivoted lightly on his shoulder. He was rather pale. His eyes, lost beneath the long black curls on his forehead, were half closed. He shook his head, once to the right, once to the left, and then walked out of the kitchen slowly; with his ceremonial step.

The door closed. The two women listened attentively; they were astonished to hear no footfalls in the living-room; suddenly the door swung silently on its hinges and Ernie Levy's tiny profile slipped into the opening. He fixed his attention on Miss

Blumenthal and absorbed her thoughtfully with his eyes. Those eyes were two wide puddles of scintillating black water. Suddenly the puddles broke up and there remained only the narrow face of a child whose cheeks were running with tears.

'I'm leaving for good,' he said in a firm voice.

'That's right, vanish,' Mother Judith agreed scornfully; 'but above all be careful not to miss supper-time!'

The head disappeared and the door closed, this time with finality.

Mother Judith declared, 'My daughter, that child has no heart.'

Miss Blumenthal thought it over. 'And yet,' she said 'he's so pretty.'

6

JUST beyond the bridge over the Schlosse, Ernie tripped over a stone, stretched out his arms and closed his eyes; he realized that his body was lying in a ditch beside the road, in the grass. It seemed to him that the darkness outside and the night within him were one. Turning over on his stomach he opened his mouth wide and let his last tears flow; for it was obvious to him that he would never catch his breath again; nor would this vast rolling motion of earth and sky ever cease, though his arms, spread wide like oars, were trying to slow it: he had run too fast, and perhaps he was going to die.

'Well, you all right like that, Ernie? You all right like that? – Well, Ernie?' he went on aloud.

A moisture rustled in his palate. Round and light, transparent as bubbles, the words came out of his mouth and flew off towards the moon, arousing in him nothing more than a feeling of dazzled surprise.

Concentrating hard, he tried a different formula: 'Hey, Ernie!' he murmured in some delight.

And immediately the person hailed turned and gave him an obsequious: 'What? What do you want?'

Rising carefully to his elbows, he knelt, sat down, and raised his knees, circling them with his arms. It all happened as if two little men were chatting inside his head, like two gossips over a cup of tea. He thought again: Hey, Ernie ... But a third Ernie appeared, hopping up on a finger, and all was confusion.

He heard a gust in the distance, and the squalling wind whipped the treetops like a wave. On the ground dead leaves raced for several yards. Beyond the meadows, the waters of the Schlosse lapped against the little stone bridge.

The wind fell as quickly as it had risen and the countryside became silent again. Motionless, the moon waited. Far off at the end of the road dim lights flickered alive, not at all menacing. On the contrary, they winked timidly, set out like a row of candles against the dark horizon; they gave off a whispering sound: it was Stillenstadt.

'*That filthy child!*'

Mother Judith's face was truly like an old cat's face. She had arched her fingers like claws, and her awesome body, leaning forward slightly, seemed prepared to pounce.

Choking back a sob, Ernie turned his back to the town and set off once more. Later on, after many years, he would return to Stillenstadt. He would know a great number of words, and the whole world would weep to hear the Just Man. Mother Judith's heart would open. There would be the yellow tablecloth with the great seven-branched candelabra. And there would be . . .

Ernie had been walking for so long he felt he couldn't be far from a great city. The green wheat he had nibbled at in his hunger had stuck in his throat. When sweat began to trickle down his feverish body, he tucked his bad arm into the opening of his shirt, as in a sling. But though his thirst became sharper every minute, the little fugitive persistently avoided the villages: they were infested with dogs, and nothing was more disagreeable than their barking and howling at night: especially at oneself.

But his thirst was turning to delirium, and he crept, step by step, into a farmyard where he reached the cattle-trough without hindrance; the water flowed from a long pipe shaped like a cane. Ernie leaned over the trough and gave his tongue to the flow.

''S not the way to drink it. Lemme show you.'

A boy of Ernie's age was standing in the moonlit clarity of the yard, in Tyrolean shorts and barefoot. His face was masked by the brim of a huge cap propped on his ears; but his leaning position suggested peaceful intentions. He slipped silently towards the frightened Ernie and, with a sign that he was to observe him carefully, drank in demonstration from the hollow of his hand. Ernie imitated him immediately, delighted.

'The fact is I always drink from glasses,' Ernie said, wiping his mouth.

The boy's cap nodded sagely. 'Sh'd think so,' he said with seriousness.

He seemed not the least surprised by the fugitive's astonishing adventures. At first their conversation took place under conditions of perfect equality; but, gradually impressed by the cap's significant silence, Ernie unconsciously allowed its ascendancy. He went so far as to admit his fears of the farmyard dogs. 'Arf a mo',' cried the cap, 'Lemme show you!' And clutching at an imaginary staff, he embarked on a very complicated pantomime at the end of which, with one masterful blow, he broke both of the hostile dog's forelegs. Then without transition he ran towards the lighted building, from which he returned a minute later, his arms laden with carrots, a chunk of brown bread, and a splendid hazelwood dowser's wand.

He hesitated, then pulled a rusty jack-knife from his pocket. ''f' ever you're 'tacked by a wolf...'

Ernie smiled: 'What do I do then?'

'For a wolf, it's zactly as for a leopard.' And wrapping his shirt around his forearm, for the claws, he said, this strange boy began another warrior's dance, this time with the jack-knife playing the role previously played by the staff.

Although the figure of the wolf was by no means unworrying, Ernie was above all aware of the nonchalance with which the peasant boy's bare feet touched the sharp pebbles that glittered in the moonlight.

The boy accompanied him to the end of the village. As they neared his calvary, he slowed down and murmured with embarrassment, 'Gotter go back. 'Cos of my ole people, see?'

'You did a lot for me,' Ernie said.

The other, suddenly melancholy: 'I'm going to go away too, one of these days.' The rim of the cap fell.

'You mean they don't love you at home?' Ernie cried in an explosion of pity.

'Oh, you know how they are: all the same.' Lugubrious: 'They don't know nothing...'

Then the boy raised one hand and folded his fingers sadly in farewell. Although his arms were loaded with provisions, Ernie imitated the gesture as well as he could, touched by the pathos of the ceremony. The children turned their backs on each other simultaneously. Ernie covered a hundred yards or so very quickly: the peasant boy had disappeared, and his village was entirely drowned in the night; it no longer seemed to be a human agglomeration. The countryside itself had melted mysteriously into the sky: trees floated in the soft air. He felt that he was miles and miles from Stillenstadt, which after all was only an insignificant idea, no larger than the point of a needle, and which Ernie could very well do without.

A nearby alfalfa field welcomed him for his first night as a vagabond.

As he chose his bed, a mosquito buzzed about his ear and lighted upon a marguerite growing at his feet. A ray of moonlight fell suddenly on the marguerite, disclosing a tiny fly on the yellow centre of the flower. Ernie held his breath, bent forward, and realized that it was a young fly, apparently female; this was obvious in the delicacy of its figure, in the slender muscles of its minute wings, and most of all in the dainty grace with which it rubbed its feet one against the other, sketching out a delightful, motionless dance step.

Slowly, in tiny steps like a little lawyer, the fly began to climb along one petal.

Ernie felt a slight twinge near the heart. He never knew how his arm executed the gesture. A cloud passed before his eyes, and the young lady threw herself stupidly into the hollow of his hand, which he closed immediately. That's it, I have her . . . he said to himself half regretfully.

The rustling of the wings attracted his attention: frantic pricking at the end of his finger like the point of a needle. He was sensitive to the jolts and jerks agitating that small particle of existence. The glimmering of moonlight on the animal's wings produced two blue sparks. Bringing the miserable jewel closer to his eyes, he went into ecstasies over the minute arrangement of the antennae, which he was noticing for the first time. Those fine filaments, they too were trembling in the gusts of the interior storm. Ernie shivered in grief. It seemed to him that the antennae were chopping the air in terror. Anguished, he wondered if the feeling that caused the fly to flutter its wings between his fingers was as important as the feeling of the grocer's daughter. At that moment part of his own being slipped insidiously into the fly, and he realized that this tiny insect, were it even infinitely tinier, invisible to the naked eye . . . its fear of death would not diminish. He opened his fingers then like a fan and for a second followed the fly with his gaze; the fly was a bit of Ernie Levy, a bit of the grocer's daughter, a bit of he knew not what . . . a fly. She didn't waste any time, she got away fast, he said to himself, amused. But immediately he missed her company, for he found himself only more alone in the middle of an alfalfa field.

A thread snapped somewhere in the night.

Kneeling on the ground, the child sniffed the ambient odours. Then he stretched out on his back and closed the eyelids of his body immediately, as a sign that it was to fall asleep as quickly as possible, to escape the circles of fear that were getting more and more closely knotted around his soul. But strangely enough, however tight he shut his eyelids, slowly, strongly, even hurting the inside of his eyes, it seemed to him that they did not separate him at all from the moon, from the stars, from the road, from the field of wheat which he sensed at a distance, or from the alfalfa ever-present with its subtle salad-smell, or from the fly, or from the wavelets of wind which drifted across his cheeks; his eyelids had become two transparent, porous partitions, enclosing only his own emptiness. Gripped by fear then, the child called himself at great length, as if hailing someone far off: Ernie Leeeevyyy, Ernie Leeeeevyyy . . . But within his head there was no answer, and the pocket of emptiness remained as transparent and black as the sky. He opened his mouth and muttered very quickly: 'Ernie! Ernie!'

He waited a brief moment.

Then he felt pierced by a rending clarity and, as his limbs melted deliciously into the alfalfa, an idea came to him, marvellous in its simplicity: since the whole world rejected him, he would be a Just Man for the flies. A stalk of alfalfa stroked his left nostril affectionately. The earth became softer. Soon both his nostrils flared, enormous, gaping, quivering with pleasure, and began to inhale the night slowly. When the night had flowed entirely into his chest, he repeated with much relief: 'Yes, a Just Man for the flies.' Then the pocket of emptiness was full of grass, and he slept.

'Hey, there! little fellow, are you playing dead?'

Ernie saw a yellow wooden shoe right up against his nose; then grey trousers, a circle of black hat surrounding a bloated, red face round as an apple. There was no threat in the voice.

With a light pull, the peasant raised Ernie from the ground and set him on his feet in the alfalfa; then he measured him for a moment, sniffed severely, and loosed a great burst of laughter in the child's face. As Ernie retreated under the avalanche, the peasant stopped abruptly and said: 'You look like a fish that got caught by the tail.'

Then, obviously feeling he had every reason to do so, he bent his knees, threw his head back and, slapping his thighs heavily flung his laughter this time against the sky.

'Which fish?' Ernie asked, interested.

'What?'

'Yes, which fish?'

The grey eyes wrapped him in a cloak of suspicion. 'First of all, what are you doing here?'

Only ten yards away, a cart with two horses stood patiently at the edge of the road. The peasant followed Ernie's gaze. 'Yes, that's mine,' he said less harshly. 'I'm going into town, and I'll bet that's where you come from. You came all the way on your knees, it looks like, they're that battered it isn't normal. And your arm ... Your folks beat you, right? You poor little shrimp, you were right to clear out.'

Ernie shook his head smiling. 'Oh no, sir, it wasn't that.'

'What was it then? Did you do something real bad, this time? Stole money, broke something valuable?'

'Oh no,' Ernie said smiling once more.

The peasant put on a thoughtful expression. 'I know: you
wanted to see the world. Tell me, did you run away very long
ago?'

'Last night,' the child said, after a moment's reflection.

The peasant hesitated, his hand fell heavily on the curly head,
and rubbed it with a kind of awkward delicacy. 'You know,
ole' pal, they'll be worried about you at home. So how about it,
do you want to tell me where you come from?'

Something stirred in Ernie's breast; there was that adult's
hand set upon his head, and that mountain of flesh casting its
shadow upon him.

'You don't look like a bad boy,' the peasant growled with
good humour.

'Stillen ... stadt,' the fugitive stammered. At the same moment
he glimpsed the full extent of his sin and melted into tears.

The cart rolled along at a good pace. From his fantastic
height, Ernie was witnessing the transformations of the countryside; when his eyes tired he came back to the solemn, swaying
stride of the cart-horses, their manes undulating like white waves
against the rock of their necks and withers, rising and falling
endlessly. 'Not that the vegetables are very heavy,' the farmer
had said: 'but I hitch them up together because they get along
well ... because they don't like to be separated. But maybe you'd
eat an apple, hey? And how do you like my apple ... like velvet,
isn't it? Ah, my friend, I'm bringing a fancy load of vegetables
to market this morning, I am.' Now and then the man traced an
arabesque with his whip above the dappled-grey rumps. When
he failed to produce a fine, sharp snap, he just clucked his
tongue against the roof of his mouth; which was far, very far,
from being as effective.

But more than anything, the parade of landscape claimed
Ernie's attention. Twisting to the four points of the compass,
he tried in vain to recognize some detail he had glimpsed the
night before. Already, a little while ago, awakening in the
alfalfa, he had lost the curious impressions of the previous night.
The sky and the trees and the road and even the least blade of

grass seemed diminished or impoverished in bright daylight. And the villages they passed through recalled nothing of the masses of shadow crumbling in the moonlight; now the houses had pink roofs and he could count the tiles clearly.

'So,' the peasant repeated, 'you're a son of the Levys in the Riggenstrasse?'

Ernie affirmed it with a sober nod.

'Not that I regret it,' the man went on in a tone of annoyance. 'There are good people and bad people everywhere ... or so they say. But just the same you have to admit it's funny ... What do you think of that, my friend!' He shot a quick glance at his passenger, and then turning away, still annoyed, said in an impersonal voice: 'I should have guessed it because ... dark little heads don't grow much in this part of the world.'

A question was burning on Ernie's lips; frowning, he risked it in a voice that was deferential, though marked by a friendly nuance of sorrow: 'You mean you're against *us*?'

From brick-red the peasant's jowls turned to rawest purple. A loud whinnying escaped his lips, and his fleshy carcass jiggled so happily on the seat that Ernie was afraid of seeing him fall overboard. 'What a little shrimp!' he exclaimed several times, 'what a cheeky little shrimp!'

More than anything, that odd epithet, 'little shrimp', cut Ernie to the quick. Resolved to show no emotion, he huddled in his seat, leaning back against a crate of potatoes; then he attempted a careless whistling. But after a minute the peasant's left hand dropped the rein, and came near him like a huge blind bird, covered with hair; landed gently on his head. The man's tone was bantering: 'Don't be afraid, little shrimp; Levy or not, we'll be there in five minutes. And after all, you don't suppose that I'd make you get out and walk. I'm not smart enough. You take a man who's really smart, it's pretty rarely he turns out to be a good fellow.'

Nevertheless, doubtless sobered, he did not speak again until they reached the Riggenstrasse. The horses snorted in front of the Levys' shop; Ernie discovered with astonishment that the narrow window had been replaced, in his absence, by badly squared-off planks. But he had no time to say anything: the peasant had grabbed him by the shoulder and, without moving from the seat, lifted him with a firm hand and deposited him gracefully on the sidewalk. Then he flung out a cheerful 'So long, shrimp,' and with a single snap of his whip started his team off at a fast trot, as if he were afraid to linger in the neighbourhood of the Levys.

At the evening meal the night before Mother Judith, pointing at Ernie's empty chair, had judged Ernie guilty *in absentia*; two hours later, she had absolved the child of all sins and loosed a volley of accusations against the rest of the universe.

She had wrapped herself suddenly in her shawl, and erupted into the streets of Stillenstadt, rousing both Jews and Gentiles as she went; and when she was quite sure that the little angel was not in the town, she had begun to plough through the surrounding fields: they found her three days later, in a quite distant farm, where she had come to rest, sick and barefoot, her dress all shredded by the brambles.

For his part, Mordecai had spent the night in a chair. At the first gleams of dawn, the shop window was shattered by a paving stone: the grocer's wife had given her husband's racial passions free rein. Mordecai hastily put together a few planks as a precaution against looters. Then he gave a long sigh, lit the oil lamp, and awaited the coming of day through the luminous cracks between the panel's ill-joined boards. 'I hope it doesn't all end in another ghetto,' he meditated secretly. Thereafter, for a thousand reasons of which one alone would have been enough, namely money, the wooden panel remained nailed to the shop front – a frontier for the Germans and a symbolic prison for the Levys.

At the sound of the cart he rushed outside; already the horses were trotting away; but on the sidewalk stood the prodigal son, dreamy, crowned with grass, filthy with earth and blood, his arms full of carrots, his bandage unrolling to his feet. He did not move an inch when the old man came rushing at him with wild gestures and a tremulous expression, as if fearing to see him disappear again.

'Don't say anything, don't be afraid any more,' Mordecai stammered. 'You understand me? Nothing happened. Oh, God is good, good, good!' he repeated furiously, clasping the boy tightly against his trousers.

Ernie seemed to have kept his calm entirely; when his mouth was free again, he asked, intrigued, 'Why is the window boarded over?'

The milkman's delivery tricycle moved away from the corner of Hindenburg Platz like a twitching insect; except for him, the Riggenstrasse was still deserted in the morning mists. Mordecai squatted on the sidewalk; laid his cheek against the child's forehead to check his temperature; and then, finding his expression a placid divinity, explained, after certain oratorical precautions, all that had happened since the night before.

'You understand,' he said tenderly, 'if you were a true Just Man, things would certainly not have come to pass this way ...'

'I understand everything,' Ernie said.

'So you must become as you were before,' the patriarch wheedled. 'Behave as you did before.'

The wide dark eyes filled with thought, and then with tears that silvered the gleaming rims.

'Why are you crying?'

'Because now I think that I'll always have trouble with everything ... even if I'm not a Just Man!'

'*Shema Israel!*'

And lifting the child against him, Mordecai rose to his full height, his head full of sunlight, thinking: 'Oh Lord, the heavens in their elevation, the earth in its depths, and the heart of a child are equally ... impenetrable.'

BOOK FIVE

MR KREMER AND MISS ILSE

1

AFTER 32 years of service, Mr Kremer's entire personality bore the serene imprint, the contemplative tinge, of democratic learning... Professorial, with a tall, elongated figure which seemed to undulate at the slightest movement, to modulate, like the shadow of a flute, some solemn, secret harmony. And that rectangular mask, stemming out of his detachable collar like a strange flower from its pot: professorial.

By the same token his smile carried an infinity of instructional nuances: half-smile, quarter-smile, one-eighth, etc. In the periods of scholastic calm, he generally displayed a cautious half-smile, circumspect, half-way between the sweetness of life and the polar rigours of duty.

From the beginning of his career, he had singularized himself through an unfortunate combination of natural suavity and superannuated pedagogical theory. The venerable Headmaster did not mince words with him: 'Don't lean over your students like that,' he cried in mid-council, 'it's the ideal position for getting a kick in the arse!' Turning purple, the young pedagogue had meditated for some thirty seconds, and then answered with much dignity:

'Despite its discourteous form, I must acknowledge that the Headmaster's opinion seems to me quite authoritative.'

And yet, although from then on he carried a switch, he had continued secretly to believe in the purity of childhood, which he would contrast with human imperfections; the child, he said to his friend Hartung, is descended from the man, yes ... in the same way that the latter is descended from the monkey! He judged that instruction in civics and the teaching of poetry, extended to the whole human race, would erect an eternal dike against barbarity. In that respect the German romantic poets seemed to him ideal nourishment, particularly Schiller, whose

209

slightest verses radiated civic consciousness. The day when Schiller was known to the entire population of the world would be a fine day. There would be no more troubles then about politics, or money, or fallen women. On that blessed day, Mr Kremer imagined, childhood would no longer be a minority on earth; every adult would remain a child, every child would become a true adult, and . . . and so forth.

These reflections made him neglect the reality of current politics to the point where suddenly he was unable to remember if Germany was a republic or still under the rule of the Hohenzollerns. He had known several regimes; none had had any profound influence on the teaching of Schiller. Besides, these governmental quarrels always came down to a question of words: republic, empire, *ad infinitum*. He had no desire to meddle with them, feeling that one day all words would fade to silence before poetry. Doubtless, like any other man, he had had his love affair, of which he retained a memory as painful as that of the wound he had received during the war – in the lower part of his belly, to be precise. 'Oh, my dear Hildegarde,' he had said blushing; 'I assure you that this . . . that that . . . at least . . . has not made me unfit for marriage. And here is proof . . .'

The years having covered the incident with the cynical patina of time, Mr Kremer wondered if it might not have been better to offer his fiancée a proof somewhat more convincing than that ridiculous medical certificate. Their meetings had become somewhat less frequent. In the end Mr Kremer had been annoyed that the girl regarded his infirmity – 'partial, oh my dear betrothed, only partial' – as the result of some vicious action in which he had been an obscure accomplice. With the help of an Iron Cross, he had been able to end his war in an administrative armchair; but the memory of another cross, unmentionable, which he carried in his flesh, had unfortunately cooled his patriotic ardour. They suspected him of defeatism. And his casual indifference to being German finally convinced the young lady that his noble parts had been reduced to nothing; as a woman of heart, she married a one-legged hero whose patriotism was rigorously intact.

As time went on, his war memories melted so intimately into

210

his sentimental reminiscences that soon Mr Kremer looked upon them both with the same wide wounded eye, confusing in one single bitterness the hole opened in his flesh by mankind, and the emptiness of his existence. And although his high opinion of love kept him from carrying the thought too far, at times it seemed to him that one and the same blow had struck him – in the heart, and in the left testicle.

'Fascism,' he judged at first, 'is the rule of the tavern in the streets and in the government. Soon they will all be sent back to their beer-cellars or their prisons; soon the old Germany will punish her bad boys.'

He greeted the first measures with the fool-proof philosophy, prudence, and tact of an old humanist. The decree on corporal punishment made him smile; but when he learned that his colleagues, for greater convenience, were applying this decree to the backs of Jewish children, a small weed started growing on that brow, so pure of any hint of evil ... And the burning of the synagogue did the rest.

The fire broke out late at night; at dawn nothing was left but blackened slices of wall. The dead synagogue smoked over Stillenstadt for two days. From his sixth-floor apartment on the courtyard, Mr Kremer noticed that a long beam, amid the tiles and the rubble, pointed like an accusing arm towards the Christian façade. Luckily, the Jews now visited their temple only occasionally since the Brown Shirt incident; so that there was only one victim, a lingering believer whom the fire suffocated as he prayed. But for a week afterwards the people of the neighbourhood complained of a subtle odour floating about the ruins, which they thought must be that of the old Jew who had gone up in smoke in the peaceful sky of Stillenstadt.

This funereal incense was very disagreeable to Mr Kremer's nostrils. He told his colleague and friend Mr Hartung, who took him to task regularly on the subject of the Jews, that his words were *full of fire*. The other pretended not to understand. But the spell was broken; and as they left school, the two friends each went his own way, walking twenty yards apart along the avenue which they had paced together, morning and evening, ever since the first of October, 1919.

Still, that mechanism had not yet been set in motion which was to send our delicate humanist to a concentration camp. And when the wheel of death began to turn, its initial motion was so slight that Mr Kremer was not even aware of it . . .

The school included about fifteen 'Jewish guests', as people affected to call them now; and about the same number of Pimpfen – pioneers in the Hitler Youth. But by an unexpected trick of the childish soul, whenever these latter launched out to attack the Jewish platoon, in the corner of the playground near the chestnut tree, many 'apolitical' students would join in with them for that small, so recreational, war. When the Jewish lines broke, they would drag their prisoners into the middle of the playground, where, under the teachers' carefully inattentive eyes, they would amuse themselves with them.

These Roman games left Mr Kremer thoughtful; but fearful of attracting some imperial lightning to his own head, he confined himself to pacing up and down along the wall opposite the Jews' chestnut tree. And yet at times, unable to plug his ears, he would retreat to the office reserved for the teaching staff and blow his nose loudly in the dark. Every time he felt the lump in his throat about to burst, he blew strongly into his handkerchief. When he came out again his nose was red and painful. This manoeuvre did not pass unobserved.

One day, in the middle of the play period, Ernie Levy came rolling in the dust at Mr Kremer's feet. There were two Pimpfen at his heels. Hans Schliemann drove a knee into his back; Ernie's arms lay limply on the ground and his palms were bleeding; his eyes were closed. Grabbing him by the hair, Hans tilted Ernie's slim face towards the sky, in a beggar's posture. 'What's the matter, don't you want to play any more?' Hans Schliemann's mouth was wide open and his teeth sparkled. He seemed indifferent to the proximity of Mr Kremer, who raised his hand to his bald head with a lost look; then sighed; pitched on his long legs; murmured between his long yellow teeth,

'Come, come, my boy,' and, grasping the Pimpfen suddenly by the collar, raised him shoulder-high and flung him several feet through the air!

At that sacrilegious sight, the entire playground fell motionless.

Mr Kremer went back to his pacing, slowly, with a dragging, harassed step, bringing his foot forward awkwardly and putting it down with caution, like an old nag too heavily loaded which verifies each step before raising the next hoof. But as he reached the corner of the wall, he sensed a light step behind him: the Jewish child was walking in his wake with his arms crossed and a look of delight, placing himself overtly under his protection. What to do? Mr Kremer resigned himself, and at the end of the play period it was two small boys and one little girl, in the seventh heaven, who trotted along behind him quite well behaved, hand in hand, forming a procession that could hardly be more compromising. The next day there were fifteen of them. Finally, three days later, Marcus Rosenberg, the great Marcus, ultimate defender of the Jewish colours, took his place in turn under the banner of Mr Kremer, carrying a steel ruler under his arm. All was ready.

That day, when he returned to his classroom, a childish inscription was sprawled all the way across the blackboard: *Out with the Jew-lover!*

He went up to the blackboard, picked up the duster and, changing his mind dropped it negligently back into its box. He remained for one full minute with his back to his pupils. When he finally turned towards the forty hostile gazes, his face was geometric and cold. And suddenly larger, harder, his jaw set forward, like the desperate muzzle of an old carriage horse (to which the shafts and a blanket flung superbly over his withers lend an illusion of vigour), Mr Kremer advanced towards his lectern solemnly, girded about by thirty-two years of everyday respectability. And as a disorderly murmur rose in the classroom, the schoolmaster picked up his switch between thumb and index finger, raised it to the vertical and tapped it against his ear, in a light, graceful movement, while his features maintained a superior impassivity. Dead silence fell immediately.

'Very good,' he articulated with a miserable smile. 'And to go on with our day's work, I propose ...' he rubbed his glasses with one hand, as if to clean away a few grains of dust; behind the metallic frames, his wide, gentle blue eyes blinked incessantly.

'... a pretty little exercise in dictation,' he went on finally. 'Take up your pens and your paper. This applies to you also, Miss Leuchner. Ready, I shall begin: one, two, three! How-sweet-it-is-comma-the-song-of-the-tomtit-comma ...'

Bent over their exercise, the pupils concentrated hard. In the first row he glimpsed the face of his favourite, Ilse Bruckner, whose green eyes flashed towards his lectern each time he began a new phrase. As for Ernie Levy, all he could see of him was a curly tuft of hair and the meditative point of a nose, far to the back of the classroom. 'All these heads are full of life,' the old man thought; 'and yet, a very special threat hangs over the four little Jewish heads ...' And as he compared the destiny of those four to that of the other pupils, Mr Kremer had the strange feeling that some unnameable monster, some kind of octopus squatting over his class, was devouring them indiscriminately ...

On the evening of that final defeat, Mr Kremer was weak enough to hold back the two elect spirits of the current year: Ernie Levy, first in German, and Ilse Bruckner, first in singing. On some vague scholarly pretext, he invited them both to tea. 'Tomorrow, Thursday, at precisely three o'clock,' he announced in order to stress, by that artificial exactitude, the official character of his invitation. 'Don't forget,' he said as he dismissed them, 'precisely three o'clock,' and he flashed a curious smile at them, trying to combine the touch of friendliness, that would make their coming pleasant, with the professorial distance that would make it an obligation.

When the two students were gone, Mr Kremer realized suddenly that they made up his entire circle of friends. Still, an instant later, the thought of tomorrow made him chuckle with pleasure; he had always known his children from far off, separated from them by the distance which his function imposed upon him; but he would not die without seeing them at close range at least once, without speaking to them, without smiling at them as if they were his own flesh. He mused that they both had the same thin legs, the same stem-like neck, the same tiny, graceful waists. Turning his gaze to the open window, he discovered the blue of the sky like a promise. The top of the chestnut tree was blossoming; he went to the window and plucked a leaf which he inspected in his palm; it was glistening in all its fresh green pith. He leaned out and received the revelation of the chestnut tree, whose myriad leaves rustled in the wind like a head of wild hair. He had lost everything, but some things went on without him: the sky, the earth, the trees, little children. 'And if I die,' he thought tenderly, 'none of that will go.' It seemed to him that he had just invented the world; of a sudden he felt extraordinarily happy; he did not know why.

2

MR Kremer's was not the house of a man of poetry. It resembled all those apartment buildings in the neighbourhood of the old synagogue, about which Mother Judith, with a doubtful grimace, had once commented with distaste: 'You can see right away what kind of fine people live in there.'

But the apartment was on the sixth floor, and this detail gave Ernie's imagination scope (no one in the Riggenstrasse lived so high up, as the houses lacked sufficient storeys); for him it was precisely the number of storeys which marked a kind of elevation of the soul. His pleasure was increased by the fact that the fifth-floor landing revealed a spiral staircase as narrow, as ambiguous, as dark, as gilded with the dust of mysterious events, as the one leading to the Levys' attic. The idea that Mr Kremer had carved his apartment out of an attic seemed full of poetry; and the thing itself worthy of such a man.

As he rang the bell, the thought of Ilse Bruckner made him hesitate; he had not spoken to a little girl for a year now. In the neighbourhood of the Riggenstrasse tongues were still wagging: some stated positively that the 'Jewboy' had pulled his little sex out of his fly, and saw in that fact a brilliant confirmation of all that had been reported of the sexual and financial devilishness of the Jews; several Nazis had demanded an investigation, but they had been able to extract no information from the little girl relative to Ernie Levy's fly . . .

'So, you have come?' said a somewhat choked voice. Mr Kremer, in a swallowtail coat and with a party face, leaned forward in the darkish rectangle of the doorway; a grey hand fluttered and came down to caress Ernie's cheek, tweaking it with infinite gentleness. Then the old schoolmaster pointed at the hatbox that Ernie was holding lightly to this chest, and said

216

with some awe: 'But what in the world can that be? I hope that you haven't brought us a bomb, at any rate?'

Ernie hesitated, understood, smiled: 'My grandmother, she doesn't make bombs.'

In the hall he felt disappointed, but the living-room amazed him: four tiny stained glass windows diffused a bluish light over the armchairs, all covered with lace, and over the golden squares that checkered the wallpaper like dead leaves. 'I shall leave you for a moment,' Mr Kremer said; and it was only then that Ernie noticed Ilse's quiet head of fair hair, set like a butterfly above the grassy plush of an armchair. Then he made out the girl herself, who rose with a quick movement and took three steps towards him, her hand outstretched at the end of an arm so smooth and white that it seemed to flow newly every moment from the short sleeve puffed at the elbow, like the disproportionately long pistil of a flower.

'How do you do, Mr First in German.'

Ernie took her hand ceremoniously, reddened, and said with much gravity: 'How do you do, Miss First in Music.'

He could not have have said exactly what it was that bothered him in those formal phrases; perhaps they seemed to him disproportionate to his own person, perhaps they sounded strange in the girl's mouth, perhaps, finally, they dampened some of the timid, vivacious pleasure he felt in gazing into Ilse's sea-blue eyes. Still, he was rather pleased with the way he had managed the greeting, so delicately, and astonishingly.

Ilse Bruckner burst out laughing.

'You had me there,' Ernie said smiling.

Ilse was anxious: 'Really?'

And as Ernie Levy's eyes continued to smile into her own, she blushed, pirouetted on the elastic tip of a toe, and flung herself into the lime-green armchair, which she filled by laying her hands on its arms. 'It's jolly nice here, isn't it?' she said with great conviction.

Then Mr Kremer was suddenly in the middle of the room; on a small iron table he set a tray bearing small china cups and other objects as preposterous in the context of his person: a sugar bowl, a teapot, etc. Opening the hatbox, he seemed surprised to find in it the tart to which Mother Judith, late at night, had added some finishing touches. The way in which he frowned seemed to indicate that this special attention was not to his taste. 'But what is this? No! ... But this is madness, pure and simple ...' And turning suddenly to a dismayed Ernie, his frown deepened while his pale eyes sparkled brightly: 'It looks delicious, it's real madness! Ah, my God!'

Then he cut the thrilling madness into slices, and poured the tea.

'What *splendour*!' Ilse Bruckner simpered, her mouth full. She was holding her teacup in three fingers, her little finger vertical, and twittering through her lips that were rounded as if to whistle.

'What do *you people* call that?' Mr Kremer asked.

Ernie Levy was jubilant: 'That's a *lechesh*!'

And Mr Kremer repeated the word over and over, saying that it was madness, but that it was delicious.

Suddenly he set his cup on the table, extracted a vast checkered handkerchief from his pocket, plunged his face into it, and blew his nose strenuously. The two children were terrified. A rending sing-song issued from Mr Kremer's nostrils; his pale, lifeless eyes once again displayed a brilliant sparkle. 'Nothing, nothing,' he stammered as he rushed out, handkerchief to his nose.

'He's really funny,' said Ilse Bruckner, who had raised herself on her elbows, to slide deeper into the chair.

'Funny,' Ernie Levy agreed.

'But he's awfully nice!'

'Nice,' Ernie said circumspectly.

His misadventure of the year before was dancing before his eyes.

'Listen,' Ilse said suddenly, 'you aren't too angry with me, are you?'

The boy choked in fear: 'Why?'

'For what happened three years ago, when we were playing Christ ...'

218

'Oh no, oh no,' Ernie said warmly.

'And you're not angry with me because of my cousin Hans either?'

'A cousin's a cousin.'

'Well,' the girl concluded, 'you're not very talkative.'

And with a thin throaty laugh she huddled up, disappearing into the depths of the armchair.

Ilse's chair squeaked. A choked laugh rose from it. Ernie felt a silky rend inside his chest. Everything was happening as if the girl were putting herself out to make him want to share her little blonde happiness, even as she deprived him of the actual possibility. For Ilse was not an animal, or a ray of sunlight in which one could bask without asking consent, and yet she was not altogether a person who could deliberately forbid one the entrance to her soul. In her face and hands there was a kind of animal or bird; in her voice and expression, a kind of person. Anything could be expected, with Ilse, Ernie thought dreamily; for she was this thing and that thing, and perhaps much more than he could even imagine . . .

'What do you see?' she asked.

'I see that you're hidden,' Ernie Levy said.

And as he finished his phrase, he burst into a laugh whose freshness surprised him, like that of a brook swirling about the stones of his mouth, the source of which within him he had never guessed at: that strange joy that Ilse had awakened.

'You laugh like a madman,' Ilse said, huddled in the armchair. And with no transition she began to warble sweetly: laaaa, liiii, laaa, as if the laughter in her had followed a delicately etched groove in her throat, very slowly and with much precision, without overflowing its banks by a drop. An extension of that crystal groove, Ernie lowered his eyelids and murmured very politely: 'You sing well.'

When he opened his eyes again the little girl's head was peeking up over the lace-covered arm of the chair, and she was making a face at Ernie Levy. But in the shadow where the eyelashes curved back like petals, Ernie made out quite clearly the ironic and tender sparks in a look like a swelling, gilded, dusty pistil, expressing the naïve subtlety of a flower.

'How are you?' Ilse said then in a velvet voice.

'I don't know,' Ernie said. At the sound of his voice, Ilse was moved; the Jewish boy's eyes were like two black cherries set into the white flesh of his cheeks; she thought that if she bit lightly at them, delicate red juice would flow, the delectable blood of cherries. 'You know,' she said confidentially, 'I want to be a singer.'

The next morning in the name of some formality which had never entered his head until then, Mr Kremer seated Ernie Levy solemnly in the first rank – right next to Ilse. The laureate took his place with an unhappy air; and did not move thereafter. She could barely hear him breathe, in light, rapid, measured little puffs. She leaned coyly forward and saw that her sweet idiot's forehead was covered with a fine sweat. She was amazed. 'Jesus, how scared he is,' she said to herself; 'yes, that's the way, that's the way, that's the way I like him!'

But during the play period she could not escape Hans Schliemann's interrogation. 'So,' he said, 'you're sitting next to a Jew now?'

Leaning back against the lavatory door, he crossed one ankle carelessly over the other. His soft blond hair hung at either side of his forehead, he was shaking his head furiously, he was handsome.

Ilse smiled scornfully: 'What's it to you? Just because old Kremer put us in the same row? You're not jealous of him?' she laughed. She brushed dust into his eyes casually, and he quivered. 'What do you suppose I can do with that idiotic little Yid, he's not a man like you? Stupid Hansi,' she simpered, making the face he loved, pouting her lower lip all moist with saliva.

'Be careful,' Hans said, 'I'm a Pimpfe. I'll bust you in the mouth, both of you . . .'

'You just try,' Ilse said. She held out her cheek at him, standing rigid and icy. 'Well?'

220

Hans wailed. 'You know I couldn't do that!'

'All right,' she said coldly. 'But remember that I'm not Sophie. I'm Ilse, and I do what I like. And that Jew is the biggest idiot in the world: if you touch him, then ... you won't touch me any more. And now go ahead, hurry up, the bell is going to ring...'

The little girl leaned forward in a bored manner; with his index finger Hans Schliemann searched for the curved flesh barely visible under her smock then, closing his eyes suddenly, he pinched quickly, simultaneously, the points of Ilse's budding breasts.

'Today it's free,' she said pushing him away. 'But remember ...'

When the school day was over she took Ernie familiarly by the arm, under Hans Schliemann's impotent gaze. Silently, they walked around the block; silently, with a timid handshake, they parted. Ilse was already arguing with herself. 'What do you see in that idiot?' the first Ilse said in exasperation. But immediately the Ilse below became tender at the memory of a detail: 'Jesus, Jesus, Jesus, he let you drag him off like a baby! He didn't ask you a single question, did he? He's not the least bit curious, that one. No, not the least bit,' she repeated to herself drunkenly. 'But what is he thinking about all the time?'

She enjoyed their walks along the Schlosse more every day; but the schoolboy community vexed her, denouncing her openly as the 'concubine', as Hans said, of a Jew: Ilse suffered brief but violent accesses of shame.

As for their Thursday visits, now ritual, they were the honey of her week: the ceremony of tasting, the little vocal concerts with which she regaled the party afterwards, the waxed parquet, the knick-knacks and the upholstered armchairs, all placed at her fingertips a world that floated way up above the family hovel. Mr Kremer varied his dress, going so far as to try a top hat; and Ernie too was invariably comical, with his vast navy-blue trousers – donned for the occasion – which, riding up almost to his armpits, nevertheless dragged along the floor, constraining him to a cautious tread that was highly amusing. Sometimes Mr Kremer disappeared briefly, sometimes he blew his nose without leaving them. And on the stroke of four o'clock (Ilse revelled in it beforehand), the old gentleman took on an artificially detached manner.

'Listen,' he said. 'If you don't feel like it today, put it off until next Thursday. As for me, I must admit that it leaves me completely indifferent.'

'You don't want to play?' Ilse said, to bait him.

'Now look here, my poor child,' he cried shrilly, 'I am only a silent partner!'

'Shall we?' the girl asked calmly.

Ernie nodded indulgently: 'Let's,' he said.

They would play dominoes.

One day Ernie took the silver tray back to the kitchen and, his absence seemed long to her, Ilse slipped into the hallway to surprise him. Raising a corner of the curtain, she saw Ernie hunched over the table, lost in contemplation of a black speck in the middle of a puddle of milk; he seized the black speck, which was a fly, and approached the red hot oven with his arm extended. Ilse had the sudden feeling that Ernie was performing a maleficent Jewish rite, and everything about him disgusted her suddenly: his thin, white wrists and ankles, the curve of his neck, even the graceful movement of his round arm above the gaping oven ... But immediately discountenanced, she saw the fly hopping about on the end of Ernie's thumb, then trotting peacefully on the palm of his hand; finally, chasing a last wisp of steam, the fly was on the ceiling in one light hop!

As Ernie moved round to gaze up at the insect, Ilse caught his expression; and if it hadn't been for the risk of getting pimples, she would have willingly have kissed him: it was the same beatific, flabbergasted expression with which he listened to her when she sang ...

As soon as she saw her mother that evening, Ilse guessed that her charming cousin Hans had spilled the beans. Because of future marriage, Mrs Bruckner's principle was never to risk her child's beauty; all the same, she used the poker. After the operation, she explained: 'From now on and beginning today, no more Thursday, no more schoolmaster, no more Jew; if he comes here to ask for you, I'll take care of him! Let me see your face, you got any pimples yet?'

'We don't kiss,' Ilse hiccupped, stretched out on her belly.

'You're lying,' Mrs Bruckner retorted, 'you smell of Jewish filth ten feet away! Ah, Jesus, Jesus, Jesus, so you had to go, and with that one too! I know all about it, Hans told me everything. That's the one who attacked her, the little girl in the Riggenstrasse, it made all those stories in the newspaper. And I suppose you didn't know it, you little whore?'

'*Yes, I knew it!*' Ilse screamed. 'But he'll never do anything to me . . .' And in a delicate whisper: 'He loves me.'

Mr Kremer listened to her in profound melancholy and said it was of no importance; because friends, he added a bit ironically, nothing in the world can separate friends. 'And our little band will continue at school, won't it?' he murmured in an engaging tone. But the next day Mr Julius Kremer arrived unshaved; and the following day, drunk.

It was Hans Schliemann who gave the signal. Hostile scrawls covered the blackboards, accompanied by obscene drawings. They also knew that neither the teachers nor the headmaster were speaking to Mr Kremer at all. The latter's manner was distraught . . . absent. One day he delivered a brief discourse on government: the following day Hans Schliemann set a lump of dry ice on the cushion of his magisterial chair.

Neither the jokes, nor the unbridled use of language, nor even the wilful missiles could persuade Mr Kremer to give up the defence of the Jews in the playground; on the contrary, he assembled them in ranks himself, by order of size, and as he convoyed them threw furious, provoking glances at the others. When Hans Schliemann told her that Mr Kremer's replacement was imminent, Ilse once again offered her chest to her cousin. Unable to persuade her to break with them, he promised (in exchange for an incursion under her dress) that he would do all he could to hold back the ardour of his *men*. 'But soon,' he added, 'that will be impossible; and for you, it will be too late.'

One fine morning the students found the headmaster in Mr Kremer's place. The latter, he explained, being no longer worthy of his position, had been obliged to leave the city at dawn. He passed over Mr Kremer very quickly, and then announced the arrival of a replacement, the next day, come straight from Berlin. 'Then,' he said with an ambiguous smile, 'order will be restored in all things.'

In a protective gesture, Ilse gripped Ernie's arm; outside, their steps led them quite naturally to the banks of the Schlosse, where Ilse suddenly sat down on the grass and broke into sobs. Then she smiled through her tears, to reassure the boy, who also sat down, a bit uneasy in spite of everything. She hesitated, then she picked a daisy; and, still smiling, plucked a petal from it delicately.

'I pluck out one eye,' she said, hardly realizing what words she spoke. For a second, the daisy's white winglet flutters; it falls into the shadowed hollow of Ilse's smock.

'I pluck out both your eyes,' she continues slowly, while her own eyes, still smiling, narrow to threads, of green light.

And her voice becomes hurried, her gesture of mutilation becomes jerky, lively, dry.

'I cut off one paw ... both!

'I eat up one hand ... both!

'I pluck out your eye again ...

'I pluck out ...' she began feverishly; but that time, her thumb and index finger came together on emptiness: not a single petal remained about the yellow, disarmed heart of the daisy.

In a panic, Ilse raised her head to see what effect her words had on Ernie. But he seemed to have guessed nothing and leaning towards her, his wide dark eyes shining with compassion, he set the ends of his fingers timidly on Ilse's palm, on the limp daisy: 'What makes you so sad?' asked the gentle idiot in a trembling voice.

Isle was in perfect despair. She said very quickly: 'It's nothing, I've already forgotten ...'

Then she raised the little finger of her right hand, and made it dance gracefully in the air to the beat of a Viennese waltz, which she began to whistle with feigned solemnity. Ernie burst into light, throaty laughter as his eyes followed the finger's dance. He has no memory, not a pennyworth, she said to herself, her heart horribly contracted. No, no, no, she could not tell him that it was all over, she had not the courage. All right, she would wait for a better time. Let him be in the wrong just once. If she had to, yes, she would create the situation herself, for, my God, it couldn't go on; truly she had not been 'living' for some time now. And under Ernie Levy's bewildered gaze, there she was sobbing again, in the middle of her song, which trailed off for an instant and then died.

3

THE new teacher burst in without ceremony; at five minutes past eight the door blew open and a short, square man sprang in like a jack-in-the-box. Paying no attention to the students, he went to the desk immediately and sat up stiffly in order to lose nothing of what height he had. The abruptness of his appearance was almost laughable, but Ernie restrained himself, for everyone seemed extremely serious. Mr Geek had a face of dried clay. Crevices lined it in all directions. The loose skin of his neck slightly overflowed his starched detachable collar. A strange smudge of moustache spread out in yellow moth wings under his nostrils. Like a peasant in his Sunday best, Ernie jeered silently.

But his joy lasted only a moment; Mr Geek was already pushing back his chair, standing to attention, and proclaiming in an angry voice: 'Attention! One, two, three, all rise!'

The tone was so aggressive, the voice so resolved to make itself heard, that Ernie felt something like the bite of a whip at the base of his spine. He rose with a haggard precipitation that surprised him and, as he stuck out his chest, he noticed that Mr Geek's eyes were shining with an unusual pallid glow between the heavy eyelids which enveloped them like the fissure of a dead veinstone.

Suddenly Mr Geek clicked his heels, and his arm rose obliquely into the air, in a swift single motion, as rigid as a beam: 'Heil Hitler!' he cried fiercely.

Mr Geek's gesture was so abrupt that the students responded without exception. Even Ernie, somewhere in the obscurity of his being, found the inspiration and the technique for a perfect clicking of heels; at the time he realized that he was crying at the top of his voice: 'Heil Hitler! Heil Hitler!' His voice was lost in the roaring of the whole class. Dumbfounded, he saw his arm pointing towards the ceiling. Slowly, he brought it

226

down and let it lie discreetly at his side, like a branch alien to his body.

'It is truly unbelieveable,' Mr Geek declared. His rural accent struck Ernie again. The lips were thin and taut like leather thongs, opening on a blackish mouth, and the words escaping them seemed to be carved out of some hard material, out of wood; brutally, with a billhook. Ernie thought that neither the lips, nor the teeth, nor the shrubbery that served him for eyebrows, nor the curious lawn of moustache, nor the bumpy ground, rutted with wrinkles, nor even, finally, the eyes, stagnant in the middle of it all like two shallow puddles of grey water, nothing about Mr Geek recalled the teacher; he looked more like a peasant, come to barter in the church square, and throwing over all things, according to his mood, a watery gaze, or an earthen one, or even one of naked, cold, bruising rock.

Suddenly, Mr Geek's face contracted altogether, some eddy blurred his expression while his mouth twisted so as to form a hole under the right nostril. A thin and trembling, ice-cold voice trickled out of the hole: 'I thought ... yes ... they told me that there were Jews in this class.' And gesturing briefly at all the arms raised in the Hitlerite salute: 'But I can see nothing but good Germans who worship their Fuehrer. Right, boys?'

A triumphant laugh shook the ranks of the Pimpfen in their brown shirts. Hans Schliemann clapped enthusiastically. Mr Geek muttered in satisfaction, turned his glance towards Hans Schliemann, and seemed to reflect for a moment. Then, spreading his enormous dark hand on the edge of the desk, he stepped calmly off the platform. At each step, half his body sagged heavily to one side. His gait was that of a man carrying a burden. Ernie noted that he seemed to tap the ground with his foot first, and then to place the full weight of his body upon it before swinging the other leg forward. But his left shoulder sloped lower than his right.

When Mr Geek had reached Hans Schliemann, he stood still and looked approvingly at the boy's uniform. 'There are only three Hitler Youth in this class?' he asked in a tone of pained astonishment. And then, as Hans Schliemann stood to attention, he went on in a voice full of severity: 'The Hitler Youth must set an example of discipline.' And without changing his benevolent expression, he slapped Hans Schliemann twice. At the second slap, the boy's head rocked back against his desk and he fell down under the bench. Ernie was surprised to hear him cry enthusiastically: 'Yes, sir! Yes, sir!'

'I like that,' Mr Geek declared suddenly.

And with his heavy, slow step, his fat hands swinging against his thighs, he walked calmly back to his desk. When he was on the platform again he stretched out his neck, took up the hazel switch, and thrust it forward in a gesture of command:

'And now,' he cried in a raging tone, '*Die Hunde, die Neger und die Juden, austreten*! Dogs, Negroes, and Jews step forward!'

For one instant, Ernie Levy attributed those words to the incomprehensible humour of Mr Geek; but as the students did not laugh, and as Mr Geek stared furiously at Ernie's dark curls, the latter understood that the phrase was directed solely at the Jews. Immediately, he slipped out sideways to take up his position as a Jew in the centre of the aisle; behind him, fat Simon Kotkowski was already sniffling.

'Jews!' Mr Geek cried. 'When I give an order to the class in general, it means that I am addressing myself to the German students and not to their guests.'

Then still in his military posture, and with only his lower jaw moving, Mr Geek launched into a confused threatening diatribe at the 'Jewish guests'. These last, moreover, must know that Mr Geek would always find a way of making himself understood when he wished to address himself to them; for example, by beginning the phrase with the name of an animal.

After the guests had retired, by order of the master of the house, to the last row in the classroom (isolated from the pure Aryans by a row of empty desks), Mr Geek relaxed, and gave a vast sigh of relief, answered by a vast burst of laughter from the Pimpfen. Then, serious again at last, he treated the German students to the brutal truth: they had all been Jewified by their former teacher; so that they were all, to some degree, suspect.

His own view was that Mr Kremer had some strain of Jewish blood in his veins, 'or elsewhere'; for a thoroughbred German would never have committed himself to such repugnant promiscuity. The hour of the Jews had struck, it was a funeral bell; and the hour of the pure and authentic Germans was beginning to sound in the heavens, and it was a victory bell, rung by him to whom we owe everything: Adolf Hitler. Finally, the students were not here *to play at learning*, but to prepare the true grandeur of the fatherland; for a day would come when the pen, transformed into a sword . . .

Here Mr Geek interupted himself sharply. The first row noticed that a pallor had spread over the new master's face.

'Uh . . . on that day . . .' he continued with an effort, 'you will all be men!'

Then a thin smile brushed his lips, and a sudden gleam appeared in his small white eyes: 'Hey, fat boy, back there,' he called brutally, his arm stretched towards the back of the room. 'Yes, you, what's your name?'

'Simon Kotkowski, sir,' answered a fearful voice.

Mr Geek's sparkling steel ruler described a slashing orbit in space, finishing at the precise point where he wished to see the Jew take his position. 'The Jew Simon Kotkowski, right here!'

Placid, resigned, huddled in his cheerful fat, the amiable Simon Kotkowski approached the blackboard. The singularly Jewish shape of his nose had struck Mr Geek who made it the subject of his first lesson. But comparisons and sarcasms, 'typological' analyses and 'bio-political' commentaries seemed to bounce off Simon Kotkowski's elastic skin, lending a clear, lively pink tone to his expression.

'Jew,' Mr Geek murmured at last, 'you and your people, you are fighting for the domination of the universe, right?'

'I don't know, sir,' the accused answered placidly.

With his arms crossed and his cheerful belly, his hair frizzy on the low forehead, he presented a picture of the most total incomprehension. The bridge of his nose like a tench's snout (like a vulture's beak, Mr Geek had said), rose and fell hesitantly. He looked extremely puzzled.

'Do you hear,' Mr Geek said softly, 'he says that he doesn't know . . .' And leaning towards the child, as if to underline the confidential character of the interview: 'Jew, Jew,' he exhaled, 'isn't Germany your mortal enemy?'

'No . . . No . . .'

'Jew, little Jew of my heart, how can I believe you, tell me?'

'It's true, sir,' Simon answered, terrified.

'The strength of the Jews,' Mr Geek went on without seeming to have heard him, 'do you mean to say that it no longer lies in the suppleness of their spinal column?'

At that Simon Kotkowski remained silent, and Mr Geek took on an expression of extreme solemnity; in a voice which all the students guessed was broken by emotion: 'Jew. Ah, little Jew. You who are still a child, tell us what fate you have reserved for us if' (here the tone of Mr Geek's voice thinned in terror) 'if . . . ah, my God! . . . if we should emerge defeated from this fight to the death? *Von der Totenschlacht?* What will you do to us?'

And the Jewish child, fascinated, caught in the play of the collective fear that swirled about his person – with the titanic struggle of the Jews and the poor Germans outlined at last upon his eyeballs – Simon answered, with a timorous desire to please: 'We won't do anything to you, sir, we won't do anything . . .'

Geek would have dearly liked to take that incorrigible idiot Kremer and split him in two before the whole class. He was a non-commissioned officer in the imperial army, recently promoted to the position of shock-instructor, and the purification of the class seemed to him a work worthy of a former trench-cleaner. From eight to ten in the morning he produced brilliant solutions to all pending problems; but the 'question' of singing proved to be infinitely more delicate . . .

Judging that the Jews would inevitably sing off-key, he decided that they would not sing at all; 'except,' he added, 'if they feel an irresistible urge. In that case since cats miaow, since dogs bark, and since pigs grunt, why shouldn't the Jews sing?'

That query split the class in two with the precision of a razor; those who laughed, and the Jews.

But soon the teacher noticed that the Jews were not singing, that the Aryan pupils were, and that the result was the ridiculous rebound of an injustice. Four recorded zeros could not console him; nor could four set impositions, or four kneeling punishments, lined up along the blackboard: the fact was incontrovertible; they were not singing.

The students were broaching the march of the Pimpfen: 'Strike, pierce and kill,' the girls in soprano and the boys in tenor to accelerate voice-break, when the solution came to Mr Geek; simple, clear and natural.

'Stop!' he commanded, his arms scissoring the air. The chorus broke off cleanly.

Then Mr Geek, smiling: 'It seems, my friends, that our guests are taking life a bit too easy. While you sing, what do they do? They calmly listen. They think they're at a concert.' Mr Geek was unable to resist pursing his lips at his little joke, and several students laughed boisterously. All the same he had to follow up that felicitous phrase; Mr Geek wiped his eyes slowly; blew his nose into a handkerchief; took in a great breath and realized with some annoyance, that the rest of his speech was not forthcoming.

A pin drop could have been heard.

Twisting their heads in his direction, the four Jews themselves seemed crushed by the silence flowing from his still half-open lips, like lava immediately frozen into soft heavy sheets over his face.

And yet the suddenness of his attack surprised them: 'Let the Jews sing,' he growled, purple with indignation. 'Let them give us a serenade!'

At which there was a new pause, but this was the pause of victory, the silence of the great German eagle, wings spread majestically; and already they were all clapping, except the Jews...

Simon Kotkowski stood up, shook a cramped leg, then

stepped forward miserably to stand before the instructional pulpit. As soon as he had received the order he rounded his mouth to a heart shape and with great good nature broke into the celebrated lament: *There is no more beautiful death on earth*, dedicated to the memory of the hero Horst Wessel. His eyes upon heaven, and his pudgy hands lying effeminately on his paunch, he was just whimpering: *Unfurl the blood-soaked flag* ... when a horrible laugh swept the class, sparing none of them, even the three Jewish souls still on their knees; all this with the swiftness of lightning.

But the singer, with his frightful voice, was serenely launching into the second verse: *Arise! that which God made German* ... when Mr Geek leaned suddenly across the lectern, shouting at him to stop and striking him with the switch to make his meaning clear. Himself in the grasp of a nervous twitch, the teacher seemed supremely shocked by such an interpretation, which was not a Jew's and yet not a German's. Simon Kotkowski went back to the blackboard and tried to find the ideal position, letting himself fall backwards so as to rest his buttocks on his heels, then clasping his hands below his round buttocks, for better support in his trial.

At a mere sign, Moses Finkelstein rose with a submissive look. He stepped forward, repressing a bird-like hiccup. When he arrived before the large lectern, a tear rolled out from beneath his glasses, a tear of shame, or suppressed hilarity, or of terror. No one really knew Moses Finkelstein; his father had abandoned his mother, who worked as a cleaner and breathed only through the nostrils of her son, which was barely at all. He placed his hands flat against his chest, in a vague gesture of defence, and broke into a sing-song on a sighing, nasal voice, almost a murmur. He was then sent back to his knees: broken and whining, licking at his tears, tasting the dregs of shame.

'I don't feel like singing,' Marcus Rosenberg said then.

He stood with his back to the blackboard, swaggering defiantly.

'Who is forcing you to sing?' Geek answered with no emotion.

Rather tall, with the thin, prominent neck of a young stag, Marcus Rosenberg could not bear humiliation. Often, in the evening, the Pimpfen organized a pack to beat him up. The scars distributed all over his face announced the score of old defeats.

'No, I won't sing,' he went on in a voice choked by his own surprise.

And as Geek limped heavily towards him, bending his adult back in order better to bring his soothing gaze to bear on Marcus Rosenberg's eyes, the latter retreated against the blackboard, which stopped him.

'But who is forcing you to sing, my friend?' Mr Geek repeated in a smooth, insinuating voice; 'Where I come from people only sing for pleasure. Ask Moses Finkelstein . . .' Then taking him from behind, Geek threw the Jewish child to his knees, twisting his wrist up in a hammerlock.

The justice of the conception and the great good taste of his execution enchanted the Pimpfen, who clapped in silence.

'So that's how it is, we have our pride?' Geek murmured affectionately; and he increased the pressure so as to force the child to groan. 'But the pride of the Jew is made to be broken. And this is how,' he added; Marcus Rosenberg wailed right inside himself, without opening his tightened lips.

Geek's voice was syrupy sweet: 'Come now, come now, *Wenn Judenblut*, when the Jewish blood . . .? when Jewish blood . . .?' At the end of five minutes, Marcus's lips were opening imperceptibly; when his mouth was wide open, a sudden howl came out, drowning in music. The proof of Jewish ignominy was achieved. Mr Geek breathed delightedly and, flinging the child to the floor he said 'Filth!'

Then he noticed Ernie, who was white: 'And that one, I almost forgot him.'

Marcus Rosenberg stayed as he was, his face to the floor, hands over his skull, mute; the Pimfpen were rejoicing that his pride had been broken.

Two tears hung on Ernie's lashes. He managed nevertheless to make out, in the first row, his friend Ilse, whose face, frozen in mineral attention, implored him to sing.

'And when will this imbecile deign to begin?'

The child turned towards the master's desk, a thin frown sunk into the root of his nose, which was pink with grief: 'Excuse me, sir ...' he stammered, rolling his eyes wildly, 'I don't know yet if I ought to ... oh ...' Then he brought his arm behind his back, offering himself without resistance to the teacher's extraordinary hold. The class was silent. The intrigued pupils in the first row heard only snatches that came out of Ernie Levy's lips: 'I don't know ... I don't know ...'

Geek suspected a trap. He advanced one hand cautiously, guarding his face with the other; but when the child did not stir, he grabbed his wrist quickly and twisted it with such vigour that the boy, helped by his lightness and his readiness to suffer, gave a little fish-like jump and fell back to his knees, imprisoned.

'You still don't know?'

But Ernie had established his whole world right there. While Mr Geek went on with the lesson, while the Aryans appreciated its clarity and the Jews its rigour, Ernie Levy was gliding at the height of a dove, crowned by the faces he would not assassinate in song: Mother Judith, the patriarch, papa, mama, Moritz and some very small faces.

4

MR Geek's oration bluntly established the fact that Ernie had not sung.

But when the cruel flamboyance of the moment had passed, a very large majority of the students secretly refused to admit that he had not *wished* to sing, so that it was impossible to go on seeing an offence in Ernie's silence; and even more impossible to see a personal triumph or – as Geek had complained – the triumph of Jews in general. According to that secret majority, neither defeat nor victory was possible for the idiot; they felt that he had no wish to conquer anyone and, not being engaged in any combat, he could not undergo any defeat comparable to Marcus Rosenberg's. And yet deep within themselves that secret majority felt a hate for 'the idiot' all the more lively in that it found no nourishment in his silence. Their hatred of Marcus was a response to his permanent defiance, and Marcus vanquished inspired nothing more than the scorn he had wished to escape. But Ernie's silence had none of these motives, and several children suspected that he would willingly have sung if he had *been able to*. From then on, their hatred of Ernie Levy was immeasurable, for it was aimed at the very gentleness which emanated from his person, and which each of the children felt within himself, confusedly, buried like a taproot.

The Jews remained on their knees until the last Aryan had left, so that each one might admire them in passing, and express that admiration by word and deed. But there was not a glance for Ernie; the students turned away as they brushed by, as if they had been exposed to a subtle danger. Ilse could not help glancing sidewise at him; surprised, she saw only a tangle of dishevelled hair, for Ernie was staring at the floor, not in fear, but ashamed and aggrieved to have become irremediably separated from both the Aryans and the Jews.

The children dispersed with all the bustle and grace of a flight of sparrows. No group was formed to speed the departing Jews on their way. The Pimpfen themselves looked at the victims joylessly. Simon Kotkowski was swearing never to come back to school – even if his father had to suffer harshly for that infraction of the law. Marcus Rosenberg was sharpening an absolute revenge. Moses Finkelstein ran home. And, with dragging steps intoxicated by the afternoon sun, Ernie Levy went to meet his friend Ilse who was waiting for him, as she did every day, beside the Schlosse, beyond the great block of houses, her blonde hair sparkling in the sun. That day when he saw the loved figure, the pain in his shoulder blinded him suddenly, and tears leapt to his eyes. Ilse was standing in the middle of the street, not far from the river bank, motionless, her head set like a pretty apple above her black smock. Without the shoulder and the tears, and that interminable distance over which every step increased his feeling of aloneness, he would doubtless never even have dreamed of kissing Ilse Bruckner on the cheek; he would have doubtless not have dared. But had he only dreamed it? It seemed to him as he approached that Ilse shared his solitude and was offering her cheek; and he could not have said if he had kissed it before she offered it or if, on the contrary, Ilse had initiated that kiss: it all happened as if the two things were only one.

'Swine!' was the first shout from Hans Schliemann, camouflaged in the shrubbery on the bank; at that signal Hans's 'men', surging out of the nearby houses or springing up from the reeds of the Schlosse, disclosed the ambush.

Ilse's eyes, gentle, blue, green, yellow, shone peacefully at him.

'Run!' Ernie cried, surrounded by the Pimpfen, hit in the face, dragged against the naked wall of an apartment building.

And as he worried about Ilse, he glimpsed her for a brief instant, still in the middle of the street, in the sunlight, her arms hanging against her short pleated skirt, observing all with a curious eye.

There was an acid voice at the back of his neck, and a tickle of breath: 'That's the second time today he's sullied the honour of Germany,' the voice announced in an extraordinary solemn tone.

Yet Ernie felt that Hans Schliemann's voice was hollow, empty as the display dumbbells which the ironmonger's children played with, the ones they lifted, contorting themselves and turning red in a thousand imaginary tortures. So he decided that Hans Schliemann's voice deserved a secret smile.

'Swine!' a Pimpfen belched against Ernie's face; 'I bet you've already kissed her on the mouth!'

'And maybe rubbed a tit or two!'

'Or stuck your hand in the little basket!'

Trembling in anger, the invisible voice of Hans Schliemann echoed against Ernie's neck: 'Or maybe the swine has already "nicked" her?'

And falling to his knees, Ernie felt the pain of his shoulder more acutely than ever; he was beaten without resistance, by a single twist from Hans Schliemann.

The pain in his shoulder became sharper; moisture blurred his eyes; then his forehead too was moist, and he imagined confusedly (as the fire in his shoulder raged hotter) that all that abundant liquid escaping from his eyes and his skull, his neck and his torso, clothing his throat with a sour pungency, filtering through lips held back by the mechanical pressure of the jaws and teeth about to break ... the child imagined confusedly that all this mass of liquid was flooding from the leaking vessel of his body, fleeing the white-hot bar of his right shoulder.

'*Schweinhund!*' Hans Schliemann cried breathlessly, 'Have you decided to sing yet?'

Drunk with indignation, Hans Schliemann could only repeat incessantly: *Hund*, dog, dog, dog, ... while the other Pimpfen spat in Ernie's face, stooping each in turn, bringing their rounded mouths to within an inch of him, spewing phlegm at him. His eyes closed, the boy imagined that the sweat, the saliva, the tears and the phlegm in which he was bathing were simply one and the same substance, welling up from some spring deep within his being, splitting open its shell now and flowing in the sunlight; all

237

those liquids emanated from his own interior substance, blue-green, shadowy, viscous, not composed of flesh and bone as he had once thought . . .

Time now seemed to him a bottomless sea.

Strangely, the floodgates opened and all waters disappeared.

Opening his eyes, Ernie found himself kneeling on the hard, dry sidewalk. A short distance away, the Pimpfen were in a huddle; they seemed to be arguing a serious point, but Ernie was more aware of their discomfited and discouraged expressions than of the mysterious words they were exchanging, with oblique vibrating glares at him from time to time. Then Ernie was delighted to discover, under the solid arch of Wolfgang Oelendorff's legs, the calm silhouette of his friend Ilse Bruckner, who seemed to be standing immobilized on the same spot, and whose sleek, blue-green gaze soon slid between Oelendorff's legs, apparently without seeing Ernie. Though her delicate features had frozen for a second, he thought, when their eyes met briefly.

'That Jew,' the redhead said, 'he looks more Jewish than the others, to me.'

'I think we should strip him in front of Bruckner,' Wolfgang Oelendorff said. 'I hear they have their pricks cut.'

'No, no, not that!' the terrified redhead cried.

'Why not?' Hans Schliemann inquired calmly. '*We can pull the devil by the tail.*'

The group burst into strained laughter, every head turning towards Ilse, who seemed to have heard nothing – although a small red spot had appeared on her cheeks – and whose eyes were becoming lightly opaque like those of a blind man, though she still stared in the direction of the boys: alternately at the Pimpfen, now silent, and at Ernie still on his knees, taking the sun's caress between Wolfgang's legs; it was turning his shoulder into gentle water.

All these things seen and heard seemed so unnatural that Ernie Levy believed the sun was coming nearer and turning over like a wheel of fireworks, only a few inches from his half-closed eyes. Yet a part of him was aware of the threat. Half rising, he propped himself sideways against the wall of the house and opened his eyes still clogged by the sun, tears, the sweat running down his forehead, saliva, and phlegm. Really, all these things were without precedent and, slowly becoming aware of the words that had been spoken, the little boy took his eyes off Ilse Bruckner in sudden embarrassment; she was still motionless in her black smock, and her huge green eyes seemed to devour her face.

The Pimpfen surrounded him in silence. The little boy did not move, staring at the sun's spinning disc. These events concerned someone else. Nothing like them had ever happened to anyone. There was not the slightest allusion to any such phantasmagoria in the Legend of the Just Men. Desperately tense, Ernie searched his memories, hoping to find a clear path, a road to help through that forest of strange circumstances, which did not seem entirely real though they bore a certain appearance of reality ... He found no road.

Hans Schliemann's arms bound him nonchalantly. Hans proceeded as if he had Ernie's complete agreement. The latter moved an elbow out of the way, allowing Hans to take a firm grip comfortably.

The redhead knelt and undid Ernie's braces.

Ernie Levy lowered his eyes and saw a red-haired neck over his belly.

With a sharp jerk, the redhead pulled Ernie's trousers half-way down his thighs; Ernie noticed that his own legs were shaking violently and, as the redhead slipped two fingers between the skin and the elastic of the pants, the little boy freed himself from Hans Schliemann's embrace in one jerk and flung his hands as high as he could, shaking them at the wheel of the sun, as if he did not know what to do with them and wished simply to express his own impotence.

Disturbed, the Pimpfen looked at those naked hands fluttering in the sunlight.

But the redhead came back to his senses immediately and pulled down the pants, uncovering Ernie's sex, and it was then that a wild animal rushed up his throat, and he bayed for the first time. Already he was falling to the redhead's feet, digging his teeth into the flesh of his calf and keeping them there. A flux of saliva rose to his mouth: his nails dug into the redhead's ankles.

Immediately Hans Schliemann set his knee into Ernie Levy's back and pulled the little boy backward violently, with his thumbs in the boy's eyes. Ernie let go, howled again, and hung by his teeth from the hand of Hans Schliemann who managed to free himself after dragging the child two or three yards along the sidewalk. Hans Schliemann took a few more steps, as if he wanted to lengthen the distance between his hands and Ernie Levy's jaw; then he changed his mind, seeing that all the Pimpfen had had the same reflex and were on the defensive now, in a compact group, out of reach of Ernie Levy's teeth; Ernie had risen quickly to his feet and was standing, back to the wall, facing them and growling in his throat, like a dog, while the tears sprang from his eyes like so many tiny, sharp knives.

'Dog shit,' said the redhead.

'Jewish shit,' said a Pimpfe.

'Jewish dog,' Hans Schliemann went on without conviction; and as he drew closer with his hand hanging limply from his arm, he added in a forced tone, 'Be careful, he may have rabies.' The Pimpfen spread out even more, but smiling, to show that they did not take the remark seriously. They could not let Ernie Levy off, and yet no one felt like breaking the evil Jewish spell they had just witnessed; Hans Schliemann's little joke seemed to offer a way out.

'Let's take him to the furrier's,' a Pimpfe said. 'They'll get rid of him for us.'

'How do they slaughter them?' a Pimpfe asked.

'They give them injections,' Hans Schliemann said, 'and they die with their mouths open.'

'Where do they do it?' a Pimpfe laughed. 'In the arse?'

'That depends,' Hans answered in the manner of an expert. 'That depends ... with Jewish dogs, they say it's in the prick.'

And as if they had been waiting for that signal, the Pimpfen roared with laughter, shoving each other enthusiastically, slapping their thighs in such an excess of hilarity that they were suddenly conscious of evading the principal question and fell silent again. The redhead picked up a stone and threw it at Ernie Levy, followed by several others. In their anger, they aimed badly. Soon Hans Schliemann gave the signal to disperse.

'You coming?' he asked Ilse.

'You in a hurry?' she said coldly.

'You looking at your darling? Watch out, he's crazy.'

'I'm not afraid of him,' Ilse Bruckner said.

Turning towards Hans, she winked conspiratorially and whispered: 'Go on, I'll catch up with you right away.'

'At the corner by the school?' Hans asked.

And at her nod, he glanced strangely at her and turned his back slowly. Soon the gang reached the end of the street. A song rose in the distance. Their voices were fresh and cheerful.

The tears had dried. Slowly the spinning sun slipped back to its natural orbit. Finally it ceased spinning and was still, infinitely far, like a candle in a room. In the meadows, a blackbird took up its song, and the Schlosse lapped among the reeds. Ernie noticed that his friend Ilse had not moved away. Her shoes had a strap with a button. She was wearing her pretty black smock, and her notebooks were on the ground, propped between her ankles. Ernie noticed that her moist eyes and everything that was *glossy* in her hair and face gave her the look of a fish. At the school fancy-dress she had worn a long robe which she could undulate like the tail of a little Chinese fish. There were also many pretty things about her nose and in her hands with their marvellously pink fingers; but no one knew what all those things meant, no one knew what to call them. Ernie smiled at her in delight, and she gazed at him with eyes dilated in fascination, in a curiosity greater than herself. Suddenly, all the green sparkle left her expression, the shadow of a smile passed fleetingly, raised her lip, reached a dimple, faded, disappeared: now the little girl was staring at him from far off, as if at a stranger to be scorned and feared. Then when Ernie looked like coming forward she went pale, stooped, picked up her notebooks, and fled like a graceful arrow in the track of the Pimpfen; twenty yards away she turned and clapped three times. The sun was so low that her silhouette, made sharper by her black smock, was like a sparkling insect in the path of its rays. And then there was nothing.

The sun began to spin again, faster and faster. Sparks leapt from the flaming wheel, shooting through the sky in multi-coloured streaks. Blonde hairs, too, shot away. Ernie pulled up his trousers. The animal in his heart was howling so horribly he was afraid he would die on the spot. As he mentally dug his teeth into the Pimpfen, he understood that he was feeling hate for the first time.

5

WHEN he reached the bridge over the Schlosse, Ernie turned and saw that he was alone.

Quite small, hunched and wrinkled, the stone bridge surmounted the Schlosse with the rustic good nature of an old peasant; tendrils of ivy gave it a flowered beard, straggling down as far as the water. Now and then Ilse and Ernie had leaned on it, to watch time pass interminably between the banks. Tench and gudgeon followed the trail of the hours, and Ilse claimed that all fish disappeared into the sea; otherwise where would they go? Ernie never contradicted her, though he knew that certain delicate species – the bleaks, for example – stopped just at the border, at the frontier between fresh and salt water.

Today the Schlosse seemed motionless in its bed, and the water as transparent and empty as air.

The little boy crossed the bridge and took the path that went down to the river's edge, to the left of the parapet, among the brambles, the nettles, the soft, green tufts of grass on the bank, and the bouquets of yellow flowers blooming in the shadow of the reeds. Half-way down, the pass curved around the famous Rock of Wotan, the Germanic god of War, of Storm, of Lords and Kings. The boulder thrust upward from the bank, ten or twelve feet high, like a cliff. Once, during the time of the republic it was said that working men had dived from its summit every Sunday in summertime. It seemed so profoundly rooted in the earth that it was impossible to imagine it alone, isolated, reduced to itself, like a simple huge stone; it was a granite tree, the stump of an oak, one might have said, still living with all its roots, decapitated but indestructible. Yet Mr Kremer had assured them that the ancestors of the Gentiles had brought it from the mountains, trimmed and chiselled on the spot, and used it as a slaughtering table, for cutting the throats of beasts and men;

the blood ran off into the Schlosse, which carried it as far as the Taunus where the witches of the Brocken came on Walpurgis-nacht and lapped it up: it was a *sacrificial altar* ... Some nights the Pimpfen and the adult members of the Party burned tree trunks on it. People in the Riggenstrasse no longer said 'the Stone', but 'Wotan's Rock' – with much respect. A professor from Berlin had found a swastika under the moss. The newspapers insisted that it was several thousand years old; and Ernie's father, shrewdly, that it was barely the age of a child in the cradle.

Ernie Levy stretched forth his arm and touched the rock with his index finger, cautiously, as if it were a sleeping animal. Then he went on down the slope and walked off ten yards or so in the late sunlight, out of reach of its fantastic shadow. The rows of reeds thinned out along a minute sandy beach. Ernie Levy dropped on one knee and noticed that the shadow of the rock extended on to the surface of the Schlosse, carried along by the movement of the water so that threads of shadow were cast up on the beach. With one knee dug into the sand, he moved a little to the left so that the two shadows, his and the rock's, became one. Leaning over the liquid shadow, from which muddy bubbles rose, he spread out his handkerchief like a raft; it drifted for a few seconds and then sank.

The ripples swirled. Ernie Levy wrung out his handkerchief slowly and started cleaning his forehead.

The metallic stick had opened a gash, that was now caked with dried blood. Ernie Levy swabbed it out with his handker-chief, and then covered it with a nettle leaf. The wound seemed absolutely painless. Running his fingers over his skull, he noted with surprise that it was covered with swollen bumps. Yet he felt none of those bumps, not even his jaw, that had been numbed by Mr Geek's fist. If he was not suffering, then he would never suffer again; the organs of suffering were abolished in him. Out of curiosity he bit into his palm, a deep bite which left toothmarks. In one of the depressions was a drop of blood, which caused him no perceptible pain; he could admire it, as something pretty. 'But the Just Men suffer,' Ernie Levy murmured suddenly.

He cupped his hands and scooped up some water, with which he softened the blood dried on his face and on his naked chest; then he dabbed it with the damp handkerchief, which he rinsed then in the hollow of his hand. The joint shadow of his body and the rock prevented him from seeing the reddened water, soon dissipated in the current. He rose and wiped off his sandy knee. Absolutely nothing stirred within him.

It was shortly after this that Ernie had his first intuition of emptiness. Not wanting to go back along Wotan's Trail, he pushed his way through the nettles on the bank; and from the height of the slope he contemplated the meadows for a moment before setting out across them, calmly, in a ceremonious tread ... Some of the grasses rose higher than his chin; the farther he pushed into the stagnant, infinitely divisible green sea of the meadow, the more it seemed to him that the waves of grass were rising about him as if they intended to drown him, or at least to imprison him by closing behind him instantly, obliterating the wake of his random steps. He could not have said if the advancing waves were swelling to drown him, or if, on the contrary, he was plunging step by step into the sea like someone deliberately abandoning the shore.

When the shore seemed far enough, he stopped and saw by the immensity of the sky that Ernie Levy was a speck of dust lost in the grasses. At that moment he experienced emptiness, as if the earth had split beneath his feet, and while his eyes rejoiced in the immensity of the heavens, these words came sweetly to his lips: 'I am nothing.' The earth around him gave off its odours. All things were fixed, enveloped in the odours of the earth. The silence had that odour, and the exhalations of the sun, and the immutable blue of the sky. A grain of dust struck his cheek and stuck to it; he took it between index finger and thumb, and submitted it to examination. It was a red ladybird, dotted with black, its paws vibrating like tiny hairs; it might have been a jewel, a pinhead cut out of a ruby, with tiny black dots inked in. With infinite gentleness, Ernie Levy set the ladybird on the end of his vertical thumb:

> Ladybird, ladybird, fly away home,
> Your house is on fire, your children will burn.
> One,
> Two,
> Three!

The childhood tradition demanded that when the word 'three' was pronounced, one should blow on the ladybird from behind. The little boy had rounded his lips but, changing his mind suddenly, he raised his index finger and squeezed it violently against his thumb. The insect's pulp cracked between his fingers. Ernie rolled the pulp into a soft, thin twist; then, with a circular movement of his index finger, he transformed the ladybird into a tiny ball, of the consistency of a breadcrumb. It seemed to him that all the emptiness in his heart was there, pinched between those two fingers. But that was not enough: setting this atom of matter in the hollow of his hand, he rubbed it between his palms at great length, until the ladybird was annihilated, leaving only a greyish stain.

Then, raising his head, he realized that the silence had just died.

... The meadow was alive with the rustling of wings, with the movement of grass, with that invisible, heavy quivering of life. The earth itself was seething defiantly. Ernie Levy noticed first a fragile grasshopper, perched on a sod, twitching its legs gently in a ray of sunlight. He leaned forward cautiously, but the grasshopper seemed not at all upset by the menace, and the child conceded that its mandibles were like the industrious nibbling of a rabbit; even better, like the alert tightening of an old woman's jaws. With that thought, he shot a hand forward and caught what he could: he grabbed the insect by one leg, between the palm and the index finger. Ernie Levy bent his thumb and crushed the grasshopper against his palm. Then he made a ball of it, then a greenish colour, abundant this time, which stained his hand right up to his fingers.

The next victim was a butterfly ... Rare are those who appreciate the butterfly at its true value; what generally lowers the butterfly in the eyes of the profane was for Ernie another reason to respect it: that it was born of the caterpillar, and that its beauty was as dust ... Balthazar Klotz collected butterflies. He ran through the fields, tilting the lance of his net; anaesthetized the victim with a flagon of ether; executed it at home, in his own good time, with a pin driven through the geometric heart of the thorax. Balthazar Klotz's room was covered with fragile trophies; examined with a magnifying glass, each of them turned out to be a cathedral, and the beauty of the wings gave them a lifelike character, the illusion of being not yet dead. Ernie would have liked to hunt butterflies for pleasure, the pleasure of seeing them; but it was impossible to release without a broken wing, a golden antenna for ever extinguished, a radiance for ever dead. So he was usually content to approach the marvel in silence, stalking it cleverly, like an Indian, then contemplating it at leisure. As he became stone, some of them fluttered about him, settling on his head, or on a finger, like a ring – a magic ring.

Now the martyr-insect was a Tiger Swallowtail with wings like stained glass. The popular name, Swallowtail, derives from the hind points of its wings, half an inch long: the immensity of its wing-spread gives it the noble flight of a bird of prey.

The Swallowtail landed on a violet; Ernie Levy enveloped the flower and the insect in his still moist handkerchief; and slipping a hand beneath it, he snatched at both things together, the butterfly and the violet, then kneaded them between his already sticky palms. After the Swallowtail came a dragonfly, a giant cricket, a beetle, a minute butterfly with pearly blue wings; other butterflies, other dragonflies, other grasshoppers. Ernie Levy ran through the meadow, arms spread wide, flapping his hands now sticky with vermin ...

Still, he was tired. Each insect's death cost him more. Each death added to the quota of soft filth that was now filling his stomach: viscous trails on his palms, but dismembered insects, seething and suffering, in his own entrails. His heart heavy with these things, he stretched out and closed his eyes, his hands flat against the grass. His belly seemed to sprawl in all directions. The victims began to swarm inside the imperfect night of his eyelids. Under cover of that darkness, the thousand chitterings of the outside world penetrated his ears, flowing insidiously into that pouch where the butterflies and other insects were still suffering. His hands, laid flat out, were dead.

Ernie raised his eyelids and drowned in the vertically falling sky.

Soon the high grasses formed a frame in the middle of which birds were gliding; the sky was swollen with them.

He tried to follow a bird with his eyes, hoping to reach it and to fly off with it. But the birds manoeuvred scornfully, indifferent to his gaze, and the distance between him and them became no smaller. How could he have pretended to reach those heights, to surpass them, even, with his Just Man's awareness, he, a puny rapacious insect, he, crawling on a heavy enormous belly, swarming with its insect nourishment? ... *I was not a Just Man, I was nothing.*

As he thought, I was nothing, the little boy buried his face against the earth and moaned out his first cry; in the same moment he felt astonished that his eyes should be empty to tears. For half an hour he cried out, his mouth against the earth. He seemed to be hailing someone far off, a being buried deep in the earth, from whom he hoped for an echo. But his cries only exaggerated the silence, and the vermin remained lively in his belly. His mouth was full of grass and dirt. Finally he knew that nothing would answer his call, for that call was born of nothing: God could not hear it. It was precisely then that the little boy, Ernie Levy, felt the burden of his body, and decided to get rid of it.

With a slow, heavy step, shuffling through the grass, he went back to the riverside to perform his funeral ablutions. The song of nature no longer disturbed him and, as he walked through the grass his only battle was against Ilse's face. With no emotion whatever he walked by Wotan's Rock. The glue of insects was so adhesive that he had to use sand to clean it from his hands, his fingers, his fingernails now darkened with a greenish ring. A head still clung to the sleeve of his smock; he examined it carefully, and recognized the Swallowtail's salt-like eyes and noble antennae: 'You too,' he thought, 'God has taken you between his hands.' When the water was quiet again he leaned over it to see his own reflection: an outline shimmered; but as his features became clear in the mirror, two drops fell from his eyelids, spreading concentric ripples over his face, which vanished. My tears fall *all by themselves*, Ernie Levy decided; but I am not crying. And when his legs trembled beneath him after he had crossed the bridge and was on the road to town: My legs are trembling, but I am not afraid.

He barely recognized the Riggenstrasse; it was a street, and human beings all walked on two feet. The people (certain people, particularly women) stopped to watch him pass; but he did not look at their faces. Similarly, as he entered the house by the door on the courtyard he did not spare a thought for the creatures whose tenuous, volatile filaments of human speech barely reached him through the veil of the corridor leading to the kitchen. His separation from the members of the Levy family – the kernel of his dead universe – was so complete that it did not occur to him for one moment to say good-bye: all farewells were far, far away.

And yet, half-way up the stairs his legs trembled so shamefully that he clutched the railing, muttering again and again: Who dares to say that you're afraid? Who dares to say that you're afraid? . . .

But the heavy iron-barred door to the attic was already before him, like a threatening creature.

The hinges squeaked; Ernie was afraid their rancorous protest would reach the kitchen through the treacherous partitions. Then when he had pushed open the worm-eaten door, the pressure of the darkness forced him backwards, so that the more adventurous foot suddenly returned to join the other on the landing; the upper part of his body made a vague gesture of retreat, for the darkness, suddenly fluid, was advancing towards him like a tidal wave. But at last the grey and black of the attic resolved into a sea-weedy twilight compounded of the ambiguous light from the landing and the now subtly busy night, that slowly offered him the skylight, with a thin rope hanging from it and holding a naked celluloid doll by the neck, two or three feet above the floor. (It was a game; Moritz and his friends had hanged it by the neck until dead; the doll was Adolf Hitler, thanks to two smears of black crayon under the nostrils. Nevertheless Ernie thought that there was something of Ilse's face in it, and derived a distant satisfaction, like the caress of an interior breeze.)

Then he made out the rows of curved tiles, their ridgebones gleaming like so many black teeth from the sloping roof; and the rubble, the pieces of string, the broken chairs, the old dining-room table (too small since the birth of Ernie's sisters and brothers), the headless teddy-bear, the basin full of dishes, reserved for Passover. Then he made out the whole attic, and he stepped forward to set a chair beneath the skylight . . .

At that very moment an aureole was born in the centre of the window; and the place was invaded by a dust-like light, yellow, tepid, flowing into his throat, and prickling it.

The little boy took the chair squarely by its back and raised it with a feeling that it had come to life at his touch: one of the thing's feet had just struck his knee. He climbed on *her*, hesitantly, stood to his full height and managed to raise the skylight as far as the notch-bar would go; then he gripped the edge of the frame, and tried a classic pull-up. Which is when an athlete raises his body by the pure strength of his wrists, taking a firm grip with both hands on the obstacle to be surmounted, and with a simple pull of his forearms lifts himself to a firm position and brings his knee over the supporting bar. Although Ernie could hardly assume he was fit for such physical triumphs, it seemed to him fair and reasonable that today his body, because of the altogether exceptional circumstances, would innocently submit to his will. But as soon as he was hanging by his hands the frame of the skylight slammed down on his fingers, pinching them to the ceiling. He kicked out wildly, then was happy enough to settle for the shock of a fall; after which, sitting in the dust, he acknowledged that the order of the universe would not yield to his misfortune.

Generally people in his situation hang themselves. Ernie had never wondered why people hang themselves in such circumstances, but now he understood that it was the most practical way. Or else they drowned themselves; for that too was a natural method, requiring few things, and more or less available to anyone. Perhaps he should have thrown himself straight into the Schlosse, a while ago; it couldn't have been so very unpleasant, especially on a fine warm day. He would have been swept along in the current like a piece of wood or a tangle of branches. But now he had to hang himself, since he was unable to get up on to the roof. But to hang yourself you need a rope, a chair, and a running knot; he had no running knot. If you don't use the running knot, you risk dangling at the end of the rope and hurting yourself badly. Feverish again, Ernie took down the doll and noticed that Moritz and his friends had simply tied the rope around its neck, but had not actually hanged it. His fingers numbed with grief, he tried various kinds of running knots; but either the knot fell apart as he pulled at it, so that when he jumped from the chair he would run the risk of smashing to the floor brutally; or else the damned knot tightened when he slipped his wrist through the noose, and became dangerously fixed. Perhaps if he persevered he might eventually perfect a good running noose, but all things considered it was not a very pleasant method. He had retained from his picture books the memory of a hanged man with a thick tongue reaching down over his chin. Of course it was probably just as unpleasant to fling oneself from the roof, but at least there was the jump beforehand; while in a hanging, there was nothing.

Since there was no longer any hurry, Ernie sat down on the chair to think things over; for this was a serious business that deserved to be examined.

The beings and things he loved and knew flowed slowly out of the window opened in his breast: Mother Judith, the patriarch, his father, mother, the second-floor room, Mr Kremer, Moritz, the infants, and the high sun floating above the trees and houses, and Ilse who was dead. Why were all these things leaving him today? And why did he feel heavier and not lighter as they abandoned him? ... It was truly as if he were falling from the sky at a great speed, and nothing but a real fall could stop this dizziness. It was therefore extremely regrettable that jumping off the roof was out of the question, on account of his inability to execute a classic pull-up.

He looked down and rediscovered the shaggy bear of his childhood, the basin full of dishes, the ropes, the heaps of rags, the old dining-room table. A broken chair caught his eye, lying on its back with its one foot smashed upwards. Ernie Levy recognized it and remembered the manner of its death, under one of Mother Judith's heady furies. One could not enter into a piece of wood; and yet Ernie had the inexplicable feeling that he and the broken chair were one.

Perhaps people ended as objects ended? ... No, certainly not, for one never knew how people contrived to die, one never had the slightest idea. Some fine day, generally at the evening meal, Mother Judith announced that So and So 'had passed away in the afternoon'; and then, sententiously, she had offered the name of a disease, as one names the culprit. According to Ernie, all those pretexts of sickness were more or less fallacious. A mere glance clearly showed that all those people had been *carried off*, under the very noses of their relations; for besides their sorrow, a very natural thing (although Ernie had often been intrigued by the extreme desolation of adults in mourning, when they themselves, not being immortal, would inevitably find their loved ones in heaven), the relatives of dead men always looked slightly but characteristically vexed.

Only the Just Men did not die in such a hasty, disobliging manner. The day came when the Just Man bore witness to his justness, and the whole universe cooperated in preparing his death bed: kings fomented invasions, noblemen pogroms. The Just Men need not lift a finger: all was foreseen, organized in its slightest detail, ever since the martyrdom of the holy Rabbi Yom Tov. No lessons could be learned from that, since none of them had tried, like Ernie, to anticipate the will of God.

And in any case neither the Just Men nor the dead and dying of the neighbourhood had ever been in a situation comparable to his own; there was no tuberculosis, no torture, no massacre: there was Ernie in the attic.

The song of a bird filtered through the skylight. Ernie Levy stood up and shook his legs, heavy with cramp: his last chance was to jump out of the small lavatory window, which also overlooked the courtyard. He stepped towards the doorway, but tripped forward: the wound on his forehead and the sharp laceration of his fingers by the frame of the skylight had suddenly blinded him with such a pain – sharp and sombre, more biting than a storm at night – that he was not at all surprised to find himself coming to on the floor. He also noticed the incisive pressure into his temples, which had suffered no violence at all. It all came from that diabolical sweet he had found a short while ago in the lining of his trousers; he had hardly set it on his tongue when the pain started flowing through his veins, under a sickly covering of pleasure. He rose to his feet with a feeling of having grown to such proportions that his head was wobbling, too heavy for the elastic delicacy of his limbs.

The banisters enabled him to control each step. The lavatory was on the floor below, opposite his parents' room. He wondered why tears had begun to streak his cheeks again: my tears fall all by themselves, but I'm not really crying. And when he reached the lavatory door he became almost visually aware of the spasmodic trembling in his legs: my legs are trembling, but I'm not at all afraid.

The lavatory was also a dressing-room; the water-closet was at the end, just beneath the small square window through which the sun beamed directly, like a river immobilized in its rectilinear bed, with a myriad flecks of dust moving gracefully like an infinity of dancing fish. Ernie raised the lavatory seat so as not to dirty it, and then climbed up on the china basin, to reach the small casement. The opening was wide enough for his shoulders, but he would have to hoist himself out head first, let his body swing over and, with the help of his own weight, hurtle down; so that, instead of truly leaping into space, he would simply be letting the window suck him out. Reflecting that he would certainly fracture his skull (which would break like an egg, leaving no trace of his face), he fell to feeling sorry again that he could not leap from the roof in a normal way.

His legs were trembling so much that he was afraid of falling from the bowl on which he was balanced. For several minutes now an evil genius seemed to be installed in his legs, simply to shatter the calm of his soul. No tears flowed from his eyes now; all the enemy uneasiness was in his legs, ordering them to do whatever they felt like. The independent will inside his legs was so far beneath his own superior will that he hardly allowed himself the right to look down at the trembling below. But, fearing that his legs would make him fall from the pan, he decided to step down cautiously, so as to give the sudden disorder in his soul a chance to calm down.

After a minute or so he noticed that he was mechanically scrutinizing the toilet articles on the shelf. As the bar of sunlight did not reach the basin, the objects lay dim in the shadow, composing a single silhouette which the little boy's eye altered, climbing peaks, skimming nonchalantly down their slopes, as it were a mountain range. Shaving tackle caught his eye. It was on the far edge of the shelf, a large part of it hanging out over the precipice. Suddenly his mind was empty of anxiety, his heart empty of fear, and he knew that his legs and eyes were once more his own.

He rose quickly and moved to the shelf. In the box was a packet of unused blades. Each of them was wrapped in a protective envelope. The naked white blade on his palm gleamed like a gem, a cameo. It was a pity that neither the patriarch nor Ernie's father used a straight razor to trim their beards. Just by shaving, certain people managed to cut their throats with an over-hasty gesture. Some claimed that straight razors were so keen that the mere setting of the blade vertically on the skin was enough to cleave the flesh. The action was so easy that one could cut one's throat without feeling even a tickle.

Ernie Levy placed his left wrist on the edge of the basin; he pierced the fragile bluish skin with a corner of the rectangle of steel, cutting as deep a groove as he could. As he withdrew the blade, he was surprised to see a drop of blood like a bead on the corner. Yet he had felt no pain, and his wrist was barely marked by a rosy thread: a mere scratch, was the phrase. He jeered to himself: a mere scratch, and suddenly the groove split into two threads that were even thinner, then spread a few millimetres apart, and opened the way for a continuous flow of blood. So the operation had been a success.

As the blood was staining the tiles, Ernie went back to the lavatory and let his arm drain over the bowl, so as not to make unnecessary work for his mother. His left hand hung down, absolutely red, and the blood flowed from the tip of his middle finger, by the same witchcraft that makes the blood of chickens slaughtered in the ritual abattoir flow through their beaks. Once, Ernie remembered, he had taken a chicken to be killed. At the blow of the razor the chicken struggled savagely at first, then with a kind of bleak despair that shook its wings in floppy jerks; then it ceased to fight, thus showing that it was still alive, since blood is life, is it not so? Ernie had eaten nothing of that chicken, nor of any later chicken or fowl, since there after he knew how they came to his plate ... And no doubt part of his own being would continue to struggle, like the chicken; perhaps that was why his legs were trembling again ...

Now his cramped hand took on the shape of a bloody beak, the open wound in his wrist being the chicken's neck; he waved his thumb against his four clenched fingers, and saw the chicken's beak chop through the air in terror, and its round eye gleam.

At what point would life leave his body? ... That was a most interesting question, and Ernie waited in delicious anguish for the moment when the passage would take place. People all got very agitated about death, because they thought one could see nothing, that it was total silence, and that nothing happens. But Ernie knew very well that that kind of death was impossible. Everything went on as before, with the sole difference that one no longer felt that painful desire to die. It was not so unpleasant, death; and in order to begin a new existence Ernie Levy imagined himself in the form of a bubble, so transparent that spinning in the sunlight it reflected all visible things. But a pin pricked the bubble at once, and he dissolved in thought . . . Then, in his desire to avoid the pin, he decided that death was really a matter of becoming invisible.

'My children,' said the patriarch, standing at the head of the table, dressed in all the pomp of religious occasions, 'my children, our beloved Ernie has left us for a better world. He did not wish to cause us grief, he left us because of the ladybirds and all the things you know of. Where he is now, he is happy, and I am sure that he is looking down upon us. Let us sing, so as not to sadden him.'

'I can't sing,' Mother Judith said.

'Neither can I,' said Ernie's father.

'Nor I,' said Miss Blumenthal.

'I loved him,' Moritz said, sobbing so pitifully that Ernie Levy, seated invisibly on the sofa in the dining-room, felt invisible tears flow from his new eyes and fall to the floor with a splosh, splosh, splosh, inaudible to all ears but his own.

Opening his real eyes, he discovered that the sound was really caused by his blood, falling drop by drop, slowly, as if the reserve stored in his veins were about to be exhausted. An intoxicating sweetness radiated from his wrist so that his whole organism was made languorous by it. Nothing was comparable to that sensation except perhaps the pleasure of strolling along the Schlosse with Ilse and glancing at her surreptitiously. Ernie imagined that once he was dead he would visit his grieving, repentant, inconsolable friend. 'I ask you to forgive me,' Ilse said. 'You're dreaming, my little friend,' Ernie said aloud, while the dripping of his blood slowed . . . splosh . . . splosh . . . splosh . . .That morning Mr Geek had said that after the battle of Verdun the spirits of the dead continued to fight in the air; in the same way Ilse's hand-claps would echo eternally behind the row of houses, and nothing, not Ilse's regrets nor Ernie's death, could make that clapping cease to exist, in every instant, in every hour, as it now echoed in Ernie's ears.

Each drop of blood was a caress to him. But what if he

yielded to that delicious desire to sleep, then awakened more alive than ever? Seized with a wild anxiety he opened his eyes again and realized that his lids had closed without his knowledge, even as he had insidiously slid to the floor and was sitting back against the wall, his naked legs gleaming in a pool of blood, Ilse's applause modulated to an ironic, light music, a music of quick, black insects, shining malignantly, each note buzzing about his ears to swoop and plunge its sting.

In the efforts he made to get up, a spray of blood gushed out. He managed to set one foot on the edge of the bowl; and, pulling with one hand on the frame of window, raised himself high enough to set the other foot beside it. Then he brought his arms together in the attitude of a diver, wriggled half his body through the gaping square of the window, and found himself suspended between heaven and earth. His left arm, dangling against the outside wall, was already trailing blood down to the first floor. Huge birds glided above the chestnut tree; their butterfly's wings, yellow, blue, green, reflected the sun like mirrors. The bird-butterflies swooped by so quickly that his eyes could not follow them; they rose so high above the roofs, the chestnut tree and the little boy, that he made fun of himself gently ... Suddenly the pungent smell of blood vanished, his arm ceased to bleed, the butterflies thinned out, and sing-song, dream-shot words could be heard, as the sun took Ernie's face in its gentle hands they were the words which the patriarch pronounced every Friday night, at the solemn meal that opens the Sabbath of glory and of peace, the words of the Poet: ' *Come, my beloved, to meet your betrothed.*'

... Ernie was already slipping down the wall, his hands high and his head raised, as if he wanted to bind himself for one second to a vision of heaven, or as if he were refusing to see the earth rushing towards him faster than he melted towards it, the earth flying up towards him, oh high-diver, oh dying swan, his skinny arms spread wide like wings ... Ernie had already taken flight, when his feet caught on the window sill, holding him back for an instant by a ridiculous reflex, as if all his will to

BOOK SIX

THE DOG

1

STATISTICS show that the percentage of suicides among
German-Jews was practically nil during the years just before the
end. It was the same in the prisons, in the ghettos, in all the caves
of darkness where the snout of the Beast poked up out of the
abyss; and even at the entrance to the gas-chambers, 'anus of the
world', as a learned Nazi eye-witness called them. But in the
years after 1934, hundreds of little German-Jewish schoolboys
became candidates in suicide; and hundreds of them passed.

So that the first death of Ernie Levy takes its humble place
in the statistics, besides dozens of similar (though more irrevocable) deaths. How admirable, that, when teaching murder
to their Aryan pupils, the schoolmasters should also have taught
the Jewish children suicide; this illustrates the German technique,
its extreme rigour and simplicity, from which no departures are
tolerated even academically.

When Mordecai discovered the child's lifeless body in the
courtyard, at the foot of the wall – a bird blasted in flight, in a
spattering of blood and feathers – he felt he was truly going mad.
His heavy grey eyes remained dry, they weighed like stones in
their sockets. As he approached the body his teeth dug deeper
into his lower lip; one red thread, then two, then three fell along
his squarish beard. He saw that Ernie was lying cheek to the
ground, like a hunting dog, his long curls covering his face
discreetly: Death had overtaken him in a position of sleep.
'Oh Lord, did you not pour him forth like milk? Did you not make
him firm like cheese? Hear me, you covered him with flesh and skin,
you wove him of bone and nerves: and now you have destroyed
him ...' Falling to his knees, Mordecai was shocked at the
buzzing of flies, circling about the thin corpse. One of them,
enormous and greenish, landed greedily on the point of a bone
which had ripped through the skin of the elbow. Mordecai

slipped his arm under the broken body and raised it from its bed of stone and blood. 'Here,' he said to the child in a calm voice, 'I cry out at the violence, and nothing answers.' At that moment the schoolboy's smock lifted, fell, lifted again with the miraculous regularity of a living organism. Mordecai felt a flood of gratitude towards a God so good. He clutched the child to him like a bleeding prey, shot through the living-room and, still in his rough brown dressing-gown, ran through the streets – with all the terrified Levys at his heels. That evening Ernie lay delirious in the hospital at Mainz – Jewish section. They had made a little plaster doll of him. Mordecai thanked God, who had been kind. He thanked him for six months, a year; but when Ernie returned to Stillenstadt, he was obliged to admit that if the Eternal, in his infinite mercy, had restored life to the little angel, he had not restored his soul.

Ernie knew at once that death had set his hand upon his spirit. Of all the suffering that outraged every cell of his body, now imprisoned in a scaffolding of straps, metal supports, and multiple tubes that distilled life through openings cut in the plaster, the most agonizing came from his one eye, as it re-discovered not only the forms and colours of the world, but also its supreme cruelty. At first, in his surprise, Ernie thought that God had withdrawn himself from things, all of which now spread colourless, dimensionless, like cast-off clothing thrown at random into the hospital room. Then he understood that he was no longer seeing them with the lying eyes of the soul. Then, although he could feel his tongue moving normally in his mouth, he decided not to respond to any overtures from this graceless world. 'He's not really awake yet,' Mordecai's voice said. Mother Judith's enormous face floated above Ernie's round eye, and tears glittered on her lashes like diamonds: '*Are you awake, my love?*' Ernie's only answer was to raise and lower his one eyelid ...

And so it was, through an incalculable number of days and nights. No word passed through the orifice contrived in his mask, for Ernie held them all back on his tongue. Only at night, amid the snoring and wailing of his neighbours, he prayed to God to change the government. But his prayer was overheard by a nurse and, as the living took advantage of it and tormented him at every opportunity, he ceased to speak even at night. At about that time, nevertheless, on a day when Mother Judith had been particularly intolerable, he saw her walking off between the rows of white beds, her head bowed, her shoulders shaken by strange tremors, then he felt a tear filter from his eye and get lost under the plaster mask, leaving a gentle trace.

That night for the first time Ernie's past invaded him like a river in flood, with torn tree trunks here and there, babies' cradles floating, animals' bellies, silhouettes on the roofs, Ilse on a boat manned by creatures making horrible faces, and the Levys' poor Noah's ark wandering among the flotsam, all of them raising their arms to God, who looked down inscrutably. The world was going to rack and ruin though no one seemed to notice. Ernie's neighbours carried on their usual conversations, always bearing on their pre-hospital lives, or on the lives they would begin when they got out, as if they had been officially assured that the river outside would politely stop its rush to wait for them. No one noticed that the river was flowing beneath the beds, carrying off the whole hospital in its slow, cruel course. Over the bed opposite, Ernie had noticed two plaques, one above the other; one, made of clay, bore this wide, handsome inscription: The Rothschild Foundation of the Meurthe. The other was a plain piece of yellow cardboard: *Reserved for Jews and Dogs*. But the invalids never referred to the square of yellow cardboard hanging above their beds; they spoke of shops to be lost or saved, of legs, arms, livers, lungs, intestines to be lost or saved, of visas for Palestine and of women and children and food and sunshine and of a thousand things to be lost or saved, as if the river were not lifting all that away with its huge black blade. Be careful, Ernie wanted to say to them, but he was silent, for death kept the words upon his tongue. And when the Levys came to visit, their mouths stuffed with projects, they too, for emigration to Eretz' Israel, with their eyes full of *serious* tears and their hands clenched in hope; Be careful, they're deceiving you, Ernie wanted to say, things are not what they seem, they are this way or that, etc. But he was more silent than ever, for in fact the Levys would have been utterly horrified to discover that muddy river under their feet, instead of the terra firma they imagined – so naïvely, the poor beloved mortals . . . With his one eye, from the wounded depths of his vision, Ernie stared at them now from a terrifying distance, that separated him from them more than the little death preceding his suicide; a distance filled very gradually by an inexplicable resentment rooted in the pity he felt for them despite – *because of?* – their blindness.

It was the same with Ilse, whom he tried in vain to dislike. Often when one bone or another ached, he passed judgement on Ilse in words borrowed from Moritz or from Mother Judith: 'She is a this,' he said with feverish industry, 'She's a that, she deserves this and that, God will rip her to pieces like a fish, etc.' But then he at once saw the swift current carrying her off without her knowledge, and all his judgements of her yielded to the horror of seeing the blonde cockle-shell of his love floating in the common waters, in a musical cry. Even when Ilse's clapping woke him at night, reminding him of the torture in his nerves and his bones, Ernie could do no more than give her a sour and distant thought, softened by commiseration. For Ilse too was being carried off by the wide river.

One day Miss Blumenthal arrived on a visit, leading her rosary of tiny Levys. The sight of Ernie seemed to petrify her. Her nose quivered like a fly in the middle of her face. Then at last she came forward and caressed her son's plaster cheeks, murmuring, 'Everything will be all right . . . You'll be home soon . . . I'll make some farfel soup . . .' Then her hand hung in a dream, and a tear splashed on the mask she could no longer see. Miss Blumenthal's tears were particularly silent and transparent. They had a way of disappearing at the slightest glance, so that Ernie always saw her with a serene face. But that day Ernie saw the drop of light fall and his tongue functioned in spite of himself: 'Everything will be all right,' he said in a harsh, rasping voice which surprised him exceedingly.

But he regretted the words at once; he felt he had just put one foot back into the old comedy.

When he returned to Stillenstadt after two years in bed, his old acquaintances did not recognize him: nothing was left of the little lamb but his curls.

Though emaciated and limping along on crutches, Ernie had come out of his bedridden years taller than Moritz. A barbed white line crossed the upper part of his forehead. A similar scar raised his right eyebrow, stretching the eyelid and making the eye seem now sad, now frozen in horror. The other eye was still as sweetly shaped as ever, but according to Miss Blumenthal who was an expert, 'Those funny little stars, you know, like summer,' no longer glittered in it: the irises were plunged in utter night for ever. As for that rasping, slow voice, so disagreeable to the soul, Benjamin claimed that it was astonishingly like the voice of the young Galician.

'The worst thing,' Mother Judith said, 'is this silence; not a word for three days. No, God shouldn't have . . .'

'All the same,' Mordecai interrupted, 'think what a miracle: if I had not been kept in by a fever, I would never have heard the sound of his fall; and if God had not inspired him with the idea of jumping from the window, he would have bled to death. Similarly, if the hospital in Stillenstadt had accepted him, even though he's Jewish he wouldn't have been taken care of half as well as in Mainz. And finally, if . . .'

Judith weighed in furiously: 'That's enough of miracles, I beg you. They hunt us up and down, children jump out of windows and break their bones and souls; and he shouts about miracles! When will God stop *miraculizing* us like that?'

'Tut tut tut,' Mordecai said reprovingly.

Ernie, who was coming down the stairs, stopped.

'Tut tut tut,' Mordecai repeated.

Now, there exists so vast a multitude of tones, expressions, chants, sing-songs, mimicries, and accents with which the idiom *tut tut tut* may be pronounced, that the Talmudists have distinguished no less than three hundred varieties, more or less debatable. Mordecai had chosen just the *tut tut tut* that could make Ernie's blood rise most quickly to his morose cheeks.

'Lord, they're still just as innocent,' he said to himself in dismay; and afraid of bursting into laughter, he went quickly back to his room where he went on with the boxing exercises he had recently begun. Ever since he had discarded his crutches, he was devoting himself seriously to the plan he had conceived in the meditative immobility of the hospital. He was to achieve a virtuosity by which he could become the defender of the Levys' ark. The latter, he had decided then, would compose his entire universe, from insects to stars. They were pure, gentle and silly, they knew only how to weep and extend their naked hands: he, Ernie, would protect them with his fists. After his return from the hospital he took an exercise-book and, basing his work on the fights he had seen, noted down all the pugilistic problems that might arise. Then in the greatest secrecy, in the first-floor room, he gave himself his first boxing lesson. There was, he had discerned immediately, a subtle way to deliver a blow, taking advantage of the whole body's momentum which, it seemed, nothing could stand up to. And dodging sharply to the side would avoid hostile blows. Etc., etc. At night he went over his notes mentally.

Several months afterwards, judging that he was in good fettle, Ernie escorted his brother Jacob to school. The first battle took him by surprise. He had the enemy – a very young Pimpfe – well in the path of his 'jab', and all he had to do was to bring his arm back slightly in order to give the blow all the desirable force. But just at that moment, he was not sure how, an enemy fist hit him full in the face. In his fall he thought that he must have forgotten something; then he stopped thinking altogether and realized that he was on his feet again, using both his fists with precision, and even both his feet, which he had never bothered to train. That first victory made him so happy that he took pity on his fleeing enemy. 'You beat him, you beat him,' Jacob kept shouting, ecstatic at his mysterious elder brother's technique.

'Yes, I beat him,' Ernie said in a strange tone.

Two days later, during a rear-guard battle, he saw a corner of the sky, very high; immediately he looked one of his assailants straight in the eyes and, thinking that they were all boys like himself, swept along in the wide river under the round, immutable eye above, he inexcusably let his arms dangle beside his body ... And this mishap occurred again. At a distance he seethed with splendid ardour; but in the fire of combat, and as soon as the *large thought* was on him, he would lay down arms forthwith. When Jacob complained, he forced himself to hate, trained himself to it. One by one he enumerated all the past and present reasons for hating the Pimpfen; but it seemed to him that even if those reasons were as numerous as the stars in the sky they would not rouse him to the feeling he needed. He went so far as to repeat to himself that the Pimpfen were animals with human faces, and he managed to believe it. But some small detail always came along to crumble the fine edifice: a child-like glance, a pout, or simply a patch of sky intruding upon the fight. So then he devised a stratagem of astonishing subtlety. When he was escorting Jacob, he would narrow his eyes slightly, so as to see all things through a mist; but then he realized it was impossible to hate a silhouette.

All this worried Ernie greatly, particularly with regard to the future of the fragile ark commanded by the patriarch. Flashes of shame shot through him. He considered himself a traitor to the cause of the Levys. His tongue became heavy again.

2

On 6 November 1938, a Jewish adolescent, Herschel Grunspan – whose parents had just been deported to Zbonszyn – bought a revolver, learnt how to use it, went to the German Embassy in Paris, and shot the First Secretary Ernst von Rath as a sacrificial victim. The news went through the Jewish hearts of Germany like a train of powder. The faithful barricaded themselves hastily and cast their most heart-rending prayers heavenward: then they waited for the storm. At Stillenstadt, around five in the afternoon, the first group of Nazi hunters appeared.

That night the whole Levy family pressed together around the small tripod stove in the kitchen, the last vestige of a vanished comfort. On the table the old oil lamp brought from Zemyock smoked without conviction; and while waiting for the string beans, the only course, the babies nibbled greedily at the chestnuts that Mother Judith respectfully extracted from the peat fire. Their faces were tired, their clothes frayed and thin, and chronic hunger kept the children quiet in spite of the close quarters.

Ernie appeared in the doorway, his face blue and crowned with snow. 'Moritz, father, grandfather, Mother Judith,' he counted off calmly. Then, casting a worried glance at the little ones, he motioned the adults to follow him into the living-room.

'And me?' Miss Blumenthal said.

Mechanically, Ernie raised his index finger to his brow and caressed the scar that ran like a pink line back to his temple. In his jacket cut from a blanket, and with the down shadowing the lower part of his face, pale and ravaged now as Mother Judith's, and with the slow, positive, meditative movement of his wide, moist, black eyes, he looked like a young Jewish workman from Warsaw or Bialystok; his beret was set squarely on the back of his head, like a skull-cap.

'No, mother, not you,' he said with a sad smile, 'this is for the grown-ups.'

The said grown-ups moved into the darkness of the living-room where Ernie, raising a corner of the curtain, showed them a reddish glow across the street, at the entrance to a hallway. A brief spark sprang out a bit further along, replaced immediately by the red dot that a cigarette makes at night.

'There are more of them,' Ernie said. 'You see, there, and there . . .?'

'Are they after us?' Mother Judith asked.

. 'Who else?' Ernie said. 'They're waiting for a signal . . . But here, I found some iron bars.'

'*For whom?*' Mordecai asked coldly. 'Neither iron nor fire will shield us from the hands of God. Let us eat.'

They went back to the kitchen. Miss Blumenthal, who had been listening at the door, retreated blushing. The meal was particularly silent. A gusty wind had passed, leaving rents of black air which did not favour conversation. Mother Judith had one eye on her plate, and the other, tender and brooding, on the frightened children; the old man was of marble, now and then emitting a growl made of falling rocks, like a great stone statue; Benjamin Levy was calculating the pros and cons of heaven knows what; and Miss Blumenthal served the meal averting her large dark eyes of a suffering female. And the little ones, aware of the threat, made themselves minute, non-existent.

Even the presence of God at the head of the table would not have induced Mother Judith to hold her tongue: 'Here's the table,' she said with emphasis, 'the bread, the knife . . . and none of us can eat.'

'What can we do?' Miss Blumenthal sighed; her lips were compressed in anxiety; 'won't God have pity on the children?'

And as she threatened to pursue that plaintive reproach to the Divinity, the patriarch interrupted her sharply: 'God does what God sees fit, but a penny in an empty bottle goes clink, clink.' And the old man stared at her with such severity that there could be no mistaking what he meant by the empty bottle; contrite, she returned to the stove, her kingdom.

269

'Ai, Ai,' Mother Judith wailed suddenly, 'Mrs Wasserman said that there isn't a country in the world that wants us Jews! Even the bits of savage territory, in Africa, in Asia, and I don't know where, won't give us visas. And Mrs Rosenberg said to Mrs Wishniak this morning that the English won't let more than two hundred Jews a month into the Holy Land. You hear that, from the whole world, two hundred Jews a month; and how many German and Austrian Jews, alas; and how many Levys? And that isn't all, they say that these merchants in human life only take the rich ones; at the border everyone has to show at least a thousand pounds. So you see, our visa . . .'

'There's no border,' Benjamin said. 'It's only the sea.'

'You want a sea, do you? I'll give you the sea,' the old woman flamed bitterly. 'It costs a thousand pounds, my friend. And how would I know, an idiot like me, whether they walk on land or on water in America, and in Africa, and in Asia? All I know, and all that matters to me, is that you need a thousand pounds to get there. Yes, for a poor Jew, land or sea, America or Palestine, the sun or the moon, it's all the same: one thousand pounds. God, God, God, the proverb is right after all: The poor man is followed everywhere by his poverty. Where can we go if we have to leave – down to the bottom of the sea with the little fishes?'

'And France?' Benjamin asked in a voice entirely devoid of irony.

'Oh, my beloved, oh, wretches that we are! In France it's another story altogether: Mrs Wasserman says that the French don't like the Germans one bit, not one bit!'

'But we're not really German,' Miss Blumenthal said innocently; 'are we not Jews?'

Benjamin could not help smiling at her naïvety, which always delighted his contemplative spirit, for he respected all the Creator's fantasies: 'Little woman, oh my own little woman,' he answered her gently, as his parents restrained their laughter, 'do you know, to the Germans we are only Jews, and to the French only Germans. Can you understand such a thing? Everywhere we are what we should not be: Jews here, Germans there . . .'

'. . . and poor in either place!' cried Mother Judith, who found it difficult to let go an idea.

Miss Blumenthal was wailing, 'My God, what a little head I have, *what a little head!* Well then, what can we do?' she added crossing her long hands over the chronic roundness of her belly, as if to calm the child within her.

'Wait a little longer,' the patriarch said.

'Cry out,' Benjamin said wryly. 'As they did in Proskurow.'

'Mercy me,' Mother Judith exclaimed, 'that man would make a joke on the guillotine!'

At those words Mordecai rose heavily and, leaning forward, with his hands together like a farmer's wife chasing chickens before her, he sent all the children out of the room in the charge of Ernie, who carried the candle. Then, closing the kitchen door, he trained the heavy anguish of his grey eyes upon Judith: 'It's not altogether a joke,' he explained in some embarrassment. 'The Jews of Proskurow cried out for seven nights. Yes, the Rabbi of Cszeln told me that the houses in the ghetto were one great cry from top to bottom. It was the Cossack Shelgin. He came every night with his White Guards. May God forget even his name – and so, whole streets cried out, one after another; they could hear our Jewish women several miles from the town. But the miracle was this: the bandits came and then went . . . because of the cries. The story is quite famous, you know,' he finished anxiously.

Miss Blumenthal's hands flew to her throat: 'And . . . and the seventh night?' she choked out.

But neither the patriarch nor Benjamin seemed to have heard her question; and doubtless they judged it unfitting to describe what happened in Proskurow, towards the end of the year 1918, on the seventh night of the Jewish clamours . . .

There was a silence.

'Do you know, I'm beginning to be really afraid,' Mother Judith said, smiling at her daughter-in-law. 'And I wonder, wouldn't it be better to be Germans in France than Jews in Germany? I know, it's a choice between the rope and the gallows, all right. But all the same . . .'

With his elbows on the table and his head resting on the heavy pedestal of his hands, Mordecai seemed to be staring off into some ultimate nothing. Suddenly he murmured with a haggard look: 'Night is falling and those beasts are prowling outside ... And our children ... our children ...'

'Do you want me to go out and have a look?' Moritz asked.

'No, no, that would be a luxury which ...' Then he returned to the conversation, plucking the thoughts one by one from his head, with the physical pain of old men remembering: 'Yes, we were talking about leaving for France,' he murmured confusedly, 'right, right? I don't think we ought to run yet. Tomorrow the Germans will calm down and the French will take up the sword of God; what did we gain by leaving Zemyock? As it is said, the wicked serve God's purposes, and all that happens is a punishment; and what then, would you escape him? (Blessed be his name throughout the centuries: Amen.) I know the Germans, and they are not altogether savages, they aren't Ukrainians; they'll take everything, but not our lives. So I say to you: Patience, children, prayer and patience.'

The old man interrupted himself suddenly and threw a brief glance of anguish towards the door.

'Ha, ha,' Judith burst out bitterly, 'I know the Germans, ha, they're not savages, not Ukrainians ...' And then as if she too wanted to forget her fears, she went on in mounting anger: 'Ha! you men, you talk and you discuss and the truth flows from your mouths like honey. I may not be *intelligent*, myself; but may I be turned inside out if you've said one sensible word tonight! And may I choke on my own bile here and now if ...'

'Enough,' Mordecai cut in. Pulling at his beard, he muttered indignantly, 'On such a night ... swearing like that ...'

Judith was afraid to look at the cold Jewish despair on his face; nevertheless she leant across the table and caressed the old man's forehead with a maternal finger, murmuring tenderly, 'Nothing will happen to them, believe me. What can happen to children? And I'm sorry for what I just said, my friend, my old friend ... It will never happen again, never again!' And carried away by her burst of good will, she added innocently: 'May I turn into a toad if I ever swear again!'

Mordecai shrugged in resignation. 'No, no,' he said, 'swear all you want, I beg of you.' He rubbed a hand across his eyes, that were pale with fatigue; then suddenly dug his lumberjack's fist into his pockets, as if to hide his face from the light. 'Children,' he murmured in a strange voice, 'my dear children, there are days when I myself don't understand the will of God too well. For a thousand years, on this land of Europe, how many of our women and children have been martyred – not with the peaceful awareness of the Just Men, but like terrified little lambs? And what good,' the old man went on in great grief, 'is suffering which does not serve to glorify the Name? Why all the *useless* persecutions?' The old Jew gave a raucous sigh, then corrected himself harshly: 'But after all, are we not the tribute of suffering that man ... uh ... offers to God? Praised be his name ... Oh Blessed ...'

'Ah, my dear father!' Benjamin said then, broken-hearted, 'if all that were God's will, who would not rejoice? But I think we are the prey of the wicked ... a mere prey. And tell me, my venerable little father, does the chicken rejoice that it serves to glorify God? No, and you know it very well, the chicken is altogether sorry – and *reasonably* so – to have been born a chicken, slaughtered a chicken, and eaten a chicken. There is my opinion of the Jewish question.'

'The Messiah ...' Mordecai began without conviction.

'Ah! the Messiah,' Judith said sharply, her head nodding suddenly and her eye dreamy. 'Yes, yes, you're right, my friend, perhaps the Messiah is about to descend. Who knows ... today, tomorrow. We need help so much, and if he does not come, who will help us? Do you know, my doves, I feel something in the air ...'

'Maybe he's behind the door,' Miss Blumenthal said.

Mechanically, all the Levys turned towards the Messiah.

On 10 November 1938, at one-twenty in the morning, Joseph Heydrich, chief of the Gestapo, announced to each of his sections by telegram that anti-Jewish demonstrations were 'to be expected' throughout the Third Reich. At two in the morning, beneath a sheet of frigid sky, a strident cry rose in the centre of a tightly

273

coiled Stillenstadt, a cry which persisted, which unfurled in the streets to the gleam of dozens of torches, like so many hateful eyes. It might have been a night-time carnival. Above the Jews was the emptiness of a winter sky, and around them was only crime. The shouts seemed to echo from house to house, a dialogue from hell. The Riggenstrasse sparkled as if in broad daylight. A wall of fire, composed of all the Jewish libraries in the street, shot skyward in purgatorial flame. Machines, bolts of cloth, even the cradle of the last-born Levy, all of Benjamin's shop was scattered over the sidewalk, delivered up to the rush for spoils. On watch behind a curtain, Benjamin declared himself *above all* grieved to recognize an old customer; savage beasts, the patriarch stated in learned tones.

When the first shocks of the batterimg ram shook the door at the end of the hallway, Benjamin suggested nailing more planks across it; and then when Mordecai simply shrugged, the two men made for the attic where the rest of the family was already huddled. Mordecai turned the key in the lock. A dusky glow filtered through the skylight on to the Levys, frozen into statues by the intense fear which made Miss Blumenthal's teeth chatter in the darkness, and the children tremble, gathered at her skirts; while Mother Judith, pressing a handkerchief gently over the mouth of the infant in her arms, muted the baby's gurgling. The noise downstairs grew louder, swelled, burst in a shattering of glass. Mordecai went to the stack of sacred books and with blind fingers made sure once more that no scripture had been abandoned to the looters. As the patriarch had ordered, Ernie held the scrolls of the Law in his arms; the same scrolls confided to the Levys' care after the synagogue had burned. Mordecai set the horns of his phylacteries on his forehead, girded his wrists with the holy thongs, and covering his head with the great prayer-shawl sat, his lips alone in motion – a sleeping mountain in profile against the shadow of the attic. Little Jacob felt a scream rising to his tongue ... 'Mother,' he groaned suddenly, 'I think I'm going to scream. Will you put your hand over my mouth?'

Ernie saw Miss Blumenthal's gesture vaguely, and then a shout blanketed everything: 'They're upstairs!' cried a piercing voice on the stairway. Ernie set the scrolls of the Law on the floor and picked up one of the iron bars he had provided for the occasion. When he saw this, the patriarch stepped towards him and slapped him. 'For life,' he said, 'would you lose all reasons to live?' Blows resounded against the attic door. There followed a lively exchange of words, and the voice of the Riggenstrasse's old mattress-maker came through the panel, bleating and begging:

'Listen, Mr Benjamin, they're *all worked up*, at least you must give them some prayer books for the fire in the street. At least you must give them that, Mr Benjamin . . .'

'Just the books?' Benjamin asked.

'The books first,' said a mocking voice.

'No,' the mattress-maker's voice interrupted, 'just the books and that's all. Over my dead body . . .' he began; then his voice was lost in the growing altercation on the landing.

Mordecai stooped down, picked up the iron bar Ernie had dropped, and with a slow but astonishingly supple step reached the door of anguish. His head was erect, he seemed larger, his shoulder rolled lightly, and when he turned towards the huddled, whimpering group in the shadow, Ernie noticed that his teeth, exposed in a grimace, gleamed silvery, while a sort of harsh laugh emerged uninterrupted, mingled with the half-insane statements he was making: 'For a thousand years, ha, the Christians have been trying to kill us every day, ha ha! And we have been trying to live every day, ha ha ha! And every day we manage it somehow my lambs. Do you know why?'

He was suddenly tall against the door, and he held the iron bar high above his head, and his phylacteries and laces of prayer-shawl fell to the floor in his anger: 'Because *we never give up our books*,' he cried with awesome strength. '*Never, never, never!*'

'. . . We prefer to give up our lives,' he added while the iron bar, swung like an axe, split the door with a deafening crash. 'We'll give you our lives, ha ha,' he finished in that same delirious tone, mingled of violence and an incomprehensible note of despair.

Then he withdrew the iron bar and stood firmly before the gashed door, his legs wide like a woodcutter drawing strength and

firmness from his axe. A flash of light came through the jagged
hole in the door. The clamour echoed again, but this time on the
stairway, and as if hesitant and dulled. Sweat gleamed on the
patriarch's cheekbones and on the points of his thick moustache;
then Ernie noticed that it was not sweat but tears; the patriarch
was sobbing sadly as he murmured, 'But the shame of it, at my
age, the shame of it . . .'

Ernie remembered these minutes all the more clearly because,
resigned to his own confusion and terror, he drove fear from his
mind by a meticulous inventory of the setting and the characters.
So, at the end of Benjamin Levy's nose, the pearl of real sweat, as
torturing as those cackles of death on the stairway; more frightening, as it gleamed, than the paving stone that suddenly won
the battle with the door; more baleful, finally, than the silence in-
augurated by the end of the pogrom.

3

ON 11 November 1938, at Buchenwald alone, over ten thousand Jews were welcomed with the customary refinements while a loudspeaker proclaimed: 'Any Jew desiring to hang himself is requested to be kind enough to put a piece of paper bearing his name into his mouth, so that we can tell who he was.' On 14 November the entire Levy family, flying the pennon of the wanderer, crossed the bridge at Kehl, carrying in their hands all that remained of their worldly goods.

But six weeks later the Levys saw their pogrom as a frankly providential nudge; Mother Judith saw in it nothing less than the hand of God. The distant reason was that everything under the skull-cap of the heavens that called itself a democracy was paying Germany back in her own coin and condemning her, by way of punishment for her anti-Semitism, to keep her Jews. The punishment was brilliant, for it was applied at the precise moment when Nazism, outraged or suffocating with Yiddishness, opened Hamburg to Yiddish emigration. Flooding into the port in tens of thousands, the German-Jews hammered painfully against democracy's order of the day: No visa. A few handfuls set sail anyway; in the name of humanity they were not sunk, but were permitted to die at anchor in London, Marseilles, New York, Tel Aviv, and Malacca and Singapore and Valparaiso and at any anchor they wished.

Since democratic regulations did not provide for funerals, pious German-Jews buried each other for better or worse in the sea. Only the natives of the island of Borneo, always Epicurean about new heads, granted the privilege of burial; but retaining – as the only condition imposed – the right to skim off the handsomest 'beards' of the lot. Called into telegraphic consultation, a famous New World Talmudist sliced (if the phrase is permissible)

277

the Gordian knot in this manner: 'Let them cut; God – blessed be his name – will put everything back in place.'

An ark in a modern deluge, the *St Louis* sailed around the world twice without evoking one flower for its women, one smile for its children, one tear for its old men. The democracies refrained from any vulgar show of emotion. After a pleasant cruise, the whole group returned by way of Hamburg to end its days in the motherland. Never in history had an embargo been so admirably observed. And long live democracy, cried the democracies. And immediately: Down with demobolshoplutojudeonegromongol . . . ocracy! brutally answered by the little corporal who, out of spite, 'dealt with' a hundred thousand Jews immediately, beginning with those from the *St Louis*. Shocking, shoooocking, the *Times* editorial ululated in answer; and, with the honourable intent of initiating this improperly constituted regime to the rules of international cant, the Royal Navy sank, eight fathoms deep, a small ship full of Jewish children which had ventured within the territorial waters of the Britannic mandate of Palestine: *but after the customary warnings.*

'Are they then everywhere, the Nazis?' Miss Blumenthal asked.

At least the Barbarians had not reached the balmy banks of the Seine, where the hours still passed so peacefully that the Levys were appalled. How could such oases exist? So God was tracing lines of demarcation upon the earth, decreeing: Here you will be hanged at any time of day, and there only at mealtimes; farther on your heads will be cut off, and elsewhere it will be France . . .?

'What a stupid vegetable I am,' Benjamin said.

'How do you mean?' Mother Judith asked.

'If I had chosen France, in Warsaw, in 1920, we would have flown without noticing it, right over a desert of tears and blood. We would never have known Stillenstadt and its delights. And yet I was offered France on a platter, like an egg from the Garden of Eden. And I said, no, I can't stand that kind of food, it doesn't agree with me. A stupid vegetable . . .'

'We would have been spared,' Miss Blumenthal said, 'all the misery we've been through.'

Benjamin stared wide-eyed at her; Mordecai said smiling, 'If you hadn't chosen Germany, you would never have met the young Galician, who would never have established you in Stillenstadt, where you would never have come to know a certain Miss Blumenthal, who would not have given you the handsomest children in the world. Now we have all that, *plus* France. Blessed be the name of him who lives in eternity. Amen.'

These considerations saw the light in a trim little summerhouse in the suburbs of Paris, where the Jewish Committee of Welcome were sheltering, as well as they could, a dozen or so refugee families. The town was called Montmorency, the house bore the name of 'Hermitage', and the city clerk was intent on making the exiles believe that it had once sheltered a vague colleague *entitled* Jean-Jacques Rousseau. But even the proximity of more illustrious shades, such as those of the great Maggid of Zloczow, or of Rabbi Yitzak of Drohobicz, would not have inhibited the survivors from savouring the exquisite, downy warmth which reigned in the garden at all hours of the day, under the leafy bower that sheltered the old stone bench where the women knitted with both fingers and mouths, heaving a long, solemn, grateful Jewish sigh at a well-turned stitch or a well-turned phrase. Still, one of the women admitted, if I were to learn that, well, for example the Baal Shem Tov in person, or the gentle rabbi Abraham the Angel, or some Just Man from Zemyock had sat here on the very spot where we have our behinds, I'd probably drop dead from shame. Mother Judith said nothing.

The whole group lived on subsidies extracted from the Paris Consistory. Mother Judith was particularly admired. She requisitioned with such authority, mingling threats and prayers, the heart of God and the lightning of the last judgement, that there was no office from which she did not commandeer something edible. And remember, she would say on the threshold as she left, it is your place to thank me. For it is written: that which you give, God will return to you a hundredfold. All I say is, until the next time . . .

But these manoeuvres cost her more than she ever admitted and it was not without a tear or two that she learned of Benjamin's employment in a Jewish tailor's workshop. Moritz followed him shortly, in the same establishment, as a presser and apprentice mechanic. And then Ernie, promoted to the rank of bicycle messenger. They lived then in such abundance that they ate only when hungry. Even Moritz, with his insatiable belly, who at first wouldn't move unless he was loaded down with snacks – he even stored them inside his shirt – would nowadays only occasionally draw a croissant from his pocket and give it a nostalgic nibble. Every morning, followed by the admiration of the whole house, the workers went to the Montmorency station and took that small, dusty blustering train that the French called *tacot*, to distinguish it from the one that goes from Enghien-les-Bains into the City of Light. The *tacot* had the great advantage of being a double-decker, with an upper level of seats, so that pitching and rolling fearfully it encouraged a Jewish imagination to sail without risk upon a furious ocean. People stared a bit at our three heroes, but no one insulted them, and no one seemed to be holding back a desire to spit in their faces. Coming back, they could go into any old bakery, now one and now another, to vary the pleasure, and without the slightest hitch buy some of those milk rolls so fragrant with French flour, so intoxicating to savour on top of a rackety little train while the countryside unrolls at your feet like an honorific carpet. And then, heartwarming thing, sometimes an old commuter would nod amiably; and they would return his greeting, all airs and graces; and Benjamin would squeeze his sons' hands tightly (both of them were a head taller than he was), as he whispered in Yiddish, in a tone implying that this was the ultimate revelation: 'My little pigeons, this is the life.'

Sometimes on Sunday Ernie accompanied the patriarch to reunions of the Paris Association of the Elders of Zemyock. The Association comprised seventeen members at that time; but as there was not room for them all in the narrow premises which served as a social hall, the reunion took place partly on the premises, partly on the staircase, and partly on the sidewalk of the Rue des Ecouffes. Since he came only under the old man's protection, Ernie never got past the staircase. But while the patriarch

palavered majestically in the 'office', and for the nth time refused
the presidency of the association, Ernie mingled with the com-
monalty on the sidewalk, snatching at gossip, memories, gilded
anecdotes of Zemyock which, to hear the refugees, was a great
metropolis, a true city of light, beside which Paris evoked only
ridiculous epithets. But occasionally the gossip bore on events in
Germany, Austria, Czechoslovakia, and the 'evil of the times'
would pierce Ernie's ribs like a needle.

'Do you know what,' someone said then, 'we would rather
talk of something gay: what news of the war?'

Ernie laughed too, but the needle pressed gently into him down
the tautness of his throat; you mustn't think, he said as he
laughed, you mustn't see, you mustn't hear *the cries*.

Knowing that everyone was waiting for her, the war made a
queenly entrance. But she was preceded by sinister heralds; a
multitude of gas-masks tha⁺ the workmen on the *tacot* slung over
their shoulders like new-style bagpipes. When it appeared that
the refugees at the Hermitage – all of whose passports were
adorned with a swastika, though bearing the further decoration:
Jew – were not to be included in the distribution of these salutary
snouts, a great cold fell upon the Levys. 'There we go again,'
Benjamin said. 'What a great God is ours,' Mother Judith declared, 'and how oddly he runs the world!' 'And you,' Mordecai
said to her, 'what a big mouth you have; and how often you
open that mouth; and do you know what comes out of your
mouth? Fire and flame, sulphur and pitch!' But when the sum-
monses came streaming in, and the police visits, the searches, the
veiled interrogations, he had to admit that in the eyes of this na-
tion so nearly at war, the gentle Levys of Stillenstadt had begun
to look terribly like enemies. In August came the first notices in-
culcating fear: Be careful, enemy ears are listening ... No one
now nodded to the three foreigners on the *tacot*. First it was gossip, murmurs. The word 'internment' was on every lip, but no
one dared pronounce it. One day the three travellers found the
little train seething. Newspapers were changing hands. War had
been declared.

In the great hall at the Gare du Nord, Ernie felt slightly sick; Moritz offered to escort him home, but at Ernie's repeated entreaties they left him in a bistro. But as soon as his brother Moritz and his father Benjamin had left him, their figures through the glass merging with the grey and blue crowd of suburban workmen, as soon as they disappeared, finally, from his field of vision, Ernie stood up, his eyes uneasy but his body suddenly hard and sharp. Half an hour later he passed through the gate of the barracks at Reuilly and took his place in the cosmopolitan line of volunteers.

'You're lucky,' the sergeant-major said. 'You're just within the age limits.'

'Luck like that,' Ernie said, 'is pretty rare.'

'You're sure you want to be a stretcher-bearer? You know, they don't give you a rifle.'

'I know that,' Ernie said. 'I don't mind.'

'All right. What instrument do you play?'

With his pen waiting, the soldier stared imperturbably at the pink enlistment form; if he wants to make jokes, Ernie said to himself, let's make jokes.

'The drum,' he said with forced gaiety.

'There's nothing to laugh about,' the sergeant-major said, 'Next.'

Outside, a little old lady pinned a starched, patriotic patch on his chest; as he thanked her and made off in confusion, she held him back by a sleeve: 'That'll be one franc twenty-five, it's a Napoleon badge.'

He was back in Montmorency before noon. The city clerk opened wide eyes but yielded to the rather extraordinary requests of the glorious conscript. In his desire to avoid any chance meeting, Ernie covered the five miles to Enghien on foot. A few flags striped the house fronts, and patriotic carnival noises came from windows open on the infinite tenderness of the sky, where small white clouds seemed to drip their milky peace upon the tiny houses at war. A little girl clapped as he passed. Ernie remembered the tricolour badge on his lapel; let's see, he said to himself, what sensations having a country procures for you ... A circle open-

282

ed about him on the train to Paris. An imposing lady leaned towards her neighbour and, contemplating Ernie Levy's devastated features, remarked acidly, 'You can't tell if he's going off to the war or coming back . . .' Someone shut her up. Ernie smiled.

He found himself in the bistro again, across from the Gare du Nord, and sat at the same table, where the secret farewells had taken place.

With the end of one finger he rubbed the corner of the table where three hours earlier Moritz's stubby, reddish, square hand had lain. The proprietress brought him paper, pen, and an envelope, and said, 'Well, *poilu*, you writing to your sweetheart before you go?'

'It's a military necessity, isn't it?' Ernie said in his strange accent, with the fleeting vowels of Yiddish rivalling the slow German palatals.

He started a first letter, but tore it up when he saw how his handwriting wavered. When he had conquered the trembling of his hand, the rapid, disorderly flight of his thoughts made a third attempt necessary. Then, taking great pains with each of the beautiful Hebrew characters, and repressing every movement of his soul, he wrote the following letter: 'Dear Parents, Grandparents, Brothers and Sisters, all well-beloved. Once more I am making you suffer. When you receive this letter I shall be in French barracks. Don't ask me how it happened, ask me no questions, ask me nothing. Moritz and father know that this morning I felt dizzy; when I felt better I took a walk and the walk led me to a barrack and there the madness fell upon me. Afterwards it was too late; hard as I pleaded with the general to return my enlistment form, he refused, the contract was signed. It is a madness that all the wisdom in the world could not resolve; so ask yourselves no questions, cease to torture yourselves, madness merits only silence. You know well that I love you and that leaving you is no pleasure for me. You must never say: Ernie didn't love us. I think that I wanted to go to war because of the Germans and because of what they did to me. But don't worry, grandfather, above all don't worry; I shall not forget that there are men opposite me; and besides I am a stretcher-bearer, I carry no rifle, I carry only men. Don't forget to give Miss Golda Fischer the volume of Bialik's poetry. Apologize to her for me about page 37 where I turned the corner down without thinking. And now something for you, venerable grandfather. I know how much I must have made you suffer since the business of the grocer's wife. I know it in my fingertips. But often it seems to me that the evil that I do is much greater than the evil which is really within me. Listen, you know what, let's talk about something gay: What news of the war? Forgive me for that joke, but I think it's good to laugh with at least one eye. Your son, grandson, and brother who loves you and kisses you and takes you in his arms with all the strength of his soul, and venerates all of you, and asks all of you once more to forgive him. Ernie. P.S. In this envelope you will find eight certificates from the city clerk. For each of you there is the proof that your son, grandson, or brother has enlisted in the French army. Take good care of them because with these you too are a little bit French, and they won't be able to put you into a concentration camp. At least for once a little good will come out of all the evil and, seeing that the madness is already upon me, at least nothing will happen to you. Let the madness do some good anyway, in return for all the suffering that I cause you today. But it's too late, because I signed my name. Your respectful and loving and sorrowful, Ernie.'

4

FORTY-EIGHT hours after this relatively inglorious volunteer
had enlisted into the French army, he became once again aware
of his limitations, in the ranks of the 429th Foreign Infantry
Regiment. Sergeants born in Dresden or Berlin trained irritated
glances upon him; and the lieutenant, a Burgundian as gnarled
as a root from his native vineyards, warned them bluntly:
He wanted none of that nonsense about the foreigner-draped-in-
the-folds-of-the-tricolour; they had better watch their step;
and consequently they were confined to quarters until further
notice.

Like colonial troops, the 429th Foreign Infantry Regiment
turned up regularly on the field of honour. Between battles
Ernie banged stoically on a drum in the regimental orchestra;
all musicians, apparently, were not stretcher-bearers, but all
stretcher-bearers were required to be musicians. In that strange
May of 1940, a letter reached Ernie on the Ardennes front,
announcing the internment of his parents, brothers and sisters,
grandfather, and even Mother Judith. It was from a neighbour
of theirs in Paris, who excelled in pointing out that the thing was
sad; and that it was painful.

All the more so, he went on, in that the precaution, though
it had struck the Levys, was not aimed at them in the least; to
tell the truth, no offence had been intended by the said 'thing'
and they had been locked up only to keep to the letter of the
law. Besides, Ernie, must, in all logic, admit that if German-Jews
were Jews, they were no less German: and it was customary in
France, etc. A letter from his father followed: less serene. The
camp at Gurs was described with great restraint, but Ernie
logically deduced from that letter that what was customary in
France conformed at times to the best German tradition. So he

yielded to the truth of Benjamin Levy's concluding remark: *To be a Jew is impossible.*

Simultaneously the letter from Gurs aroused the analytic verve of the captain, who read his foreigners' mail willingly: 'It's in code!' he thundered desperately. 'It might as well be Hebrew for all I can make of it.'

'It *is* Hebrew, captain,' Ernie said without malice; but with a touch of a Yiddish accent.

Amazement, questions, it must be translated. By chance Nightingale Company also boasted its Jew; they looked for him, they found him, and in all essentials he confirmed Ernie's version.

'And yet, Major,' the second Hebrew specified. 'There's just one thing, a very little thing . . .'

'In the eyes of France there are no little things; speak, soldier!' the officer cried, stern and dignified.

'It's just this, General,' the Second Hebrew said, deeply disturbed. '"Delicacy" is really an imperfect translation of "hemdah"; much better would be . . .'

The rest of his lecture was lost in a colourful outburst, predominantly purple.

The whole affair would have ended in the customary rites and ceremonies of the military art if, as he rewarded both Hebrews, one with two, and one with eight days of guardhouse meditation, a singular thought had not crossed the officer's mind. It was this: if Corporal Ernie Levy's entire family had been *rendered harmless*, his continued existence as a uniformed soldier was a sort of furious, outrageous anomaly unprecedented in the annals. Should he, should he not arrest Levy on the spot? In that cruel dilemma, with the question taking on national dimensions, he decided immediately to refer it to higher authority.

A courier is dispatched, goes full speed ahead, gets worried, gets frightened, is seized with terror. But all the terror in the world is of no avail: the higher authority has vanished. Mortified, he grabs at random an orderly from headquarters who was about to flee by bicycle. Grimly clutching his orderly, the courier climbs up to the battalion: no major; goes back down to company: no captain.

The rest can be read in the History of France. But not this: that Ernie Levy, placed in the custody of the battalion C.S.M. (who had solemnly received him from the Officer Cadet; upon whom he had been bestowed by the sub-lieutenant; who had inherited him directly from the captain) . . . that Ernie then slid so smoothly down the hierarchical ladder that he finally landed in the arms of a private; who disappeared suddenly and in a most shameful manner and without passing the orders along, even to a Pole.

After that, his decision was easy; knowing there was an excellent bicycle in a certain nearby depot, he judged that, with his nourishment and means of transport arranged for, all he needed now was an honest travelling companion. But the Second Hebrew, after a fond embrace, addressed him in approximately these words: 'My dear sir, I shall never be able to tell you how deeply touched I am by your proposition; for I feel quite sure that it was not made simply to a coreligionary, but somehow to the man *personally*. Let me therefore thank you for that mark of consideration; and yet . . .'

'And yet?' murmured Ernie, much more saddened by that flowery preamble, from a mouth recently converted to French grammar, than by the approach of the barrage.

'. . . And yet, considering that aside from you I remain the last follower of Moses in the battalion, it seems to me of the highest necessity not to leave the non-Jews with the impression that Israel is no longer with them.'

'But there isn't even the shadow of a Frenchman in the battalion!' Ernie cried, losing patience at last.

'There is me,' said the Second Hebrew. 'I've been in France since 1926 and I'm about to be naturalized.'

Ernie smiled bitterly:

'All right, we'll be naturalized together. And stuffed, if you think it would be impressive. By the way, do you know the prayer of the dying?'

'I know it. But . . .'

'So do I,' Ernie Levy said gently.

'Don't be a defeatist,' said the Second Hebrew. 'Man is

weaker than the fly and harder than iron. Tomorrow the soldiers of Verdun, Waterloo, Valmy, Rocroi, Marignan . . .'

The next day the Nazi pocket burst open, showering an infinity of tanks on the Ardennes flank. Reduced to the able-bodied of one company, and lacking officers altogether, the 429th Foreign Infantry Regiment elected three veterans from the International Brigades to its command. At the ceremony every man swigged down a large, last gulp of eau-de-vie; after which Ernie was surprised to see the Second Hebrew raise his thin fist above all the others, high above them, towards heaven, while his features expressed his most lively satisfaction with himself and with everyone else. At that moment the elected Spaniard cried, '*Compañeros!*' at the end of a black speech in which despair welled up like a bruise, 'Comrades, among us there are Garibaldians, Austrian socialists, German communists, Spanish anarchists, Jews, refugees from all over Europe. We've been retreating for years, kicked from border to border. France was the last country; but today France too is betrayed, and the French are rushing towards the sea like sheep. We know that, we know the taste of treason; the ex-communist comrades here tasted it a while ago with the Molotov pact. *Compañeros*, I don't say this to revive old arguments; I'm about to breathe my last, and I feel hazy and silly, like an old lady's travelling companion. This speech is just to tell you that there's no retreat for us, there's no more emigration, France was the last bastion. Those with thin skin, can move out now. To the others, by way of a joke, I can offer this proverb from my own country (Catalonia): The man who has a tough heart is never beaten until he is dead. And to those of you who fought for the Republic, I recall the words of Dolores Ibarruri, la Passionaria . . .' Then a fit of hilarity bent the dark little man, with a face more wrinkled than a walnut shell; he whinnied, 'We're in great shape! From now on these words sum up our whole . . . hi . . . strategy, and all our . . . ha, ha . . . revolutionary tactics!'

'What? What did she say?' asked several dissatisfied voices.

The little Spaniard recovered some of his seriousness. 'My

friends,' he announced with some difficulty, 'in Madrid la Passionaria told us that it was better to live on our knees – no – better to live on our feet – no – *better to die on our feet than live on our knees!'* he shouted suddenly and tensely.

A phrase that the fifty men echoed in one breath, while the tiny, tipsy, triumphant Second Hebrew wept quite obviously for joy.

A time of waiting followed. Stretched out in a ditch with his rifle beside him, his heart heavy with the thought of the camp at Gurs, Ernie felt the same old amazement that there was no rhyme or reason to the universe ... The patriarch would hesitate for a second, his soul taut, then pluck a perfectly ripe quotation from the Talmud. Less austere, Ernie's father was happy with a legend gleaned here, with an anecdote picked up there: fruits fallen from the great tree of Jewish knowledge. One of those anecdotes sang in Ernie Levy's memory. It sang with the feverish, ironic voice of Ernie's father; with his bespectacled rabbit's face and his fingers, skilled at analysis as much as at needlework ...

'Hear me, brothers. A village rabbi in his sermon taught the perfection of all things: "And why would the Most High – blessed be his name – why, I ask you humbly, why would he have produced imperfect work? So, my lambs, the earth is so perfectly round so that the sun may freely and comfortably circle about it. So, you see, the sun is so perfectly round so that its rays, darting out in all directions, shine for everyone, *without exception*; and so that neither the bears at one end, nor the Negroes at the other, will be left out. And the moon? But what does the moon matter; let it be enough for you to know that although the moon is not always round, it is always perfect.

' "Hear me, brothers ..." "And the onions?" asked a child; the onions too, answered the rabbi. "And radishes with butter?" a second child asked; it is just the same for radishes with butter, answered the rabbi. But above all, he added, fiddling with his beard, remember that after Him (blessed be his name), man is the most perfect thing in all creation. Man, my little goats, ah! man ...

' "And me, oh excellent rabbi?" cried out a tiny hunchback.

'The rabbi thought quickly: "But little animal, sweet little soul," he murmured with an aeriel nuance of reproach; "*for a hunchback, you're as perfect as can be . . . you know?*" '

The bitterest delights of that philosophy suddenly repelled Ernie. That the world bore a fantastic, enormous hump of suffering was not a fit matter for joking. For his part, he knew that the Most High – blessed be his name throughout the centuries – had endowed him notably with a matrix made to measure, crystalline and cold and transparent as glass, imprisoning him body and soul, and reflecting with tearless perfection the white ward in the hospital; the gleaming lights of the pogrom; the delicately blue sky of suburban Paris; this dawn, stinking delicately of blood, and gnawed by a swarm of Junkers . . .

And this was added to his memories a few hours later: the dazzling end of the Second Hebrew, hit by a missile in that region which the Zohar calls the Third Eye, or the Eye of the Centre, or the Eye of the Interior Vision; for the obvious reason that, situated as it is precisely between the external eyes, with it is extinguished all human consciousness, 'be it noble as the sun, be it pure as light, be it innocent as childhood,' as was demonstrated to the Second Hebrew that morning. And this was added to his memories: the ritual burial of the Second Hebrew, in a grave dug miraculously by a bomb: arms crossed upon his chest, phylacteries clinging like ivy to his forehead and, above them, enveloping him as if for the Prayer of Forgiveness, the gentle black and white shroud of the prayer-shawl. And this was added to his memories: the no less admirable annihilation of the 429th Foreign Infantry Regiment. And these were added to his memories: a retreat of an altogether Celtic innocence, half on the magic steeds of Providence, half on the bicycle noted above. The burial of a human trunk lying at the roadside near Chalon-sur-Saône. The last respects paid to a child lying face down under a squall diving from the sky obliquely. Italian fashion. The bicycle fraternity of a yellow-gloved officer who said to him: My dear fellow, the situation is desperate, but not serious.

And then was added the announcement of the French army's capitulation. The discovery of the sempiternal blue of the Riviera. The announcement that France had ceded half of herself to the conqueror. The apprenticeship in disintegration.

And finally, the announcement in 1941 of the complete surrender – including the terms and conditions of transport – of the internees at Gurs to Nazi extermination camps.

Though buried in his protective matrix, Ernie Levy felt that this was the last straw; now, for the second time, the happy thought of hanging himself came to him. We hasten to add that he did nothing of the kind. 'And why did he want to hang himself? and why didn't he hang himself?' Interesting questions indeed. But, our space being limited, we merely point out that he never forgave himself for not going through with it.

5

In a dizzy spell, Ernie Levy invoked the domestic shades in these words: 'Oh my father, oh my mother, oh my brothers, oh my sisters, oh patriarch, oh Mother Judith ... How is it that losing you I cannot lose myself with you? If it is the will of the eternal, our God, I damn his name and beg him to gather me up close enough to spit in his face. And if, as all my comrades in the 429th Foreign Infantry Regiment taught me, we must see the will of nature everywhere and in all things, I ask her humbly to make me an animal as quickly as possible: oh my loved ones; Ernie exiled from Levy is a plant without light.

'Which is why, with your permission, I shall do everything humanly possible from now on to become a dog. So, my beloved family, I ask you to consider this message my last farewell.'

We may mention discreetly, to his discredit, that a certain Indian summer, of a kind unique to the Mediterranean, added greatly to the sweetness of life.

'Come now, brother,' Ernie Levy was soon asking himself, 'how does one become a dog in this part of the world?'

So doing he adopted a way of life whose logical refinement will be obvious to the reader. Ever since Tarde's experimental work we know that imitation is at least second nature, if not all nature. Following that line of thought, and if it is established that the various ways of looking at life, the plucking of rose leaves or the cutting up of a chicken are strict respecters of frontiers, we may agree without cavil that, if Ernie wished to lose his human identity, he could do no better than to concentrate on wholly absorbing the local manner of being a dog.

To begin his apprenticeship, the later Ernie Levy decided to take on the surname of 'Bastard', which seemed rather appropriate to his new position; first name, Ernest. Whether man or dog, it would be offending the creature uselessly to take it on anything but its own terms.

But baptism entails sacramental rites; and as he had once been circumcised in his now-rejected Levy's skin, he redeemed that secret heresy by the gradual addition of a moustache most Catholic in its form, consistency, and grooming. Having thus acknowledged Rome, he could not help finding these fantasy wisps a bit ridiculous, indeed frivolous, without the strong support of a beard. Not the least effect of his moustache was to give him the look of a poodle. And his walk, until then a gloomy slouch, took on a *friskiness* which is surely not found once in a century among Polish Jews, even converted.

At the end of August, 1941, three months after his conversion to the canine species, the late Ernie Levy and his new charms entered a small bistro in the Vieux-Port in Marseilles, where he was now lodging ... His entrance triggered a few laughs. Despite a torried heat he was crammed into his old, mangy, tattered, patched army tunic, far more repellent than the coat of a dog with ringworm. His collar was fastened with a safety pin. A string supported his trousers at the waist. And below the forage cap and the unkempt hair, a hairy sort of face with drooping eyes seemed to be in search of some old bone to gnaw on in a corner. Reeling with hunger, he stepped up to the bar and asked for a glass of water. The barman, a fat, ruddy, and facetious man, claimed at first – to the indescribable joy of other customers – that he did not stock one drop of that dangerous 'medicine'. Then he served the vagabond with a beer-glass full of the local red and, seeing him hesitate, pushed his nose into the wine, inciting him to drink. The poor fellow's gurglings inspired the barman, who raised Ernie's head by the scruff of the neck and offered to 'bottle-feed' him. Two red furrows ran from the corners of Ernie's mouth to his chin and neck. Carried away by the joke, a customer slapped him on the back 'to make it go down better' and the liquid sprayed all over his face.

'That's enough,' a voice said from the end of the room.

The barman froze with respect; Ernie wiped his face on his sleeve and saw an elegant, swarthy, curly-haired gentleman standing with his back to a cheerful table where convivial characters of both sexes were enjoying a midday pastis.

'We didn't mean any harm, Monsieur Mario,' the barman's disintegrating voice said at Ernie's ear.

'Holy Virgin,' the man said with his sing-song accent, 'just to look at you makes me feel bloodthirsty, you fat pig!' Then, coming towards Ernie in a slow, majestic stride which seemed to consist entirely in the motion of his shoulders, 'What's the matter, soldier, famine in the army? Couldn't you have pushed his face in, that son of a bitch? Ha! You're no great specimen of manhood. It wasn't with heroes like you we could have won the war. Want to drink a pastis with us? We're all veterans of the bicycle brigades, except for the ladies. You haven't got fleas, have you?'

An hour later, with his hair combed, his body clean and wearing a two-toned shirt, Ernie was actively participating in a kind of family banquet on the first floor of a shabby restaurant. Monsieur Mario had developed a strange affection for him from the moment he caught sight of the beggar's wrist, with its rosy bracelet of suicide. Later on, Ernie was to discover an identical symbol on Monsieur Mario's right wrist; Monsieur Mario was left-handed. But for the moment he asked no questions, and gave himself over altogether to mastication tenderly supervised by Monsieur Mario, who leaned confidentially towards him: 'Now let me tell you again, you eat, and you let it settle a little; and then you drink, and pee a little if you want to. Otherwise, my friend, you're a goner. I've been through it in my time, you know . . .'

Monsieur Mario's friends seemed to be celebrating recent high profits. At first restrained by the presence of a guest, they were soon engaged in an eloquent debate on business in general and, in particular, on the traffic in cigarettes, milk products, leather and medicine. The men loosened their belts and the women gave rich, thick laughs that ended shrilly. Mélanie came and went, up and down the stairs that led to the kitchen. She was an imposing woman, youngish still; and Ernie did not understand why, every time she went by, the men –

under the blissful gazes of their wives – felt the need to make extremely bold passes at her, passes which she did not seem to notice, keeping her head erect above the dishes. Yet he too fell to laughing at it and, intoxicated with joy, drunken-eyed, he decided to be a dog.

At first it was with vigorous woof-woofs that he barked over his plateful of bones; then a spectacular tumble that got him down on all fours and, amid general hilarity, he trotted grotesquely round the large table. One of the girls threw him a bone, which he dug into, teeth flashing, in perfect mimicry. Screams of laughter. Women writhing ecstatically. Then he rushes at Mélanie, still on all fours, to take a bite at her fair chunk of flesh. With her back to the wall the waitress defends her virtue, appealing to his higher feelings. Waves of laughter. At last Ernie gives in to her stirring pleas, sits up begging, delicately pinches Mélanie on the cheek, and barks in her face. But suddenly he feels the extravagant sweetness of a human face between his thumb and his index finger, and cries, 'Melanie!' flinging himself backward as if his fingers have burnt at the contact. Laughter all around which stops suddenly when they see that Ernie's gallop round the table has taken on a frantic, desperate gait, and that tears from the depths of his drunken soul are running down his cheeks, as he barks hoarsely, to the death, barks, barks, endlessly . . .

The band of 'Veterans', as they called themselves ironically, held its gathering in a little house at the end of the Joliette overlooking the wharves. They were a dozen or so young men brought together by the military disappointments of the Exodus, in a common awareness of absurdity and of the secret shame of those who are defeated ingloriously. We were sold, some of them would say, enumerating the proofs of it. We were weak and naïve, retorted others, more aware of moral frailty. We were cowards, insisted a third group, mostly escaped prisoners, who drank more than the first two groups to forget what treason, weakness, and naïvety could not absolve them of. These last seemed to be waiting, watching for a sign of a new fulfilment. The black market gilded it all with a comfortable tolerable varnish. Under their influence Ernie discovered in himself a treasurer's talent for petty cash, and the sensitive antennae of a 'universal snoop'. But the prime reason for the high esteem in which they held him was his ability to drink cold; the second, his ability to eat raw. Although this last talent offended the delicacy of some people, Ernie's 'raw meal' was a real circus act: bloody meats, black puddings of all kinds, great bags of solid blood, filled him up to the ears. Strangers who had been invited without explanation were frightened.

'The blood will be running out of your eyes,' his protector said to him one day, amused. 'Don't you like anything else?'

'Only animal's blood, Monsieur Mario,' Ernie excused himself.

'All right, all right, what I was saying was for your own good...'

The Jews do not slaughter their animals; a kind of holy executioner does the job according to an age-old ritual. Blood being the basis of life, the animal is bled to the last drop; then its blood, collected down a ridge, is buried; this symbolic funeral of a chicken, a duck, or a calf marks the respect due to all forms of creation. In appearance Ernie had been stringy, gloomy, and puny as a result of the vegetarianism he had been condemned to after his enlistment, by the strict observance of Judaic laws; now he was taking on the look of a tubby, good-natured, gluttonous, Rabelaisian personality. A huge paunch of fat had formed over his belly, a pouch popularly called a 'brioche' in France, as much for its characteristic shape as for the gentle good humour to which it disposes its owner. But was the word brioche really appropriate to the potency of Ernie's belly? Intellectual honesty forces us to set down a reservation on that point. For the brioche, that superfluous furnishing, settles pianissimo (to grow a brioche), in a context that is always harmonious (pink, round, laughing, etc.) ... For all that Ernie's face, carefully observed, retained its chronic sickly emaciation, and his eyes revealed nothing of the warm and pleasing brightness of a tranquil soul in perfect repose. Certain people (whose testimony we cannot trust absolutely) claim to have noticed that

the more the brioche of the late Ernie Levy grew fat the more his
face grew thin. And his companions accused him of masticating
stiffly, sadly even. And then, they wondered, how was it that
he could take so much inspiring nourishment and yet not devote
the slightest part of all that vital energy to love? In fact, despite
his age, despite a certain vigour and his extraordinary appetite,
the late Ernie Levy seemed determined to remain without any
kind of *love-life*.

In truth, the late Ernie Levy had deceived his audience from
the first day; passion was smouldering in his heart. Strangely
drunk on the night of the fatal banquet, he lay sleepless afterwards, with the feeling that between his thumb and finger there
had momentarily been something supernaturally soft and smooth.
Whether that sweet, tender something in Mélanie's face had
clung to his fingers, or his fingers had been made tender by her
cheek, he could not say. When he awoke the next morning, he
knew, though he was still a dog, that some new force was at work
in his world. While he mused upon it, the lustral sweetness of
Mélanie's face at his fingertips reminded him of her presence. He
rubbed his fingers together quickly, to make her disappear;
but in vain.

This tenderness refused to leave him; wherever he went from
then on, whatever he did, even when they believed him lost,
body and soul, in one of his orgies, he found himself sadly
caressing Mélanie's face. When he saw her again a few days
later he thought her transformed; all the facets of her careworn
person glowed for him. She felt the difference, and showed
him the kind of little attentions that deceive only the most
indifferent glances. But Ernie was sounding himself anxiously.
He suspected that even at the lowest levels of love there occurred
phenomena that could trick the imagination and tempt even
a dog to thoughts dangerous for his future. And yet the more
he pondered, the more that frightening languor crept up his arm,
weaving its threads one by one, enveloping it in a sheath that
quivered at the slightest breath, at the most gentle motion.
When the gentleness of Mélanie's face had reached his shoulder,
several months later, and invaded his breast, and made his heart

beat heavily, the late Ernie Levy realized with terror that he had fallen in love with the woman Mélanie! . . .

Fearing the worst, he decided to pay his respects as soon as possible to some young lady of the streets. But as she left her post in the dark doorway he was moved by her animal lassitude and when she stood before him in her garret, prattling affably under the naked bulb that cruelly sharpened her features, the young madman felt an excruciating pain tear through his chest.

'Excuse me, dear lady prostitute,' he said in his strange accent, 'I've changed my mind. Be kind enough to take this money and let me go.'

'You ill? You in trouble? Don't you like me? How sad your eyes are? You're a stranger, you're not from around here.'

'Sadness,' Ernie said, 'is not for me.'

'So something's bothering you?'

Ernie sat down on the bed, considered, invented an autobiography; when he had finished telling her about his family in Marseilles, he went on to his grandparents from Toulon, to the numerous relatives he had in the area of Nîmes, reeling it all off like so many titles that would make him a man in the eyes of the world. 'And you?' he asked finally.

The girl hesitated, invented a child for herself, then another; then augmented them by an aged mother, for these are among the props that emphasize the pathetic. Then she began to joke, and between wisecracks and caresses she turned out the light with a kind of loving discretion. She babbled on even as she submitted the poor madman to a fate worse than death.

When he came to his senses in the street, feeling a certain new and more complete sweetness, Ernie realized that he was indubitably in love with the prostitute; or at least considerably more taken with her than with Mélanie, who ran a poor second now, and for whom, in all honesty, he no longer felt more than a small tingling in one finger. Then an outdoor café cooled his enthusiasm. As he sat down, his legs moist with tenderness, he noticed sitting near him one of the girls from the Negro quarter in the Belle-de-Mai with gilded whalebone combs in her chignon, and a swept-up hairstyle that seemed woven of black silk above a face carved of Eastern island wood. Immediately all the false softness, all the impious tinglings disappeared, giving way to a yet stranger intoxication, this time centred in his eyes; and he knew that the young Negress had inspired eternal love in him. Then another, white as milk, who was gliding along the sidewalk like a sailing ship in the wind, ravished his heart no less thoroughly. Then it was another; then still another. In the next few days he lost all his capacity for drinking cold and eating raw; Ernie wandered like a troubled soul among the streets infested with faces, dotted with eyes like so many stars twinkling in his night. Finally he decided to leave the city as soon as he could. For if a dog, he said to himself in his delirium, gives in to love just once, he soon thinks nothing of going without his feed; and from fasting he backslides to temperance and to breaking his siesta, and from there to daydreaming and the impulse to write poetry. And once on the downward trail, no one knew where it might end. Doubtless more than one dog could date his fall from some passing fancy that seemed quite unimportant at the time.

6

ERNIE spent the whole winter of 1942 roaming the Rhône Valley, working upstream against the season's furious mistral; at night, its screaming winds mingled strangely with the harsh, dark shrieking wind that swept through his wounded brain. His diet in Marseilles had filled him out; he had no trouble finding work in a countryside depleted of its men by the German prison camps. That period was a black hole. He systematically cultivated his lowest instincts. Now and then he brawled like an animal. His object, though unformulated, was to prevent any infiltration of light into the hole. One day he caught his reflection in a mirror. He was pleased to note that his former face had in some way been left behind on the gallows of Marseilles. All the features which ordinarily compose a face, nose, mouth, eyes, ears, were there in their proper shapes and usual places; but they did not constitute a human face. They seemed detached one from the others, and the late Ernie Levy suspected that it would have made no difference if he had worn his ears where his eyes were, or his eyes in his dark nostrils, for example.

He wound up near St-Sylvestre on a small farm owned by a prisoner's wife who, from the height of her weakness, ruled with a rod of iron over the waifs and strays whom the invasion periodically sent her way. In a woman too weak to dominate her fate, and too demanding to give in to it, delicacy is easily transformed into treachery. Madame Trochu had become somewhat independent since her husband's incarceration; she breathed a bit more easily, regarding herself even as a free woman and, between one parcel to Germany and another, she slept with all comers among her hired hands, waiting for the man she now knew how to tame, if he didn't kill her first. She was a woman of Provence with eyes like acid black raisins and a harsh mouth; but wholly and paradoxically carved in fire and ice. Ernie saw at a glance that she could never make him lose his head; so he gazed at her fearlessly, and she at once took a fancy to him. Intent on his bloody meats, he let precious time slip by; then she commanded, and he obeyed.

Since he did not love her in the least, the late Ernie Levy imposed upon himself the penance of displaying a Herculean passion, which she accepted without question. She was a modest soul, so exquisitely constituted that in love she sought only the proofs of love, provided they were repeated: she was called The Glutton. It would be easy enough to show how, as the late Ernie Levy established those proofs, and as his unsubtle mare lapped them up, nothing happened between them that did not relate to the disposition and management of those proofs. But we will pass along; such common things are not worth discussion.

'My love,' the excellent lady asked, 'a little more kidney?'

'A pepper?'

'A little pheasant? It's three weeks old. It does that little jesus of yours so much good. Peter Piper picked a peck of pickled pepper.'

The late Ernie did not answer, opening his mouth only to masticate. But now and then, dreamily, helped along by nostalgia, he tried to figure out which meat, raw, roasted, or simply boiled, was most compatible with a bestiality which was aboriginal and therefore his own.

For the rest, lodged, laundered, stuffed, honoured by the whole village and respected in the bedroom, he was what we on earth call (and have called, since time immemorial) a happy mortal. Even better: his amorous benefactress, fearing to overwork him, worked out by some private arithmetic various ways of sparing him the pains of sowing, spading, planting, clearing fields, harvesting, digging potatoes, etc.; the trouble of drinking cold; and even the inconvenience of getting out of bed.

'Look at the geese!' she cried on a note of triumph. 'Follow their example!'

At which the late Ernie Levy would fall obediently on all fours; stump out to the front yard; salute colleague rooster on his dunghill; his cousins the geese in their coop; throw an envious glance at the current capon; and finally, as always, push along to the pigsty, which evoked a cold fascination mingled with a hate so excruciating that at times, in a fury, he spat Judaically upon the impure beast.

That night he had a strange dream. As usual he was embracing a thoroughbred Airedale, and as usual he was amazed at the intensity of the pleasure he took in his beloved; if, he said to himself, the appearance of man had been denied him, at least his essence remained spiritual. The proof lay in the high level of the pleasure the bitch gave him.

But at the very moment when, as the Zohar says, 'All visible things die to be born again invisible,' the bitch was transformed into a splendid cat whose eyes shone in the night; embodying the thousand twists and turns of desire, she enticed Ernie into the dance again. And why, too, by what malicious spell, did the cat, at the moment spoken of in the Zohar, become a rat, and then a beetle, a cockroach, a snail, etc., finally to melt against him in a living, seething mass, in a drunken, amoeboid crawl towards oblivion in the sea of infinity?

Though she was inordinately proud of Ernie's proofs, the farmer's wife began to look at him with a new respect when he told her that he didn't like to think about the man whose bed and wife he was occupying. That's the height of *cynicism*, she told herself, impressed. For a long time she tried to make him admit it, acknowledge his cynicism, but when the sly fox refused, her respect became even greater.

Similarly, he never admitted that he was not from Bordeaux (as a certain identity card in the name of Ernest Bastard falsely stated). So that his admirable loyalty to his 'Alsatian' accent made the woman think that he was an escaped prisoner. Giving her curiosity full rein, she deduced from a certain detail of the bedchamber that he was an Israelite; but as she preached the greatest tolerance in religious matters, she never mentioned her discovery – and anyway that peculiarity, taking one thing with another, added a certain spice. Since girlhood she had dreamed of meeting a circumcised man. The desire dated from her early catechism, the priest having imprudently mentioned the circumcision of the heart; at which the little Dumoulin girl had sneered, as she did often under the influence of her father, the teacher, who, unable to keep his pious wife from going to church, obliged his daughter, a little lady of no religion at all, to attend catechism and heckle the priest. A secret conference had united the catechumens on the theme of circumcision. Miss Dumoulin explained, on her father's orders, that the Israelites, the first monotheists, customarily sacrified a small piece of their bodies to their God. And that the priests, the second monotheists, not wishing to be behindhand and in any case rather timid, confined themselves to removing a small circle of hair from the skull.

Monsieur Dumoulin, a perfect layman, never called the Jews anything but Israelites. Deep down he half believed that the word Jew had been invented by the Jesuits to annoy the Freemasons. And out of all this emerged one consequence that was unfortunate for the late Ernie Levy, who fell from his heights when, towards the end of an afternoon, he was resting on the bed, and his farmer's wife rushed in, her face afire, exclaiming: 'You lied to me, you're a Jew.'

'Oh, come, surely you must have guessed?'

'I know that you're an Israelite, because ... yes. But I was just talking to the town clerk, and he told me that all Israelites were *automatically* Jews.'

'Maybe. But what's the difference?'

'What's the difference?' she cried indignantly. 'I can't have a Jew sleeping in my Pierre's bed, and sitting in his armchair, and wearing his clothes and his shirts! Ah no, no, what you did was very bad!'

'All right,' said the late Ernie. He got up.

'Where are you going?'

'Away.'

'But why? I can make up a nice bed for you in the barn.'

'And the rest?' asked the young madman.

'Well, we'll have to be careful. You can't see poor old Pierre –' (she always said 'poor old Pierre', indicating as much her grief at knowing him a prisoner as the strange compassion that swept over her when she reflected that he was being deceived) '– You can't see poor old Pierre finding out that we – that I – did it – with a Jew? No, no we'll do it in the stable.

'And anyway,' she added suddenly, 'you've been taking it a little too easy lately. You'll have to do what I say now. And put a little less butter on your bread, etc.'

'And if I don't like it that way?'

'What's this I hear?' she said dryly.

'All right,' said the madman.

With those slight alterations, life went on as before. The mistral had dropped. A slow heat rose from the earth. Even the olive trees were no longer tormented, and sometimes, in the evening, all things seemed to rise into the liveliness of the peaceful sky. On Sunday Ernie went into town, heard Mass vacantly, and then, between two dreamy pastis, went to watch the living play *pétanque* in the shadow of the church porch. One of the players threw a glance at him once which made him turn pale. It was the village blacksmith; he was a returned prisoner, and he bowled with his body rigid from the effects of a burst grenade. Ernie saw him again at his forge. By tacit agreement both kept silence about the mysterious thing which had brought them together. The blacksmith had a northern face with two warm, subtle, constantly flickering southern eyes; he was a big fellow with long limbs which ended in wide feet and thick hands, and he balanced himself carefully, like a tightrope walker, when he moved. When he spread his hands flat, they took up an impressive amount of space. Long fingers, pudgy at the base, tapered to flat ends with odd fingernails; Ernie thought they were like very sturdy pliers with the sensitivity of antennae. It was obvious that he had not been born with those two machine tools, with their thick, grey skin, stitched with 'welding scars', and with nerves and muscles far more complicated, Ernie guessed, than any animal paw. Ernie watched them move precisely through the forest of controls of a multiple drill, or withdraw a glowing diamond from a wreath of sparks, and he felt that a part of the blacksmith's intelligence had shifted to his fingertips, because he made his living with them. Which is why he followed their movements with more respect at each visit.

The blacksmith never asked him the questions that make a man construct a more and more complicated scaffolding, at the mercy of the slightest truth. Only the future seemed to interest the artisan, who occasionally let slip phrases heavy with meanings, but without looking at Ernie: 'My boy,' he said, 'there are things that make us feel they'll never end, like a good stiff mistral after a week of steady blowing. And then one morning the sun comes out. You understand?' Then he would invite Ernie to a 'drop' of pastis; they would go down the three steps at the far end of the smithy, and the fat beribboned woman would bring them a well cooled flask; nor did she, any more than the other, question Ernie about his past; it was as if she had instinctively joined her husband's conspiracy of silence. When the children came back from school their guest was often pressed to stay to dinner; and even the children seemed to retreat from any innocent inquisitions, wanting only to amuse the mad young man who would occasionally emerge from his delirium and in a heartrending flash discover that astonishing world under his very eyes, that unsuspected France, simple and good as bread. And though he was obscurely afraid that they would melt away the chains weighing on his soul, he could not keep himself from returning to that dangerous source of light.

'Listen,' he said to his friend the blacksmith one day, 'I feel somehow that you know me from somewhere. Even the first time...'

The blacksmith hesitated for a second: 'My boy, my boy,' he murmured gently, without raising his glance from the anvil, 'I never saw you before, believe me. But I knew right away that you were Jewish.'

'But I'm not!' Ernie cried in panic.

The man left his hammer on the anvil, and crossed the room to place his heavy hands on the young Jew's shoulders.

'So it's as obvious as that,' Ernie said in an odd voice, a slow, musical voice, flowing from his throat with the moving ease of a rediscovered melody.

At which, the blacksmith spoke. 'I don't know what a Jew looks like,' he said. 'All I can see is the man. We had some in Stalag 17, but I never thought about it until afterwards, after the Fritzes came and took them away. But when I got back from the prison camp I made a detour round by Paris, because of the wife of a dead pal who lived in Drancy. It was pretty early in the morning, and German motorcycle troops told us to line up on the sidewalk, and we saw buses hurrying by, full of Jewish kids with stars all over. They were all at the windows, and they stared and stared at us. And their hands were gently clawing at the glass like they were trying to get out. And I couldn't see any one face very clearly, but they all had eyes like I'd never seen before, and like I hope I'll never see again in this life. And when I saw you for the first time, my boy, it wasn't when we were playing *pétanque*, but in church, at High Mass. And I couldn't see your face very well, but right away I *recognized your eyes*. You understand?'

'Ah,' Ernie said, touched to the heart.

He got up and staggered out. Outside he heard the first cry, not right against his ear as before, but far off, still kept small by the tough shell of dogginess which he was holding together with all his strength, though it was already crumbling. At the top of the path to the Trochu farm the cries, heedless of the flowering almond trees and all the other things which often distracted him, had become so loud that he stopped his ears several times. First he recognized the patriarch's cry, then Mother Judith's. Then he seemed to be coming out of a long dream, and suddenly he wondered whether he was entirely sane; that question, as soon as framed, caused him such abominable suffering that he brought both hands to his throat as if to give it more air. The farmer's wife thought he was ill. He stretched out in the barn, and tried to escape the cries by covering himself entirely with straw. Now and then he went out to breathe the night air of Provence. When he fell asleep nothing within him had loosened; it was simply that the cries came from within him now. He dreamed that he was a dog running the streets of a great city while passers-by pointed at him, surprised but

306

nonchalant: Look, a dog with Jewish eyes! The hunt began without his knowledge, and already people were running towards him from everywhere, brandishing nets that covered the whole sky. A cellar sheltered him, and he thought he was safe until the sound of pursuers came through the door, demanding that he give them at least his eyes. My eyes? But that's ridiculous. And suddenly screaming at the top of his voice: 'We won't! We'll never give up our eyes, never, never, never. *We'd sooner give up our lives*, woof, woof!'

Ernie Levy got dressed in the darkness and left the barn. The whole farm, the fence, the nearby olive grove, were bathed in black water, vibrating with milky eddies. He opened the wooden gate, changed his mind, and went to the house. A man's voice preceded Madame Trochu's anxious exclamation, 'I've come to say good-bye,' he said through the door.

A light gleamed; Madame Trochu opened the door, furious: 'What do you mean, running off in the night like a thief?' She had thrown on a bathrobe that smothered her in red flowers, and over her shoulder Ernie could see, in his former place, the naked body of a man he did not know. But though he recognized every object in the room, the luxurious oaken bed, the lampshade throwing that greenish light to the ceiling, the slippers into which he had placed his feverish feet so many times, the nauseating odour of flesh against flesh in a room that was never properly aired, it seemed to him that the whole picture had detached itself from him and was floating before his eyes like a dead fish. Madame Trochu too seemed dispossessed of her customary personality; she was neither beautiful nor ugly, as he had previously tried in vain to define her; she pitched and rolled gently in her poor female flesh, without destination, without moorings, drifting with the current.

'I wanted to say good-bye,' he repeated. 'I thought it was only right.' He had spoken in a sweet, low voice which made her quiver. Bringing her hands suddenly to her exposed chest, she cried, 'My God, what have I done!' She wrung her hands furiously.

'Come, come, you mustn't cry,' Ernie said. He took a step into the bedroom, towards the farmer's wife who was petrified by some unnameable grief. 'You know very well that a fine woman like you will never want for men, don't you?'

'But he's a child! *He's a child!*' the woman exclaimed, staring at Ernie with wide eyes. Then she said nothing, and only her hands spoke, twisting together in fury against her breast while Ernie retreated timorously towards the door. At the last moment he turned for a farewell smile, but the woman's lips were twisting soundlessly.

On the wooded path that led down to the village, he again had the feeling he had forgotten something at the farm: but he did not know what.

'Dirty dog,' he murmured suddenly.

And sitting down in the middle of the dark path, surrounded by shadows that seemed to be the shadows of his life itself, he hunched forward and scattered earth upon his hair, following the immemorial Jewish technique of humiliation.

That too left him dissatisfied.

Then he stretched out a hand in the darkness and slapped his face several times. But soon he felt that the slapper was himself, and the slapped one was another himself, and it was like beating someone else – in spite of his cheek, which still stung. For which reason, he remained dissatisfied.

Ernie scratched his left hand with his right, then his right hand with his left to cancel out the pleasure that the latter might have derived; so that neither hand could be considered the victor. But always there was born a third hand. Then he tried to remember all the old-fashioned methods of self-abasement. And he invoked the name of God. And he saw nothing there before which he could reasonably debase himself. And he evoked the image of his own people; but doubtless they were too long dead for the image to be of much use.

Then he remained motionless and dry. Then he stooped and picked up a stone and, in the pain he felt as it cracked open his cheek, a tear finally escaped his eyes. Then two. Then three. And as he laid his cheek against the earth, sobbing, rediscovering deep within himself the source of tears which he thought had run dry when little Ilse had clapped three times; and while Ernie Levy felt himself die, and come to life, and die again; his heart sweetly opened to the light of days gone by.

BOOK SEVEN

THE MARRIAGE OF ERNIE LEVY

It happens that nations lose their sons:
That is a great loss, surely, and there is no
easy consolation; but here comes Doctor
Soifer, with his own loss . . . For he is
one of those who are in the process of
      losing their nation . . .
What ? . . . What is he losing ? . . . No one has
ever heard of such a loss!

*David Bergelson. A Candle for the Dead.
Translated from the Yiddish. Posthumous.*

1

THE old quarter of the Marais, once a resort of noble ladies, is probably the most dilapidated in Paris; and so the Jews had their ghetto there. On every shop window a six-pointed star alerted the Christian stroller. These stars were also displayed on the breasts of furtive pedestrians, who glided along the walls like shadows; except that they were made of yellow cloth, the size of a starfish, sewn above the heart and bearing the hallmark of human manufacture: Jew. Ernie noticed that the children's badges were of the same size as the adults' and seemed to devour their frail chests with those six points dug in like claws. A wave of incredulity swept over him at the sight of these miniature branded cattle; he thought he could see a dim halo of fear above them. But the disbelief faded fast.

The Association was on the Rue des Ecouffes, which seemed to him the most 'picturesque' in the neighbourhood; and the building in which it was quartered, the most leaning and woebegone.

His heart pounding with curiosity, and with the moist anguish that a certain kind of moribund staircase can distil, he knocked at the narrow door on the sixth floor. A little old man opened it. Over his shoulder, Ernie made out three little old men standing in line, as if to review him. The master of the house raised a hand to his skull-cap and tilted it forward a quarter of an inch, then pushed it back to its ritual position.

'Pray come in,' murmured the first little old man: his thin ceremonious voice reminded Ernie of the acid, temperately courteous voice of his father Benjamin. When his host had closed the door behind Ernie, he took a step forward, bowed imperceptibly, extended his right hand and said, '*Bonjour, monsieur!*' Then the second, the third, the fourth old man greeted him. They all had the same pointed beard, the same small eyes buried deep beneath the majestic slope of the Israelite forehead. But the first attested his culture by pronouncing 'Monsieur' in perfect harmony with its spelling and etymology; while the others were more easily satisfied, one with 'Mossieu', another with 'Moussi', and lastly and oddly, the third with 'Missiou'.

The master of the house introduced him soberly to those three personalities, who proved to be, in order of enunciation, vice-president, secretary-general, and treasurer of the Association. 'As for ourselves,' he finished, raising a hand to his heart (this impersonal 'ourselves' seemed much more fitting than a 'me' steeped in pride and complacency), 'we are the president.'

As his host was completing this ceremony, punctuating each introduction with a respectful pause, Ernie took the liberty of examining the headquarters of the Paris Association of the Elders of Zemyock: a cube seven foot square, a dormer window on the courtyard, a jug and a basin, a sewing machine with an unfinished garment lying over it, some fifty books on a shelf – Hebrew, French, German, Russian, perhaps Yiddish – a minute table, a tiny wall-cupboard, an oil stove in a corner, with a pot and a plate on it; a bed, a chair. All this meticulously disposed in the room's dark daylight, and bathing in the odour of antiquity.

'May I ask the object of the gentleman's visit?' inquired the president in a voice made thin by his worry at Ernie's silence ...

Abashed, Ernie could only answer, yes, yes, then fell silent immediately, with a confused feeling of being an intruder.

'Come, speak, have no fear,' said the president with a smile full of subtle melancholy. 'You have come no doubt, as I have guessed, in order to arrest us, have you not?' he finished, with that same shrewd melancholy smile in his small shining eyes.

'Oh,' Ernie murmured.

'Have no fear, sir, we are quite ready,' the president went on, staring at him in a sad fascination. 'We were expecting you ...'

And with a gentle sweep of his foot, he pointed out four small bundles carefully lined up on the floor near the door.

'*I beg of you*,' Ernie said in Yiddish. And unburdening himself beneath the calm gaze of the small shining eyes, he added, 'I am the grandson of Mordecai Levy, my grandfather brought me here before the war. And ... and ...' he sobbed, 'I beg of you ...'

The four old men immediately began talking at the same time, and their voices, at first restrained by their emotion at Ernie's presence, soon rose to extraordinary heights, reaching the shrill-ness peculiar to old men and children, as the discordant, plaintive concert mingled in rhythm with a dance of lamentation, arms raised to heaven, hands contorting, and small, skinny bodies swaying back and forth. Their eyes, turned towards a heaven momentarily quite close, shed the thin, transparent old men's tears that linger on the eyelids, then burst and vanish into hair and wrinkles.

When the first wave of emotion had passed, the old gentlemen suddenly returned to Ernie. A ballet began, each attempting to show the greater respect for the descendant of the Levys, and to invent the most delicate tribute. The master of the house pulled a handkerchief from his pocket, dusted off the only chair as care-fully as if it were a religious relic, covered it with a cushion of aged silk, and begged Ernie at great length to do him the honour of sitting upon it; as Ernie brushed back a tear the old man leaned towards him and stroked his cheek paternally, murmuring with a regretful smile, 'Forgive us, we are so *permanently* afraid. May I hope ...?' The vice-president extracted a slightly flattened cigarette from a metal box and extended it to Ernie, his arm stret-ched to its full length, as an offering. The secretary-general open-ed a small bag of peppermints. And the treasurer finally trotted to Ernie, stared unbearably into his eyes, took his right hand in his own two gnarled ones and said, 'Missiou, Missiou,' and was then shaken by a brief sob. Ernie noticed that they were all cos-tumed for the slow, miserly death of old men; Missiou's shoes were dissimilar, one high and one low. But it also seemed to him that on their caftans gleaming with age the four yellow stars, sewn in great awkward stitches, were floating, even fluttering, with the fragile, disarmed grace of butterflies.

He had taken a seat on the cushion, and the four old men were sitting in a row on the edge of the bed.

'We had no idea,' the president began, trying to put Ernie at his ease, 'no idea at all that your father had a son thirty years old. It is true that before the war we were not yet president, but simply assistant treasurer (which office no longer exists today). Alas! the day is not far when the Association will be extinguished, gently, but physically, as a candle is extinguished; first myself, I hope, then another, then another, then the fourth. And tell me, what will be important then? Dead flesh cannot feel the sword.'

Ernie wiped a hand across his eyes and murmured, as if to himself, 'But what are you saying? My father has no thirty-year-old son.'

'Then how old are you?' the four cried together.

Ernie smiled to see them so lively and impetuous; so young, he thought irreverently. 'Sometimes,' he said, still smiling, 'I feel a thousand years old. But from my father's point of view, may God take him into his gentle hands, I'm only twenty.'

The president examined him with horrified attention, turned to the other three, and launched a passionate debate in Polish, during which Ernie forced himself to remain politely detached.

Then renewing conversation with the visitor: 'Then you escaped from *their* hell?'

'I've just come from the unoccupied zone,' Ernie said flatly, 'this morning. What hell were you speaking of?'

'Do you mean that you've come from *out there*?' the president asked, examining Ernie's face again, as if a terrifying story were to be read upon it.

'My God,' the secretary-general echoed, 'he hasn't come from *out there*!'

'Then where has he come from?' asked Missiou in a barely audible voice.

The president was still leaning towards Ernie, sadness glowing from his discoloured, grey-green, rainbowed eyes, like those ancient objects whose colours have melted into the patina of time. Because he was so close, Ernie saw the first sudden stirrings in the refracting liquid of his gaze – like a fish whose existence is signalled first by a kind of watery tremor – a submerged idea, rising slowly to the surface. 'You wouldn't be Ernie?' the old man asked very gently.

316

Surprised, Ernie assented with a silent nod.

'Ah,' the other said in a tone of sudden remembrance, while tears of shame ran down Ernie's face, 'the old man spoke of you often. He always came to the meetings on Sunday morning, he was a real ... Jew. Forgive me, I remember, he spoke of his grandson – I mean, the son of his son – as if he were quite certain that the little one would be called upon to become a Just Man. Not a Just Man of the Levys, he said, but a true Unknown Just, an Inconsolable, one of those whom God dares not even caress with his little finger. But we are a long way from all that now, aren't we? Still, if I'm not being indiscreet, my child, my dear child, why have you come back to us, into the flames? Perhaps you don't know. They tell stories that raise every hair on your head ...'

'I know all that can be known,' Ernie said. 'Some of us read clandestine leaflets, some of us heard forbidden broadcasts. But the stories they whisper are too much for the human spirit. They tell you, this is what's been happening to us; but they don't believe it themselves.'

'Do you believe it?' the president exhaled.

Ernie Levy seemed extremely upset.

'Then why did you come back?'

'That,' the boy said, 'I don't know.'

'What you have done is very bad,' the president said. 'In Paris, nowadays, life is shorter by a baby's gown. And you're so young, you don't look Jewish, the whole future is running through your veins. It's really surprising how little Jewish you seem. Listen to me, I'm telling you the truth,' he said in exaltation, 'you look exactly like anybody at all!'

Then, examining Ernie's disfigured face, he restrained a shudder: 'My child,' he went on in a different voice, 'it's true, you know, you don't resemble anything or anyone. Were you the little curly-haired boy who used to come with old Levy? Don't say anything, don't wake up, don't wake up ... True, it was in the old days, in the world that used to be, in my old, dead memories, and if I didn't know that only three years had passed ... Was it really you?' He gestured absurdly in denial. 'No, I beseech you, don't answer, don't ever answer me; my aged soul prefers to remain in doubt about the hell they speak of and the hell they do not speak of. Child Levy, do you know, it seems that I am not a Just Man, for I cannot abide any sort of hell.' And dropping his gaze from the visitor suddenly, as if he could no longer bear the sight, he clapped his skinny hands to his wrinkled face and cried out, in a kind of plaintive caterwauling: '*Oh God, when will you cease to stare down at us, when will you grant us the time to swallow our saliva? Oh Lord, Father of men, when will you forgive us our sins, and when will you forget our iniquity? For we Jews sleep in the dust; and one day you will seek us . . .*'

'Tut tut tut,' Missiou interrupted reprovingly.

'*. . . and we will no longer exist,*' finished the president of the Paris Association of the Elders of Zemyock.

Furious, the three little old men advanced upon him, Missiou going so far as to pinch at the president's elbow: 'What is this? Have you no shame? Who do you think you are, Job? And in front of a Levy, too . . .'

At the magic name the four old men fell silent on the edge of the bed, some crossing their arms, some twisting their beards in shame. The president lowered his eyes.

'We argue,' he muttered, without daring to look at the visitor. 'We jaw at each other like the old women we have become. But that's because all four of us live in this room, two on the bed and two on the mattress we spread on the floor at night . . .'

'Taking turns,' Missiou echoed.

'And the venerable Levy,' the president explained, more and more embarrassed, 'will perhaps understand that our forced cohabitation leads us into excessive familiarity, which of course we are the first to regret . . .'

'Me especially,' the secretary-general punctuated earnestly while Ernie Levy, squirming on his chair, thoroughly ashamed to see himself transformed into a supreme Judge of these four harried lives, searched vainly for a polite formula that would restore their dignity without removing his own insignificance.

'What am I,' he said finally, 'that my glance troubles four noble patriarchs like you? If you knew . . .'

At these words, Missiou brightened; and chortling enthusiastically, 'These Levys!' he cried. 'They're all the same!
Ai, ai, ai, patriarchs, did you hear him!'

'There is milk and honey upon their tongues!'

'If you ground up a Levy with a pestle,' the president ac-
quiesced without daring to look at Ernie, 'his gentleness would
yet remain with him. Patriarchs, my God ...' And with his nose
still pointed at the floor he went on in a more peaceful voice:
'My child, my dear child, it is not one, but four, miracles that
we are here alive. If no miracle had come about, you would
have found only the shadow of our precious Association; and
in that case what would you have done?'

'I don't know that either,' Ernie said smiling.

'Is it possible that ...?'

Missiou interrupted violently: 'Don't interrogate,' he yapped,
'don't ask questions of a Levy, let him go on; he knows his own
way by heart! As they used to say at home, do you remember;
It is useless pushing a drunkard, he'll fall down all by himself;
useless pushing a Levy, he'll *fly on* all by himself! Hee, hee, hee!'

'Stay with us,' the president said; he seemed to be speaking
to the floorboards. 'Truthfully, this room belongs to no one,
it belonged to the Association; and as you see, we have made it
our hiding-place. They may come tomorrow, tonight: but today
you are at home here. May we adopt you then? Perfect. Excellent.
The perfection of excellence.'

'But I –'

'Ah,' Missiou said, 'perhaps we're a bit too old for you,
hey? It may be not too cheerful with four old sardines like us;
I understand. But before, you know, there were young people
in the Association too. My God, is that possible! I can remember
a year when we had twenty-seven members enrolled in the Paris
region!'

'*And the dances* ...' the secretary-general said ecstatically.

Missiou did not let him finish: 'Ah, ah,' he yapped in excitement, 'I remember the annual dances we used to have. Can it
be? ... We held them in Belleville; simple family dances, not
like the madness of big cities, like Warsaw, Lodz, Bialystok,

where nobody knew anybody else. And even so we had quite a few people, because people from Zemyock are known and loved in the whole of Jewish Poland . . .'

'What a sardine you are,' the president said coldly.

Missiou rolled wild eyes; then, carefully, 'Ah, ah,' he said, 'I beg your pardon, I meant to say, *were* loved. Because from what I hear there is no one left to be loved in Jewish Poland, nor anyone to love . . .'

The president raised his face at last, revealing a nostalgic moisture in his shining little eyes: 'Do you accept our invitation?'

'It would be . . . my great happiness.'

Trotting around the table, the president shuffled papers behind his guest's back; later Ernie was to notice the cupboard cut into the wall, which contained the Association's archives. Returning to his place almost immediately, the president spread a black-bound register on the tiny table; and as he leafed through it gently his lips went on plucking at his memories . . .

'You understand, I was living with my son before the war. A handsome apartment, with a tailor's workshop. And you know, they left me and tried to reach the unoccupied zone. I crossed quite a few frontiers in my youth, but I had no more desire to run; so I stayed in the apartment. *May they rest in peace.* The concierge took the machines, and then the furniture, and then the dishes, and then the apartment. But she didn't turn me in . . . We stayed on, the old books, the papers, and myself. Do you know? God amuses himself. No, no, no, no, I think maybe it was 1938. Ah! do you see? Mordecai Levy, 37 Rue de l'Ermitage, Montmorency, Seine-et-Oise. Shall I put your name next to his? Perfect, excellent; the perfection of excellence.'

'Only,' Missiou interrupted worriedly, 'you'll have to hurry and sew on your star.'

'With pleasure,' Ernie Levy said.

2

ERNIE was amazed that the men of the Marais never tired of God. In a tiny block of houses condemned to disappear shortly in the great flood of death, they went on waving their arms to heaven, clinging to it in all their fervour, in all their torment, in all their pious despair. Every day a new raid netted friends or relatives, next-door neighbours, flesh and blood beings with whom only yesterday words had been exchanged; but the little synagogues in the rue du Roi-de-Sicile, in the Rue des Rosiers or in the rue Pavée were never empty. The four little old men dragged their guest there regularly, so that he should participate in their fiery prayers. Sometimes young people adorned with fleurs de lys were waiting for them when they came out, bludgeons in hand, elegant sarcasms on their lips. 'It's like that every day now,' the little old men moaned, trotting along close to the wall. 'And yet we can't miss the Office. That's what they want, you know.'

Between raids a swarming fish-pond of an existence continued in the branded alleyways and cul-de-sacs. Communal cauldrons of soup appeared; no one knew how. In those springtime days of 1943 even the starred scum of the earth enjoyed the privilege of the pale sun that shone dimly through the grey, medieval waters of the Marais. Ernie had found work, with a furrier who had a green identity card. People were already passing word along that it was the turn of the white cards next; but it was the red ones. Thus the anglers on the bank confused their prey with the painful bait of survival.

In the narrow garret on the sixth floor the row of little bundles belonging to the castaways had been lengthened with Ernie's bundle, which contained, like the other four, a prayer-book, a prayer-shawl, prayer-ribbons, a spare skullcap, and six lumps of sugar. When he got back from work one day he found the door sealed with a strip of cloth bearing a German stamp. He hesitated, undid the seal and entered the room, which was essentially unchanged; only the four little parcels belonging to the last four survivors of the Paris Association of the Elders of Zemyock were missing. They left a terrible vacuum around his own untouched bundle.

Stretched out on the bed and shivering with a strange fever, Ernie waited his turn for forty-eight hours. His relatives and friends paraded before his eyes. Occasionally he felt like going down to join one of the movements now forming in the ghetto and outside. There had been stories of exploits by certain young Jewish heroes. But all the Germans on earth could not pay for one innocent head; and then he told himself, for him it would have been a luxurious death. He had no wish to singularize himself, or detach himself from the humble procession of the Jewish people.

When he realized that the Germans were not ready for him, Ernie walked down the six flights to go back to work. That day as he tottered along the sidewalk a little Frenchwoman in mourning came up to him and shook his hand. The next week, in the Métro, another delight: an old workman in overalls offered him a seat. 'They're human beings too,' he burst out, glaring furiously around him. 'And my God, nobody chooses his mother's belly!' Ernie declined that charming invitation, but he was still smiling as he went to the synagogue at the Rue Pavée for evening Office. He found it almost deserted, and deduced that there had been a raid during the afternoon. Only a few old men in permanent devotion haunted the dim stalls, and two or three women weeping behind the segregating partition. Again Ernie wondered what attracted him to the place. In spite of all his efforts he had not once been able to reach the person of God, from whom he felt separated, for ever, by the wall of Jewish lamentations that rose all the way to heaven.

Outside, a crew of elegant youngsters were amusing themselves. One of them tried to tug at the beard of an old worshipper who, afraid of dropping his prayer-book, defended himself fiercely.

'Montjoie Saint-Denis!' the young man shouted spitefully; and an enthusiastic crowd came running to the rescue, crying, '*Pour Dieu et mon droit!*'

Drifting away from these exploits, Ernie noticed a bestarred young girl in a doorway fighting desperately, caught by two French 'patriots' who were caressing her and laughing. For a moment he tolerated the sight then, moving forward mechanically, he dispersed the two by the suddenness of his attack, grabbed the girl's hand, and raced madly with her through the mysteriously empty alleyways of the Marais.

At the Rue de Rivoli, as they slowed for the traffic, Ernie noticed with surprise that the girl limped.

'I owe you many thanks,' she said in Yiddish as they paused near the empty site at the rue Geoffroy-l'Asnier. She was panting, and the beads of sweat were pouring down her forehead; Ernie thought she looked a bit bohemian, with her devilish red hair, her cotton dress that floated round her like a sack, and, in the middle of those high, lustreless, Provençal cheekbones, the same look of impertinence and candour that had attracted him in the vagabond women along the roads from the Camargue to Saintes-Maries-de-la-Mer. The yellow star was like a gaudy trinket over her heart, a gypsy-woman's showy jewel. 'Not that they would have done much to me,' she added with a smile; 'I'm not pretty enough.'

Ernie stared at her uncomprehending, their hands separated in embarrassment; the girl began to speak rapidly, breathing out, as if blowing soap-bubbles, vague acknowledgements of her *eternal* gratitude, etc.

'You're not too tired?' he asked, interrupting her brusquely but gently.

'No, why? Oh,' she said quite naturally, 'because of my leg?'

The young man hesitated, 'Yes,' he said finally, 'because of your leg.'

'Don't worry about that. People think so, to look at it. But it's even stronger than the other. You got yourself broken once, my girl, but it won't happen again!' Bent over the offending leg she rebuked it gaily, even punishing it with a light slap.

Ernie said quickly, as if to divert her attention from it, 'Do you live far from here, may I ask?'

She interrupted her game, raised her head, smiled. 'No, no, it's just around the corner.'

'Take my arm all the same, would you? Please?'

Abashed, suddenly blushing, the cripple slipped her arm word-lessly into Ernie's and the two young people followed the Rue Geoffroy-l'Asnier as far as the banks of the Seine, where they walked under the bewildered eyes of the other strollers. Though she had taken his arm, the odd young lady chose not to lean on him, so that their arms touched only when she stepped on her shorter leg, in a light skip, which nevertheless made her rest her weight against Ernie for a brief instant. 'It's only a tiny bit shorter than the other one, you know,' he said naïvely, in an ordinary conversational tone. But hardly had the words escaped his lips, when the girl laughed gaily in answer, let go of Ernie's arm, and took a few steps alone, in a deliberately limping gait, as her glance maliciously took him to witness. 'Only a tiny bit?' she said cheer-fully. Then she was silent, for Ernie came up to her, took her arm without permission, and led her off again; but supporting her this time so that she rested much of her weight on him, quiet, be-mused, following him unresistingly, her limp abolished. Suddenly they burst out laughing together, then were quiet; then laughed again, happy and embarrassed by this cascade of coincidences.

Ernie said dreamily, 'And now, does it still feel shorter?'

'No, no,' she answered in the same tone.

The sidewalk along the bank was strewn with feathery seed-pods; they stirred at the slightest breeze, mingling with others that dropped from the plane trees, in delicate spirals. Ten yards below them ran the waters of the river, imprisoned by the city. A chance taxi passed them, bearing away the vision of a cyclist with his tongue hanging out, and his passenger, a fat lady regally en-throned in the sidecar, who seemed to be sniffing pleasurably at Paris in the spring. A few soldiers of the Wehrmacht were also strolling along the bank, and Golda – that was her name – pointed out to Ernie that, by thus supporting her with both hands, he was dangerously masking part of his yellow star. Then she went on to create fantastic tales, among others that she was now in her second marriage and had decided not to stop there, if new opportunities offered. Ernie let himself float along the stream of this prattle, concentrating exclusively on the pleasure he felt in breathing, slowly, deliberately, with all the suddenly reborn vessels deep within his chest. That's enough, she said every five minutes, you can let me go now, why are you taking all this trouble? But those words too left Ernie unimpressed; they seemed subordinated to the pleasant shift that Golda's presence imposed on all things, making houses dance in the warm air, turning the Seine to a modest village stream, melting the noises of Paris into a single triumphal harmony; at the most, when Golda recited such nonsenses, Ernie straightened her up a bit with his right hand, holding tightly to her upper arm, and lifting her from the ground slightly, as if to raise her words to a more aerial flight.

Moving away from the bank, she led him towards one of the numerous blind alleys cut like drains into the rotten flanks of the blocks bordering the Seine behind the Bastille. She trifled when he asked if he might see her again, as though this were a joke of the first order; and still trifling she agreed, asking about his work schedule, apparently juggling with the preposterous idea that her 'saviour', as she said sweetly, would tomorrow be at such and such a place, at such and such a time, awaiting her good pleasure. But as she stood before the narrow iron door and offered her hand casually, she made a funny face and murmured, like a hostess, 'You will come, won't you, Mr Ernie?'

'Of course I will,' Ernie said calmly. 'I can't very well send my shadow.'

Attentive then, her voice trembling uneasily, 'But why?'

'I beg your pardon?'

'I asked you,' she went on gravely, 'why will you come?'

'To see you,' Ernie said softly, though with a slight hint of reproach.

At these words a second face appeared beneath Golda's features, etched in surprising clarity; a face of real beauty, expressing a happiness so innocent that Ernie lowered his eyes in spite of himself. When he looked up, the girl was moving away with her

3

GOLDA was not born with a limp. When the passports of emigrating Polish Jews were revoked in 1938, and the new 'Austrian' government sent them back to the Polish border, the Engelbaum family was included in the general expulsion. The story was well covered in the international press; on the first night the Jews were deported to Czechoslovakia; the next day the Czechs sent them along to Hungary; from there they went to Germany and then to Czechoslovakia again. They travelled in endless circles. Finally they got into some old boats on the Danube. Most of them drowned themselves in the Black Sea; wherever they landed, they were expelled. In a violent eddy of the Danube Golda was flung overboard, then held back at the last moment when her leg got crushed between the hull and a flat rock. They set the leg in a wooden splint: she sang to drown her pain. After complicated wanderings a few of the castaways found a footing on Italian soil, where they finally dispersed. One group entered France illegally, with Golda riding on a man's back; the wounded leg ceased to grow; that was all.

But Golda never considered herself normal after that and, although there was no bitterness in her, the fine veil of that renunciation fell over her still smiling face, her still carefree, happy manner, her character no less avid for life; she was thenceforth shadowed by an imperceptible reserve that transformed her former waiflike prettiness into beauty. She had occasional accesses of greed, eating fruit until she was sick, or intoxicating herself on the melancholy strains of a harmonica, from which she drew unbidden love-songs. She did all things without restraint, and bit into a wrinkled apple as though the whole world were between her teeth. Or she gulped vast quantities of water with no apparent thirst, in a dreamy frenzy that terrified her mother. Each excess left her satisfied on the banks of her desire, with no sadness

327

and no regrets, as though she had truly slaked her thirst at the most exhilarating springs of life. 'You're a feather-head,' her mother told her. 'You'll never find a husband if you go on like that.'

'And if I didn't, do you suppose? ... Who'd want me with a leg like that?' And Golda would burst out laughing as her mother, a woman that life seemed to have shaped to an angular character as well as shape, protested harshly and stubbornly. 'I'll choke in my own juices before I understand this little animal! If you were as ugly as a toad you could find a man to take care of you if you wanted one! And what do you think I raised you for? So you could rot where you stand? Look at me, and I managed to find your father, didn't I?'

When Mr Engelbaum was there he would throw his hands up fatalistically: 'You found me, I found you, we were both lucky ...' And sarcastically, under his breath, 'God save you from that kind of luck ... come here, my little one, and tell me what kind of husband you want.'

All these things passed over Golda's head without affecting her, without even upsetting her, and it was only in deference to parental eccentricity that she joined the game of matrimonial hide-and-seek, asking her father, 'But you're my husband, aren't you?' as she glanced in friendly mockery at her mother; and she would add these words, which never failed to infuriate her mother, 'and you're my wife, my delicious little wife. What more could I want?' And gradually as if to show her indifference with regard to her own femininity, she fell into the habit of treating her parents in this way, as if she wanted to make them feel that having married both of them she was doubly happy to be with them. Her imagination never dwelt on the future; but rather on the richer and fuller and more mysterious satisfaction of the present, which bounded her world. Her 'hungers', as she called them, her 'thirsts', her sudden 'desires', bore only on objects near at hand. When the cupboard was bare she treated herself to a marvellous 'hunger' for dry crusts. Later, when her relationship with Ernie became more tender, he asked her sometimes what thing she might desire. Ask me for something impossible, something I can't give you . . . In the beginning she answered him with hugs. And then, as she came to know Ernie's odd personality, she asked him for things which in her own mind existed only on the borderline between the possible and the impossible, such as a toilet article, some unrationed bit of food, or a pear. Her lack of imagination was the despair of Ernie, who read into it the grey humbleness of the poor. And sometimes he saw in it a kind of calculated wisdom, the spiritual fruit of suffering. Which is how he interpreted Golda's resignation to misfortune, her own and others'. He often called her 'simpleton', but one day after a long conversation on that subject, in which she had insisted on accepting and he on denying, the will of God, he said dreamily, 'It's because I don't yet know the first thing about even the beginning of what suffering is; but you, you know more than a rabbi.' At a loss, she stared at him. Another time, in the Rue Pavée, when he asked her to name a 'wish', she felt a sudden desire: to walk through Paris together without their cloth stars. They did, the whole afternoon; that was her only impossible 'desire'.

The walk took place on a Sunday in August. Since all their clothes bore a star over the left breast, Golda suggested that they should quite simply go out in shirtsleeves. The weather was fine, finer than it would ever be again in their lives. Ernie and Golda went down to the bank of the Seine and in the shadows under the arch of a bridge doffed their compromising jackets, which Golda stuffed into a shopping-basket, covering it with a newspaper. Holding hands, they strolled down the Seine as far as the Pont-Neuf where, in delicious anguish, they climbed the stone steps to the surface of the Christian world.

In those days Ernie stood very straight on his two legs, having reassumed the solemn stride of his childhood, and his long black curls – carefully combed by Golda – fell over either side of his forehead, screening the scars. His white shirt was bright under the sun, his slim body had the sinewy grace of a young cedar, and he looked like any young man with his life before him, his fingers restraining, like a casual leash, the youthful frisking of a reddish fawn with an equal claim on life. Golda seemed to dance. She

glowed with a peasant beauty; her hair tied up like a sheaf and
still glossy from the water of the Seine; a trace of lipstick that
she caressed now and then with an amazed finger, and a blouse
out of a dream, brilliant white, dazzlingly starched, which for
two weeks had promoted her to the rank of 'young lady', and
which she had insisted on ironing herself, with a delicate and
skilful touch that came straight from the heart, according to
Mr Engelbaum.

In mingled agony and delight, not daring to look at each
other, they strolled peacefully, knowing each other there, like
two birds who fly in perfect formation by instinct. Forgetting
his promise occasionally, Ernie swayed slightly towards Golda,
who brought him to order with a slight pressure of the hand.
They reached the Place Saint-Michel, and lingered in front of a
cinema. Golda broke the silence suddenly: 'I've never been to
the cinema. Have you?'

'Neither have I,' Ernie realized in surprise. 'But as we don't
have our stars,' he whispered softly in Yiddish, 'we can go in for
once: I can't even imagine what it's like. Look, I have four,
five, seven francs left.'

'It's much too expensive,' Golda said. 'And anyway I like
it better outside, where life is.'

She made a sweeping, possessive gesture. Ernie told her to
wait for him, then came back with two ice-cream cones. She
chose the green one and, twisting her neck to avoid spotting her
blouse, she bit into the ice-cream and choked, strangled, spat
up the delicious surprise. Then she followed Ernie's learned
example and, as she ran her tongue around the cone, he thought
she must be savouring her very self in the ice-cream, as she
seemed to do in all things, in her slightest word or gesture,
even in the greedy glances she trained on the nearby stalls of a
street, on the festive Boulevard Saint-Michel, and on Ernie – who
felt that he was dreaming with his whole body, and that there
was no longer the slightest trace of self-hate within him.

When they had devoured the ice-creams, they followed
the Boulevard Saint-Michel and came to the lion in the Place
Denfert, as majestic and dominant as the Lion of Judah, guardian

of the Ark of the Holy of Holies. Tempered then by the local charm of a small street, they emerged in the Avenue du Maine and saw an enchanting little square, a true oasis surrounded by sun-struck buildings with all their shutters closed, which seemed to have fallen into a final sleep. They took their time choosing their bench; Golda set down her basket; and in the immemorial attitudes of lovers in Paris they watched – without seeing them – the children, housemaids, and old ladies who were also soaking in the happiness of the Square Mouton-Duvernet.

'Imagine,' Ernie said, 'thousands of people have sat here before us; it's funny to think about it . . .'

'Listen,' Golda said, 'I existed before Adam was created. I have always alternated the two colours of my garment. Thousands of years have gone by and I haven't changed at all. What am I?'

Ernie said, 'My father had anecdotes for every occasion. Yours has riddles.'

'I'm Time,' Golda said dreamily, 'and my colours are Day and Night.'

The same thought drew them together, while Time hurtled by around them with cruel speed, branding their happiness with a star.

'I wonder why they forbid us even the squares,' Golda whispered. 'It's nature, after all . . .'

A cloud of pink silk crossed the sky of Paris, just above the tall building outlined behind the foliage, on the other side of an empty Avenue du Maine, and in his imagination Ernie followed it all the way to Poland, where, under the same evanescent August sky, the Jewish people were dying.

'Oh, Ernie,' Golda said, 'you know them; tell me why, why the Christians hate us the way they do. They seem nice enough when one can look at them without a star.'

Ernie put his arm around her shoulders solemnly. 'It's very mysterious,' he murmured in Yiddish. 'They don't know exactly why, themselves. I've been in their churches and I've read their gospel. Do you know who the Christ was? A simple Jew like your father. A kind of Hasid.'

331

Golda smiled gently, 'You're laughing at me.'

'No, no, believe me, and I bet they would have got on very well the two of them, because he was really a good Jew, you know, sort of like the Baal Shem Tov: a merciful man, and gentle. The Christians say they love him, but I think they hate him without knowing it; so they take the cross by the other end and make a sword out of it, and strike us with it! You understand, Golda,' he cried suddenly, strangely excited, '*they take the cross and turn it around, they turn it around, my God . . .*'

'Shsh,' Golda said. 'They'll hear you.' And stroking the scars on Ernie's forehead, as she often liked to do, she smiled: 'And you promised you wouldn't "think" all the afternoon . . .'

Ernie kissed the hand that had soothed his forehead, and went on stubbornly: 'Poor Jesus, if he came back to earth and saw that the pagans had made a sword out of him and used it against his brothers and sisters, he'd be sad, sad for ever more. And maybe he does see it; they say that some of the Just Men remain outside the gates of Paradise, that they don't want to forget humanity, that they too await the Messiah. Yes, maybe he sees it, who knows . . . You understand, *Goldelé*, he was a little old-fashioned Jew, a real Just Man, you know, no more or less than . . . all our Just Men. And it's true, he and your father would have got on together. I can see them *so* well together, you know: Now, your father would say, now my good rabbi, doesn't it break your heart to see all that? And the other would tug at his beard and say, But you know very well, my good Samuel, that the Jewish heart must break a thousand times for the greater good of all nations. *That* is why we were chosen, didn't you know? And your father would say, Oi, oi, didn't I know? didn't I know? Oh excellent rabbi, that's all I *do* know, alas . . .'

They laughed. Golda took her harmonica from the bottom of the basket, flashed sunlight from it under Ernie's nose and smiling still, brought it to her lips and started mouthing soft and secret tunes; it was the Hatikvah, the ancient chant of hope, and as she scrutinized the Square Mouton-Duvernet with anxious eyes, she tasted the sweetness of forbidden fruit. Ernie leaned down and plucked a tuft of slightly mildewed grass,

332

and planted the blades in Golda's still moist hair. As they got up to leave he tried to strip her of that poor garland, but she stopped his hand: 'Who cares what people think,' she said. 'And who cares about the Germans, too! Today I say who cares about everybody. Everybody . . .' she repeated, suddenly solemn.

'Ernie, Ernie,' the girl modulated tenderly, 'you know that we're condemned.'

She was sitting very erect, almost rigid, on the small, grey-blanketed bed in the room on the sixth floor, and her clasped hands lay trembling on her knees, in an attitude of supplication. The hem of her skirt was a modest half-circle. Her red woollen jacket was an explosion against the sombre shades of the room that had once been home to the four old men from Zemyock, and a random assortment of buttons fastened it up to the gleaming, starched white collar of her blouse. A few blades of grass still hung in her hair, dry now after their walk, with golden glints lending it, in the shadowy room, an autumnal red.

'Condemned, Ernie, condemned,' she repeated, suddenly cold, and Ernie discovered the same tear in the corner of her eye that he had surprised during their silent return from the river, the same bitter clearness that had edged her eyes when, under the bridge, she had put on the red jacket marked with its star; the same wilful desperate spark that had livened her face a while before, when he had almost begged her to visit his room. And now, seated on the only chair, facing Golda as two months before he had faced the four little old men since gone from him for ever, now, his hands heavy and flat against his trembling knees, Ernie Levy heard the mute cry exploding from Golda's lips, lips still stained with that scant touch of lipstick.

'Of course,' he murmured, forcing himself to smile; 'we're friends to the end.'

'No, no,' she insisted, 'you know what I mean. The end isn't far.' She leaned forward and grasped his hands, then leaned back slowly, their arms a bridge between them.

'At the moment,' Ernie said, 'it isn't far from anybody.'

'Ernie, Ernie. But us, we're . . . sort of engaged, aren't we?'

333

'At the moment,' Ernie said, very pale, 'are we the only engaged couple in the world?'

The tear Golda had been holding back since the Square Mouton-Duvernet slipped delicately down the shadowed curve of her cheek, and while she maintained her stiff, hieratic pose her lower lip sagged and she blurted, 'No, no, there are others, so many others.' Ernie had never seen Golda cry, and he found the tears of a girl one loves are more bitter than death; and he thought, look now, my God, the oppressed weep and there is no one to console them! They are naked to the violence of their oppressors, and there is no one to console them! And while Golda's tears flowed silently he discovered that the dead who were already dead were happier than the living who were still alive, and he pressed Golda's hands so tightly that she raised her eyes and smiled through the tears and said, 'Ernie, Ernie, I want to be your wife today.'

He was breathless for a moment.

'Perfect,' he said acidly. 'Excellent. The perfection of excellence. And where will you find a rabbi at this time of day?'

Golda laughed, and threw him a glance full of reproach. 'You know very well,' she said with heavy significance, 'that there is no rabbi in my heart.'

'Perfect. Excellent. Then who is in your heart?'

'Please,' Golda said.

Ernie closed his eyes, opened them, and seemed to recover his powers of speech with a jolt. 'Tomorrow,' he said abruptly, 'you'll be sorry not to have been . . . before God.'

'Tomorrow,' Golda said calmly, 'it may be too late.'

She detached one hand from the bridge of their arms, still stretched between the chair and little grey bed, and with a flutter of the free hand above their heads she added, 'And aren't we before God now? Would he abandon us at a moment like this? You know it as well as I do: when death knocks at the door, God is always there.'

'If you want,' Ernie said. 'If you want . . .'

In spite of its customary gentleness his voice carried a distant condescension which displeased Golda. 'If God wasn't here,' she breathed in a tiny, indignant voice, 'how would people stand it? You're crazy, Ernie, if you believe ... If God wasn't here, right now, if he weren't helping us all the time, we'd melt into one tear, we Jews, as my father says. *Ernie, do you understand me?* Or else,' she added distractedly, 'we'd all become dogs, like the Just Man of Saragossa when God abandoned him for only one minute. Or we'd disappear into thin air. *Do you hear me, Ernie, do you hear me?*'

Worried, she set her free hand on the quivering bridge of their arms, and while he murmured, jolted out of his dream, 'Of course, of course God is here ...' she surprised so cold a gleam in his eyes that she withdrew her hands, threw herself back on the bed, against the whitewashed wall, and sighed in desolation, 'Then you don't want me for a wife?'

'Want you?' Ernie said.

He stood up suddenly, and as he hissed, 'Want you! Want you?' his eyes glazed and his cheeks seemed to soften, to swell. Then he cried in a rasping voice, 'But my poor Goldelé, don't you know who I am?'

'Yes, yes, I know who you are,' Golda said, frightened. She felt as though she were in the presence of a shrewd madman; his conversation is a black night bristling with sharp points, one's own uneasiness is hard to define because he is gentle, sensitive, cultivated; suddenly one finds that he lacks only rationality.

'No!' Ernie repeated harshly. 'You don't know who I am! I...'

Then that abominable voice thickened and a third voice emerged, so slight that Golda had to lean forward to hear it: 'Listen, Golda,' it was whispering, 'you have to know, believe me, there is no worse Jew on earth than I, truly, truly ... Because I ... an animal wouldn't have ... you understand? ... And you, you're so ... And I'm so ... Now do you understand? Oh, Golda!'

'Don't say another word,' she told him calmly.

And as he contemplated the girl who seemed not at all alarmed, who smiled frankly at him, Ernie raised his hands; they seemed

to float in the air for an instant before he fell, the whole weight
of his shame crashing down at once, his head on Golda's knees,
her hand combing through his hair, gently smoothing the black
curls dishevelled in the storm, the girl herself unembarrassed,
feeling Ernie's breath against her thighs, savouring it, happy to
know herself so fully loved.

'I know who you are, I know who you are,' she repeated in
delight.

Ernie discovered that his old mask of blood and earth was
dissolving in Golda's words; pulling back, he looked at her,
and saw something like a distant reflection of his own face deep
in the girl's eyes. He did not know what his true face was composed of, the interior face he could sense, confusedly, within him;
but Golda's eyes seemed to be smiling simply at the face of a
man, and, liberated, Ernie smiled.

'Maybe we should kiss at least once,' Golda said.

'That is necessary,' Ernie said. 'Absolutely.'

Facing each other, seated on the edge of the bed, they made
an arch of their four hands, and each looked at the other's
mouth; but the occasion was one of such gravity that finally
Golda, confused, rose and retreated slowly towards the small
square-paned window, against which her tawny head was framed
on a background of sky.

'And now,' she said, 'what do I have to do?' As she spoke
she saw an almost imperceptible smile flit across Ernie's lips
like the stroke of a child's crayon. 'Oh yes,' she sighed, stirred
by that smile, 'I've read that men undress their women. But
what would you like, to undress me, or to have me undress
myself?'

'And you, which would you prefer?'

Golda burst into cheerful laughter: 'I'd rather undress
myself.' And then frowning, worried, 'But maybe you want to
watch me?'

'I want it if you want it,' Ernie smiled.

Her laugh was more relaxed: 'I'd rather you didn't.'

When he too was naked Ernie turned, and saw that Golda
was a taut little face, lying like a flower on the upper part of

the bed; the grey blanket covered her to the chin. Suddenly regretful about his body, he was sorry for the long, livid scars on his legs and arms and trunk, the marks of old open fractures. Then he knelt near the bed, laid his cheek against the pillow, and rubbed his black hair against Golda's russet curls. 'There is no tomorrow,' he murmured low. At these words the girl brought a milky arm from beneath the covers, and while she caressed Ernie's moist chest hesitantly her eyes opened upon him and she said, observantly: 'You're as handsome as King David, do you know that?'

4

THE night was a transparent blue when the two children came back to this world. It was past the hour of the Jewish curfew and, though Golda forbade it, Ernie could not resist following her, twenty yards behind, through the dark and deserted alleys of the Marais. At the metallic tread of a patrol she dived into a doorway; flat against a shadowed wall, Ernie congratulated himself that he had not let her face arrest alone. But the patrol passed, and Golda's halting figure took up its journey through the night. When she reached the cul-de-sac she turned and, to Ernie's amazement, waved one arm, and disappeared.

Ernie made his way back to the Rue des Ecouffes without trouble, and fell asleep the moment he closed his eyes. In the morning he found a few blades of grass on his pillow, left behind by his beloved. He rolled them carefully in a handkerchief which he slipped between his shirt and his skin. Then he went off to work, and began to construct plans for the future, plans which rose and fell in ruins, one after another, in his mind. His work consisted of stretching and tacking down untanned sheepskins, which Mr Zwingler, happy owner of a green card, delivered to the German army as waistcoats. His mouth full of tacks, the tiny furrier's hammer in his hand, Ernie fought off the rising temptations of the 'simple human happiness'. According to logic, he had claimed the night before, we shall all be arrested. According to logic, Golda had answered, I love you and I shall stay with my parents. According to logic? In the long run they were risking death with that logic. And yet Golda was right: they couldn't run away, they could only love each other, on the brink of their common fate, a few days, a few weeks. 'Maybe even a few months, who knows?' Ernie cried enthusiastically, causing a stir among his fellow workers.

The girl was not waiting on the other side of the street at

midday; and yet she knew the price of a moment's anguish. Had her parents kept her home? Had she . . .?

At twelve-thirty Ernie set out slowly for the cul-de-sac; he took the last hundred yards at a run; but when he reached the corner he stopped. An hour passed. His back to the wall, he suppressed the beating of his heart. When he entered the alleyway at last, the concierge looked out of a kind of port-hole, opened her mouth, closed it. On the second floor Ernie had to cling to the banisters; then he seemed to go up effortlessly, as if drawn by a rope fixed somewhere inside his belly, like an umbilical cord; all he had to do was to let himself be hoisted up by the horrible thing, and he was standing outside the un-assuming, iron-latched door, on a corner of which he saw the seal of the Engelbaums' doom.

The concierge was waiting for him on the ground floor. Golda's harmonica lay in the flat of her hand. She was one of those Paris concierges, in a dressing-gown, with corkscrew curls, who never forgive you for confining them to a perpetual sentry-box. The first time Ernie had disturbed her to ask where the Engelbaums lived, she had pushed her head out of the porthole and answered, furiously, Still in the same place! But today she stood modestly at the foot of the stairs, against the brass knob of the banister, with her limp stringy hair falling over her fore-head as if to hide the woodlouse grey of her flesh; and in the hollow of her palm Golda's little harmonica, broken, twisted as if by an iron hand, expressed all that the concierge might have said. But Ernie's silence was disconcerting: 'I wanted to tell you before,' she explained, 'but this is the third time I've had Jews, and it's better to let people go upstairs first. I'm not very good at saying things, though I'm not so wicked as people think. Here.'

Stunned, Ernie raised the harmonica to his lips; a shrill, unpleasant hiss came out of it.

'They stamped on it. She threw it to me and she said, "The young man," and I knew she meant you; because I know about life, I do. And one of the gentlemen picked it up to see what it was. Maybe he thought it was jewellery, or maybe just to see what it was. And he *trampled* on it. And then they all got into the truck. And . . . well, you know how it is!'

'It's nothing,' Ernie offered. 'It can be mended.' As she stared at him in amazement, he added, 'Don't worry about it, madame, all your Jews will be back. Besides, all the Jews everywhere will be back. All of them.' Then suppressing a shudder, 'And if they don't come back, you'll still have the Negroes, or the Algerians . . . or the hunchbacks.'

'What are you talking about?'

'You're right,' Ernie said. 'Excuse me, I really don't know how to apologize. And thank you, thank you. It's . . . really I don't know how to apologize!'

'Get out of here,' she said, 'before my charity runs out.'

'Re-excuse me,' the Jew insisted awkwardly. 'The words simply come out of my mouth. Sincerely. Just like that. Pop.'

The name 'Drancy' was merely an insignificant sign on the pediment of an ordinary station in suburban Paris; with its open-air platforms, its patriarchal clock through which time seemed to flow gently, *à la française*, and its sleepy little crowd of travellers, and that man in a cap who collected tickets without even looking at them, leaning back on the concrete barrier beyond which the whole town basked in the mellow caress of an Ile-de-France sun – nothing about all this seemed to betray, even to knowing eyes, the existence of the camp, the mere name of which terrified Jewish children more than any tale of devils. Ernie felt once again as he had several times in his life: stupefied, overburdened by the extraordinary power of humanity to create suffering out of nothing, or almost nothing. The sky above the roofs of Drancy was no less sweet and pure and woven with promises than the sky that had witnessed the blossoming of a juvenile Hell on the banks of the Schlosse; no less serene than the clouds contemplating the annihilation of the 429th Foreign Infantry Regiment; the Exodus, the dog's death of Ernie's despair. The day after a flared bombing by American planes, the city of St. Nazaire, almost annihilated according to the newspapers, awoke beneath a silken sky. Things took no part in the mischief of men. Somewhere Drancy harboured an abscess from which oozed an unbelievable quantity of suffering; but the town showed nothing of it, nor did its sky. Ernie followed the ticket-collector's directions, walked for a long time, saw a mass of concrete rising to dominate the low roofs around it, turned down a badly paved road, and was suddenly standing before the huge double block of buildings which seemed to have sprung fully armed from the vast emptiness of backyard gardens and vacant lots among which it stood like a bronze fortress. A cyclist coming up behind him passed at a leisurely pace, riding half-way between the barbed-wire wall and the small, snug homes opposite the concentration camp. As he passed, the cyclist threw a brief gesture of greeting at the squad of policemen posted in front of the gate (more precisely, in front of a tiny door of white wood), then, slanting off to the left, he dismounted, left his bicycle on the sidewalk, and entered the neighbouring café whistling, his cheeks sunburned and his eyes shining with thirst and life. The shadow of the barbed-wire grazed the sidewalk.

Ernie halted before the two policemen on duty and said, 'I'd like to get into the camp, please. I'm Jewish.' Then he wedged his little Zemyock bundle firmly under one arm, and bowed.

'Hear that?' the first policeman said, pointing to Ernie's star. 'He's Jewish. So it follows naturally that I'm a policeman.'

'Visits are not permitted,' the other said sententiously. 'But you can leave packages; we could make a deal . . .' And he winked heavily at the first policeman, who clapped Ernie on the shoulder banteringly: 'You can get in, but you can't get out!'

Ernie waited until their laughter had receded. 'That's precisely what I want,' he said then, his voice altogether deferential. 'To go in and not come out.' And inspired by the fat policeman's previous wink, he winked conspiratorially at the two of them, and then bowed his head slightly, smiling, as if inviting them to make fun of him freely.

From the appalled silence that greeted his words Ernie knew at once that these two characters had not received his proposal kindly; and from the angry outburst that followed their silence he understood with dismay that the policemen saw themselves only as guardians of the cattle rounded up by the Gestapo, and were greatly offended at being classed among the hunters. 'That's not our job! Go and ask somebody else! Here we only receive the goods, and that's all!' But beyond the vehement phrases of refusal Ernie could also hear a muffled reproach for the sacrilege he had committed in thus surrendering himself to the will of the German gods; instead of waiting, humbly, like all the others of his race, for the day and hour appointed by the competent authority. Finally the policeman with the more officious face (Ernie suddenly noticed a sergeant-major's triangular badge on his sleeve) raised the butt of his carbine with a nervous gesture, and pushed Ernie roughly into the middle of the street with the lacerating phrase: 'Don't you be too bloody clever.'

The bead curtains in the café door parted, and a few drinkers, one of them glass in hand, gathered around the sentries to hear what had happened. And as their suburban accents rose in the warm air, mingling with the policemen's oaths, Ernie Levy, sweating with fear, with suppressed grief, and with the heat engendered by the black wood-fibre suit he had inherited from the little old men of Zemyock, Ernie Levy stood in the middle of the road and wiped his cheeks slowly with the bundle, his eyes closed, his tongue out, like one drowning in the eternal immediacy of suffering.

One, two, three drinkers surrounded him, trying to drag this haggard, silent Jew towards the café. Close to his blurry eyes, stinging with sweat, Ernie saw the woebegone face of the young cyclist who had been whistling ten minutes before, and who could now only repeat, with the feverish assiduity of a child, 'Come along, come along, we'll talk, we'll talk . . .' while Ernie, touched by the awkward compassion of these ordinary Frenchmen, clung to the café frontage, smiled at the workingmen who were trying to drag him inside, and assured them calmly, without the slightest intonation of reproach, as if he were stating a naked fact: 'But you can't understand, you can't understand . . .'

He was not sure how it happened: the hands released him, a purring throb echoed in his skull, and while he stood, amazed to find himself alone before the sunlit façade of the café, with the bead curtain still rustling near him, a low black sedan, gleaming like a beetle, came out of nowhere and glided to a halt at the camp gate, which opened with a shrill metallic screech. Then a short man in a Tyrolean hat stepped out of the car, and examined the motionless Ernie with small, cold, official eyes; examined the young cyclist who was still on the sidewalk, his arms dangling in fear; examined the two policemen at stiff attention, whose rigidity masked the obsequious agitation behind their eyes fixed fearfully on the German inspector. Ernie raised a hand to his heart and tried to undo one of the points of the yellow star sewn to his jacket; but Mr Zwingler, a man of caution, had crowded his tight stitches too densely; exasperated, Ernie grasped the centre of the star in his right hand, as though he were sinking claws into it, and ripped it whole from the jacket in one strenuous jerk; with it came a shapeless patch of the thin and brittle wooden cloth. Then, with a slow, deliberate gesture that expressed a kind of nostalgia, he flung this shred of stuff into the middle of the street. The paving-stones glittered in the raw sunlight, which touched all things with its enchantment, the street, the policemen, the great black insect purring outside the open gate of the Drancy concentration camp, inside which he could see with heart-rending clarity, a kind of pathetic swarming at the base of the fearful concrete blocks. '*Was ist das?*' cried a harsh, angry and curiously one-pitched voice, the voice of the little man in the Tyrolean hat.

A young S.S. man in the death's-head uniform jumped out of the car and, at a sign from the Tyrolean hat, dragged Ernie into the camp, raining blows all the while on his back; they burst into the guardroom, followed by a short procession consisting of the Tyrolean hat complaining in German about the 'unheard of impudence', and the two policemen trailing along behind, wailing, in voices low enough to imply humility but high enough to be heard, 'With your permission, Herr Inspector! With your permission!'

The 'correction' Ernie received in the guard-room seemed

to him, if not justly deserved, at least in the normal order of things; but when it appeared that the Tyrolean hat did not yet consider that he had paid for his 'impertinence', and was disposed, after methodically interrogating the two policemen through an interpreter, to 'beat it out of him', as he said, to force a confession of his 'real reasons' for demanding entry to the camp, Ernie could not repress a thin smile. He nevertheless answered, with an earnest goodwill that might have seemed cowardly, that he wanted to see someone, a person very close to him, from whom the camp had unfortunately separated him. He excused himself; he had never dreamed that it would create such complications; it had seemed to him that the simplest way was to present himself at the camp gate. Whom did he want to see ...? But what good would it do to make trouble for that person; couldn't they take his word for it? What harm was there in a Jew wanting to get into the camp? he cried finally, in mingled tones of vindictive bitterness and simple irony.

A few minutes later he was on the first floor of a building situated behind one of the two huge concentration blocks; they invited him into a luxurious room, illuminated – thanks to a steel shutter – only by a single arc-lamp; the walls were of square white tiles, and the tiled floor was gently concave in the centre, where Ernie stood: a narrow drain, as in a bath-room, vanished into a hole at the prisoner's feet.

'Tell the *creature* to undress,' said the little man in the Tyrolean hat.

Violence lurked in the paraphernalia with which he surrounded himself, and in the torpid eyes of the S.S. aide (now in his shirtsleeves and nervously striking the lash against one of his boots), but, more even than in these, violence lay coiled in the thick, fair face of the seated inspector, a face rigid beneath the ludicrous hat; and in his eyes, seemingly cut from the soft gauze of German sentimentality, but in which, behind the veil of his glasses, slender serpents ringed in green stirred every now and again. And above all, violence radiated from his small, childlike mouth, moistened as if by raspberry juice, which since the beginning of the interrogation, had been riddling Ernie with

344

icy demands that would have seemed harmless enough if the use of the word 'creature', to designate the Jew, had not lent them a devilish significance. 'Let the *creature*,' said the little man in the Tyrolean hat, 'let the *creature* explain the reasons for his request more clearly. Does the *creature* have friends in the camp? What messages was he to transmit, and to whom? To what organization does the *creature* belong? Hans, explain to the *creature* that all this is just an hors-d'oeuvre, calling for a main course. Now, does the *creature* understand?' And so on and on, as if, in some inverted delirium, believing his victim and not himself possessed by a devil, the inspector wished to strengthen the barrage of violence with that bizarre form of verbal exorcism; or as if, fearing the sudden manifestation of a human face in that lump of flesh offered up to his good pleasure, he wanted to drive Ernie down all the steps that lead to nothingness, making him less than a Jew, less even than an animal, reducing him to a mere visual appearance.

'Let the *creature* strip,' he said again softly, as the slender green rings writhed frantically, savagely even in the now troubled waters of his eyes.

His aide leaned forward smiling. 'Should I help him?'

Then he stepped back into the shadows, reading in his superior's angry features that he had just transgressed against some unwritten rule of the ceremony.

The techniques of torture are ridiculously limited; the boldest, the most 'concentrated' imagination can but restrict itself to variations on a few fundamental themes bearing on the five senses: by the end of the afternoon Ernie Levy was chattering, chattering, chattering tirelessly.

Rolled up in a ball against the door, he was wriggling like a wounded caterpillar in its own juices. He had been stripped of all shame, his eyes were staring whitely, and the only defence he offered was to cup his hands around his genitals. No Jewish name, no Jewish address, nothing but that babble of infantile confabulation, like a rushing spring, irresistible.

'What do you think of it?' the little man in the Tyrolean hat asked suddenly in a soft voice.

The aide snapped to attention. 'I don't think anything of it, Herr Stoekel,' he said in a panic.

The little man wallowed in the armchair he had occupied all the afternoon, and smiled. 'Oh yes, yes, I'm convinced that you think something. I permit you to state it. I even order you to.'

'Really?' said the aide.

And when the little man shot an imperative glance at him, the aide shuffled his feet, embarrassed and coy, and at length said timidly, 'With your permission, Herr Stoekel ... When I was in Poland, at every outdoor *Aktion*, there was always at the last minute – when the whole sector had already been "handled", you know? – there was always a shit or two who came out of some hole and calmly walked up to the ditch or the truck, and who also wanted the "special treatment". And this reminds me of it ... That's all.'

The little man leaned back in the armchair and chuckled in pleasure. 'And just when did you think of that?'

'With your permission, Herr Stoekel ... it was when the animal,' he pointed to the now unconscious body, 'said "Where are you? Where are you?" It was then, Herr Stoekel.'

'And I,' the little man said, 'I thought so from the beginning.'

'Really?' his aide cried, dumbfounded. He shook his head to recover from the shock; and then, guessing from his superior's chuckles that he was expected to show admiration for a *Witz* so well contrived, the aide raised a hand to his mouth politely and said, 'With your permission, Herr Stoekel, I feel a tremendous laugh coming on.'

5

WHEN he came to he thought that he had been carried back several years, to the hospital at Mainz; not so much because of the whispering Jewish voices busy around his bed, but because his body felt as it had then, because he recognized the old desire not to cry out, though his mouth was exhaling God knew what larval gurgling that might have been a cry. Then he made out the deep grey of the concrete ceiling, the yellow stars gleaming on the attendants' white tunics. A hypodermic needle of fantastic proportions danced above his body which lay on the bloody sheets; he felt it enter his thigh, and with it a trickle of cool silence invading the already vanquished citadel of his body. He closed his eyes on that liquid sensation, and fell asleep. And while they inspected all the wounds of his flesh, while they washed and disinfected and anointed his skin, while they checked his stitches and his bones, he dreamed that he was being married, as trumpets of joy sounded upon the air:

... That morning, before dawn, before the morning star, he bathed himself so thoroughly that no human (or spiritual) being was ever as pure in the flesh as Ernie Levy is at this moment, a unique moment, when the dream is an official promise of happiness. Oh God, guided by a spirit, the crystal cake of soap slides over his skin, and he makes no movement, except to raise himself, most gracefully, when the soap seems about to lave his back. (With a gesture of his red beard the doorman at the baths points the way to the synagogue.) Do not believe, Ernie says, that my gratitude ends as I leave the baths; I am not one of those young bridegrooms who strangle the universe within a wedding ring, and I beg you to permit me never to forget your beard. What will it profit you to sell cakes of soap, if no one in the world cherishes you in memory? ... Then cherish my beard, the

347

doorman answers simply; and yet, he adds, permit me to thank you for having expressed your gratitude. I shall never forget the cake of soap I sold you. Mazel Tov.

As the doorman of the baths offers that benediction, Mazel Tov, two stars of David illuminate his eyelids and Ernie knows that the doorman is a Just Man. So, he thinks, my ancestors are rejoicing with me, and I deduce from that that I am the just heir of the Just Men and that I must be happy for all of them with my beloved. Rejoice in your fragile glass of elegant crystal, the doorman goes on, smiling in approval; *even if it is only for a single day.*

Do not believe, Ernie says immediately, that I have any desire to rejoice in my beloved; my beloved is not a fragile glass of elegant crystal, for drinking wine of the best vintages. Nor is she . . .

But the doorman clucks ironically, while his two stars stare at Ernie as if to say, You, my boy, you would teach me how the seed of the Eternal is planted? . . . and then, as a fat yellow-grey bird, he flies off towards the mouldings of the ceiling, wings trailing through the shadows of the synagogue.

The rabbi's pointed red beard is also like a beak and the black flaps of his *taleth* reveal his swallow's belly. Ernie prays, in order to drive all Christian entreaty from his body, from his heart, from his soul; and that he may receive his beloved as a beggar receives the light of the Lord. Here, on the rabbi's left, is Mother Judith, smiling, her wig unfurled in long tresses that wrap her naked body like a dress with a train; in her right eye is a tear of blood, in her left eye, a pearl of milk. And in a corner of the synagogue, surrounded by a dozen friends, is the bride, so beautiful that everything around her disappears, so beautiful that she herself blurs and becomes invisible, leaving an admirable hollow in the air so burdened with faces.

'Let us have music,' the rabbi says, 'let us celebrate'; he extends a glass of wine to the beloved, who drinks a modest half, her lower lip thrust forward like a little spoon. Ernie wets his lips in turn, then flings the glass of fragile crystal to the floor at his feet and turns to the beloved, whose soft and tender flesh is visible now, though the contours of her face remain unknown. 'So that no woman,' he says boldly, 'will ever drink from the cup on which you have set your lips, and so that no man will ever set his lips on the cup from which I have drunk. And may this broken cup be resurrected in spirit in our hearts, and may the spirit of the cup remain inviolate in our life and our death. For it is made, my beloved, of a matter that the human eye cannot grasp, and that the human foot cannot crush. Amen.'

They all applaud so vigorously that Ernie is convinced he has invented the words. It's a beautiful wedding, Mrs Feigelson says. May the evil eye stay away, Mother Judith answers; since heaven has been heaven, and earth has been earth, Ilse and Ernie were made for each other.

'I thought,' Mrs Feigelson says, 'that her name was Golda?'

'Didn't I say Golda?' Mother Judith answers gently.

And as the procession arrives at the Riggenstrasse, exposed to the four winds although the day is gaily sunny, tinted with blue and with the green of the chestnut trees, Mother Judith wraps the garment of her wig more tightly about herself; the tresses of her train are studded with apple-blossoms and with those winged seed-pods that flutter down from the plane trees upon the whole procession. Behind Mother Judith, the beloved advances on Benjamin Levy's arm; he struts and puffs as though he were the groom, instead of his son, Ernie the Blessed. And then comes the beloved's mother, a celestial creature whose hands, on Ernie's elbow, are as light as cobwebs. Her face cannot be seen, for it is entirely veiled by pink, fresh, happy tears. They sense that she is flattered to have a son-in-law like Ernie Levy.

And, marvel of marvels, the fiddler appears, with a white belly and a light, black prayer-shawl. He dances and flutters and pirouettes and turns, as if he thought he was truly a swallow. A sharp stroke of his bow opens the nuptial song: 'Who is she that comes up from the desert, holding the arm of her beloved? . . . Oi weh, oi weh, oi weh . . .'

And here is our swallow now, that stops in the middle of the road, waits for the procession, stands aside, then follows it with

tiny steps, as for a cold Catholic procession, while heads appear
at the windows, and fists spring out.

> Set a seal upon your heart, ha ha!
> Like a seal upon your arm, ho ho!
> For love is like death . . .

Each of them would now prefer the fiddler to manifest the nuptial joy more discreetly; but one cannot, alas, stop singing, merely
because fists are rising. Ernie thinks it would be fitting if one of
those fists were to come up politely: My dear Jewish ladies, my
dear Jewish gentlemen, the Fist would say, the world is not gay
enough to warrant so many violins; each stroke of the bow pierces
our hearts. Have you no pity?

But as the fists always rise at a distance, stubborn, silent, the
procession continues imperturbably, each couple talking courteously and casually, with the lazy gait of a purposeless stroll.
Even that swallow-fiddler has slowed his flight, to show his disapproval of the fists; and he enters the Levys' living-room with a
long stroke of the bow, and with a long, heart-rending voice:

> The great seas cannot reach love
> And the river cannot drown it
> Oi weh . . . Oi weh weh
> But who is she that comes up from the desert
> Holding the arm of her beloved?

Where did Mr Rajzman find that sumptuous top hat? And
dear Mrs Tuszynski the fox bonnet that so ineptly hides her
withered dewlaps? And that poor beggar of a Solomon Wish-
niack, the gold-headed cane that he holds between his legs with
both hands as if he were afraid it would fly away?

Happily the little whore from Marseilles answered his invitation in a quite simple dress; and the Second Hebrew, in his muddy
uniform. But alas, he keeps pouring out excuses each time the
drop of blood falls to his plate. Why does he make excuses? One
could die of hearing such a pure and gentle fellow excuse himself
that way. All the same, he is not too shy to sing. He gets up on his
chair at once and in a piping mousy little voice he starts learnedly
intoning a peculiar love-song no one has heard of until now. Be-

tween verses, and with numerous apologies for the interruption, he wipes away the trickle of blood running into his mouth. And when the last verse ends in the death of the lovers, he smiles charmingly to beg forgiveness for that sad ending: 'Excuse me,' he says before sitting down, 'excuse me, my friends; it's only an old local song, a penny ditty, you know, the kind that has to have a bad ending . . . to have a good ending.'

The Second Hebrew sits down to thunderous applause. Then Mr Benjamin Levy, red as a cherry, undertakes to explain something to the groom. But he is constantly interrupted by the malicious laughter of the women, and can say only this: 'My son, I recommend to you . . . For the divine instinct . . . enlightened by a shadow of worldly knowledge . . .' Upon which he collapses into his chair, also generously applauded. Ernie thanks him with a brief nod, and then concentrates his attention on the fiddler, who has sprung on to the table and is hopping about among the dishes, scraping vigorously at his instrument, his mouth shaped like an O. After a zithery ghetto tune the fiddler climbs up on to the neck of a bottle and starts dancing the old-fashioned way, on tiptoe. Entranced by the spectacle, Ernie has not glanced once at his beloved, whose elbow pressure he nevertheless senses as a kind of mist on his left. 'May I die on the spot,' Mother Judith says, 'if the lovers have spoken one single word!'

'And yet I have not ceased to speak to my beloved,' Ernie says.

'Nor I to hear him,' says the young bride.

'May my insides rot!' Mother Judith begins, indignantly: but Ernie interrupts her with a smile, his eyes still staring straight ahead: 'Where are the words?' he asks in a tone of amused confidence.

'Yes, where are they?' murmurs the beloved in echo.

'At least look at her once,' Mother Judith says plaintively.

'I have not ceased to,' Ernie says.

'He has not ceased to,' the voice says.

'Then all happiness!' Mother Judith says, embracing him.

And the whole company lines up instantly behind the plump woman, waiting for her to finish so that they may do as much. All happiness, all happiness, they all say weeping, one after another.

And then in the hallway that leads to the couple's room, the beloved murmurs: 'My feet are bearing me to the place that I love.'

The bridal chamber is so small there is hardly room for a sewing-machine, a bundle, and a miserable cot with a grey blanket. But as Ernie and Golda enter, the room, as if by the pressure of their calm breathing, distends, swells, grows to the dimensions of the couple's happiness. Now it is the immense hall of a palace, in the centre of which reigns a canopied bed, under a sky glittering with stars, a few of which drop softly to the sheets. Golda glides towards the bed with the requisite humility and good breeding, and truly Mrs Levy is right to say that she has been brought up to share the bed of a prophet (although Mordecai claims that the prophets would look upon her, even a girl of such saintly beauty, with only the cold eye of the spirit). And now Ernie takes his beloved by the hand, and between their fingers dappled butterflies are born, fluttering off into the sky of the bed. And now Golda's hand is lost in Ernie's, and from the warmth of their hands a dove is born, and gazes at them for a moment with a wide, peaceful eye. Then a hen, a white rooster, ruby-crested, a fish squirming with life, spring up between the lovers. But when Ernie draws Golda's body to himself the body is suddenly cold; he opens his eyes to find that he is embracing a scant handful of faded grass.

What has happened? Can such things occur on the banks of the Seine? And the wedding, what has become of it? Dropping the handful of grass Ernie rushes into the corridor, moaning sadly, Where are you? Where are you? ... But the corridor is as empty as the bridal chamber, and empty the dining-room, deserted by the wedding-guests years ago, perhaps, for cobwebs cover the walls and veil the corners of the ceiling, while scrolls of mildew rise from the once-joyous banquet table. Ernie now rushes out into the Riggenstrasse stark naked, pleading with passers-by to tell him which way the procession went. But why do the passers-by answer with comments about the weather? And with indifferent shrugs, with looks that pass through Ernie as though he were made of glass, phantom looks, mere absences of looks? Lowering his eyes, he suddenly discovers the bleeding, lacerated surface of his body, as in anatomy textbooks, muscles and nerves exposed.

Demoralized by that discovery (or perhaps deriving fresh strength from it), Ernie makes his way, without falling too often, to the modest waiting-room of the Drancy station, that shimmers with pleasure as it bathes, undulating and ceremonious, in the syrupy stream of sunlight. But no railway clerk will offer him the slightest information; it is a point of honour with them to close their wickets in his face; one of them is even preparing to have the skinned monster thrown out, on the grounds that the sight of him is offensive to the travellers, when Ernie feels a hand on his streaked shoulder-muscle: 'So the creature kept us waiting,' the German soldier says, 'let him hurry up. The *little train* is about to leave.'

The little train stands patiently in a station within the station, a sort of secret station; Ernie is barely on the platform when the little train quivers passionately, spitting and thundering on both levels. Ernie leaps on to the last step, pushes open a door. The whole wedding party is in the compartment.

'We were waiting for you,' they shout enthusiastically. 'We thought you weren't coming ...'

'Shall I be the only Jew left?' Ernie sighs. 'Every drop of my blood cries out for you. Know that where you are, there am I. If they beat you, am I not in pain? If they gouge out your eyes, am I not blind? And if you take the little train, am I not aboard?'

'You are, you are,' the wedding company cries, all but Miss Blumenthal, huddled in a corner with the newborn at her breast and her bundle timidly lodged between her knees; she wails in a timid, despairing voice. Oh, my angel of God, I had so hoped that you wouldn't come ...

'But why?' Ernie asks. 'Don't I belong among you any more?'

'Put on this garment,' says the patriarch, 'and instead of listening to empty bottles, sit down with Golda, who saved a place for you like the good Jewish wife she is, even though she is not the daughter of a prophet.'

'I too,' Ernie says to Golda. 'I too saved you a place.'

The girl presses his hand without answering, then, leaning from the window, shows him the extraordinary length of the little train. Other trains appear in the distance, smaller and smaller as far as the eye can see, all converging towards a central point far ahead of the locomotives, in Poland, according to Mordecai.

'I don't know where we're going,' Mother Judith says. 'I'm not a seer like some; but we're going there together, and that's good.'

'It's in Poland,' Mordecai repeats. 'God is calling us all to him, great and small, Just Men or not.'

'Yes, there will be an emptiness in the shape of a star,' says the Second Hebrew sententiously.

'But God will make them pay for it,' Moritz growls, 'he'll crush them all, like us.'

At that point Ernie feels constrained to reveal the great thought which has come to him long before: 'Moritz, Moritz, if God exists, he will forgive everyone; for he threw us all blind into the stream, and he will pluck us out of it blind, as on the day of our birth.'

'Then what will he do with us, if he forgives the others? Will he put us in a special luxury paradise?'

'No, no,' Ernie declares calmly. 'He will say to us: See now, my beloved people, I have made you the lamb of the Nations, so that your hearts may be forever pure.'

'Oh, but my friend,' the Second Hebrew cuts in, 'even so, why this journey? Why?'

No, no, no, none of Ernie's words can calm the Second Hebrew's heart, or halt the terrified rolling in the eyes of the little ones who remain silent between Mother Judith and the patriarch, each clinging solemnly to their exile's bundle. Shivering suddenly, Ernie moves closer to Golda, who slips her hand lovingly beneath his jacket, seeking the hollow of his chest. But in spite of the happiness in his soul, the touch of that hand upon his nerves and his skinned flesh is so insidiously cruel that Ernie chokes back a cry as he smiles at Golda, who is all garlanded with grass. The fiddler strikes a note then that reduces the whole wedding party to tears; his voice swells in a fullness they have never before known:

354

Oh! Can we rise as far as heaven
To ask God why things are as they are?

The train disappears along the track; but the violin music rises like smoke in the sky. Flung back into his solitude, naked and bleeding on the gravel with his legs spread wide between the rails and the wind plucking at every naked fibre of his body, Ernie thinks that separation from a loved one is the most painful foretaste of death. Then the smoke of the violin also disappears, and Ernie starts crying out in his dream. Crying. Crying. Crying.

BOOK EIGHT

NEVER AGAIN

The sun, rising over a town in Poland,
in Lithuania, will never again greet an old Jew
murmuring psalms at his window, or another
on his way to the synagogue...

Isaac Kacenelson.
Song of the Assassinated Jewish People.
Translated from the Yiddish. Posthumous.

1

A FEW freight trains, a few engineers, a few chemists got the better of that old scapegoat, the Jewish people of Poland. Along strange roads, the ancient procession to the stake ends in the crematorium; rivers to the sea, where all is engulfed, the river, the boat, and man.

In the general extermination of the Jewish race, the camp at Drancy was only one of the many drains inserted into Europe's passive flanks, one of the assembly-points for the herd being led to the slaughter, quietly and without fuss, towards the discreet plains of Silesia, the new pastures of heaven. The Germans reached such perfection in *Vernichtungswissenschaft*, the science of massacre, the art of extermination, that for a majority of the condemned the ultimate revelation came only in the gas chambers. From profane measures to sacred, from registration to the star, from assignment to transit camps, a prelude to the final mopping-up, the mechanism functioned admirably, extorting obedience from the human animal, before whom a shred of hope was dangled to the very end.

So that in the Drancy camp many believed in a distant kingdom called Pichipoi, where the Jews, under the crooks of their blond shepherds, would be permitted to graze laboriously on the grass of newer times.

And even those who had heard wind of the 'final solution' did not trust their senses, their memory, their alerted minds. An interior voice reassured them, arguing plausibly that these things did not exist, that they could not exist, that they would never exist as long as the Nazis retained the faces of human beings. But when that voice was silent they took refuge in madness, or flung themselves from a seventh-storey window on to a certain cement slab which became sadly famous in the camp. And yet they were silent to the end, leaping with their lips sealed on their terrible

359

secret; and if they had spoken it aloud none would have believed them, for the soul is the slave of life.

In the infirmary Ernie was offered a review of all the mental and physical distress that can afflict the human creature: from sick old men plucked out of homes for aged Jews in Paris to madmen plucked from their asylums, women in childbirth and·scab-bed, purulent children whose seraphic faces, like those of the women, were deformed by the venomous bites of bedbugs; day and night the long room's crude cement walls echoed with complaints that were eased by the yellow-starred attendants, all reputable physicians, once occupants of important professorial chairs, who contemplated the double- or triple-decker beds with impotent, terrified, blind expressions. Hell, Ernie discovered in the infirmary, the real Hell, is simply the vision of a Hell; nothing more than that; and to struggle in Hell, he understood as he watched the fights break out around the garbage-cans that served them as cooking-pots, is to play the Devil's game.

The 'attendants' had nicknamed him Gribouille, which means simpleton; one of them particularly, a Catholic of vaguely Jewish ancestry, hovered constantly at Ernie's bedside, as though he were fascinated by the insane act which had led the young Jew to the infirmary. 'But it's madness,' he said, raising his gold-rimmed glasses as if to get a better look at the prostrate patient; 'not content with just being Jewish, you came straight to the camp?'

'And everything that's happening now,' Ernie answered one day, 'don't you think that's madness too? Look, you've got a medal of the Virgin hanging around your neck and you have a yellow star on your jacket; is it reasonable to be born one-eighth Jewish?'

'I know, I know,' the attendant said. 'In the old days if you people disliked being persecuted you could escape it by baptism; but now it isn't your souls that they're after, it's your blood. They think you don't have souls.'

'And do you still believe in . . . uh . . . ?'

The madman on the upper bed of the double-decker bayed

loudly from deep down in his belly; without changing his heavily dignified expression the Judaeo-Christian doctor excused himself to Ernie, set one foot on the bed, hoisted himself up and said a few words to the madman, who had only wanted to make his existence known and who, satisfied, was then silent for an hour. The attendant came down to Ernie's bed again, and as he gently answered his patient's question the latter, ill at ease, a bit distracted by the veneer of pedantry with which the ex-professor masked his prisoner status, suddenly saw a slight trembling behind the gold-rimmed glasses in the big myopic eyes that were so Frenchly blue, a vague terror which revealed, like a tear in a tapestry, the compact suffering mass of the man's being.

'Do I still believe, my poor Gribouille? ... It depends on the times. When I was a gentleman, as you put it, one of my friends used to tease me by asking if God, in his omnipotence, could create a stone so heavy that he couldn't lift it. Which is more or less my position: I believe in God, and I believe in the stone.'

Ernie thought it over; decided to smile: 'I don't understand at all, Mr Jouffroy. You're not angry with me?'

It was said in such a way that the attendant did not consider it undignified to chuckle several times, covering his mouth courteously with one hand. 'Gribouille,' he said finally, 'Gribouille ... you're right; we French are often *intelligent for nothing* – that's the expression you use, isn't it? To tell the truth, I don't know any more whether I'm Catholic or not. When I found out a year ago that I was one-eighth Jewish, at first I was very ashamed; I couldn't help it, I had the feeling that I'd crucified Our Lord, that ... you understand don't you? I was still on *the other side*. And then I came here, and I began to be ashamed of the part of me that isn't Jewish. Terribly ashamed. I kept thinking of those two thousand years of catechism that prepared ... the ground ... that allowed ... you understand, don't you?' The torn gap in his glance widened. 'Two thousand years of Christology,' he said dreamily, as if to himself. 'And yet, I know it's absurd, but I still believe, and I love the person of the Christ more than ever. Except that he's not the blond Christ of the cathedrals any more, the glorious Saviour put to death by the Jews. He's ...' Gesturing

at the infirmary, he leaned over Ernie's stinking bunk and looking quite disintegrated, 'He's *something else*,' he whispered in a
suddenly Jewish tone, the miserable tone of a prisoner.

And then, to the great surprise of Ernie, the neighbouring
patients and perhaps himself, he raised his hands to his temples
to hold his glasses firm, and broke into sobs.

The October sky was like a sheet of dirty snow ready to fall
into large empty space in the courtyard; gusts of wind with
human voices raised black dust from the slag that carpeted
the entire camp. Only a few children were running around,
mufflers flapping, on the square of cement reserved for prisoners'
walks outside the 'normal' building. Near the gate S.S. men
gleamed in all their leather and all their steel; they had replaced
the French policemen, who in the end were found to be seriously
lacking in enthusiasm. Doctor Louis Jouffroy, one-eighth Jew,
supported an emaciated, pallid Ernie, grotesque in his black suit,
whose condition no longer justified the privilege of a stay in the
infirmary. They ambled along beside the Technical Building,
past the little red-brick kiosks, and joined the 'normals' in their
walk.

Ernie's head was shaved, but a quarter-inch fuzz covered
all traces of torture; his lobe of right ear, though, had been
imperfectly sewn up and flapped loosely, as if exhausted, and
his smile disclosed several black gaps that gave him an old man's
mouth. As they came up to one of the doors a boy of about
fifteen emerged excitedly, his hair savage in the wind, his face
blue with chilblains, and waved a pair of huge gloves tied to his
forearm, shouting triumphantly, 'I'm not cold any more,
with my gloves! I'm not cold!' He ran the length of the promen-
ade, screaming, 'I'm not cold. I'm not cold!' and disappeared
into another doorway.

The one-eighth Jew commended Ernie to the care of the
floor supervisor, Stairway A, Second Floor. But when they heard
the name Gribouille they surrounded his bed, laughing, and
brought him bread, soup, vitaminized biscuit, all seasoned
with a generous sprinkling of advice on how to avoid hunger,

thirst, sickness, death, etc. The room differed from the infirmary only in that it was calm and silent by contrast; some played cards, read, prayed aloud; one little group huddled around a stove that radiated nothing but smoke. When they left him alone for a while, Ernie slipped from beneath his single blanket, shivering, and went upstairs, where he haunted the women's dormitories, inquiring whether anyone had seen, some three months before, a *pretty redhead named Golda.* Only once did he dare to mention that she *hopped* a bit, but in such a pretty way, so amusingly ... They answered him evasively; in three months so many convoys had left so much emptiness, so quickly filled by new arrivals; they didn't know, no one could keep track, no one remembered anyone. And behind his back, they whispered. At the door to Stairway B he hesitated; he was intoxicated with all these feminine dormitories and their indescribable disorder, in which innumerable little signs betrayed the desire to preserve, to the last moment, this fur coat, that make-up kit, this ludicrous or charming knick-knack – the flotsam of the sex. Then, as he entered a new room, his heart beat rapidly even before he recognized Golda's hair under a distant bunk, in the shadows of the row opposite the windows.

She was sitting quite still on the edge of the bunk, with her head in her hands, and did not hear him approach; he touched the hem of her red jacket, to make sure it was real, and only then did she unveil a face that was both swollen by fleas and bedbugs, and hollow, gaunt, yellow with wretchedness. Chilblains had purpled her beautiful hands, which she brought to her mouth to quench a cry. Ernie sat down beside her and wept. When he looked at her again he realized that her eyes were dry, examining him with the sad indifference common to all the internees.

'You too,' she articulated coldly.

'And your parents?' Ernie said.

'Gone a long time ago. Pichipoi.' She paid no attention whatsoever to the despair with which Ernie was wringing his swollen, reddened, frozen hands.

'Have you been here long?' she asked politely; and without

363

staying for an answer she went on in the same neutral tone, 'I can hardly recognize you, you poor thing. You look as though you'd been run over. All you have left is your eyes. And what about me, do you still think I'm pretty?'

'Golda, Golda,' Ernie said.

Curious groups gathered at a distance; a woman with dishevelled hair peered down from the upper bunk. The girl nodded slowly. 'There's no more Golda,' she said, 'it's every man for himself here. But I'm glad to see you anyway. You mustn't think . . .'

'Are you hungry?' Ernie asked.

She stared helplessly, a dawn of understanding in her eyes.

'Wait,' Ernie said, rising.

And tapping her nose in good humour, he managed to reach the exit door without betraying his weakness. But outside, in the icy wind of the roll-call ground, the after-effects of his dysentery bent him double, hands clawing at his belly. Yet there was a strange peace within him, for it seemed to him that nothing, not men, not the circumstances that make and unmake men willy-nilly, could ever again exile him from that great Jewish ark where, since his admission to the infirmary, he had come to rest side by side with the invisible shadows of his own people; where, in the last few moments, he had been able to touch Golda, even though ugly, soured, indifferent to the past. With joyful gestures he raised his blanket and found the chunk of bread, the vitaminized biscuits, intact; then with a grin that tried to be a smile, and in a very natural voice, he asked whether anyone would be good enough to give him a piece of chocolate or some other delicacy that might 'gladden a heart'. His immediate neighbours turned round scandalized.

'You were right,' a card-player said in Yiddish, 'this one's a comedian. You could split your sides.'

'But it's not for me,' Ernie protested, tears in his eyes; 'I swear it, it's to give away!'

The laughter increased; in a flash Gribouille's latest performance had reached the far end of the room. But a man with grey temples, stretched out on a near-by bunk, slipped a hand into

364

a secret opening in his straw mattress and extracted a spectacle-case containing two lumps of sugar and a few acid drops. He emptied it into his hand, paused to reflect, then slowly replaced one of the sweets into the case. Shuffling up to Ernie, who stood haggard and trembling at the foot of his bed, shoulders bowed under their gibes, he smiled and handed the boy his small fortune. 'Brother,' he murmured with a note of almost imperceptible regret, 'brother, little brother, you're the one who's right; it's very important to give ...' he hesitated, his smile widened, '... when you have nothing.'

Ernie guessed immediately that their attitudes had changed while he was gone; a group of women awaited him on the landing, and they all stared at him with a melancholy, familiar, emphatic gaze. One of them, a tiny, hooded dumpling, withdrew her hands from the blanket that shrouded her like a burnous, clapped vigorously, and shouted stupidly, 'Bravo!' Then the others giggled conspiratorially, but there was nothing disagreeable about all this strange behaviour, and when he went into the dormitory Ernie had another surprise; a troop of magpies chattering around an embellished Golda, to whose lips a young internee was solemnly applying rouge. At his approach the whole group fluttered away, and even the tenants of the neighbouring beds strolled to the far end of the dormitory, abandoning Golda, dolled-up like a madwoman in the middle of the aisle that separated the cubicles of white wood. When she saw the lump of black bread and the sweets he was clutching to his chest, her eyes, all veined with purple, gleamed so brightly that she looked beautiful again. She beckoned to Ernie and made him sit down; and as he silently removed her make-up, with his saliva-damped handkerchief and an artist's care, she kept repeating, only half embarrassed, 'They wanted to make me pretty ... They did it ...' And then she had to laugh, a velvety, gentle laugh, and rubbed Ernie's hand against her cheek, saying, 'I didn't know that Gribouille was you ... Did you come to the camp because of me?'

'No, of course not,' Ernie said in a tiny voice.

Under the powder and the hideous whiteness of her face the girl's eyes were as loving, as clear, as mysteriously bubbling with life as under the arch of foliage that had shaded them in the Square Mouton-Duvernet. 'Then there are other skies,' she sighed, 'another earth, other thoughts than the ones that come to you in Drancy?'

Towards the middle of October the Feldgrau buses deposited fifteen hundred orphans in the middle of the snow-covered roll-call ground, orphans between four and twelve years old, arriving from the collection camp at Pithiviers; they were jammed like insects into the special stall-like dormitories of the Technical Building and, as they went on screaming pathetically for their parents, it was decided to tell them that they would meet them again soon in Pichipoi, which was evidently the next, if not the last, site of their incarnation on this earth. Many of the smaller ones did not know their own names, so their companions were questioned, and supplied bits of information; names and surnames thus established were inscribed on small wooden medallions strung around the children's necks. A few hours later some of the little boys were bearing medallions inscribed Estelle or Sarah, as the children played innocently with the medallions, swapping them for fun.

Five hundred adults were added to them for the shipment scheduled at dawn the next day but one. When he learned that Golda was on the list, Ernie paid a discreet visit to the secretariat, where he found a dozen postulants like himself, but female: some wanted to join their husbands in a common fate, others felt pity for the children. The superintendent of documents sat in a tiny office at the end of a corridor on the ground floor, a kind of depot for forms and dossiers, illuminated by a single red bulb which gleamed like a bloodshot eye over a funny little puppet with pince-nez, the sleeve-garters of a city clerk, a skull of glittering, soft, pink skin, and tiny porcelain-blue eyes that examined you with the disincarnated benevolence of a nineteenth-century photograph. The yellow star on his meticulously pleated shirt seemed a stroke of pure malice.

'But you're out of your mind,' he murmured in a thoroughly French voice when Ernie stated his strange request.

'Yes, that's right,' Ernie agreed, breaking into an idiotic laugh, 'I'm completely crazy, you guessed it.'

The bureaucrat's charming eyes narrowed in suspicion. 'Unless,' he said, pointing his pen at Ernie, 'you believe in that kingdom of the Jews? But suppose it was ... *something else?*'

Overplaying his part slightly, Ernie applauded three times, alarmed the superintendent altogether with an attempt at an entrechat (his toothless smile and emaciated body, ghostly in the black suit, made the gesture perfectly demented), and let out a piercing laugh: 'Mr Blum, wherever there are Jews, there is my kingdom!' The little man shrugged, and when it became clear that the candidate for that kingdom obstinately refused to choose postponement, the superintendent hunched over his lists, sucked at his pen, and suddenly noticing a namesake of the young madman, struck out the word Hermann and wrote in, above it, in a good round hand: Ernie.

The search took place early in the afternoon.

As usual, the inspectors of the French Police for Jewish Problems officiated in the barracks adjoining the S.S. building. A table was set up near the door and there, all the afternoon, volunteers untied and retied, as best they could, the children's bundles. The little girls' brooches, earrings, and bracelets went the way of the adults' jewels. A ten-year-old girl left the barracks with a bloody ear: a searcher had ripped off an earring which, in her terror, she was unable to remove quickly enough. Ernie also noticed a six-year-old boy, tousled, dirty, wearing a nice little jacket ripped at the shoulders, with a good shoe on his left foot and none at all on his right, barehanded, the proud possessor of nothing under the sun.

After the search the two thousand souls were herded into the Technical Building, thenceforth isolated from the rest of the camp. The stalls in these special dormitories were not even furnished with straw. The tumult soon became indescribable; terrified by the search, the children were out of their minds. But the adults were forming teams, and Ernie, with the help of a woman doctor and a few nurses and teachers, arranged the distribution of children around nuclei of adults. Then, until night fell, the few owners of pens or pencils which had escaped the search filled in the farewell cards. Thoughtful housewives and little old illiterate ladies crowded around Ernie, who could do no more than repeat the same formula, or an atrocious banality: *We leave tomorrow for an unknown destination ...*

'My handwriting is a little shaky,' he said, smiling, 'but that's because I have a tiny pencil.'

Golda and he slept with two children between them. In the darkness he stretched out a hand and found Golda's, waiting for it. Now and then a breath of panic followed a shriek, and forests of little arms rose in the suddenly clamourous darkness. He had to get up and spread the balm of an adult voice. But women too, turning their backs on life, were losing their reason, dying of fear in the shadows, and the only remedy, the only way to quiet the storms swelling in their throats, was to place a child in their arms. Occasionally a neighbouring roomful of people exploded in the night and then, jerked out of their torpor, restored to the cold, to the hunger, to the incomprehensible destiny hovering above them, the children answered with equally horrified wails, launching the strange dialogue that several old internees had described in Ernie's presence, but of which he had never suspected the colossal horror. At dawn the children were sleeping so deeply that the S.S. Death's-heads had to drag them out of the room before they once again became aware of what was happening in the adult world. But in the courtyard all turned silent, as if by magic. Quietly clutching an adult's hand or arm, they answered the roll-call as distinctly as possible. Those who did not know their names took their cues from the adults, who deciphered the medallions in the yellowish clarity of the floodlights set up on observation towers. Then the stars were snipped off and thrown to the centre of the courtyard, which was soon like a plain carpeted with buttercups; finally the machine-guns were trained on the flock, the gates opened, and the first transport buses drove into the yard.

At the last moment the Germans rushed at an internee who

wore a bowler and sported a display handkerchief in his breast pocket. He was flung down in the snow, stamped on, struck with rifle butts, but seemed outraged only by the way an S.S. man, to start things off, had bashed his fist into his bowler on his very head, thus flattening the last vestige of his dignity. A few children gave in to shrill laughter. Ernie realized quite clearly that he was entering the last circle of the Levys' hell. And when, an hour later at the Drancy station, the sliding doors closed over the dark night of the Jews packed into freight-trucks, even Ernie could not help shouting with all the herd howling its terror in one single breath: Help! Help! Help! As if he too wanted, for one last time, to stir up a void in which the human voice could echo – however feebly.

2

His head on Golda's knees, he emerged from his icy torpor, and thought that the soul must be woven of nothingness, in order to bear, without breaking, the trials that God reserves for men of flesh and blood. 'You were crying in your sleep,' Golda's remote voice said, 'your tears never stopped. Can't you dream?' she finished in a plaintively reproachful tone as Ernie arched up on his elbows, incredulously rediscovered the fantastic darkness of the freight-truck, which seemed to be rolling alone, in a clacking of wheels and axles, delivered up companionless to the engine, an antediluvian beast breathing fire, dragging to its lair the hundred or so bodies stretched out on the jolting floor. They were like congealed corpses, though there were only a few dozen who had found true consolation, cadavers heaped up pell-mell, limbs intertwined and skulls knocking, in a corner of the car first established for sick children, which had imperceptibly become a morgue. 'Wait, let me wipe your eyes first. They're all red.' Laying his head in her lap, the girl blew on her stiff, cold handkerchief and wiped her lover's inflamed eyes; suddenly aware of a presence, he woke up completely and discovered the circle of children scattered round the couple. There were about fifteen of them, of all ages, crammed together in various attitudes, their bodies interlaced by the same reflex that brought men and women together in compact masses under the shared blankets; their eyes, in blue faces ravaged by dysentery, were black in the shadows, all staring at Ernie with the same animal patience; some opened their mouths, or let hang their lower jaws, and threads of vapour, grey as smoke, escaped a silent gash of lips.

'They're waiting for you to say something,' Golda told him. Moved by the fierce, somewhat childish, rancour that had raged in her for twenty-four hours, while most of the beings imprisoned in their compartment of doom had ceased to be human, she added spitefully, 'I can't even have you to myself any more.' As she said it, other childish figures emerged from the gloom, moving closer on their knees or crawling on their elbows across the straw blackened by the soot and soiled by human filth. 'What time is it?' Ernie asked. 'It's the third morning,' Golda articulated with an effort. 'And it still hasn't rained?' 'No, but the dew made icicles.' And with numb fingers, she ripped off one of the stalactites that the night had infiltrated through the cracks in the truck, and held it to Ernie's lips. Before the envious eyes of the children Ernie, still dulled by sleep, sucked at it slowly, sadly, deliciously, his palate seared by the cold, his thirst slaked in unspeakable joy. 'So I'm nothing to you?' Golda said. Ernie understood that she wanted consolation before he turned to the children; he jacked himself to a sitting position, put his arms tightly round the mass of blankets that enveloped her, parted the woollen things she had borrowed from the dead to hood her face, and kissed her marbled blue cheek, then clung to her, cheek against cheek. 'You're everything to me,' he began in the slow, chanting voice that was his only balm for the flayed nerves of the wretches in his charge; 'you're more to me than bread and water and salt, more than fire, more than life . . .' He went on, without paying much attention to the meaning of his words, trying only to recapture the solemn, soothing rhythm of Biblical verses, while Golda, exhausted by her sleepless night, set her forehead against Ernie's shoulder and sank into the oblivion of tears. 'All this,' Ernie said – the children were hanging on his words – 'is because you believe in this train and everything that's happening, when in fact they don't really exist . . . do they, children? . . . All this is because you believe your eyes and your ears and your hands . . .' As he spoke the children in the first rows let their jaws drop, and some of them started to wag their heads left and right, as if to sink more quickly into the dream flowing from Ernie's mouth, but others came closer, greedily, craning their necks, lips already moist.

'You're not talking for me,' Golda sobbed, 'you're talking for the children.'

Frightened, the nearest children retreated with a horrifying, slow passivity, backing away on their elbows or knees, without a word, while they stared intently at Ernie's mouth; and Ernie was once more amazed at the extraordinary toughness of his soul. O God, he thought, you have given me the soul of a cat, that must be killed nine times before it dies. Golda was still lying against his shoulder; he stroked her cheek, scantily stretched his lips in a sweet, blackish smile, winked cunningly at the first row, and murmured in Yiddish, 'Don't run away, little ones, don't mind her; come closer, and I'll tell you what our kingdom is like . . .' A little boy in the first row opened an eye – swollen by a blow he had received in the explosion of panic the night before – and whispered tonelessly, as though his tongue were unable to reach his dry palate, 'It's not for us, mister, it's for the other one, the one who's sick, he's asking for you,' 'Why didn't you wake me up?' Ernie asked. 'I thought, as it was only the first time . . .' Golda said, ashamed. Ernie released her without answering and, with a sudden acute awareness of the tearing in all his limbs, crawled through the crowd of children, who edged away to make room for him, or over whom he climbed so as not to make them lose the advantages of immobility; the child was lying two yards from the morgue, and the old woman doctor was sitting next to him, her back to the wall, her rigid face like a mask beneath the red cross cap which some strange aberration compelled her to wear, although her functions had been reduced, since the night before, to rubbing the icy bodies of dysentery victims and watching them die; her eyes were fixed on some invisible point in the dimness of the sealed freight-truck, and did not even blink at Ernie's approach. 'He's dead,' she said simply. The old woman's face was a desiccated bone, blue in the cold, and her nostrils were as pinched as those of the dead child. Sensing the children's stares behind him Ernie said, clearly and emphatically, so that there would be no mistaking him, '*He's asleep* . . .' Then he picked up the child's corpse and with infinite gentleness laid it on the growing heap of Jewish men, Jewish women, Jewish children, joggled in their last sleep by the jolting of the train.

'He was my brother,' a little girl said hesitantly, anxiously, as though she had not decided what attitude it would be best to take in front of Ernie.

He sat down next to her and set her on his knees. 'He'll wake up too, in a little while, with all the others, when we reach the Kingdom of Israel. There, children can find their parents, and everybody is happy. Because the country we're going to, that's our kingdom, you know. There, the sun never sets, and you may eat anything you can think of. There, an eternal joy will crown your heads; cheerfulness and gaiety will come and greet you, and all the pains and all the moans will run away . . .'

'*There*,' a child interrupted happily, repeating the words rhythmically as though he had already said, or thought, or heard, them several times, '*there, we'll be able to get warm day and night.*'

'Yes,' Ernie nodded, 'that is how it will be.'

'*There*,' said a second voice in the gloom, '*there are no Germans or railway-trucks or anything that hurts.*'

'No, not you,' an enervated little girl interrupted, 'let the rabbi talk, it's better when he does it.'

Still cradling the dead boy's sister on his knees, Ernie went on. Around him the heads of his young audience nodded weakly on their shoulders, and he noticed that further off a few men and women had begun to eavesdrop; their eyes gleamed vaguely with the same delirium that was exciting the children. The girl on his knees broke into a tearless weeping, like several others who had wept too much in the first two days; and with her eyes wide open on Ernie, and her blue fists balled against her chest, she fell asleep.

'And me too, mister,' a dying voice whispered, 'won't you make me sleep? I haven't slept since the beginning.' The voice belonged to a boy of about twelve, with a face so emaciated that his protruding eyes seemed to hang in place only by a miracle.

'And why?' Ernie asked.

'I'm afraid.'

'But you're a bit big for me to rock you to sleep,' Ernie said, smiling in spite of himself, 'I wouldn't know how to do it.'

'Just the same,' the dysenteric begged, 'even if I'm big, I want to sleep.'

Ernie slipped the little girl under the blankets and after strenuous efforts on both sides he managed to hoist the boy on to his thighs; but he himself was so weak that, instead of rocking him, all he could do was alternately to raise the sick boy's head and then his knees, all glistening with excrement. With the help of a few women who had somehow contrived to stand up, Golda began rubbing the limbs of the most threatened children. '*When we reach the Kingdom of Israel* ...' Ernie murmured, hunched over the boy, whose eyes were filming over, yellowish, dreamy, peaceful. Then suddenly the doctor's arid, ravaged face was close to his own. 'What are you doing?' she whispered in his ear, while the children retreated in fear. Ernie looked down and discovered that the living corpse he was rocking had become a dead corpse. The doctor clutched at his shoulder, her fingernails digging into what remained of Ernie's flesh.

'How can you tell them it's only a dream?' she breathed, with hate in her voice.

Rocking the child mechanically, Ernie gave way to dry sobs. 'Madame,' he said at last, 'there is no room for truth here.' Then he stopped rocking the child, turned, and saw that the old woman's face had altered.

'Then what is there room for?' she began. And taking a closer look at Ernie, registering all the slightest details of his face, she murmured softly. 'Then you don't believe what you're saying at all? Not at all?'

She was weeping with a kind of bitter regret, and laughed a short, terrified, demented laugh.

3

THE hours that Ernie Levy lived through in the sealed freight-truck were lived through by a host of his contemporaries. When the fourth night fell on the chaos of tangled bodies, a Polish night pressing its whole dark and icy weight on their crushed souls like some fantastic beast – against which some of the adults were still struggling, blowing on their hands or rubbing some frostbitten limb – not a single complaint, not a protest, not a single moan came out of the children's half-open mouths. Even gentleness was powerless to make them speak. They just stared at you long and expressionlessly; now and then those who were cramped against adults' bodies scratched at random with insensible claws, like little animals, not to remind the world of their existence, but rather from some reflex born in the still tepid depths of their entrails, a kind of dimmed pulsation that slid new blood along their veins, a vague trickle of life perpetuating itself in bodies abandoned by their extinct souls but as yet uncomforted by God. Inert, his back to the wall, Ernie did not dare to look and see whether Golda's face, resting against his shoulder, still concealed some breath of life or whether she had been silently drained of what made her – because of, in spite of, the horrors of the flesh – the object of his love; but for some time he had been incapable of the slightest movement, and only the upper part of his body floated above the mass of little bodies clinging to him, bodies which had slowly surrounded him, clambering over each other, attracted by the memory of his words, freezing in position then, as they were now, a wave of cold flesh settled at the level of his heart, binding him in a network of hands, flat upon his skin or clawing deep into his flesh. Occasionally, thinking that one of them might be able to hear him, Ernie created gentle, happy words in the ice-palace of his mind, but in spite of all his efforts the words were now incapable of passing the threshold of his duly sealed lips.

The engine whistled, shuddered, ground reluctantly to a halt. A sluggish tremor ran through the truck. But when the first barking of dogs was heard, an electrifying fluid terror spread into the outstretched bodies one by one, and Ernie stirred too, thunderstruck, supporting Golda, who had been jolted out of her stupor. The surviving children started yelling with all their poisonous breath, surrounding Ernie with a gaseous ring of decomposing entrails. Outside, pliers were already snipping through the seals set at Drancy, and the doors slid back, admitting a blinding flow of light and the first silhouettes of the S.S. Death's-heads, carrying whips and bludgeons, restraining black mastiffs on taut leashes, plunging their gleaming boots into the stormy tide of deportees, scouring it out to the platform with shouts and blows that roused even the dying, set them suddenly into motion, like a flock of sheep, jostling and crushing each other. At dawn the platforms seemed unreal beneath the floodlights, and the jerry-built station opened out on a strange square, bounded by a chain of S.S. men, dogs, and a barracks dimly visible in the agonizing fog. Ernie never knew how, with Golda and a child clinging to his arms, he too managed to run the length of the platform, caught in the mad panic of the survivors, many of whom were absurdly dragging bundles or suitcases. In front of them a woman tripped into her suddenly open suitcase, her skirts flying up to her waist. Immediately a German stepped forward with one of those savage animals baying on his leash and, visibly addressing the animal he shouted, before the terrified eyes of the motionless group, *Man, destroy that dog!* Under the poor woman's shrieks Ernie started running again, aware of nothing but the crackle of his brain on fire and the pressure of Golda's hand and the child's hand, wondering suddenly if that sharp small cry belonged to a girl or a boy . . .

In the dawn's black heights, the square, trampled by hundreds of Jewish feet, also seemed unreal. But Ernie's alert eye was soon noting fearful details: here and there on the pavement – obviously swept in haste just before the train's arrival – abandoned objects still lay around, bundles of clothing, open suitcases, shaving-brushes, enamelled pots ... Where had they come from? And why, beyond the platform, did the tracks end suddenly? Why the yellowish grass and the ten-foot barbed-wire? Why were the new guards sneering incomprehensibly at the new arrivals, who, recovering their breath, were trying to settle into their new life – the men mopping their brows with handkerchiefs, the girls smoothing their hair and holding their skirts when a breeze sprang up, the old men and women laboriously trying to sit down on their suitcases, silent, all of them, in a terrible silence that had fallen over the entire herd. Apart from the sneering and the knowing laughter, the guards seemed to have exhausted their anger, and as they calmly gave orders, blows and kicks, Ernie understood that they were no longer driven by hate, but were going through the motions with the remote sympathy one feels for a dog, even when beating him; if the beaten animal is a dog it may be supposed, with a fair degree of probability, that the beater is a man. But as he re-examined the barrack building a vague gleam shone through the fog, high in the grey sky, capped by a cloud of black smoke; and suddenly he became aware of the nauseating smell that hovered in the square, a smell that was quite different from the stagnant fumes of dysentery, an acrid smell of organic matter in combustion. 'You're weeping blood,' Golda said suddenly in amazement. 'Don't be silly,' Ernie said, 'nobody weeps blood.' And wiping off the tears of blood that furrowed his cheeks, he turned away from the girl, to hide from her the death of the Jewish people, which was written clearly, he knew, in the flesh of his face.

The crowd was thinning out in front of them. One by one the deportees passed before an S.S. officer who was framed between two manned machine-guns; the officer was directing the prisoners with the end of his swagger-stick, distractedly, left or right, gauging them with a quick, practised glance. Those on the left, men between twenty and forty-five, whose outward aspect was relatively sturdy, went to line up behind

377

the chain of S.S. men, along a row of roofless trucks which the vanishing fog had just revealed to Ernie's haggard attention; on one of those open trucks he even noticed a group of men apparently wearing pyjamas, each of whom was holding a musical instrument; they composed a kind of ambulant orchestra that farcically waited in the truck, wind instruments to their lips, drumsticks and cymbals raised, ready to blare forth. The prisoners on the right, all children, women, old men and invalids, huddled together raggedly near the barracks, shrinking before a wide grating set directly into the wall of that strange building. 'They're going to separate us,' Golda said coldly. And as if echoing her fears, the few children who had mysteriously found Ernie's trail through the crowd pressed closer around him, some of them simply offering the mute reproach of their heavy eyes, swollen like abscesses, others clinging to his sleeve or the tail of his pitiful black jacket. Ernie caressed their little heads, quite sure now of their imminent destiny, and contemplating Golda's anxious face, widening his eyes fogged by the blood congealing under the lids, he dizzied his heart one last time with the girl's beloved features, with her soul so well made for the simple marvels that earth dispenses to men, from which the curt movement of the S.S. doctor's swagger-stick would shortly separate him for ever. 'No, no,' he said, smiling at Golda, as a fresh flow of blood streamed from his eyes, 'we'll stay together, I swear it.' And to the children, many of whom were now risking feeble moans, 'Children, children,' he reassured them, 'now that we've come to the kingdom, do you think I would stay out of it? *We shall enter the kingdom together,*' he went on in the grave, inspired voice which alone could touch their souls so full of darkness and terror, '*in a little while we shall enter it hand in hand, and there, a banquet of succulent foods awaits us, a banquet of old wines, of succulent foods full of pith, and of old wines, decanted ... Over there, my little lambs ...*'

They listened without understanding, gentle smiles shadowing their tortured lips.

shit' which had just pronounced those words. 'Well,' he said, 'we shall look after you.'

The swagger-stick made a semi-circle. The two young S.S. men smiled slyly. Staggering with relief Ernie reached the sad human sea that lapped the edges of the barrack; and with Golda hugging him and the children's little hands tugging at him, he went in, and they waited. At last, all were assembled. Then an Unterscharfuehrer invited them, loudly and clearly, to leave their baggage where it was and to proceed to the baths, taking with them only their papers, their valuables, and the minimum necessary for washing. Dozens of questions rose to their lips: should they take underwear? could they open their bundles? would their baggage be returned? would anything be stolen? But the condemned hardly knew what strange force made them hold their tongues, and proceed quickly, without a word or even a look behind them, towards the breach in the ten-foot wall of barbed-wire by the barrack with the grating. At the far end of the square the orchestra suddenly struck up another tune and the first purring of engines was heard, rising into a sky still heavy with morning fog, then disappearing in the distance. Squads of armed S.S. men divided the condemned into groups of a hundred. The corridor of barbed-wire seemed endless. Every ten steps, a sign: To the Baths and Inhalations. Then the herd passed by a row of anti-tank spikes, then along an anti-tank trench, then by a hedge of coiled thin steel wire; finally, down a long, open-air corridor between yards and yards of barbed-wire. Ernie was carrying a little boy who had fainted. Many were supporting one another. And in the crowd's more and more crushing silence, in its more and more pestilential stench, smooth and graceful words sprang to his lips, scanning the children's steps with reverie, and Golda's with love. It seemed to him that an eternal silence was closing down upon the Jewish cattle as it was led to the slaughter; that no heir, no memory would supervene to prolong the silent parade of victims; no faithful dog would shudder, no bell would toll; only the stars would remain, gliding through a cold sky. 'O God,' the Just Man Ernie Levy said to himself, as the blood of pity streamed from his eyes again, 'O Lord, we went forth like this thousands of years ago. We walked across arid deserts, through the Red Sea of blood, in a deluge of salt and bitter tears. We are very old. We are still walking. Oh, we would like to arrive at last!'

The building resembled a huge bath-house; to left and right large concrete pots cupped the stems of faded flowers. At the foot of the small wooden stairway an S.S. man, moustachioed and benevolent, told the condemned, 'Nothing painful will happen! You just have to breathe very deeply. It strengthens the lungs. It's a way of preventing contagious diseases. It disinfects.' Most of them went on in silently, pressed forward by those behind. Inside, numbered coat-hooks garnished the walls of a kind of gigantic cloakroom where the herd undressed one way or another, encouraged by their S.S. cicerones, who advised them to remember the numbers carefully; cakes of stony soap were distributed. Golda begged Ernie not to look at her, and he went through the sliding door of the second room with his eyes closed, led by the young woman, and by the children, whose soft hands clung to his naked thighs; there, under the shower-heads embedded in the ceiling, in the blue light of screened bulbs glowing in recesses of the concrete walls, Jewish men and women, children and patriarchs, were huddled together; his eyes still closed, he felt the pressure of the last packets of flesh that the S.S. men were clubbing now into the gas chamber; and his eyes still closed, he knew that the lights had been extinguished on the living, on the hundreds of Jewish women suddenly shrieking in terror, on the old men whose prayers rose immediately, growing in strength, on the martyred children who were rediscovering in their last agonies the fresh innocence of older anguishes, in a chorus of identical exclamations: *Mummy! But I was a good boy! it's dark! it's dark!* . . . And when the first waves of 'Cyclon B' gas billowed among the sweating bodies, drifting down towards the squirming carpet of children's heads, Ernie freed himself from the girl's mute embrace and leaned out into the darkness towards the children invisible even at his knees, and shouted, with all the gentleness and all the strength of his soul, 'Breathe deeply, my lambs, and quickly!'

When the layers of gas had covered everything, there was silence in the dark sky of the room for perhaps a minute, broken only by shrill, racking coughs and the gasps of those too far gone in their agonies to offer a devotion. And first as a stream, then a cascade, then an irrepressible, majestic torrent, the poem which, through the smoke of fires and above the funeral pyres of history, the Jews – who for two thousand years never bore arms and never had either missionary empires or coloured slaves – the old love poem which the Jews traced in letters of blood on the earth's hard crust unfurled in the gas chamber, surrounded it, dominated its dark, abysmal sneer: 'SHEMA ISRAEL ADONAI ELOHENU ADONAI EH'OTH ... Hear O Israel, the Eternal our God, the Eternal is One. O Lord by your grace you nourish the living, and by your great pity you resurrect the dead; and you uphold the weak, cure the sick, break the chains of slaves; and faithfully you keep your promises to those who sleep in the dust. Who is like unto you, O merciful Father, and who could be like unto you? ...'

The voices died one by one along the unfinished poem; the dying children had already dug their nails into Ernie's thighs, and Golda's embrace was already weaker, her kisses were blurred, when suddenly she clung fiercely to her beloved's neck and whispered hoarsely: 'Then I'll never see you again? Never again?'

Ernie managed to spit up the needle of fire jabbing at his throat and, as the girl's body slumped against him, its eyes wide in the opaque night, he shouted against her unconscious ear, 'In a little while, *I swear it!* ...' And then he knew that he could do nothing more for anyone in the world, and in the flash that preceded his own annihilation he remembered, happily, the legend of Rabbi Chanina ben Teradion, as Mordecai had joyfully recited it: when the gentle rabbi, wrapped in the scrolls of the Torah, was flung upon the pyre by the Romans for having taught the Law, and when they lit the faggots, branches still green to make his torture last, his pupils said, Master, what do you see? And Rabbi

Chanina answered, I see the parchment burning, but the letters are taking wing ... *Ah, yes, surely, the letters are taking wing*, Ernie repeated as the flame blazing in his chest suddenly invaded his brain. With dying arms he embraced Golda's body in an already unconscious gesture of loving protection, and they were found in this position half-an-hour later by the team of Sonderkommando responsible for burning the Jews in the crematory ovens. And so it was for millions, who from *Luftmensch* became *Luft*. I shall not translate. So this story will not finish with some tomb to be visited in pious memory. For the smoke that rises from crematoria obeys physical laws like any other: the particles come together and disperse according to the wind, which propels them. The only pilgrimage, dear reader, would be to look sadly at a stormy sky now and then.

And praised be Auschwitz. So be it. Maidanek. The Eternal. Treblinka. And praised be Buchenwald. So be it. Mauthausen. The Eternal. Belzec. And praised be Sobibor. So be it. Chelmno. The Eternal. Ponary. And praised be Theresienstadt. So be it, Warsaw. The Eternal. Wilno. And praised be Skarzysko. So be it. Bergen-Belsen. The Eternal. Janow. And praised be Dora. So be it. Neuengamme. The Eternal. Pustkow. And praised be ...

At times, it is true, one's heart could break in sorrow. But often too, preferably in the evening, I cannot help thinking that Ernie Levy, dead six million times, is still alive, somewhere, I don't know where ... Yesterday, as I stood in the street trembling in despair, rooted to the spot, a drop of pity fell from above upon my face; but there was no breeze in the air, no cloud in the sky ... there was only a presence.